It was a June evening, heady with the scents of summer, especially of fresh hay in one of the barns. And she'd been as sure that the young monk would come as she was that the sun, now sinking in the west, would rise again tomorrow. He came, carrying his measuring-rod and looking very businesslike.

So, on a bed of sweet hay, she committed adultery, and he broke the vows of celibacy which he had taken in ignorance of what he was forgoing. It was all hurried and secret and sinful and all the more delicious, like the apple in Eden.

There were moments, usually before the consummation, when she could think of nothing but the joy to come. Afterwards it was different, and hard sense took over.

In one of these afterwards she said bluntly, "I have betrayed Edman, and you, my love, have cuckolded him."

Fawcett Crest Books
by Norah Lofts

A Wayside Tavern

Norah Lofts

FAWCETT CREST • NEW YORK

Library of Congress Catalog Card Number: 80-954

ISBN 0-449-20140-6

Printed in the United States of America

First Fawcett Crest Edition: September 1983

10 9 8 7 6 5 4 3 2 1

Contents

And as the cock crew, those who stood before
The Tavern shouted—"Open then the door!
You know how little time we have to stay,
And, once departed, may return no more."

OMAR KHAYYAM

...the present, like a note in music is nothing
save as it appertains to the past and what is to come.

W. S. LANDOR

I

1 Paulus

A.D. 384

"DESERTED,"ONE OF THE MEN IN THE FRONT RANK SAID AS THE little settlement came into view. Men sighed or groaned or were silent according to their nature and training. Paulus strode forward to see for himself, and with a little sinking of the heart saw that the place certainly looked deserted, not a light showing, though within doors it would now be deep dusk, and no smoke rising into the clear, frost-threatening sky.

He called out in his loud, strong voice, "It offers shelter. And there may be food—abandoned." Mithras grant that there might be, for it was forty-eight hours since they had last eaten, and then only a few beans, less than a handful each, and of the coarsest kind, sometimes fed to horses, more calculated to upset a man's bowels than to provide sustenance.

Paulus had travelled this road twice before and knew that it ran through inhospitable country, partly untouched forest land, partly heath. Very few Romans had been tempted to settle and farm in such a district, and what few there had been were gone. Of this place, a posting-stage called Mala after the apple trees which flourished there, Paulus had had great hopes; it was well south of the Iceni border and far enough from a river to have escaped the sea-raiders. The last such posting-stage had been a heap of ashes with a few charred beams lying about. Mala, except for the absence of any sign of human life, looked just as it had done when Paulus last saw it, four—no, five years ago: a complex of buildings centred about the wineshop— stables, a smithy, a bakehouse, huts for servants and slaves. Only the wineshop was tiled, red and warm in this cold light, and, if Paulus remembered rightly, the main room had boasted a tesselated floor of which the owner had been immensely proud.

Because the road sloped downwards, or because his remark about food being abandoned had heartened them, the men moved

3

more easily now. Paulus fell into step beside Marius, one of the half-dozen veterans in this group of conscripts.

"It may be ambushed. I think it is unlikely, but we'll take precautions. The usual drill."

That meant that men with armour, even so little as a breast-plate, and men with shields, went first to attract the enemy's attention. They were not greatly at risk, for the enemy, if he lurked in this seemingly peaceful place, would be obliged to fire his arrows through window openings that restricted his range, and a man even in half-armour was vulnerable only in certain places, face and throat, forearm, and below the knee.

The dozen or so armoured men marched into the forecourt of the wineshop, deliberately exposing themselves, deliberately inviting attack. And nothing stirred. Mala was as deserted as it looked.

Paulus had been one of those who had taken the admittedly slight risk, though he had had some doubts as to the wisdom of his action. Certainly it was his duty to lead, to set a good example, but it was equally his duty to stay alive and carry out his extremely difficult orders, which were to get as many men as possible to Walton, where, protected by a stout castle, one embarkation place was still open. All the rest, in this section of what was called the Saxon Shore, had been abandoned. The barbarians from the sea were free to come and go. At two mustering-places, Brancaster on the coast and Norwich on a river, it had been they whom Paulus had feared, rather than the native Icene who were themselves afraid. Later, on the march, especially in well-wooded country, it had been the Icene. Never anything approaching a direct confrontation: a few arrows despatched from the shelter of the trees, and those who had despatched them vanished. So far, since Norwich, two men had been killed and five wounded. Walking wounded, fortunately, for this hurried march must not be impeded by the need to carry stretchers.

In the forecourt of the wineshop he halted his men and divided them into search parties, giving each its target. He hoped that the bakehouse would yield flour or meal, the barn some sort of grain. Some living thing might have been left behind. He visualised a few fowls, gone to roost and easily taken, caged rabbits, a fattening pig, even—for this had been a place which served delicacies—a hutch of dormice.

With four chosen men, one of them bearing a torch, Paulus

undertook to search the wineshop himself. It was the place most likely to offer food abandoned and readily edible, and wine. Of any such thing he must take control, for he was not in command of trained, disciplined men accustomed to fair rationing.

He found no food, but in a room behind the kitchen there was liquor. Two tall wine-jars, still sealed, one opened but half-full. There were also two casks which might contain either cider or the native brew known as barley-wine. This discovery justified his making a personal search, accompanied by four men he considered trustworthy. If the undisciplined element in his small force had stumbled upon this potential treasure, there could have been trouble. They'd have begun to drink without thinking. Wine on an empty belly would be comforting, but almost instantly intoxicating, and in the morning they would feel far worse than they did now. On the other hand, if no food turned up . . .

"We'll drink later," he said, and left two men to guard the door. He stepped back into the kitchen, which had a wide hearth, and passed on to the main room which had a smaller but still serviceable one. The people who had evacuated this place, taking all food stores with them, had at least left fuel behind, wood logs *and* charcoal. Yet it had occurred to none of the men not detailed to the search parties to get a fire going. Tired, dispirited and hungry, they'd slumped down, waiting. Sheep looking to their shepherd; domesticated men with whom eating was a habit. Not for the first time Paulus wondered whether, safely embarked at Walton and taken to some so-far-unknown destination on the Continent, they'd serve any purpose, or merely be, as they were now, so many mouths to feed. However, such speculation was outside his sphere of duty. He snapped out orders to get the fires going. "We can at least lie warm."

Nothing. Nothing. Paulus steeled himself to accept the negative reports without showing dismay. He had himself survived a siege in Mauritania and had heard tales of many others. Chewing leather gave some satisfaction, though no actual nourishment, and, had he been dealing with ordinary legionaries, he'd have suggested it, with a grim joke about everybody having an inch or two of belt to spare. As it was he prayed again. After all, Mithras was the soldiers' god; he knew what men needed, and he should give some heed to Paulus who, unlike many who professed the creed, had been properly initiated. He could remember standing under the platform in an underground temple in Antioch, and feeling the warm blood of the sacrificial bull showering down upon his head and shoulders.

All the searchers were back now except Marius, and when he and his party approached, everybody knew that they'd struck lucky; they sounded hilarious. They carried the bloodied, disembowelled bodies of eight little piglets.

"Not more than two days old, sir. Every bit edible."

"The sow?"

"I thought," Marius spoke with fitting diffidence, "I'd slaughter her later. There's tomorrow to think of."

"Say nothing of her," Paulus said, addressing his search party as a group. The eight sucklings, no larger than rabbits, eaten without bread, would not fully satisfy the hunger of fifty-three men, and if the sow's existence were known the improvident would wish to eat her tonight. "Kill her later and joint the carcass small, no piece more than four pounds."

On makeshift spits, over clear charcoal fires, the meat cooked quickly and smelt rather better than it tasted. Too young to have much flavour, Paulus thought, chewing his own portion, but it was food, and now he could begin the distribution of the wine. That at least was excellent. Imported stuff, probably Cyprian. Vines had been planted in Britain and were prolific, but the summers, though sometimes hot enough, were too short for perfect ripening; just as the grapes were almost ready, down came the rain or up sprang the wind; even frost was not unknown in late August. The home-produced wine was consequently thin, sour stuff, much inferior to the cider or the brew made from barley.

The thought reminded Paulus that he had plans for whatever the casks contained. Tomorrow half the men would carry water for drinking at midday, and the other half would carry whatever the casks contained. So, with the sow-meat, tomorrow was provided for, and by the end of the day after, failing any delay, they'd be in Walton, and his immediate responsibility would end. He'd have done his job, and probably nobody would ever recognise how difficult it had been, getting a rabble of old men and boys—conscription age ranged from sixteen to sixty— through what was virtually chaos: ravaged country, hostile country.

Mind you, he said to himself, the rebel tribes and the sea-raiders would be sorry, presently. When the troubles on the Continent were settled, Rome would come back in strength, as indeed she had left, with Maximus taking all the crack troops with him and making himself emperor, a title that he had been obliged to fight for, so that even the second-rate, left-to-hold-the-fort legionaries had been recalled. And finally isolated groups like the one which Paulus now commanded and was responsible for.

The weight of responsibility lifted a little as Paulus saw his contingent settling down for the night. The men had been fed, adequately if not fully, and the wine was taking its effect; the boys and the older men were settling down to sleep; a few, neither young nor old, were beginning to rattle the dice. The ideal campaigning age, Paulus reflected, was between twenty-five and forty. He was himself approaching the latter age.

Marius was killing the old sow; sentries had been posted. One thing remained to do—broach the barrels, see what they contained, and draw off whatever it was into jugs, ready to be transferred into the selected water-bottles at daybreak. He went into the wine-store and closed the door behind him.

It was an accepted fact that close concentration upon one subject made a man blind to the significance of others. When he first stepped into the wine-store Paulus had been thinking about the remote possibility of an ambush; then he had begun to think about the wine and how and when to distribute it. It would have been wrong to say that he had not *noticed* that one of the casks on its cross-legged trestles stood athwart a doorway; it was just that he had regarded it as unimportant, since no hidden enemy could have gone through a doorway and then blockaded it on this side. Nor had he considered the possibility of food being hidden behind this door. Why should it be? To what purpose? The evacuation of this place had been so thorough, so leisurely, that even the bed-linen and the table-ware had been taken. Paulus could understand why the sow had been left; she'd be too heavy to keep up with the other livestock on foot and too bulky to be transported by other means. So she had been abandoned. Strictly rational, yet, with a little pang, Paulus now remembered that he had not—with so many things to think of—rendered thanks to Mithras. He did so now, with words and with a libation, knocking out the wooden bung of the barrel and letting about a pint of the liquid stream out on to the bricked floor. He thought: Mithras will understand why I cannot spare more.

(One day, when things righted themselves and he had earned honourable retirement and the emoluments that went with it, Paulus intended to make a proper offering to his god. Every veteran, after twenty or, better still, twenty-five years of service, was entitled to so many acres—the number varied according to the density of the population in the area in which he chose to settle. He intended to choose Spain, his native land, and one of the first things he reared should be a bull-calf, a proper offering to Mithras.)

He tasted the contents of the first cask and recognised the barley-wine, very potent stuff indeed. It must be served to the men well watered. He took another appreciative sip, and a third, and felt it speed through his veins, warming and uplifting, making his assumed optimism and certainty real, and presenting the temptation to drink more. Pot-valiant, he thought scornfully, and set the temptation aside.

Then, when a voice called "Pollio! Pollio!" from behind the cask, from behind the door, he doubted his own sobriety or the purity of the beverage of which he had taken exactly three sips. There were liquors known, especially in the East, which could confound a man so that his senses were untrustworthy. How could anyone behind a closed door, barricaded by a heavy trestle bearing a heavy cask, be calling a name?

A trick of acoustics. Somebody calling "Paulus" in the outer room and the sound bouncing back, mangled. He opened the door and looked out. On the kitchen floor the men lay like dead men; even the dice-players had fallen asleep with the faint rose-coloured glow of the dying fire lying over them like a benediction. Nobody there had called his name.

He turned back, closing the door again, pulled aside the cask on its trestle, opened the half-hidden door, and found himself confronted by what seemed for a second to be a supernatural being. The light from the torch, which he had placed in the iron ring on the wall, shed its light on a figure, all white and shimmering, and on a cascade of truly golden hair. At the same time another sense came into play and his nose recognised two odours, sharply contrasting: the fragrance of carefully pampered woman flesh and the stench of untended sickness.

She moved first, putting up a hand to shield her eyes from the torchlight. And she spoke first, knowing him for what he was, in his own tongue but curiously and attractively accented. She said, "I thought you were Pollio. He promised to come back for me. Is he . . . is he . . . dead?"

"I cannot tell you. I know nothing of Pollio."

She reached for the wall, seeking support, and said almost apologetically, "I was too ill to go with them. Pollio left me some food and promised . . . I think Livia barred the door. Have you any food?"

"We had, but it is all eaten." A statement of plain fact; the skeletons of the little pigs had been gristle rather than bone. "I have a little wine—the dregs." No need to worry, he thought, about the effect of drinking on an empty stomach where she was concerned. Then the full implication of the thought struck him. Her voice was weak, without carrying-power, but he had been speaking in his ordinary tone; somebody in the kitchen might have heard and wondered, be about to look in. And the presence of one female amidst a crowd of men was a guarantee of the worst kind of trouble. In a gruff whisper he said, "Go back. I will bring you something to drink."

What was left at the bottom of the wine-jars was undrinkable; so he poured some of the fierce barley-brew and added water. Then he waited long enough for anyone, who had heard him speaking, and felt curious, to arrive. Nobody stirred; so, taking the torch in one hand and the cup in the other, he stepped into the little lobby, off which three arches opened. The curtains of one were drawn, those of the other two open, and the girl lay in the further one on a luxuriously appointed bed. The marble-topped table nearby bore a small copper lamp, a silver cup, a plate and a tall jug. The oil in the lamp had been used; whatever food and drink had been there, consumed.

"Thank you," she said, and sipped. Stopped and smiled. "Not dregs! That was kind." She then drank in a curious way, not gulping but savouring each mouthful, rather as though she were eating as well. Now that the full light of the torch fell upon her, Paulus saw that she was woefully thin but that, given more flesh, she would be pretty.

"You must stay out of sight," he said. "I have fifty men with me—and you know what men are."

She smiled in a different way and said, "I know," in a tone that implied that what she knew did men as a whole little credit.

"We leave at first light. The sow has been killed. I will leave a piece for you out there," he jerked his head towards the wine-store. "For your safety's sake I shall put the barrier back tonight, but I shall remove it before I go."

"To Colchester?"

"Walton."

"I wish you well."

"Thank you. I wish you well, too." It was a leave-taking of a sort, but near the curtain he paused, thinking that he needed something in which to wrap the pork. But certain plagues were so contagious that even material could carry them. And the stench coming from the curtained cubicle was not reassuring.

"What ailed you?" he asked abruptly.

"I had a baby. It was dead and things went wrong with me. I had child-bed fever."

"Then I'll take this," he said and ripped down the curtain. In the wine-store he slashed and ripped the thin stuff into pieces each sizable enough to wrap a four-pound joint. He supervised the first change of sentries; then, with the practised ease of an old campaigner who could sleep anywhere, instantly, and wake in the same way, he slept.

The watchers on the far side of the road were all that remained of a hunting-party which had set out some days earlier in search of food and excitement. The original party had consisted of eight men, none too many when, in pursuit of a deer, one could rouse a wild boar or even a bear. The party was now reduced to three, for the older men had gone home when they had meat sufficient for their needs. The three young men had stayed on, and presently discovered another sport, harassing the Romans, who seemed to be in retreat and had no means of retaliation, for every Iceni boy in this part of the country was at home in the forest, but the Romans belonged to the roads and to open battlefields.

There was no real malice in this harassment; none of the boys had a personal grudge against any Roman. Many, many years ago Rome had learned that the Iceni were not a people to be oppressed with impunity, or even ruled directly. Indirect rule through their own chiefs had been adopted, once some now almost legendary rebellion had been avenged. There were, of course, the taxes, but so long as the money could be seen to be spent usefully on forts and ships to keep the sea-raiders at bay, taxes were paid with grumbling but without real resentment. All that was changing now.

They were running short of arrows; for one thing the older men, at heart disapproving of the boys' decision to prolong the hunting-trip, since it meant three backs fewer to carry the load of meat, had left them only a limited number, and whereas an arrow which landed in an animal could usually be recovered, an arrow sent flying into the Roman ranks was an arrow lost. Still, they had killed two men and wounded five, and were on the whole well pleased with themselves.

The old sow had had strength left in her to squeal just before Marius slit her throat, and in the quiet of the night the sound had carried to the verge of the forest where the three Iceni boys lay hidden. Their leader, leader by virtue of his age, was named Ceretic; at the next midsummer day he would be sixteen, and thenceforth count as a man. His tactics were better than his marksmanship. He wanted to kill the centurion, the man so obviously in charge of the half-century, and he had twice failed, though one arrow had not been wasted; it had hit and lamed another man. Both the other boys, however, had killed a man. By the old tribal standards, they had therefore excelled him, and by the old tribal standards, only very thinly overlain by the imposed Romanisation, they would be held in higher regard. The thought troubled him, but he found a way to evade the worst shame.

"We have but three arrows, each one," he said, "so we *all* aim at the centurion. Then we hide and wait until they have straggled away. We shall then return, and the liver and kidneys of the pig will be there on the table. We eat the kidneys, cook the liver, but carry it for tomorrow and tomorrow, and so home, where roast venison will await us."

Morning came, a lightening of the sky followed by a rosy flush which was supposed to foretell a wet day. The wineshop came to life as men came out, yawning and stretching, to relieve bladders and bowels. Until he was fully accoutred, the centurion was indistinguishable from the others, and so the boys waited while Marius and the other veterans, acting as temporary uncommissioned officers, ran about barking orders and distributing gaily-wrapped parcels.

At the last minute Paulus, who had been filling some water-bottles with the barley-brew and handing them out, remembered the existence of the girl and the promise he had made to her. From the doorway he called, "Lucius, bring me your bundle." One of the choicer joints, so far as any part of a breeding and half-starved sow could be called choice. Using his sword, he cut off what he estimated would constitute his own supper, carried it back, placed it in a prominent place on top of the empty barrel, and moved barrel and cask away from the door. Then, promise kept, duty fulfilled, he went out and was near the well, hearing Marius say, "All in marching order, sir," when one of the arrows struck him. Two others bounced harmlessly off the ornamental stone surround of the well.

At first, no pain. Almost every sudden wound brought its momentary, merciful anaesthesia. But there was blood and the feeling of having no leg below the knee. And there was the arrow, still quivering, its barbed head sticking out of one side of his knee, its unfeathered shaft on the other. Between the two his shattered knee-cap.

With a stumbling hop, before Marius could reach him, Paulus got to the rim of the well and lowered himself into a sitting position. Some instinct deeper even than self-preservation made him sweep his cloak over the injured knee and the arrow that had done the damage. "A trivial wound," he said loudly. The men were lined up, facing in the direction of the march, and sunk in early-morning apathy. Few had witnessed the incident. "Lucius, take charge. Marius and I will follow. Proceed!"

At that Marius protested. "We need stretcher-bearers, sir."

"To carry me would slow down the march, and already time is short." The pain was beginning now, and also the despair. He would never be useful again. Even if he lived. He'd never sit—an honourably retired man—under his own olive-trees in faraway Spain, never marry and beget children, never sacrifice that bull-calf to Mithras. Time enough to think such weakening thoughts when he was alone. As alone as he would soon be, and in obviously hostile terrain.

He said, keeping his voice steady and cool, "You can free the arrow, Marius. Use your knife if you must."

Ability, if not actual willingness, to bear pain and inflict it was part of their common training, yet Marius said, "Take a good drink of this." He had naturally been one of those trusted to carry the barley-wine. Paulus drank, but allowed no time for the liquor to take effect. "Hurry," he said, "or they'll be out of sight."

Marius pulled at the arrow-head and the straight, unfeathered shaft slid out with comparative ease. He thought, not irrelevantly: And *we* taught them, barbarian brutes, to make arrows heavy enough in the head to need no flight aid! He produced one of the bandage-rolls which he, as a trained man, was allowed to carry; inexperienced fellows were inclined to take fright at anything which implied that wounds were likely. But as he twisted and tied the coarse linen he asked himself: To what end? That Paulus, his leg useless, his wound staunched, should stay here and starve?

"They are still within call," he said, "and I, personally, will carry one corner of the stretcher until the day's end."

"To what purpose? You can do better, Marius. Get that mob to Walton. There are a few good men ... Go now, Marius. That is an order."

Marius, an excellent man for taking orders, felt that when he gave them, he needed backing. So he invented the story that Paulus, only slightly wounded, only slightly handicapped, was just behind them, just about to catch up and resume command. This pretence gave him the necessary assurance.

Rome had never been race-conscious, and among the men now under Marius's rather uncertain command here were some who had had Celtic mothers or grandmothers, able to see what an ordinary person could not. Such a gift was uncertainly transmitted, and tended to be the inheritance of women rather than men; but at least four men, having tramped twenty miles, eaten the tougher but more flavoursome flesh of the old sow and drunk the diluted barley-wine, claimed to have seen Paulus moving about the camp that they made that evening. Since he was not there in the morning, they explained, solemnly, that he was dead and that what they had seen was his Other Body. Everybody and everything—even a tree—had this other body, sometimes called the spirit, but only the very powerful could make themselves visible. This theory was acceptable to the few Christians in the group—Christ had been powerful, and He had been seen after his death—and it was equally acceptable to Marius for strictly practical reasons: so he encouraged it, and a simple incident passed into folklore.

Paulus might well have died for any number of reasons; loss of blood, the fever following an untreated wound, lack of food, or suicide. He could have died dramatically, torn to pieces by wolves, of which there were a good many in the forest on the other side of the road; or in a moment of weakness he could have tipped over from his perch on the well-rim into the water.

He was saved by the girl.

Her name was Gilda, and she was a second-generation slave who never, in a lifetime of seventeen years, had made a decision of her own.

Her mother had been a kitchen slave and, until she was ten and showed some promise of comeliness, she had worked with her mother and taken orders from her. At ten she was judged to be capable of waiting on guests, taking orders from them, from Pollio and from Livia, his wife. At fourteen she had gained the dubious promotion of becoming one of the three prostitutes in the wineshop's little brothel. That, too, had demanded compliance and little more.

On this fateful day she emerged from her cubicle as soon as the place was quiet, and, walking feebly, supporting herself on anything that was handy, she went into the wine-store. The Roman soldier had kept his promise and left her a piece of pork. Only a slight gap separated her from those of her ancestors who would have eaten the meat raw after giving it—if time allowed—a good hammering to soften it, but the gap was there, and Gilda, using her own discrimination for the first time, decided that the meat must be cooked, and how. It was a piece of meat to be boiled rather than roasted. Boiling would render it more edible and would also shrink it less.

First she must make a fire, and that seemed to be an impossible task without flint and tinder, unless, somewhere under the grey ashes, some ember lived. It did, but she had no bellows and too little strength to blow. "Stay alive," she implored it, and made her feeble way to the rear door of the kitchen. It was the season of windy weather, and dry leaves and dead twigs had drifted into corners. She gathered a handful. The core of embers had stayed alive, and now accepted her offering. Presently she had a fire, but of a fragile kind, in as much need of sustenance as she was herself. She needed wood and, unless the soldiers had used it all, she knew where it could be found, stacked under a kind of awning at the far end of the yard. But could she walk so far? Carry logs back? Not without something to strengthen her. Barley-wine! Would they have left so much as a drop?

They had left more; half a caskful. She drew some into a cup and drank it, without water, and was almost instantly strong enough to do anything. Resourceful, too. Barrels would roll. They did not need to be carried. She rolled the empty one into the kitchen, and pushed it on to the struggling fire. There was a burst of flame and a roar; the staves caved in, and there was just the fire to roast an ox, had an ox been available. As it was, having placed in the longest-handled pan the meat and some of the water which the soldiers had drawn and left behind, she was obliged to approach the fire cautiously. The heat was so fierce that the water in the pan began to bubble almost immediately.

Her liquor-inspired energy was then almost exhausted, and she was content to sit on a stool, watching the pot boil, and now and then pushing pieces of the cask, which tended to fall away, back into the centre of the fire.

Her thoughts were with Pollio, who had promised to come back for her once he had conducted his family, his slaves and livestock to Colchester, which he thought of as a safer place. He had left her provisions enough for three days or four. "You'll feel like eating soon," he'd said. But how long ago he had said it she had really no means of knowing for, as the fever mounted, she'd lost count of time, had drifted about in a dream world. Then she had come back to this one, and been first thirsty and then hungry. Food and water were to hand. She had not then noticed how hard and stale the bread was or how even the honey cakes had lost their freshness. But she remembered it now. And she remembered too, the terrible moment when she tried to get out and found the door more than she could manage. Livia's doing, of course. Always jealous.

"Condemning me to a living death. But thanks to a stranger, here I am with meat enough, if carefully handled, for three days. Then Pollio will come as he promised . . ."

The bright morning, with its false promise, gave way to heavy cloud, and Gilda, not yet completely re-oriented to the ordinary world, thought that evening was falling, and realised that she had used to put into the pot the last of the water drawn by soldiers. When she had eaten, she would need to drink, and the barley-wine, of which there was still plenty, was not thirst-quenching unless mingled with water. So she must make the vast effort to get to the well. Before dark. Because of the wolves. She'd never actually seen a live one. She'd seen two dead ones: one shot by an arrow and one caught in a trap. Both rather pitiable than fearsome, but the dread of wolves was part of her heritage, and at night, even within walls, safe by the fire or snug in bed, the sound of wolves howling in the forest could set the atavisic fear crawling cold in her blood.

Paulus had managed to lower himself to the ground so that his shoulders rested against the raised rim of the well, and the danger of falling backwards and drowning was eliminated. The pain in his knee seemed to come and go; while it burned and gnawed and stabbed, he was aware of the hopelessness of his situation; when it receded he seemed to be enjoying already the Mithraic idea of heaven, which closely resembled any soldier's dream of bliss on earth: peace and plenty, good food, good wine, good women, good company for ever and for ever. When each semi-conscious interlude ended, he thought: Still here! And was dismayed.

Gilda did not recognise him; his back was towards her as she stepped into the forecourt, but she saw that he was a soldier, a Roman, and from such a one there was little to fear. Both in the wineshop and in the little brothel the Romans were known to be good customers, men with simple tastes, easily satisfied, usually young and always clean. Officials and merchants were on the whole older, greasier, and more prone to have curious ideas about what a girl was for.

She went unsteadily around the well, recognised him and said, "You! Why didn't you leave with the others?"

"As you see," he said, twitching the cloak aside and showing the rough bandage, "I cannot walk."

"Does it hurt much?" She had an abnormal susceptibility to pain, both her own and that of others. Every month she'd gone about suffering terrible cramps in the stomach and stupefying pains in the head. The loss of her maidenhead had been agonising, and childbirth, which everybody said was nothing, had been two days of torture.

"It hurts."

"Wait here," she said. Had it been merely a shattered knee and not the general desperate situation, Paulus would have laughed. Wait here! What else could he do?

She went away and presently came back, dragging a stout branch which forked at the top.

"If you could get this under one arm, and on the other side lean on me, you could come into the house. The meat is ready for eating. *Your* meat," she said as a courteous afterthought.

It sounded a simple operation, but it took a long time and some contortionist feats. He weighed just about what he should for his height and build—a hundred and sixty pounds—and his left leg was not merely useless, neutral, it was an active enemy. The girl's shoulder under his hand seemed to have no substance, to be merely an arrangement of sharp brittle bones, likely to collapse under pressure.

By the time they were inside the house both were breathless, and Paulus was sweating heavily. He dropped down, stiff-legged, on to a bench just inside the door, and they looked at one another with the satisfaction that comes from a shared achievement, however small. Yet what, he asked himself, had been achieved? A night's safety from a wolf-pack? A staving off of starvation until tomorrow?

"I will bring the food," she said as soon as she could speak. "And some barley-wine. Pollio may come today. Or tomorrow. And he will ride. He hates to walk."

She brought the meat, apologising. "No onions, no peas or beans. No bread. But it will keep us alive until tomorrow when Pollio . . ." Paulus had said nothing, and he was accustomed to controlling his expression, but she broke off her latest profession of faith in Pollio and said, "You think he will not come?"

"How can I know? But perhaps you should not count upon it too much. In fact, I think you should try to get back to your own people."

"What people?"

"You're Iceni, aren't you?"

"It was they who sold my mother into slavery. Of all people they are most false." For the first time her manner became animated, and her sunken blue eyes flashed. The story was old, but the hurt remained. "My grandfather was from the sea; he was a trader, bringing things the Iceni did not know, or could not make. Like this . . ." She pushed back her sleeve and displayed, above the elbow of her thin arm, a bracelet of amber. "He was well known and respected, and when he wished to settle he was permitted to buy land. He prospered and bought more land, and he bred many sons. As my mother told it, people began to talk against the family, and to say that the land was wrongfully sold to a foreigner and should be taken back, with the well he had dug and the house he had built. So there was a fight, and only my mother lived. The father of Pollio bought her for a house slave." A commonplace story enough, but in telling it she had neglected her food, and in listening to it Paulus had found an excuse to eat very slowly

indeed. The flaccid meat cooled on the plates; both were being
deliberately sparing. Both aware of the morrow. Their attitudes
differed; Paulus had had for years some authority and the responsibility that went with it; Gilda until today had had as little
control of her own destiny as a domestic animal.

"Pollio and the others were making for Colchester?" he
asked.

"It was fortified, he said."

True enough; but when a system suffered even a temporary
collapse, it was the bigger things that went first. Colchester,
that once proud place, had had its garrison withdrawn, and was
probably now like other formerly fortified places, a helpless,
dying town, hopelessly overcrowded by people like Pollio. In
his time, Paulus had seen dozens of them, or what remained
of them. Often the abandoned fortress, standing strong and
prepared to last forever, and, all around, makeshift huts, disease
and famine.

Confused, in great pain, for the barley-brew had not yet had
time to soothe him, Paulus faced the complete hopelessness of
his own case, and concentrated upon the girl's. All the while
wondering why he should bother.

"Walton would be safer for you, I think. The last port open
along this shore. Eat your meat; then set out, carrying this,"
he indicated his own portion of the meat.

"On the road?" she asked, with apparent stupidity. "I dare
not do that. Even before, before everything went wrong, it was
hardly safe for a woman to walk alone."

"Walk in the wood, but keep parallel to the road."

"That would be worse. I am afraid of wolves." It was a
rational fear enough, but pain made him irritable and he said,
"Then you must stay here and starve."

"Pollio . . ." She cut the sentence short, and, hope of rescue
abandoned, fell back, not upon the inheritance of her own
sheltered experience, but upon the accumulated race memory,
never stirred until now, and even now not recognised for what
it was. "We shall not starve," she said.

She went away, and after a long time came back, out of
breath again. "I have pulled a bed for you into the kitchen. It
is warmer there."

The journey from the wineshop's main room to the kitchen
was shorter than that from the well-head, but more difficult
because the tesselated floor, of which Pollio had been so proud,

offered no grip for the crutch. Once he lurched and they would have fallen, doing more damage, but she reached out and clutched at a table's edge and steadied both herself and him with unbelievable resilience, and presently he was installed, in what comfort his hurt knee allowed, on the first feather-bed he had ever occupied. In the country of his birth, in Syria and Mauritania, the feather-bed had never been needed and was therefore unknown. In this colder, northern land, feather-beds were not provided for soldiers, and even a man on leave, able to pay for and be welcome to the best a post-stage house could offer, avoided the feather-bed, unhygienic and possibly verminous.

After these exertions, she rested again, but briefly; then came back with a small cup containing a little dark, viscous fluid, and a cup of water. She poured some water into the cup and stirred vigorously, producing a liquid the colour of mud.

"Claudia knew of these things and, when the pain was at its worst she gave me some. So Livia blamed her for the baby's death and my not being able to walk." She offered the cup tentatively, saying, as though to a child, "It is vile-tasting, but effective." Within minutes the pain was in retreat and he was asleep.

The world of dreams had seldom been for him a pleasant one, too thickly beset by muddles for which he was responsible yet had no way of sorting out; he dreamed of battles going badly, through no fault of his own, though he knew he would be blamed. Above all, he dreamed of the dead, men with whom he had served, good men, dead untimely and not liking the other world, the paradise of soldiers in which they found themselves.

Therefore, as a general rule, he woke gladly, back in his own world once more, and ready to splash cold water over his face and head to wash away the last of the night's miasma.

On the first morning of his entirely new life, he woke, was as usual glad to be awake, and then made a forgetful move which set the pain flaring, not perhaps quite so savagely as it had been occasionally on the previous day, but sufficiently to remind him of his desperate position. At the same time he could smell food.

"I am glad to see you awake, Paulus," Gilda said in that lilting voice which made even an expression of gladness hold something of grieving, "It is not good to awake too suddenly. The spirit is not ready."

She had been up and busy since first light. On the big table, where so many good meals had been prepared, stood a basket half-full of beech-nuts. Alongside stood a stone pestle and mortar. The discarded husks of the beech-nuts she had stripped lay drying in the hearth, and in a pan over the revived fire the pork, now cut into small cubes like dice, frizzled alongside flat cakes of the beech-mast, crushed into powder and moistened with water. Also in the pan, between the sizzling meat and the flat cakes, were sprigs of greenstuff.

"The meal is ready," Gilda said, "but first you will wish . . ." She knew what men most need on waking, and was not coy on the subject, though adhering to the thought that men who could get outside should go outside. "I will help you."

"Thank you, but no. I should like to see how well I can manage on my own." He managed well because, although the front of the wineshop had its tiled roof, its plastered walls and the elaborate well-head, the remainder of the building was in native style, roughly-trimmed tree-trunks as uprights and crossbeams, the interstices filled with clay, offering plenty of handholds. And because he was a healthy man in good training, accustomed to an active life, to handling weapons and doing things, he found the management of the crutch becoming easier.

"Nettles," Gilda said, laying on his plate some of the green sprays between the sizzling meat cubes and two beech-cakes on his plate. "Some people think it as good as spinach." She spoke with the obvious intention to please, but Paulus did not know what she was talking about. The Roman soldier's rations were simple—bread, meat, fruit in due season, and such trimmings as travelled well—onions, garlic, dried grapes, figs and dates. The whole thing was geared to the exigencies of the march, and long spells of garrison duty had done little to change it. Paulus cut a little of the greenstuff, balanced it on a piece of the beech-cake and chewed experimentally. Bitter and pappy, he decided, and did not try again.

"You do not care for it?"

"To be truthful, no." She reached out her knife and transferred the greenstuff to her own plate and gave him instead three of the little meat dice. "No need for that," he said, but she had her answer ready, as polished an axiom as though it had been bandied about for years. "Only in justice can friendship flourish."

He lay on the bed, the wounded knee stretched rigid, and on his lap a bowl of unshelled beech-nuts. She showed him how to separate the husks from the kernels, and he worked at it diligently, amazed at the tininess of what was edible compared with the amount that must be discarded. He was also amazed by the temerity the girl showed on her nut-hunting forays, she who had confessed to being afraid of wolves. With his career ended and inactivity forced upon him, Paulus had time for thought and speculation, and sometimes, seeing her set off with such apparent boldness, he wondered whether an indifference to danger could be a thing of natural growth—like the calluses that developed upon harshly-used hands or whether, as day followed day and Pollio did not come, she'd lost the hope, the certainty of a better tomorrow which alone made life worth living.

One day she brought back, in addition to the beech-nuts, some larger, harder-shelled ones, called hazels, which could be cracked and eaten raw; a pleasant change from the gruel, but disturbing in that it aroused a desire to chew, for something to bite upon, something to make eating more than a dutiful, almost tasteless exercise in keeping alive.

Neither Paulus nor Gilda spoke of this carnivorous longing; in fact, for two people marooned as they were, they talked very little, and always about practicalities. Then one evening, instead of eating all her beech-mast gruel, she set some aside, mixed in a little more of the dry pounded stuff in the pestle, and, when the paste was solid enough, rounded bits of it into balls, about the size of a pea.

"What are you making?" he asked.

"Something that came to my mind," she said. "It may not work. If it does, you shall know."

It occurred to him that it was just one day short of three weeks since he received his wound. There was an unwritten rule that a hurt severe enough to need a bandage should be left undisturbed for about that length of time unless something went wrong with it and interference—usually the surgeon's knife— was called for. His wound had healed well; there'd been none of that almost invariably lethal stench of flesh rotting while still attached to the living body. He had not fallen into a fever, and, thanks to the dark medicine which Gilda had administered so long as it lasted, he had not suffered unbearable pain. He was practically certain that his leg would be useless, but a limp, flexible leg would be less of a handicap than a rigid one. Tomorrow he would test it.

Blood and what was called healing pus had seeped into the coarse linen, and hardened it into a carapace; he was obliged to use his knife to cut the inmost fold away. The knee thus exposed was curiously shaped, the convex knee-cap fallen in, the skin, white as a woman's, rigid and puckered. In two places fragments of bone, more silvery white than the skin, protruded. An excellent sign! Bits of bone loose in a joint could burrow about and fester, and cause almost constant pain. The splinters of his shattered knee-cap were almost so near the surface that at a pull they came away, hurting no more than a wasp's sting.

Now, could he bend his leg? At first it seemed impossible, and was so painful that he sweated again, although the kitchen was cold, because Gilda said they must be sparing of firewood. Each night she placed a single log over what remained of the suppertime fire, and then heaped ashes over it. It was of the fire and the fire's needs that Paulus was thinking as he forced the long-immobilised joint into action. Bend. Straighten. One. Two. It seemed that each movement hurt a trifle less. Presently he ventured to stand. Not bad, he thought, not bad at all. He needed the crutch still, but now in a different way, as a support of a limb which would grow stronger with use, not as a substitute for a useless impediment.

Slowly and carefully he began to make his way towards the woodshed, giving a sideways glance of distaste at the heap of ordure which had accumulated in three weeks. The standard of hygiene in the Roman army was high; even the most temporary camping-place had its latrines. Paulus was wondering how soon he could use a spade, when he reached the woodshed and saw the immediate need to use another tool. And he understood why Gilda had been so sparing of fuel. Wood enough here for a year or more, but most of it not in immediately accessible form: sturdy tree trunks laid neatly along one wall, awaiting the saw; rows of logs already sawn, each a load for a man or two boys. But the significant and to him, pitiable, thing was the log off which two sizable pieces had been split, and into whose main body the axe had been driven with force enough almost to bury its head, but with no resultant split.

Bracing himself—a tripod thing, one good leg, one weak

one, and the crutch—he tugged out the axe, wondering that she had power enough to drive it in so far. His own strength was not what it had been, for, although heaving himself about on the crutch had kept the muscles of his arms and shoulders in trim, a steady diet of beech-mast gruel was not conducive to physical power, but he persevered and presently had manageable logs enough for two days. He could have left them there for her to find, but he remembered that she invariably returned from her foodhunt tired and, since the weather worsened, cold. For once he would surprise her.

She surprised him. She came in, her thin face blue-white from cold, but her eyes, her bearing, all redolent of triumph. In one hand she carried a cock-pheasant, and in the basket, instead of beech-nuts, some pale roots.

"Parsnips," she said. "And how could you know? How could you manage?" She looked with pleasure at the fire.

"How could *you*?" He nodded towards the dead bird.

"Pollio kept a few," she said, already beginning to pluck the bright body. "They lived in a pen, and had one wing cut so that they could not fly. When I was young," she spoke as though that time were long past, "one of my duties was to feed them. They knew me. Wing feathers grow again, you know, and perhaps Pollio forgot. Some flew away and went into the woods. Yesterday I saw one, this or another. I called and he knew me, but he was shy. And I had no enticement, only the beech-nuts which he could find for himself. He wanted corn, or peas. So I made what looked like peas, and he followed. Then I . . . I caught him and killed him." Suddenly her matter-of-fact voice shook, some tears splashed down to her hands, which never for a second ceased their plucking action. "I betrayed him," she said.

Such a sentiment was beyond the understanding of Paulus, and in his mind he labelled it womanish, and then thought he was being illogical, remembering how, at the games and at bull-fights, the females in the audience often seemed the more excited, the less inclined to show mercy. And not merely women of the rougher kind; he had seen great ladies, clad in gossamer, give the death-sign with their jewelled hands on occasions when at least half the men around the arena would have spared the gladiator who had put on a brave show.

Nor could soft-heartedness be regarded as an Iceni attribute; in places not yet fully Romanised, human sacrifice was still

practised. Not that Gilda was, by her own account, a member
of the Iceni tribe. It occurred to him that the girl's behaviour,
weeping over what would be a good meal, using the word
"betrayed" over a bird she had deliberately lured to death, might
be a thing peculiar to herself. And for the first time he regarded
her as something other than a fellow castaway, a girl whose
life he had inadvertently saved and who, in turn, had saved his.

For the free birds in the forest the season of hunger had barely
started and this pheasant was fat. Grease and vital juices dripped
down the spit and into a pan where the sliced parsnips lay.
They were wild ones, therefore small, but they had been frosted
and were sweet. No meal that Paulus and Gilda had shared had
been so delicious, so satisfying, or so evocative of the question,
What next? From the moment when Gilda accepted the fact
that Pollio would not be coming to her rescue, the future had
narrowed down to the business of surviving from this day to
the next. The one good meal and the heat and warmth of the
fire, which for once need not be doused as soon as the beech-
nut gruel was cooked, had an invigorating effect on them both.

"Now that you are less lame, how soon can we set out for
Colchester?"

"You think of Pollio still?"

"We were lovers," she said simply. "And since he has been
prevented from coming to find me, I must go to him. A hundred
things may have prevented him—Livia most of all; she could
keep ten men busy from dawn to dusk, and," malice came into
her face, into her voice, "from dusk to dawn! Also, bear in
mind that Pollio did not know that I was barred in. He left
food and water. He may think that I am already on my way."

"Or that Colchester was no place for you."

"Because of Livia?"

Paulus had had singularly little experience of women; he
could not remember his mother, had had no sisters. He'd patronised brothels when the need took him, but his knowledge
of women, apart from their bodies, was all hearsay and on the
whole derogatory. It was difficult to get an idea into a woman's
head—and equally difficult to dislodge it once it was there.
Women were not unlike dogs, either embarrassingly faithful
or shamelessly faithless. They had invented and diligently cultivated something called love. Their minds were narrow. Of
the last fault this young woman was giving ample proof when

she thought that Pollio's failure to keep his promise to her was due to another woman's machinations, and not to the general state of things. But then, he thought, instantly excusing her, how could she know; she'd never seen a garrison town deserted; never seen the refugees pouring in, inspired by the false hope that a place which had once seemed to be impregnable must still be so, or would soon be so again.

Better be frank, he thought; kinder in the end, and, although kindness was to him part of the small change in life's currency, rating far lower than courage and duty and the enforcement of sanitary rules, she had been kind to him, deliberately, whereas his kindness to her had been inadvertent. He had simply happened to come along and release her; she had shared her pitiable food with him, and she had stayed with him, never once mentioning the idea of going to Colchester until he had proved that he could walk. In return he must be frank with her.

"I do not *know* what has happened to Colchester. I have seen Ancaster and Brancaster and Norwich, and I see no reason why Colchester should be different. Wherever there was a fortress or a garrison, however small, people looked to it; they lost the art of self-defence. *And we encouraged that loss.* It made for peace. Then, when the first legions were withdrawn, old quarrels broke out; those who had lost their taste for fighting—even handed in their arms—were at a sore disadvantage. They looked for protection, which the few of us left could no longer provide." He forgot that he was talking to a girl, and an unusually ignorant one at that. "At first it was not too bad. Few in numbers, but with arms and experience, we had authority. We were training auxiliaries . . ." His mind reached back to the time when faith in Maximus had been strong, and justified. For the leader of the Roman legions in Britain had attained his ambition and made himself emperor. Then things had gone wrong; the holding forces were recalled, finally even such near-useless fellows as those whom Paulus had been trying to get down to Walton.

"How old was Pollio?" he asked.

"Old. Older than you." Paulus neither winced nor smiled. He had his full share of vanity, but it was not concerned with looking younger than his years. "Why?" she asked.

"Because if he's under sixty and able-bodied, he may have been conscripted."

"At Colchester?" she said, unbelieving. Colchester was to

her the place to which Pollio went once or twice a year to buy such necessities as the little settlement could not produce, and pretty things and trinkets. Then, more lately, Colchester had seemed to be a place of safety. Over and over again she had heard somebody say, "If we can only get to Colchester! . . ."

Gilda sat thoughtful for a minute or two, and then offered him the results of her reflections.

"If the army took Pollio, I should be Livia's slave. And without Pollio . . ." Her always pale face blanched at the prospect of such a fate. "No. I shall not go there. What was the name of the other place you mentioned?"

"Walton?" A smile, of the grim kind, twitched at his mouth. "The galleys will have left long since. We were making a forced march to reach there at a certain time." He had the professional soldier's unacknowledged but positive scorn of the sailor's craft. "Something to do with the moon and the tide . . . There would be nothing, I am afraid, for you in Walton, except to beg from those who had little themselves."

"And *you*?"

"At the pace I go I might reach Walton by the equinox, and by that time the Horned Men will be there."

"Or here. It was they whom Pollio feared most. I must think," she said.

I, too, Paulus thought, taking the first essential step towards being a thinking man. He, as well as Gilda, had gone through life on a simple pattern: do this; don't do that; stick to the rules, even in calamity. In calamity he had stuck to the rules, handed over to Marius, concealed his own hurt, and for three weeks this sticking to the rules had been, in strange fashion, rewarded—a man wounded in action had a right to care and attention from the able-bodied. Now that time of immunity was ended. He must begin to think for himself.

Round and round; a problem incapable of solution. Here I am, a man no longer young, and trained to no trade but war; a man irrevocably maimed—nobody would employ me, even as a night-watchman.

Things would change, of course; the internal dissensions in Rome itself, which Paulus did not pretend to understand; the barbarian threat from without, which he thought he did, would end as all such things ended—in the increase of Roman power. Rome would return in strength, and a man with Paulus's record would get his just dues. But it would all take time, five, ten years. How to stay alive so long? No satisfactory answer, and round and round his thoughts would go again.

In the morning Gilda said, "We have wood; we have half the pheasant left; but we need beech-nuts. I have another plan for today, but it may fail. Could you make shift to gather what we need?"

He said, "Yes," without thinking. After all, yesterday he had split and carried logs. The task now assigned him seemed simple. When he moved, however, he found himself rather lamer than he had been yesterday, because his leg muscles, so long unused, had stiffened. But such pains, he knew, were trivial; the knee hurt very little, but it was still weak, and he needed the crutch. He made his way across the road and into the verge of the forest, and almost immediately learned that gathering beech-nuts was not so easy as it sounded. For one thing, beech-trees were few in comparison with oaks—what a pity, he thought, that human beings could not live on acorns! Then, again, the beech-trees shed their leaves and their fruit at about the same time, and both were of the same colour. Search was necessary. And Gilda, fearful of wolves, had not penetrated far into the forest, and she had not been the only hungry thing on the hunt: four-footed animals had stamped and rooted about.

The most telling thing against him was, of course, his knee. He was unable to kneel and scrabble about amongst the leaves, the hoof-marks, the ridges of overturned soil, and the droppings. In order to retrieve a few nuts upon which tomorrow's meal depended, he was obliged to lower himself clumsily into a sitting position and then, having made sure that not one of the tiny brown things had escaped him, heave himself, even more slowly and clumsily, on to his feet again.

It was a gruelling experience, but Gilda had left him the basket which she usually carried and brought back almost full, and he felt a compulsion to do at least as well. He had seldom been so exhausted in his life, for those in authority knew exactly how far a man, even on a forced match, could go without dropping nearly dead of fatigue, or how long a sentry could keep watch without falling asleep. This was the time of the shortest days, and this one was edging into dusk when he emerged from the trees, and saw Mala as he had hoped to see it three weeks earlier. Streaks of light showed from gaps in the shutters and a steady column of smoke rose into the air. She had reached home first, and he felt a curious shame because, in a longer day, he had gathered less than she usually did in a shorter time. He would have to tell her, perhaps even demonstrate to her, how awkward it was for him to gather anything from the ground . . . Simple, natural thoughts, but new to him; never before had he thought of the wineshop as *home*; it had been a place of shelter while his knee mended, and never before had he thought of Gilda as a person whose approval he needed.

As he stumbled in, she looked up from what she was doing—kneading dough made from real flour—and smiled.

"I was beginning to fear for you, thinking that you had lost your way, or fallen." She glanced at the willow basket, only three-quarters filled by the gleanings of an exhausting day, and said, "Tonight we shall have bread, *real* bread." She had said that she had a new plan, but that it might fail, and he had refrained from asking what she had in mind. Now, dropping down to his bed, he watched with interest her primitive baking. All around the glowing fire she placed bricks and, when they had heated, put on to each a lump of dough about the size of a man's clenched fist. She squatted down within arm's reach of the fire and, from time to time, using two knives, turned the little loaves about, and presently the kitchen was filled with the appetising odour of baking bread, and the loaves were expanding.

After a long silence, for she was exhausted, too, she said, "I thought correctly. The miller was there and he had flour in abundance." She laughed. "He could not carry away the river, or the grinding-stones. And many of his customers—like Pollio—had taken their corn to be ground and then run away before they could collect it."

Still thinking in the terms of his training, Paulus asked, "What river?" For it was by river that the sea-raiders, the Horned Men, came.

"It has a bird's name. The Lark."

"How far distant from here?"

"Ten miles. In that direction." She indicated the level heathland. She turned the loaves, and Paulus saw that, on a low stool near the door, stood a gaping sack, a hundred pounds' weight of flour at the least.

"Who helped you?"

"Who could? A large village—ten houses at least—and

only the miller left." She eyed her loaves, and said in an unemotional voice, "At the sight of me he wept, for joy. And again, for sorrow, when I left."

Twenty miles was reckoned a fair day's march, and sixty pounds of equipment a fair burden for a man in prime condition; this wraith of a girl, weighing, he estimated rather less than the sack, had carried it for ten miles. Amazing! Almost at once she contradicted what he had not said. "Much of the way I dragged it. The miller wished me to stay with him," she said, turning the loaves again. "He says that whatever happens, whoever comes, they will need bread, and the mill is so old that it would not work for any new master." She speared a loaf on a knife and held it to her ear, listening as though to a lover's voice. "It is ready."

In the course of his life he had eaten many strange things, some regarded as luxuries, for when a city was taken or an enemy camp overrun there was always a moment when everything was free for all, but never had he enjoyed anything so much as this freshly-made bread. When the first hunger was satisfied, he said, "The miller was right. Bread is the one thing . . . And his offer was good. Why did you not accept it?"

She hesitated before replying.

Then, speaking slowly but very firmly, "You would not understand, being born free . . . You set me free when you left the door unbarred, and in return I fed you with what poor stuff I could gather, when without me you would have died. A life for a life. I prefer it so. Then there is no obligation."

Very dimly he began to understand what her life had been and how valuable freedom, which the free man took for granted, could appear to some of those to whom it was denied. It was a matter to which he had never before given a thought, and, in his daydreams about retiring to a farm in Spain, it had always been slaves who tilled the ground, tended the livestock, gathered in the harvest, trod the winepress.

He turned his mind to more immediate things, since the dream was unlikely now to come true—or at least only in a future too remote to be considered.

"From whom did the other villagers flee?"

"The Horned Men in their beaked ships had been seen lower down the river. But it was low then, the summer having been so dry; and then the winds were against them. They will come back, of course. I know from my mother . . . Their own land is so poor, rock-strewn or swampy. Here even the heathland can be made rich. In three generations." She gave him a look oddly compounded of understanding, a kind of pity, a kind of scorn. "You have not seen what Pollio's grandfather made behind this house?"

"No."

"There is an orchard and fields. All that rough land needed was dung. Pollio's grandfather penned his animals narrowly to dung the earth and dig it in with their hooves." She looked thoughtful, and then said with sudden decision, "I shall regard it as mine and look after it well. I have kept count of the days and I know now, I *know* that Pollio is dead. Had he been alive, he would have come, or sent."

"Had he no children?"

"No. My son, had he lived, would have been heir to all."

"Livia, as his wife . . ." Gilda made a grimace, not a smile, a drawing back of the lips which exposed white teeth, the canines exceptionally sharp.

"She was not his wife. A wife would not have had such fear of being supplanted. You are a Roman; you know the law. If Livia had been his wife and he liked me better—which he did, and she knew it—he could have divorced her, given back her dowry and made an end. But she was one of us, you understand me? For a long time the favourite. Then she grew fat and bad-tempered, and Pollio . . . he was a kind man and liked peace in his household." Unaware that she was expressing a profound truth, she said, "Those who value peace above all things are the last to obtain it."

Paulus had an imagination as chequered as a chess-board. This he understood and accepted; this he did not understand and therefore refuted. He'd never owned a house under whose roof peace must be kept at any price, never had anything to do with women's squabbles. Here he was, by his own stern standards a useless man. But now he could keep the fire going, the more easily after he had applied on the most resistant logs the principle of the wedge. When the snow fell in the two-faced month of January, he and Gilda had a fire; they had bread, and the half-tamed pheasants, so far from needing enticement, came seeking food at the kitchen door. Out of a shredded blanket he made a net and caught several. He remembered that as a boy he had been handy with a sling, and, after some failures, brought down other birds, such as pigeons and rooks.

At some point during that winter he discarded his crutch, for the stiffened leg developed a strength of its own, and he developed a peculiar gait, not unlike that which he had seen in various places with those who had survived crude amputations and been fitted with wooden legs. He could walk, though awkwardly, but at least unaided.

So the spring, the growing season, came to Britain suddenly, as was its habit, and Gilda said, "Now is the time for planting seed. And we have none. Perhaps—the miller . . ."

2 Paulus and Gilda

HE SAW HER OFF NEXT MORNING WITHOUT MISGIVING, THINKING that the worst that could happen would be that the miller had, after all, decided to move away, that the village would be truly deserted and she would come back empty-handed. But when it was dusk, then dead dark, and she had not come, he grew worried. Mental agitation over a matter about which a man could do nothing was something that had been trained out of him; like most of his kind he could sleep on a night before a battle or walk unperturbed through the streets of a plague-smitten city. But tonight he worried. Even in spring the evenings were chill, but he set the shutters wide, and made a fire calculated to give more light than heat, so that she should see the house from a distance. He explained to himself that it was the not knowing which disturbed his nerves. On the eve of battle or some other perilous venture like crossing a river in dangerously frail-looking boats, a man knew what he must face. Death itself did not inflict the agony of uncertainty; to a man who had lived by the rules, death was merely a removal from this camp, as it were, to another, more comfortable one.

This was different; it set his imagination to work. So many things could have happened to her, ranging from her collapse under too heavy a load to the miller holding her by force. There were men who could not live without women...Other possibilities occurred to him, always accompanied by the detestable realisation that against whatever, whoever it was, he could do nothing.

At first light in the morning, he set out without any very clear idea of where he was going. The village of the miller and the ten deserted houses lay, Gilda had indicated by a gesture, across the heath—towards the east, and it was ten miles distant. That was all he knew, and to go wandering off, exhausting himself and probably losing his way, seemed senseless, yet better than sitting and waiting.

The land was flat, with a definite slope to the east, slanting down towards the river, he thought. Once he was off the cultivated ground, walking was not easy; coarse grass and, in places, bracken hampered his stumbling progress, and he was unable to steer a straight course because he was obliged to circle around clumps of brambles. When Gilda had said the village was ten miles away: did she mean as the crow flew, or as a man must walk? Had he covered a mile yet? He looked back, and was dismayed to see how close the wineshop still seemed. In the house and around the yard he had lately managed without his crutch; now he was glad he had brought it—was, in fact, relying upon it more and more.

Counting paces helped, he knew, when a man was tired. A mile was a thousand paces—but the paces of an able-bodied man. Still, he took a thousand blundering steps before looking back again, and now he could not see the winehouse, though its invisibility was probably due to the bramble bushes rather than to the distance he had covered. Another mile, or at least another thousand steps, and pains which had departed weeks ago began to make themselves felt in his knee. Sit down and rest it for a while? He remembered the difficulty he had experienced when gathering the beech-nuts.

There were marching-songs, but they were all designed to encourage and to synchronise the paces of men with two sound legs—even to think of them now was a grim parody. The sun travelled in the sky, upwards and southwards; it would soon be noon. Half the day gone. The complete folly of this expedition came home to him. Whatever had happened to Gilda had happened now, and what could he do about it, tottering old wreck? Silly old fool! It was even possible that the miller had detained her for the night and then let her go. In that case she might even now be making her way across this heath where there were no beaten tracks and apparently no landmarks. Or the miller might have had no hand in the matter at all; perhaps Gilda had simply lost her way, or was now making for home, to an empty house and a fire damped down as though for the night. Should he turn back? But it seemed that the power of making such a decision had deserted him, and presently he ceased to think at all, but plodded on, intent only upon keeping on the move and ignoring the pain.

The nature of the land changed; there were trees, the grass was finer and dotted with clumps of primroses. Riverside country, but he hardly noticed it, and the river itself, one shining loop partially overhung by willows, was a surprise to him. He associated the river with the mill and, even had he been feeling optimistic, he could not have persuaded himself that he had staggered ten miles.

He had, at least, made in the right direction, but he was immediately confronted with a problem. Did the mill lie upstream or down? That needed thinking about and, while he thought, he was entitled to a little rest. He chose a tree with a low branch by which he could heave himself up when he had reached his decision, and lowered himself to the ground. Almost immediately the worst of the dagger pains ceased. That easement, the cessation of effort, and the sun, now just past its zenith, shining warm on his right shoulder, induced a kind of waking sleep, but he saw and heard them before they were aware of him: the sun shone full on them.

A curious procession. Gilda walking between two tall men. The likeness between them was astounding, not only in the bright yellow hair but also in the set of the head, the way they walked, free and easy, though all bore burdens. Paulus was accustomed to associating age with bulk, and the man who seemed to be the older of the two carried a calf, draped across his shoulders like a scarf. The beast was alive; every now and then it added a plaintive little cry to the chatter between the two men, which seemed to be of a hilarious nature. The younger man carried a sack on one shoulder and had various bundles

hung about him. Even Gilda was laden with a basket, lidded
over, and, from the way she held it, containing something
precious—eggs, perhaps. A lean, long-legged dog bounded
around them. Both men wore belts from which depended swords.
Yet they looked neither wary nor hostile, and Gilda seemed to
be all right, until she saw him as he heaved himself up, pushed
the crutch under his left arm, and stood to await what happened
next.

What happened was that Gilda set down the basket and,
thus lightened of her load, ran, embraced him with the most
curious combination of fervour and respect, and hissed—there
was no other word for it—into his ear, "You are, for the
moment deaf and dumb. And my father. There is no other way.
No Latin, if you would live."

There was no time for more, for the two men, the younger
having stooped and taken up the basket and added it to his
load, were now close to where Paulus, utterly bewildered, stood
under the tree. There followed the most elaborate bit of dumb
show which Paulus, who had seen some of the best, had ever
witnessed. He could hear, and his ears told him, that the language which the two yellow-haired men spoke with fluency,
Gilda spoke just as a child learning to speak would talk—a
few isolated words, probably mispronounced, but accepted with
pleasure and admiration. Eking out her few words and gestures,
she introduced a man, apparently deaf and dumb, to two men
with whom she seemed to be on friendly terms, and yet not to
trust. Making what was obviously an introduction, she smiled
and spoke a few words with the utmost amiability, but her eyes
were wary. An infantry man himself, Paulus yet knew enough
about horses to draw a comparison—a frightened horse might
look in just that way.

Yet the two men were behaving deferentially. Paulus recognised respect when he saw it and, though these men showed
it differently, it was almost as though they were saluting him.
The elder laid his hand to his own breast and then offered it
to Paulus. He smiled, lifted down the calf and laid it at Paulus's
feet. Its front and hind hooves were tethered, but it struggled
to rise, and both the strangers laughed. Gilda produced one of
her limited smiles, said something, and held up two fingers.
The man who had carried the calf laughed and smote his right
fist into his left palm twice and made a sound that seemed to
Paulus like "Ja!" Then the younger man, bowing his yellow-

haired head, presented his offering. The sack contained sound, good wheat grain, neither shrivelled nor mouldy. To it he added smaller bags—a bunch of onions, a smoked ham, a large wooden bottle. In the basket which Gilda had carried so carefully and abandoned so carelessly, sat a speckled hen intent upon nothing but brooding.

Gilda signed to him to register pleasure, which he did as far as his complete bewilderment allowed, for they were now presenting him with the dog!

Paulus pretended to be pleased, and Gilda was undoubtedly pleased, everything having gone as planned.

Few men did their twenty years of service without incurring some wounds; for Paulus the last and most harmful had been that to his knee, but there were others, trivial things which had hardly put him out of action for a day. But they had left scars. One, the oldest, yet the worst looking because it had been dressed with rock salt, which hardened tissue, had not been gained in honourable battle. It dated back to his time in training, when he was learning sword-play in the arena at Nimes. The non-commissioned officer in charge of that exercise had had caustic things to say about that.

The scar was actually not much of a disfigurement, following as it did the line of his jaw, and it was so much a part of him that he had forgotten it. Gilda, however, had noticed it, and now she put aside the collar of the worn old sheepskin jerkin which even Livia had not thought worth taking away, and exposed it. She mimed a knife-slash, and the two men nodded and made sympathetic noises. She then drew attention to his knee. Their response indicated that they regarded this as a much graver matter, a serious disablement.

Gilda gestured towards home and spread her hands in an unmistakable gesture of invitation. She picked up the basket and was ready, but the men did a little shuffling of their loads, so that the younger was less encumbered and had an arm free to offer Paulus. He shook his head violently. Gilda gave him a reproachful look and glanced at the sky. "No Latin, if you would live," she had whispered; so he had said nothing, acted like a deaf and dumb idiot, but he had his Roman pride. He set himself to counting paces again, but now the slope of the ground was against him; even the smoother, primrose-scattered grass was exhausting, and the thought of the rough, tussocky heathland still to come filled him with dismay.

They courteously matched their pace to his, but were growing impatient. Despite the pain and the mounting fatigue, he had one pleasurable thought—the men had thought the destination to which Gilda was leading them was far nearer than it was, believing that a man so crippled could not have walked so far from home. Presently he touched Gilda on the shoulder and mimed that she and the men should go ahead, leaving him to struggle, to retain his self-respect. She shook her head, and indicated that he should take the arm of the younger man and abandon the crutch. He shook his head, and they had made a little more slow progress when disaster overtook them. The end of his crutch sank into a mole-hole, ruining his carefully preserved balance; he lurched and fell and heard the bough crack under him.

The next thing he knew was that he was being carried on the back of the older man. The younger now bore the calf and the sack: Gilda bore more than the basket, and they were all trotting literally, at a fresh pony's pace, across the rough ground, through the darkling pasture, the untilled fields and the orchard which had once been Pollio's, his father's, his grandfather's.

Paulus wondered vaguely that this man whose back he rode should carry him so easily, forgetting that months of near-starvation diet had reduced his weight.

He noticed that the man carrying him wore a thick collar of what looked like gold. Some time later he noticed that the fire he had damped down had survived, and that the kitchen window which he had left unshuttered to guide Gilda home last night now glowed with its golden welcome. And presently, inside the house, comfortably seated, he realised that, though he had been carried—how far?—like a tethered calf, like a cornsack, he had not lost status. For him, as usual, were the best place by the fire, the first of the meat, hastily fried over the fire, and the first draught of the liquor, cloyingly sweet, poured from the wooden bottle. Gilda waited upon them all, and it seemed to Paulus that they ate prodigiously, for he had lived so meagrely in the last months that his belly had shrunk, and the pretence that he could not hear or speak imposed a kind of blockage, so that even swallowing was not easy. They talked, Gilda joining in with a word or two, like a child. Except for her occasional wary look and his pretended inability to understand anything, the meal and the drinking afterwards could have been said to be amiable. But it seemed to Paulus that the two men had moved in. And by what right?

Paulus found himself longing for the moment when he would be alone with Gilda, listening to what she had to tell him, hearing her explanation. It came when they separated for the night.

He no longer slept on the small bed by the kitchen fire, upon which she had installed him at first, but in a side room, formerly occupied by the master of the house. She occupied another. Never again, she had told him emphatically, did she wish to enter the cubicles beyond the wine-store. In one of them, she explained, she had borne her dead child and been ill. Later—still waiting for Pollio to come and release her—she had moved into another as soon as she found that she was a prisoner, and had used the one already soiled as a latrine. But she had spent the greater part of a cold winter day in giving the place a thorough cleaning, and it was towards this part of the house that she now conducted the visitors, smiling, making agreeable noises, and lighting the way with a flaming resinous pine-twig stuck into a narrow-necked jug.

She was back almost immediately, and Paulus said, "Now tell me." She gestured to him to be silent, and waited, listening. Once she went into the wine-store and came back, closing the door softly behind her. "After mead they sleep soundly," she said.

"Who are they?"

"Angles—from the sea. They are my own people, the people of my mother. I told you, did I not, how the Iceni pretended to be friendly, and then turned enemy and killed all but the young girls, apt for slavery, of whom my mother was one." She hugged herself, each hand on the upper part of the opposite arm, and leaned forward, rocking herself in a gesture of despair. Then she tackled her story from another angle. "I went to the mill. It was working—but the miller was not there. Instead eight, ten men roistering. I was saved by my hair." She moved a hand and touched one of the plaits in which, since that first night, she had worn her hair. "And the amazing thing," she said speaking with astonishment yet with detachment, as though describing another person's experience, "is that after the first minute I understood some of their words . . . My mother, to my memory, spoke seldom and then in Latin, but I understood. And I lied to them."

"Saying that you were my daughter?"

"To save you from harm," she said quickly. "They need women. You saw with what respect they behaved to you, the gifts they brought. To please you. The younger one—Sweyn is his name—wishes to have me for his wife."

"And you wish to have him for your husband?"

"We must live." She spoke quietly but with violence. "We have a garden, but no seed to sow in it; a meadow, but no animal to graze. There are fields; can we dig or plough?" It was not an answer to his question, but he saw the point of it. "What is more," she said with a certain reluctance. "I *could* have said that we were married. But I *know*, just as I know some of their words, that they are ruthless; what they want they take. I should have soon been a widow!"

He saw the point of that, too—a young woman and desirable, married to a useless man.

"What other lies did you tell about me?"

"They hate the Romans and despise the Iceni. I told them that you had come in from the sea, married my mother who had the wineshop and a little property, and that, when the Romans left, the Iceni attacked, from envy. I gave you a good reputation. I said that single-handed you killed five. And then were robbed. I was obliged to explain quickly. There was no time to invent. The Iceni did hate my family—and Livia took all that could be carried."

"The best lies always contain some element of truth."

"You are angry with me?"

"Why should I be? You did very well."

Disconcertingly, she began to cry.

He looked back over the time they had spent together; the months of mere survival—and from her never a whimper. He thought of her kindness to him when he was helpless, her courage in facing the wolf-threatening woods. He thought of his own utter helplessness. He could neither provide nor protect. The known world, of which he had been a part, had vanished.

He put out a hand and touched her shoulder. "Gilda, don't cry. For you . . . things should be . . . easier now." The one called Sweyn was young, healthy and seemed amiable.

"And for you," she said, twisting under his hand and burying her face against his chest. "And for *you*."

He was denied even the small satisfaction of self-abnegation; he could not say, "Think of yourself, not of me."

"As my father," she said, still sobbing, "you will be honoured. Sweyn shall work for us both. But I . . . but I . . . I love you, Paulus."

The statement struck him dumb as he had this day pretended to be, for it was a phrase out of time, out of place. There were a few stories, a few songs—but not the ones sung by soldiers—which exalted the feeling between man and woman, woman and man, as something above the coupling of animals or the huckstering in a market. When, the ground of the Roman Empire solid under his feet and the weight of his commitment to it on his shoulders, Paulus had visualised himself, honourably retired with his allocation of acres in sunny Spain, he had also visualised a wife; young, not ill-looking, full-bosomed, wide-hipped, a potential good breeder of children. Men who asked or expected more were mad, or bewitched, like Menelaus sacking Troy because, of all the thousands of women in the world, only one, called Helen, could content him. Antony and Cleopatra . . . That kind of thing had no part in ordinary life, nothing to do with ordinary people, like him and the girl who now clung to him, gulping and shuddering. "I thought I loved Pollio—but that was only because he was kind and gave me presents and made promises. This is different. Tomorrow will be different again, but, my love, *tonight is ours*."

And he went mad, or was enchanted—overwhelmed by an emotion he had not known existed.

3 Paulus, Gilda and Sweyn

PAULUS HAD BEEN RIGHT IN SAYING THAT THINGS WOULD BE easier when Mala was in the hands of a young, active man. Never again were they reduced to a diet of beech-mast, or obliged to go begging for flour to make bread, but for some years life at Mala was hard and exacting. Partly this was because of its position: it was too far from the main settlement which centred about the mill.

The distance between the two places was far less than Gilda had said and then Paulus had believed. Pollio had always said that the mill was ten miles away and to the east, but he always used the road as far as he could and then turned off. Gilda had cut across country and to her, uncertain of her way on her outgoing journey, heavily laden on her return, the distance had seemed a full ten miles. It was actually five. Paulus was astonished to learn that, on that momentous day, he had almost reached his objective.

The road made and used by the Romans was generally avoided, as was everything else Roman, except the mill, which had to be accepted because it was there, in the exactly right position, and a thing which could not be picked up and moved. The newcomers seemed to be superstitious about anything Roman; even the ten houses in the deserted village were used only as temporary shelters while new houses were being erected. The new houses, all near the river and built north or south of the mill, made a settlement now called Beofricsworth, named for Sweyn's father, the man with the golden collar. Sweyn was his fourth son, youngest and favourite, and he was delighted to see him married and provided for. But Sweyn often felt cut off, remote from his community, and handicapped by being a

40

man on his own. Around the main settlement, though a few individuals built their own houses, living was largely communal and the land was cultivated in the traditional way, each man holding strips, many or few, in the big open fields. Ox-power and man-power were pooled at busy seasons. Sweyn owned one ox, and had no neighbour from whom to borrow, and so his ploughing was slow, in a season already late. And for help he had a cripple and a woman, soon pregnant.

Paulus—now known as Alfred, a name bestowed upon him by Gilda and seemingly acceptable to all—did his best, was indeed indomitable. As Sweyn ploughed the rich, clayey soil, Alfred limped and lurched behind, casting the seed from the bag suspended from his neck. His progress was slow and painful to watch, and sometimes Sweyn, from sheer pity, would halt the ox at a turn, and indicate that Alfred should take a rest. More often than not he was met by a stubborn refusal, but sometimes Paulus would allow him to take the bag and would lower himself to the grassy headland and watch as the young man, lithe and apparently tireless, took the uneven ground in his stride. Paulus tried to reason with himself, thinking that had things gone well with him and he had achieved retirement to his acres in Spain, one day he would have become old and feeble, and envious of youth. He'd merely grown old before his time. He also told himself that to be envious of Sweyn was ungrateful. But for him, he and Gilda would have died of starvation.

It was also arguable that he had no real reason to be jealous of Sweyn; Sweyn had not robbed him. Until that memorable evening, Paulus had not recognised that his feelings for Gilda were anything but admiration, a gratitude and liking. None the less, it was impossible not to feel envious to the point of hatred each night when the bedroom door closed behind them, or during the day when, as he often did, Sweyn made some gesture of uxoriousness, patting her with a possessive touch, winding one of her thick shining plaits around his arm or neck. Nothing wrong in a man showing affection for his wife in front of her father. Yet up would come the feeling, sour as bile.

Gilda seemed never to invite such gestures. She usually looked amiable enough, rapidly improved her knowledge of Sweyn's language, and often made jokes, but she was always rather ostentatiously busy, especially in the time after supper when Sweyn, his day's work done, was relaxed and inclined to be playful. She had a way of saying, "I must just..." and then name some pressing duty. The broody hen had hatched her clutch, all twelve, little balls of yellow fluff; then leggy and half-feathered things; then full-fledged. Three were cock-erels; one would be kept for breeding next year, two were doomed to the pot next winter, but all must be protected now, against foxes, against wolves. "I must just see to the fowls," Gilda would say. There was also the calf, part of the bride-gift— a bull-calf who presently would be able to defend him-self, but for a time must be protected. And there was the oven in the old bakehouse.

With flour at her disposal and three instead of two to feed, Gilda was no longer content to bake tiny loaves on bricks around the kitchen fire. And why should she, with a real oven in the old bakehouse just across the yard? Since she no longer had to gather beech-mast in order to survive, she could gather sticks, make a faggot, put it in the brick-lined oven, light it and allow it to burn out while she made the bread dough. If she timed it well, the dough was just ready for the oven when the oven was ready for it, the faggot burned out, the bricks retaining their heat. Bread made in this fashion was more evenly cooked through, more palatable, but the business involved a lot of running to and fro, and often an after-supper errand, since one spark left could be dangerous. "I must just..." Gilda would say.

With the ploughing done and the evenings growing lighter, Sweyn fell into the habit of slipping down to Beofricsworth, seeking the company of his fellows, and making bargains. To Paulus and to Gilda, who had both lived in a civilisation where coin was currency, this method of bargaining seemed clumsy, though just—provided you could trust the one with whom the bargain was made, and had faith in the future. On one occasion Sweyn came home with a sow, guaranteed to be in pig but lively enough to walk five miles with a string tied around a hind leg. The animal had belonged to his brother Osric, who could claim, for the next four years, the pick of any litter she bore. Some similar arrangement, more complicated because it involved a portion of his corn crop, gave Sweyn possession of a cow. The ox had been a free gift from his father. Beofrics-worth seemed to be well stocked; some of the animals had made the voyage in the beak-prowed ships; others had been captured in raids.

When Sweyn was absent during the evening, Paulus and Gilda practised, without a word being spoken, a mutual avoidance, each finding some demanding and urgent job in different parts of the holding. They would both begin to be ostentatiously busy as soon as Sweyn mentioned "stepping across," as he called it. The work, deliberately prolonged, would last until bedtime, when they might meet and exchange a few words—always in Latin. Once Paulus ventured to ask, "Are you happy?" She gave him a look which could easily have been mistaken for dislike, though he did not so mistake it. She said, "I have a kind husband, and by the year's end I shall have a baby. Should I not be happy?"

"Ours?"

"So long as you continue to think in Latin and speak it as soon as you have a chance, you will never make progress in their tongue. Good night," she said.

Playing deaf-mute had demanded such intense concentration and posed such difficulties that Paulus had soon indicated that he could hear again, and then ventured on trying his voice with a word or two in the language which would seem to him, to the end of his days, a barbarous one, all clicks and grunts. Animal talk.

When Sweyn went to Beofricsworth on a real or a concocted errand, Beofric always asked, most courteously, about Alfred. And Sweyn always reported faithfully, speaking in the highest terms of the man who seemed to him to be old and who bore such afflictions with such fortitude.

"He can hear now. Less than he pretends," he said of the man whose hearing had always been excellent. "I know he is still rather deaf. The other day I called, 'Alfred,' across the width of the field, no more, and he did not hear."

"He has regained some speech," Sweyn said, "but to talk is still an effort."

Then Sweyn would revert to how indomitable the old man had been in following the plough. And how quickly he had learned to milk the cow.

A more critical audience—or one which had taken less mead—might have wondered why Alfred must learn how to take milk from a cow. But in an all-male company, merry on mead, such a thought, if it occurred, slipped easily in and out. There was plenty else to think and talk about: weather, crops, animals, an expedition back to what they still regarded as home, to fetch women, more livestock, household gear. The settlement was now regarded as established, a fit place for family life to be resumed, and in every way it must be regarded as a fortunate place, one upon which all the gods had looked kindly. There'd been no opposition, because the land was virtually uninhabited. In fact, the depopulation of the area between the two rivers, the Lark and the Wren, had given rise to the theory that the natives had fled from a plague of some kind, and this accounted in part for the reluctance of the newcomers to live in what houses were available. Sweyn's brothers and cousins might call him the Lucky One because he had gained himself a wife, young and comely and soon with child, as well as some land and a father-in-law who seemed amiable, but they did not envy his dwelling, in which, on all their visits, they had felt in a curious way ill-at-ease. A place so plainly alien—one room with a picture on the floor and on the walls. Osric said that if he were in Sweyn's place he would choose to live in the barn, and Beofric said that, once the harvest and the expedition were over, they'd all join forces, come to Mallow— the Angle's name for Mala—and build Sweyn a proper, timbered house. With timber so readily available and so many willing hands at work, a house could be reared in a week.

It was a good harvest, for the heavy soil, though hard to plough, was rewarding, and the summer had been—to Paulus and Gilda—exceptionally sunny, but the newcomers took it for granted, part of the legend which had always drawn adventurers to the west. Except for their chanted songs, dealing either with the honourable genealogy of the living or the remembered exploits of the dead, the Angles had no history, but they knew with the certainty of instinct that every migration—and they had made many—had been towards the west, to some land of promise. It seemed to Beofric and his followers that they had found it in this well-watered, gently rolling, rich soil. Back in Friesland they would praise the new home so highly that other men would be tempted to emigrate; the little settlement would grow strong and great, until it warranted the title of kingdom, with Beofricsworth as its capital.

The fundamental weakness in the matter of numbers was never more clearly illuminated than in the discussions which took place just before the expedition set out. Enough men must go to make the little fleet unassailable; enough men must remain to guarantee the safety of the settlement itself. A good many of the decisions were left to personal choice; any real differences were settled, as others were, by a straw ballot. Beofric held in his fist two pieces of straw, one longer than the other, each projecting about an inch. Men took their choice, and another man, so placed that he could see nothing of the procedure, would call, "Short to stay," or "Short to go," as the fancy took him. Such decisions were never questioned—it was the gods who made the choice.

Sweyn, the married man, with a wife growing heavy with child, had no wish to go from the place he regarded as home, but he agreed to move himself and his family and his animals down into the settlement, to tend the livestock of some of those who were leaving, and, in the event of any attack, to help with the defence of the settlement. No such attack was expected, but it was always wise to be prepared. A pony was provided for Alfred and all Mallow moved down into Beofric's hall— the proper Anglian house which Sweyn hoped Gilda and Alfred would like so much that, when the time came, they would welcome the building of a similar, though smaller one, at Mallow. So far, they had shown little enthusiasm for the proposed new house, and Sweyn, with his sea-roving blood, failed to understand an attachment to a place, especially one so strange and unhomelike.

Paulus had never seen the mill or the little Romanised village of which it had been the centre, and so he was unable to estimate the change, wrought by sheer physical labour, which had been brought about in so short a time. Gilda, who had seen it, once when the miller was mourning over his surplus of flour and once when the Angles were in occupation—what had become of the miller?—did stare about her with astonishment; at the one big house and the few small ones, all much resembling barns; at the wide field, just harvested and being pecked over and scratched by fowls. Gilda had brought her own, the three cocks in an osier cage—where the cocks went or were taken, the hens would always follow. Sweyn turned his animals out into the common ground which had been useless heath. A donkey or two, several goats and some geese had devoured what cows and cattle despised, and allowed the grass to push through. The whole place gave the impression of an orderly and modestly prosperous way of life.

Sweyn led the way to Beofric's hall and said, "Welcome
to my father's house. Regard it as your own." The whole place
smelt of new timber. In the centre of the floor ran a clay-lined
trough containing the fire. The hall was furnished, after a fashion; there was a table, a large slab of wood that had not been
planed, merely given some smoothness by someone skilful with
his axe. There were stools and benches made in the same way.
The floor itself was covered with rushes. They grew plentifully
alongside the river above the mill where the water ran more
sluggishly. The rushes were freshly laid and emitted a pleasant
odour when stepped upon, but Gilda regarded them dubiously;
how dirty they would become—unless changed daily—compared with the pretty tiled floor of the wineshop, the plain red
tiles of the kitchen!

"My father built wide," Sweyn said proudly. "He looked
to the future when fifty men could feast in his hall."

Prodded by something which was not pride of ownership in
a personal way, Paulus made an incautious statement. "I have
known fifty men take supper at Mallow." Gilda gave him a
warning look. Apart from the information volunteered within
the first hour of the two cultures coming together, the past was
a thing not to be mentioned. Beofric and Sweyn had been so
delighted by the acquisition of a woman, not only marriageable
but pretty, not only pretty but well dowered, that they had
asked few questions.

And even now Sweyn said, "But not the same fire, around
the same board, Alfred."

Sweyn had the happy feeling of being back where he belonged, and, having shown Gilda the lean-to which served, not
as a kitchen, having no hearth, but as a storage-place for food
and a few household utensils, he hurried out to join in the corn-
threshing. Each man left behind had undertaken to thresh for
some of the men who had gone away, and though the work
was a communal exercise, strict tally was kept. "That's Brad's
done," the man in charge said. "Bring on Otto's."

The threshing was done out of doors on a hard-stamped
floor; the wind helped with the winnowing. The flails beat in
unison and the men whistled or hummed tunes which helped
to keep the rhythm.

"My corn is still in the barn," Sweyn said, without breaking
the rhythm. "Afterwards you must all come and help me thresh

it. And I'll kill a pig." They said, "Oh, yes!" and "Good, good!"

There were four women besides Gilda in the settlement; one was old and had come with the raiders because her son—her only relative—had considered it unfilial to leave her behind. One man had brought his daughter, a girl of about ten, and two of the men had acquired women since landing, both typical Iceni, short in stature, with black hair and greeny-brown eyes. For the first time since the exodus from Mallow, Gilda found herself in the company of women, and at first she did not enjoy it much. Women asked so many questions, personal things, about which men did not bother. The old woman, Ethelreda, was regarded as a wise woman, able to read signs and portents in almost anything from the stars to the way a bird flew, and she professed to be skilled in the use of herbs. She was far more agreeable to Gilda than to the two Iceni girls, whom she seemed to regard with some contempt. She said that she could promise Gilda that her child would be a boy, but she did not reveal upon what premise she based this certainty. She did, however, ask the most probing questions about the past, about Gilda's maternal ancestry, and about Alfred. And once, either by guesswork or by the peculiar second sight which she claimed to possess, she came very near the mark, asking Gilda a question which could not be given an evasive answer. "Were you a slave?"

Gilda said, "No!" and to back up the lie, "How dare you ask such a question?"

"I speak as the spirit directs me. Your son, on his father's side, will be son of Sweyn, son of Beofric, son of Eric, back and back for ten generations. But a boy has also a mother; he will be the son of Gilda, daughter of Alfred, son of . . . ?"

"My father and I lived through troubled times," Gilda said with what she hoped with dignity. And she remembered things that Paulus had spoken of when there was nothing but talk to enliven a supper of beech-mast porridge. One thing had seemed to hold great importance—the Wall. "My father," she said, "comes from beyond the Wall."

That silenced even Ethelreda, for even in the twilight which was descending upon the known world, even upon the fringes of it, in places where Ethelreda had spent her life, the Wall had been heard of, and the people beyond it, never conquered, were regarded with respect.

Fortunately it was the time of the blackberry harvest, and all around and over the common land the fruit ripened, filling the air with its sultry, late-summer fragrance. Ethelreda knew how to make the best of this free harvest, and although she was secretive about some of the leaves and roots which she used for her medicines, she was glad of the girls' help in gathering enough blackberries to be preserved, made into wine, or added to anything bitter or sour to make it palatable. Gilda was especially eager to learn what she could because, transferred from kitchen to brothel at an early age, she had acquired only simple domestic skills. "Sweyn's mother should be pleased with you," the old woman said, adding cryptically, "despite all."

When the corn was all threshed, other preparations for the winter were made. Then men went hunting in the forest—not that part of it which lay beyond Mallow, but just upriver. And some went downstream to fish. There were fish in the river, and in times of hunger anything edible was welcome, but riverfish had a flat, insipid flavour whereas sea-fish, either fresh-caught or dried, was tasty and, with the sea only four miles away, was hardly a luxury except for the fact that fishing took time. Now, in the short interval between the threshing and the first ploughing, there was time to fish and to hunt.

The first fishing expedition was extremely successful, made while the calm left-over-from-summer weather continued, with mornings slightly chill and rather misty, but then the day clearing and blooming, without wind. And the sea here was so rich in fish that a net dropped three boat-lengths from the shore and dragged around for quite a short time gave a rich haul. Everybody ate to full capacity, and Ethelreda had the pleasure of instructing ignorant girls in the art of smoking fish—using Beofric's hall, because the fire was longest. Gilda watched how it was done, and helped with the doing. In the trough a good fire was prepared and over it a layer of oak-bark was laid—Ethelreda, the wise woman, said that only oak would do. Over the oak went some damp straw and some turf. Above this, suspended like washing on a line, were the fish, detted and spread wide, changing colour.

A few days later the wind changed, blowing strongly from the east, and everybody in the settlement welcomed it, for it was now about time for the long ships to be setting out, heavily laden, from the old home; a following wind would help. Ethelreda did not actually claim credit in words for this wind from the east, but every time it was mentioned she looked smug, and she whistled a great deal. Paulus, who resented her questions, remarked sourly that some people regarded a whistling woman as an ill omen, as unnatural as a crowing hen. Sweyn laughed and said that anything as old as Ethelreda must be regarded as sexless. As he made this remark he gave Gilda a glance which most people would not have noticed. Now well into her seventh month, she too could be regarded as sexless, but the look spoke of remembered intimacies and others to come, once the child was born. Paulus saw it and writhed inwardly.

A second fishing expedition was now due, and Osric, Sweyn's brother, should have gone with it, but he had been fortunate enough to kill a bear on one of the hunting-trips, and was busy dressing the pelt as a gift for the bride whom the home-coming ships would bring him. He and Gerta had been pledged for some time, and he had been content with the arrangement made between his parents and hers, but she was too young for marriage when the venture to Britain was being mounted, and secretly Osric had once thought that his father had dealt unfairly when he arranged for Sweyn to marry Gilda. He had actually voiced a protest, and Beofric had dismissed it. "My son, you are pledged; Sweyn is not." And then, when Osric had seen the place called Mallow, so isolated and so alien, he had ceased to envy his brother, and had seen that his father had been wise after all.

It took three men to go fishing: two to row the shallow-drafted boat, one to manage the net, to cast and haul in. Sweyn on that morning was to be the fisherman.

There was often some turbulence where river ran into sea, current fighting against tide, and sometimes, as now, the wind taking part, but the boat, though small, was sturdy and passed through the disturbed waters, buoyant as a feather. Brad said, "Now!" and Sweyn stood up, the neatly folded net in his hands, his legs braced. For him the horizon widened by as great a distance as young, clear-sighted eyes could see, and he sat down suddenly, saying, "*Three* ships!"

"Ours?"

"Too far away to tell yet," Sweyn said. "But my father left with *two*."

"A third could have joined him," Brad said, but with no

great assurance. He stood up, squinting, then cupping his eyes with his hands. Even so, against the glare of the morning light he could see nothing, a fact he was unwilling to admit, failing sight being one of the signs of age. "Yes. Three," he said. The third man, Eric, then stood up and stared. Seen from a distance, and head-on, long ships were not easily distinguishable from one another, but these were coming fast, each with its single square sail spread, and doubtless rowers at work as well. After what seemed a long silence, Eric said, "No. Not our colour or mark." Sweyn stood up to confirm this, which he did with one word, "Yellow." His father's sails were reddish brown. He lowered himself, and took Brad's oar. He was younger and, having been chosen as caster, had not exerted himself on the outward journey.

The three men did not speak; their shared anxiety needed no words. It was possible that the strangers were friendly; it was also highly unlikely. Even if they had no evil intentions now, were would-be settlers and not raiders, things would change as soon as they saw the settlement with so much of the hard work already done and containing so many animals. And all to be defended by a handful of men—fourteen, fifteen, if you counted old Alfred. Three ships meant sixty men at least. And that sixty men should leave fourteen in possession of something desirable was unthinkable. They would not have done it themselves; they did not expect it of others.

A council of war must be called, plans made, the settlement defended, to the last man if necessary, but, being so comparatively weak, they would not take the offensive and, if it so chanced that the newcomers intended to settle and not to raid and were content to make use of land seaward to Beofricsworth, a mutual tolerance would develop and become a kind of good-neighbourliness.

There was another possibility, too. Hard on the heels of the yellow sails might come the russet ones, with Beofric's two ships, perhaps reinforced, as Brad had suggested, by a third. Then Beofric would dictate the terms, either offering bloody war or exacting some kind of tribute.

Thinking these things as he rowed, Sweyn looked out on the land on either side of the river, and doubted whether the newcomers would find it attractive; it was low and marshy and susceptible to flooding. He remembered how, in the previous year, his father had pushed on inland and been rewarded by finding the mill, land that had already been cleared and cultivated with plentiful timber nearby.

The council gathered in Beofric's hall; Paulus was present, but he took no part. He was one of the tribe up to a point: father-in-law to one of the chief's sons and thus acceptable, but he was not really one of them; he was not in a condition to fight, and although at his age and with his record he doubtless had experience, it was not of the kind to benefit them now.

He was, indeed, deeply concerned, even frightened and not ashamed of being so, since his fear was for Gilda and then for the fourteen men and the four other women. What happened to him did not matter. He'd had the better share of his life; his body was crippled and his spirit was being eaten away by jealousy.

He had hobbled about the settlement and looked at it with an old soldier's eye for defensibility. It had seemed to him to be pitiably vulnerable. He was a Roman, with all the Roman belief in defences, fortresses, walls, even stockade posts planted around one-night camps. The Angles planned to build a solid fence around the houses, and had actually begun to do so, fifteen to twenty feet on the river side; but they had been busy— and careless, considering the land around them to be uninhabited, and not expecting an attack from the sea so soon.

At such a meeting as this every man had the right to speak: it was a free and egalitarian society, but things were done in order, and Osric, as Beofric's eldest son, was allowed to speak first; after that priority went by age. Paulus thought it typical of the kind of impracticality which he had noticed before in these extremely practical people that, before settling down to business, Osric sent for Ethelreda and said, "Old woman, whistle up a wind from the west to delay them."

She said, sullenly, "I never claimed to command the winds."

"Try," he said. She went away, muttering to herself.

In the talk that followed, only one man suggested—and that very tentatively—the possibility of flight, carrying as much food as possible, driving or leading their animals and taking to the woods. It was significant that he was married to one of the Iceni girls, and the policy he proposed was exactly what the Iceni had done and were doing. What he said was rejected by everyone. Nobody wished to leave the land over which he had sweated and which he had reaped with rejoicing, or the little raw wooden houses that were homes. They were only first-year settlers, but the sense of ownership was already at work in them—that, and another thing, utterly different: the lust for a fight, the legacy of their blood. Never mind the atrocious odds; everybody knew that one man of this tribe was worth ten of any other. If the strangers wanted a fight, by all the gods in Valhalla they should have one. And what a fight it would be!

They were all sober; last year's mead and ale had been consumed and this year's not yet prepared; yet to Paulus watching it was as though they were all suddenly intoxicated. They yelled, waved their arms about, gave each other playful buffets. One man shouted, "Why wait? We could go now and take them by surprise." Wildly fantastic as the suggestion was, it was not rejected with the unanimity that flight had been. There were supporting cries. "Aye! Aye! Fall upon them as they land!"

Osric remained calm. The strangers might not land, he pointed out. Neither their intentions nor their plans were yet known. Until the newcomers showed themselves to be hostile, the best plan was to wait and prepare, get arms in order, and lengthen the stockade. A young man of good sense, Paulus thought. A good leader, but in a cause already lost. "We need a spy," Osric went on. "Who will volunteer?" Fourteen right hands shot into the air.

Something moved in Paulus and he wished that he could volunteer, too. He had never seen the river below Beofricsworth, but he had heard it described and he knew from the description that flat, marshy, treeless land would offer little cover. Whoever took on the task of reconnaissance was risking capture and a death more painful and protracted than that met in battle. A spy evoked no sympathy; a brave opponent was often granted the mercy of a last, killing thrust.

The spy was chosen by some mysterious consensus—a boy named Wulf the Orphan. He was in his middle teens, very little and slim. A good choice.

It took a little time to make him ready—a task handed to Ethelreda—and Paulus, despite the despair in his heart, was interested to see that, when the boy was prepared, he was, as nearly as possible, made invisible. He wore only a pair of short breeches, and from the top of his yellow head to his rawhide shoes, he was coloured a brownish green.

"You look like an elf," Ethelreda said, "and the elves will

aid their own." Men commended him to Thor or Woden, to Fria or Tew. Paulus consigned him to the keeping of Mithras. Then, when the boy had slipped away, he began to consider what part he could and must play if the hopeless confrontation came about.

Until he was posted to Britain, Paulus had never been north of the Rhine, but he had talked with men who had fought the barbarians on that frontier, and who had had lurid tales to tell of the ferocity and tenacity of the tribes there. Nobody had mentioned how they behaved to women taken captive. And although he had now lived among a sub-section of such a barbarian tribe, and seen the two Iceni girls kindly treated, he feared for Gilda. Would she be spared? Enslaved again? And the child, which could be his own. Would she prefer to die? Could he offer her the choice? In what words?

These thoughts ran round and round in his head all the afternoon as he helped with the lengthening of the stockade. He could not dig holes for the stakes which seemed such a poor defence, but, propped firmly on his crutch, he could hammer stakes home.

Evening fell and there was no sign of the boy. The stake-driving went on by the light of a huge fire, which once, when replenished, sent a long plume of smoke flying upriver: a plume which then turned back on itself, hung turbulently as though trying to make a pattern on the sky, then settled and streamed towards the sea. At the same moment bits of straw and chaff from the threshing floor spiralled up and fell flat.

Ethelreda cried, "The gods have spoken and earth has spoken. Ours will be the victory." She and the other women began handing out water and bits of bread and hard cheese to the men who were still toiling, bringing the stockade in a curve like a strung bow, the string being Beofric's hall.

Gilda paused by Paulus, and startled him by speaking in Latin and using his own name. "It is effort wasted, is it not, Paulus?"

"Unless help comes."

"But from where? I want you to promise me one thing, my dearest love. Do not let me be taken. Kill me. Promise!"

He answered her indirectly. "My sword and my equipment are at Mallow."

"I know. I will fetch them. I will take the pony. It is the hunter's moon. Light as day."

Before he could protest, she had moved on to the next toiling man, offering food and water. Then she seemed to vanish.

Something very like superstitious fear touched him. He wondered if it could be that she bore a charmed life. Locked in and left to starve, she'd been saved; stumbling all alone into the Angles' camp, she'd been kindly received. And now, if the attack came tonight, she would at least not be *here*, where the most danger was. Such things were beyond man's understanding and must be left to the gods. Again he prayed to Mithras, this time promising no bull, promising only that, when the butchery that he thought inevitable came about, he would fight and die as a follower of Mithras, as a soldier, should do.

Wulf slithered back soon after first light. Over the green plastering he now wore a coat of mud; in the mask that it made of his face his eyes shone very blue. The news he brought was not good. "They speak our tongue but they are not friends. They will not attack today, nor in the night, but tomorrow. They wait for a special tide." All the men, knowledgeable about the sea, nodded. Wulf described how the ships were anchored, one behind the other, well into the river, and how parties of the men from them had landed and gone down to the beach, hunting for shellfish; and how he had lain in a mud flat, listening to their talk as they came and went. He had heard a great deal. The strangers came from an island into whose harbour Beofric's ships had been forced by a storm. The islanders had pretended to be friendly, and Beofric had talked, boasting about the rich soil and good climate of his new home. "They joked," Wulf said in a pained way, "about the warmth of the welcome he will find when he returns." Beofric had plainly talked too much—even the number in the settlement was known. "Less than twenty men."

If such news evoked panic, none was evident, and Paulus, who had spent his life in the company of brave men, was impressed, without ceasing to think them ridiculous and pitiable.

Gilda had returned, giving him his sword, and saying that she had hidden the rest of his gear in a bush. "I thought it better, until the last moment." They had always been careful to keep his equipment hidden, it was so distinctly Roman, and, although the men of Beofricsworth might not ever have fought the legions, they might have heard talk. Now, when the last moment for all was so near, Paulus thought that, when it came, his nationality would not matter. He would die in his own uniform, his only wish being that he had his own century behind him.

The tribesmen showed a childish interest in his sword, comparing it with their own, which were cruder in workmanship, and heavier. They had swords, but their favourite weapon was the battle-axe. Some axes had names, like domestic pets—Skull-splitter, Blood-seeker, Thor's Finger... The men who handled them were brave as bulls—and like bulls would be slaughtered.

For the first time Paulus saw war, which had been his career, as an iniquitous thing. Then he told himself, cynically, that he only felt so because defeat was this time certain. He looked at Gilda and thought how wise of Rome to forbid acting soldiers to marry. Then, with despair at its depths, the idea came. An idea he had heard talked about but never seen in action. He had a short talk with Wulf, asking him to scratch on the ground with a stick, to show the disposition of the three ships. Then he talked to Osric, who said, without any great faith, "It would be worth trying. I will have everything made ready."

Paulus said, "It may be but a frail hope, but not so frail as manning the stockade against such a number."

Osric scowled. He knew as well as anyone how hopeless the approaching conflict seemed, but saying so did no good.

He said, rather haughtily, "This idea means *certain* death to one man."

"And I shall be that man, Osric. It is *my* idea. And whom can you so easily spare? Now I will talk to Gilda."

What was said during that talk was to remain a secret for more than fifty years.

Gilda came from her last talk with Alfred in a state of obvious distress, her face very pale and tears welling from her eyes. It was understandable. He was her father. What she concealed from Paulus—and from everybody else until the suicidal venture was launched—was that the birth-pangs had begun. She did not want him going to his death worried about her and his child being exposed to all the dangers that a premature birth involved.

Wulf tried to comfort her. "Alfred will come back. Last night they were all drunk before moonrise. And tonight there is no moon." All day the wind, coming out of the far west, had been piling up clouds and hurrying them on before they shed rain. With such a wind and the river's current, Alfred would need only to steer. Pray that the rain holds off.

At last all was ready. There, tied to its post, was the fireboat. Amidship it carried the biggest iron cauldron the settlement could provide; all around lay everything that could be easily ignited—bits of clothing soaked in tallow, brittle dry twigs from the forest, splinters of resinous pine, little bundles of straw. There was a good fire in the cauldron and some sound firewood to keep it going as the boat drifted downstream, guided by Alfred using one oar as a paddle. But the fire on the bank was so fierce and bright that the one in the cauldron was dimmed.

The Angles, to whom this was all new and strange, were almost silent with awe. What Alfred was about to do was very different from fighting, as they understood it. None of the headiness of battle, none of the noise, none of the company. In battle, a man could sustain a severe wound and not notice it, the blood-lust being so strong. To go alone and in silence to certain death had something uncanny about it. Osric himself, now that the moment had come, felt a creepiness between his shoulder-blades.

"We must send him off well," he said. "Call on the gods, and roar!"

Yet when Alfred emerged from Beofric's hall there was a deeper silence. For this was not the old man who was the father of Sweyn's wife; who was lame, who had been deaf and dumb and unimportant.

Paulus seemed to move more easily, one hand on his daughter's shoulder. On his high-held head the Roman helmet gleamed; the scarlet cloak streamed in the wind, revealing the harness below. The traditional enemy, recognised, even if never before actually seen: one who had lived among them for almost a year and was now about to die for them.

Osric ceremoniously helped him into the boat and, stepping back, freed it. Paulus stood for a second, his arm uplifted in the salute he would have given to his emperor. Then he sat down and, with the oar, pushed the boat away from the bank. Then, the spell broken, they roared and called on the gods to bless him and take him, Roman though he was, straight to Valhalla.

* * *

In the midst of the uproar, Ethelreda took Gilda by the arm and said, "Come with me." They went to Osric's little house, more private than the hall, and there, on the half-cured bearskin, Gilda's son was born, premature—Ethelreda took special notice of his nails—but a good baby for all that. "Had he gone full time," Ethelreda said, "you would not have got rid of him so easily."

Gilda managed to gasp. "He must be called Paulus—for his grandfather."

To this suggestion, in any other circumstances, there would have been objections, but this was no ordinary time. In the morning, Wulf, in elfin guise again, stole away and, before the baby Paulus was one day old, was back again with a tale as wonderful as any recounted in a saga. It was plain that the Roman had not been content to do merely what he had at first suggested, and what everyone had imagined he was about to do—set the boat on fire and steer it towards the anchored ships. He had flung shovelsful of blazing stuff into the midst of each one. The strangers were all asleep or drunk, and the confusion had been absolute. Men had jumped overboard into the river or into the mud-flats; believing themselves to be attacked, they had fought each other.

"And how," Osric asked, "can you know all this?"

"I talked with some of the survivors."

"*Talked* to them?"

"They speak our tongue. I told them many lies. Great lies." Wulf spoke proudly. By tradition the small lie was despicable, the great lie admirable. "I said I was from the Little People, who had seen their plight and pitied them. I offered to lead them to Elfland, but they were afraid. They said they would come here, to Beofricsworth. So then I warned them that you were many and very fierce. I said that Beofric had returned, with *four* ships, sailing another river. I offered to lead them, again. Then as they talked about it, I vanished."

"How many are they now?"

"Perhaps twenty-four. Some burned. Some wounded. I do not think that they will come this way."

And if they did, who cared? The fourteen who had been prepared to repel sixty could deal easily with twenty-four.

Four days later, Beofric did return, by chance with four ships. There was a great feast to celebrate the victory-without-a-battle and the safe return of old members of the tribe and a welcome to the new. The ships brought mead and ale, and everybody was drunk for two days and two nights. And then the ploughing began.

4 Gilda and Fergus

THE OLD WOMAN AT MALLOW WAS VERY ANCIENT INDEED AND, like most old people, very cantankerous. But then, had she not always been? As the daughter of a hero about whom tales were still told and songs sung, she had always had an impregnable position in the tribe, and to this she had added by becoming the wise woman, the repository of old Ethelreda's wisdom. And as though that were not enough, she had proved to be a termagant.

Very few still living had any first-hand memory of Paulus or Ethelreda, but they knew through Wulf's songs what they had been and what they had done. Wulf was still alive, but now so old that his memory was gone, and in ordinary life it was unwise to rely upon a word he said, but put a harp in his hands and he would begin to chant about the great happenings fifty or more seasons ago, not neglecting the part he had himself played. Of his doings on that memorable occasion proof had come in a curious way: a man from another, smaller tribe, established on what to the people of Beofricsworth was always known as the Other River, had once said that he remembered his grandfather telling him about a green man suddenly appearing and offering to take him and his fellows to Elfland. The green man was no larger than a tall child, and seemed to come out of and vanish into the earth. (The people on the Other River were friendly now, old feuds forgotten. There had been intermarriages.)

Gilda, the woman who ruled at Mallow, never claimed to be able to control the winds or the weather, but she made the best brews and wine and cider and ale. In some ways she was an excellent wife; she bore Sweyn two more sons after Paulus— usually called Pauli—and two daughters. Daughters were as good as currency in a tribe where men still outnumbered women. Gilda was a good housewife, made excellent bread, wove good cloth, and had somehow retained her looks and her shape to what must be an advanced age. Her one fault was an over-fondness for having her own way.

She was exceptionally stubborn about the house. In the year of the great gales, the roof at Mallow lost many of the red, foreign-looking tiles. Sweyn, who had never liked the house with its many small rooms and its painted walls and pictured floor, snatched at the chance of building a new house, a little larger than his brother Osric's, much smaller than his father's. Gilda refused to hear of it. The tiles must be gathered up carefully and replaced. "And if you won't do it, I'll do it myself."

"And she would," Sweyn said to his brothers. "Four months gone as she is. What can one do with a woman like that?"

They were ready with suggestions—mostly facetious, all unworkable. Sweyn could not imagine himself beating the daughter of Paulus. He replaced the tiles, and went on living in the alien place for another five years. Then he achieved his ambition and built a proper house, and Gilda refused to move into it. "You," she said, "can live where you like. I stay here. And I would remind you of the time when you were glad of a roof over your head."

To that he had answer. "And you were glad of a mouthful of bread."

"So was my father," said Gilda in a voice which reminded him of how Paulus had paid any debt he owed to the tribe.

Point-blank argument having failed, Sweyn tried cajolery, and when that failed, too, took her at her word and moved all that was his—and that surely included the five children—into the new house. Pauli was then just over fifteen, Ethelburga, the eldest girl, almost fourteen, far too old, Gilda said, for the communal sleeping customary with the Angles. What was implied by this remark was so disgusting that Sweyn was shocked. He roared at her, "Can you think *that* of your own children?

Many of us slept together in my father's hall. Did you see any wrong-doing there?"

"No. But it is a barbarous custom." Ever since Paulus had revealed himself as a Roman—and a hero—Gilda had felt free to pretend that she was half Roman by blood, free to denounce certain customs as barbarous, certain people as barbarians. The words never failed to sting.

"Barbarian I may be," Sweyn said, "but I am the head of this house . . ."

"Of the house across the road," she corrected him, and dared him with a flash of her blue eyes to lay claim to this house, too: the place he'd never liked, the place which for years he had called a leaky old wreck. He took refuge in dignity. "I have said that you can stay here."

"*I* said I would," she corrected him again.

The community was shocked when it heard that Gilda and Sweyn were no longer sharing bed and board, that Ethelburga had charge in the new house and Gilda lived alone in the old one. Such an arrangement had never been known. Some of the men said that Sweyn must be happier out of the range of Gilda's tongue, but even they admitted that Sweyn, not yet forty, would find celibate life hard.

Sweyn, who had long ago formed the habit of slipping down to Beofricsworth to air his woes, said that he did, but he wasn't going to give in, this time. When the ridiculous arrangement had lasted almost two months he said that he believed that Gilda had put a spell on him and the children. Sweyn, the youngest, aged six, had waked in the night, crouping and gasping for breath. "A terrible thing to see. I had to send for his mother."

"And she came?"

"Oh, yes. Whatever her faults, nobody can say that Gilda is not a good mother." Nobody had said it. "She knew what to bring, too." He sounded half admiring and half suspicious. "She put a handful of stuff in a pan and boiled it and made the child breathe the steam. He was eased at once."

For young Sweyn's attack of croup, Gilda blamed the new house. It was damp, standing as it did so near the forest trees. Sweyn, she said, had been in such a hurry to move that he had not cleared enough land. She insisted upon taking the child to the old house.

Then Osric, who was ten, and clumsy, let an axe fall on

his foot and had to go across the road to be taken care of. But the sorriest accident befell Ethelburga, who scalded her arm, and really nothing much could be expected of Edda, who was only eight. So everybody went to the old house to eat, and then to sleep, and the new house was used only when Sweyn entertained his friends from the village.

Sweyn died at what seemed, to those who survived him, a comparatively early age, and in a way Gilda was to blame. Fifty years earlier the men on the Other River had settled with no women folk at all, but they had found wives, chiefly Iceni women still living in little isolated communities, and they had bred sons and daughters. Deep instinct, if not any openly acknowledged rules, warned all the tribes of the dangers of too much inbreeding. So a man from the Other River tried to make a bargain with Sweyn; his daughter should marry Pauli, his son marry Ethelburga. Gilda objected so violently and so loudly that some people claimed to have heard her across the five miles between Mallow and Beofricsworth, which was, of course, nonsense, but it showed how people felt. Never, never, never, she said, should any child of hers mate with the Other River people. If everybody else chose to forget, she remembered. It was the intrusion of the men now settled on the Other River, but fifty years ago bent on taking Beofricsworth, who had been the direct reason for Paulus's self-sacrificing action. No Other River man should have her daughter, no Other River girl have her son. It was left to Sweyn to refuse the offers and bear the ill-feeling which resulted. He did so quite calmly. Similiar offers were made or rejected every day. But the Other River man chose to be offended, and said an unforgivable thing. "Perhaps it is as well. Who would willingly be kin to a witch?"

It was then incumbent upon Sweyn, for his honour's sake, and for Gilda's, to challenge the Other River man to a bout of fisticuffs, no weapons to be used. They fought until both men were prone, and neither the winner. The Other River man was carried to his home and survived, but Sweyn, carried home not to his own house but to the old one which he had always hated, died on the second day, despite all that Gilda could do.

After that there were no more disputes at Mallow. Pauli had always been, in a curious way, his mother's boy. They seemed to have a link stronger even than that usual between a mother and her first-born, her favourite. They shared jokes which nobody else thought amusing, and sometimes failed to see the humour in things which sent other people into roars of laughter. There was, naturally, a strong physical resemblance between them, and, since Gilda retained her youthful look beyond the ordinary span, there was a time when they might have been brother and elder sister, but as Pauli aged he grew tall and muscular, not quite in the tribal way; he was lighter in structure, less hairy, nimbler on his feet. He had inherited his mother's hot temper rather than his father's amiability, yet he and his mother never clashed.

Pauli married when he was eighteen. His wife was Brad's daughter and her full name was Hyldegyth, but she was more generally known as Hilda. When he married, Pauli moved into the house that Sweyn had built, and eventually added to it a room to which women and children could retire. It was known as a bower.

Gilda had her way over the inheritance of her sons after Sweyn's death. The usual custom was a just division between sons, but Gilda insisted that Pauli should take full possession of the land which belonged to Mallow and which had once been—she said—the property of Paulus. Osric and Eric could divide between them the acres which Sweyn, with some help from them, had brought under the plough, and if they found that too little to support them, they could take in more of the heathland. They accepted the arrangement without protest.

Beofricsworth was expanding in a similiar way and for similar reasons. When a man's acres were divided, however justly, among *all* his sons, their individual holdings were too small to be viable; so in addition to what they owned in the big communal fields, many men tilled patches of what they called intake land. With Mallow expanding towards the river, and the intake lands extending towards Mallow, the distance between the two communities decreased.

There was a good deal of coming and going between the two places, some inspired by a natural gregariousness, some for less obvious reasons. People came to consult the wise woman about ailments, for most of which she could offer, if not a cure, a palliative. Young women came with requests for love potions and general advice. Gilda was free with it when it concerned ordinary things like brewing and baking, but further probing invariably drew a blank stony look and the remark that some things which Gilda had learned from Ethelreda she would pass on, intact, to Edda, who would also inherit, in due time, the red-roofed house. Ethelburga married Garth's son and went to live in Beofricsworth.

When Gilda was, by all known standards, a very old woman, with only Wulf left of her contemporaries—and he at least a couple of years younger—she grew, all suddenly, very frail. "My legs have failed me," she said. She would not stay in bed, she would not be carried, but every morning Pauli had to cross the road from what was still called the New House, to help Edda to get their mother up and into her chair in the room with the painted walls and the curious floor. To look at her, one would have said that she weighed nothing, and Pauli, though now past his prime, could have lifted her easily, but she would not be lifted; she would only be helped.

One morning, bleak and grey, for it was nearing the time of year when the sun died and must be strengthened and encouraged by the lighting of great fires, the eating of huge meals—both symbolic—the old woman said, as soon as she was seated, "Pauli, the winter solstice, what they call the time of wassail, is upon us. It will be my last, and I shall keep it here."

He was about to say, looking around the painted room, that it was impossible, the place was too small, when she said, "Not all; there is not room. I want only the kin of Paulus. Our sons and grandsons . . . with their womanfolk, of course." Pauli was glad that his mother added the last five words, for over the years Hilda had often complained about Gilda and the power she exerted. But when his mother said, "And we shall kill the bull," he thought she had lost her senses. He reflected, sadly, because he loved her, that old age must strike this blow or that, and that the gods were inclined to give with one hand and snatch away with the other; his mother, active of body to extreme old age and then made almost helpless, had now, with the same suddenness, lost her wits.

Nobody killed a bull, four years old and in his prime. Very few bull-calves were left intact for long; some were castrated early and turned into bullocks or steers; some were left until they had developed the thick necks and heavy shoulders of their sex, then castrated and turned into oxen, capable of dragging ploughs and wagons. A few, very few, were allowed to grow up and fulfil their proper function in life—the begetting of progeny. And the bull at Mallow was one of the few—famous, sought after. He had a reputation—a good breeder, and he had a history: he was one of the animals directly descended from the few brought over by the first settlers; he was the direct descendant of the bull-calf which Beofric had carried to Mallow, part of the bride-price offered to Paulus.

When Gilda suggested that such a valuable animal should be killed and eaten at a feast, Pauli did not protest. People whose wits failed forgot from one minute to the next, and she would forget that she had ever made such an unthinkable suggestion. He said, "Will you be warm enough? Would you like a rug? It is a sharp morning." And she, as though reading his mind, ignored this question and proceeded to give proof that her wits were not a-wander. She named, without hesitation, all her descendants—quite a feat of memory; Pauli had three sons and three daughters and four grandchildren, all boys; Ethelburga had been even more prolific: four sons and three daughters, six grandchildren; Osric's family was comparatively small, for his first wife had died young and he had had difficulty in finding another, because Gilda was so set against the Other River people where a likely girl was available, but he had in the end married into a third tribe, founded by a man called Wipped, settled at Wippedtun, ten miles upriver. The second marriage had given Osric three sons, so far, but no grandsons. Eric, four years younger than Osric, had four sons, one daughter and two grandsons. And Gilda remembered them all.

Of her own brood only Edda remained unmarried, and now, nearing forty, seemed doomed to die childless, if not a virgin. When Gilda died, as die she surely must, some widower, wanting a housekeeper, might choose Edda. Nobody would speak for her while her mother lived, such dreadful things befell those who wished to marry Edda. She had been a pretty girl—was in fact still comely, having inherited Gilda's ability to carry the years lightly—and she had been sought after by three men. Gilda never said, or in any way indicated, that she wished Edda not to marry. In fact, she seemed to take pride in displaying what Edda would inherit: not only the red-tiled house but also the household goods, some old, some new. "And in addition my daughter has learned all that I could teach her. You are indeed a fortunate man."

But they were not fortunate. Three men had struck marriage bargains; two had met with fatal accidents, and one had been smitten with that infirmity of the spine which was openly called the witch's strike. After that there were no more offers, and on this cold morning Edda listened unmoved to the recital of her kin, fetched the rug and tucked it around the thing of skin and bones which her mother had become, and then listened to the first argument that her mother and her brother had ever had.

"The bull," Gilda said, "must be slaughtered on the day before the feast. And with ceremony, about which I will inform you when the time comes."

"Mother, I cannot kill that bull. Think of his worth! Every man who brings his cow to be served brings the price, in goods or in silver. I will kill a pig—or a young steer. Not the bull."

"Whose is the bull?"

Confounded, because the question of who owned what at Mallow had never yet arisen, Pauli said, "Well . . . mine."

"You are mistaken, my son. Long years ago, before you were born—*just* before—I made a solemn vow to your father. I promised that as soon as I was able, I would see that his vow was kept. A bull for Mithras . . . Those were his words."

"But my father," Pauli said, thinking of Sweyn, "would never have exacted such a promise when he was sober."

Gilda raised her hand to her head, and the light from the fire shone through it, showing the bones.

"*My* tongue fails me, too. It was your *grandfather*, Paulus, who exacted that promise. As you must know from the song Wulf sings, Paulus was about to embark on a desperate enterprise. He needed help from his god, Mithras. He told me what must be done. And never until now could I do what he and what I promised. Never before could a bull be spared. Now this one can; he has already sown his seed."

"To kill him would be a great pity, a great waste."

"Not to do so would be to break a promise. It would also be an insult to the gods and invite misfortune."

"This Mithras," Pauli said thoughtfully, "is not one of *our* gods. Will they not be offended by so costly a sacrifice being made to another?" He still had hopes of dissuading her without being defiant.

"The bull will be sacrificed on Woden's day, eaten on Thor's. That should content them. Only the actual killing and a few minutes' ceremony will be in honour of Mithras and of a promise made long ago."

Forced to be blunt, Pauli said, "I cannot agree to it."

"You mean you will not! I am ashamed of you, Pauli. My son, my best beloved, opposing me in what may be the last thing I ask of you. But very well; spare the bull, shame your mother and be cursed! This is one thing I cannot do for myself; but I have other sons . . . I now realise that I have dealt unfairly with them, running contrary to custom and denying them their rights to Mallow. A bull will be sacrificed if I have to buy one. And if I am so forced, you, your sons and grandsons will have no part in the ceremony or the blessing which should follow it. You may go now."

Pauli went, but only to inform every member of the family of what the old woman was planning: a purely family gathering for the first two wassail days, and the slaughter of the Mallow bull. He did not mention Mithras.

There were many ways of killing a bull when his usefulness ended. He could be baited by dogs—a grand sport to watch— and then, when he was weary and temporarily harmless, despatched by a sword-thrust to the heart: he could be killed by a blow from a battle-axe, heavy enough to stun him, and then his throat could be cut; he could be entangled with a net so that every attempt he made to free himself bonded him more securely. But the Mallow bull, by Gilda's order, was to be killed in a manner which was new, and which demanded the ultimate in man-power and in courage. He was to be roped and then heaved on to a platform, sturdily built and high enough for a tall man to stand under it. Then his throat was to be cut, and all the males of Gilda's family, ranging from Pauli in his fifties to Eric's toddling youngest grandson, were to pass under the platform so that the blood of the bull, dripping through spaces between the planks, could drip upon them.

Nobody knew what this ceremony meant, and Gilda made no attempt to explain. She was acting, she said, in obedience to orders given her just before Paulus, the founder of this family, went to his death. But when Pauli asked who was to perform the actual sacrifice and slit the bull's throat, she said, "I shall. Who else?" Pauli then completed his unfilial performance by laughing in her face. He lifted one of her hands, always delicate despite all the hard work she had done and now nothing but pale skin and fragile bone. "How could you?" he asked. "The bull's hide is tough as undressed leather."

"I shall do it with Paulus's sword. See to it that it is well sharpened." She went on to give orders about the digging of the hole for the charcoal over which the carcass would roast.

Afterwards Pauli said to Edda, "Our mother is out of her mind. The effort will kill her."

"Death comes to all," Edda said, her voice cool, her eyes stony. In her heart she pleaded with the gods: Let it be soon. Let it be before the courses cease and my chances of child-bearing are lost forever. Edda hated the mother whom she now tended so carefully, and she knew enough about lethal herbal brews to have killed her, any day. Something had made her hold her hand, for no good could come of such an action by which Edda meant no child when she married Alwyn, a widower who had caught her eye and to whom she had said most urgently, "Keep away from Mallow, as you value your life." If only the old woman could die as the result of her own wilfulness—and what end could be more fitting?

News about the extraordinary thing which was to take place at Mallow had spread through Beofricsworth and to the most outlying of the intake land; so, although the bull was to be killed at sunrise on Woden's day and nobody outside the family had been invited, a crowd had gathered. A mannerly crowd, just come to stare, and some of them making bets upon whether Gilda, so very frail, could or could not cut a bull's throat with a sword, however well ground on the communal whetstone.

The platform had been erected in front of the old house, between the well and the road, little used at first but gradually coming to be recognised as the shortest way to Wippedtun and other small settlements. In the grey pre-dawn light the watchers, invited and uninvited, saw the bull's helpless bulk hoisted up and fastened down to the framework of the platform. Then they saw Gilda carried out, a little cloth-wrapped bundle, and some of the older people gave small sighs, remembering her as she had been, and how, until she was quite old, she had seemed young.

Pauli carried her out, past the well which had such memories for her, and Osric, her second son, already on the platform beside the supine bull, reached down and took her into his arms. The transfer could not have been more easily made if it had concerned a child of, say, five years. Her third son, Eric, handed up the sword which Paulus had left behind when he went down the river to defeat sixty men. He'd left it partly because to him it could only be an encumbrance, and partly because, if he failed and the enemy came, the sword might be handled by young Wulf who had no weapon of his own. Afterwards Gilda had reclaimed it, and here it was, its silver-embellished hilt catching the light, its well-honed blade agleam.

Could she use it effectively, or would one of those who stood by—all her kin—be called upon to use their knives? They had them ready.

Wulf—he needed no invitation, for as a singer and a maker of songs he was welcome anywhere—took a step forward from the crowd and began to play his harp, and to sing. All the male progeny of Paulus—looking rather shabby, for their best clothes were to be worn tomorrow at the feast—lined up in order of age, ready to pass under the platform.

The bull had huge horns, and as it lay on its side, Gilda rested her hand on the one that was uppermost, steadying herself. She made a sign to Wulf, who silenced his harp and his voice. In an astoundingly clear voice, with the little lilt which she had never lost, she said, "I dedicate this bull to Mithras and to the memory of Paulus." She placed the blade against the great artery of the neck, and the bull, warned by instinct, managed, despite the ropes, to make one last convulsive heave which pressed the point deeper. The blood showered down, and the twenty-five males of Paulus's breed were baptised into a faith about which they knew nothing.

"The vow is fulfilled," Gilda said, adding mystification to mystification. Now die, Edda thought. Die now!

But Gilda did not die. Although she did not know it, there was still something left for her to do in this life.

Pauli lifted her down and carried her into the house, where, strengthened by a cup of her own blackberry wine, she relented a little her ruling that only the family should feast tomorrow.

"Hurry out, Edda, and invite all those who came to watch, this morning. It is a large beast and there will be meat for all."

Such a widespread invitation was only possible, she thought scornfully, in a barbarian society where plates were seldom used, where everybody would come provided with a drinking-vessel and a knife. Her guests would all hold hacked-off lumps of the roasted meat and gnaw on it. Like dogs!

It was the custom, at this time of the year, to encourage the ailing sun not only with feasts and fires but also by the bringing into the house of evergreens, the leaves which did not acknowledge the change of season. In this, as in other ways, Gilda conformed, and the younger women of the family dragged in and hung up great boughs of yew and holly, long trails of ivy. The young men and boys tended the meat, feeding the fire with charcoal all through the night, and laboriously turning the great carcass which was transfixed by an iron bar resting on others shaped like a forked bough. To turn the body they used pitchforks, and, with each piercing, fresh juices and fat ran down to splutter on the glowing fire. To say that the smell of this quite exceptional feast could be detected a mile away was no exaggeration. One man, uninvited, sniffed it more than a mile away.

Ordinarily the main meal of the day was eaten at noon, but the wassail feasts were always timed to take place when the sun, weak because of the season, was weakest because his daily decline was at hand.

At last everything was ready. The sun, ailing and failing, but still more rosy than the moon, tipped down below the dark ridge of the forest, and the feast began. There was meat for everyone, bread for those who desired it, ale in plenty, mead, cider and, for the few who preferred it, wine. The cooking-fire, once its work was done, was replenished with fuel that gave light as well as heat, and inside the house, in the room with the painted walls, another great fire burned.

Nobody took much notice of the newcomer who slipped into place just inside the room where Gilda, her immediate family and elder members of the tribe were feasting. The room was crowded and there was always some coming and going in the doorway, with meat being brought in and liquor being taken out. It was an inconspicuous spot that he occupied, but he was not overlooked; both meat and ale were offered to him, and he accepted. He had not broken his fast for a long time.

Because Gilda was now so small and must remain seated, her chair and the table upon which she insisted—just as she insisted upon using a plate—had been set high on a little platform, so that she dominated the room, a tiny, rather bizarre figure, to whom most of her guests were accustomed, but at whom the stranger looked with interest and a certain calculation. She wore silk, not homespun, and although her face was that of an old woman, her hair was still plentiful and not grey; when a flame leaped on the hearth, her hair shone with the colour of a primrose. Surrounded by tall men—sons, grand-

sons, and privileged guests—there was something almost royal
about her. With a word, a slight movement of the head or of
the hand, she appeared to give orders, instantly obeyed. A
good sign, the stranger thought; experience had taught him that
women were more susceptible to the message he carried.

There was a great deal of hubbub in the room, ale being a
loosener of tongues, and when the harp music started it was at
first barely audible, but the harpist—an old man—knew his
audience and struck several discordant, jangling notes, demanding silence which, beginning with those nearest the table,
gradually spread outwards until even those who had been obliged
to eat outside fell quiet.

Wulf said, "This is the saga of Paulus . . ."

The man in the doorway gave a start, thinking of St. Paul.
Was it possible that the Gospel had reached this isolated area?
Was this crowd about to be entertained with a recital of Paul's
journeys—especially appealing to a maritime people—or of
his experience on the road to Damascus—especially attractive
to people who liked a touch of the supernatural?

It was neither. And yet as Fergus listened to the saga of
Paulus, he was struck rather by the likeness than by the differences. Paulus, the song said, was a Roman, and had not St.
Paul been proud of, made use of, his Roman citizenship? Paulus, when they first knew him, the song said, had been unable
to speak. Hadn't St. Paul been smitten dumb? Paulus had been
lame. And hadn't St. Paul suffered some unspecified infirmity
of the flesh? Still, these were trivialities, the passing thoughts
of an active mind. When the long saga ended it was upon a
note of which Fergus could make immediate use. "And so he
died," Wulf declaimed, "and by dying saved us."

There was always a little silence after that for, though Beofricsworth and its people had enjoyed peace for fifty years, apart
from a minor brawl or two, memories ran in the inherited blood,
and every man and woman could now see how great the danger
had been, how great the odds, how important to all their forebears Paulus's self-sacrificing action had been. The Angles,
except when the blood-lust intoxicated them, were exceptionally logical and reasonable people. So even at a feast like this,
with most of the men drunk, they were prepared to pay that
little tribute of silence to the hero of the tale, and, of course,
to Wulf, the Great Liar. When the silence ended, the clamour

would begin again, some of it boastful talk. Counter-boasts, challenges.

Tonight there was no chance, for Fergus, taking advantage of the small silence and of his position in the doorway, so that if he spoke loudly enough all within the house and those without could hear, raised his powerful voice. He spoke English, but not as they spoke it, nor as Gilda did. There was no lilt to his voice, and no fluency to his speech. Sometimes he halted a little, but he pressed on, telling, without any rhythm and with no accomplishment of music, another story, about another man who had died to save others: not a few others, as Paulus had done, but all the world.

To minds affected by mead and ale, what Fergus said about a man-god, called Jesus, made little sense. And it seemed to decry their own hero. Now that the man had drawn attention to himself, it was obvious that he was a stranger. He wore homespun, not as a tunic and breeches, but as an ankle-length robe, resembling a woman's dress; it was girded, not with a belt of leather, but with a length of rope. Before he began to speak he had pushed back his hood, revealing a head almost hairless: no beard, and only a circlet of short hair surrounding the bald patch on his scalp. An absolute stranger, daring to push in amongst the invited guests, and talking nonsense about a man born of a god and a virgin, and dying for all men's sins!

The fire inside the room had been allowed to die down a little, while that outside, in the chill of the night had been replenished, so that Fergus stood dark against the brightness. An excellent target. Pauli's eldest son flung the first bone, half a well-gnawed rib. As he flung it he shouted, "Be off with you. We want no such talk here."

That bone, aimed with deliberation, struck Fergus on the face, at the top of his cheekbone a little to one side of his eye. It drew blood, and the sight of it roused something of the terrible excitement of the first blood drawn in battle. Other bones flew, amid shouts of derision and roars of disapproval.

Fergus had been warned, before he set out from Iona, that his mission might end in death, and he had already had some narrow escapes. To himself he said, "This is the end!" And to Christ he said, "Jesus, to thee I commit my soul." But his nature was practical rather than mystical, and, even as he prayed, he raised his arms to shield his head, and began to push his way through the hostile crowd towards the place where Gilda sat. It might offer only a temporary sanctuary, but nobody was likely to throw a bone which might hit the woman who was plainly a chieftainess, or at least a matriarch.

His progress towards the high table was opposed and slow, and he was still at some distance from it when Gilda, becoming aware of what was happening, raised the wine-jug which stood ready to her hand, and brought it down on the table with a crash. It was a glass jug, one of the few things which Livia had inadvertently left behind. It shattered with a noise of such unfamiliar quality that it exacted a startled silence. Into it she spoke, communing with this stranger in a tongue which she had not used for more than fifty years.

"You are a Christian?"

"I am, madam. And you?"

"A hard question to answer," she said. Pollio and Livia had professed to be Christians, Christianity being the acknowledged state religion of the Empire. But ever since Christianity had been promoted, it was considered to be rather too good for slaves and the poor, the very people who had first practised it and only the merest smattering had brushed off on to Gilda. She had found it difficult to understand how Pollio—so kindly—and Livia—so heartless—could share a creed, but she had always been too busy to spare much thought for such matters. She could, however, now say, from pride in her good memory rather than any other emotion, "I can say the paternoster."

"You delight my heart, madam," Fergus said, not without cunning.

"Come nearer," she said. "Make way there! Make way!"

Seen near to, she was very old, and so frail that the shattered wine-jug and the strength in her voice were triumphs of will over body.

"What is your name?"

"Fergus. I am a missionary, come to bring the Gospel to those who sit in darkness."

"Let us speak now in English, so that all can understand. These are my family. I apologise for my son who flung the first bone; it is a weakness with him to act without thinking. Now, stand here by me and tell them again, very simply. They are simple people..." She lowered her voice as she said that. "And say nothing about Christ which would seem to lessen Paulus, whose saga you heard."

"From the saga I gathered that he was a Roman and a very brave man indeed. Was he a Christian?"

"No. He served Mithras. But it would do your cause no harm to..." Here, as so often, the language defeated her, though she had spoken no other for more than fifty years. It had little subtlety and did not deal in abstractions. "...to link the two," she said. "Both were brave men. Both went to death alone and to save others. Bear on that. I speak as an old woman, to whom life has taught one lesson above all. *Make the best use of what you have.*"

He gave her a little smile and a nod to show that he understood, and then, raising his voice again, launched into a discourse which left the slower-minded and the more drunken members of his audience slightly confused. Was he speaking of their hero, Paulus? Or of another man who had died, bravely and alone? This time what he said was received, if not with approval, without any overt hostility. When he finished, Gilda said, "Now what is your wish? To dwell among us?"

"For a time," he said cautiously. "Until the faith is rooted here."

She considered this and said, "There are stables, not much used since Mallow ceased to be a posting-stage. You may have one for your use."

"Nothing could be more suitable. Our Saviour was born in a stable."

"That I had not heard. You must tell me more, but now I must speak to them."

She spoke and they listened, courteously, being her guests. "This man, whose name is Fergus, has come to live with us and teach us things we do not know. Listen or not as you choose; you are free people. But any person who insults him or injures him will do so at the risk of my displeasure." And they all knew what *that* meant.

Now she was very tired and ready to be helped to bed. The two last days had been strenuous, and she felt very old. Edda, with hatred and admiration warring within her, came to one side and Pauli moved to the other, but she rejected his aid and asked, "Where is Alwyn? I saw him a minute since. You, my dear Pauli, show Fergus the small stable which I have given him."

Alwyn, awkward because he was unskilled in handling the helpless old and the helpless young, and Edda, nimbly but with hatred getting the upper hand, helped Gilda to bed in the room which held for her a memory never to be shared. And then she surprised them. Reviving as soon as she was prone, she said, "Alwyn, you have land?"

"Yes, a fourth part of my father's holding and some intake land."

"Where?"

"About a mile this side of the settlement."

"Then it would be no great hardship for you to renounce your rights in the common fields, keep your intake, and give your attention to what land goes with this house, the few acres which were my dowry?" The lilt in her voice tipped up into a question.

"No hardship. But Pauli might have something to say about that."

"Pauli is my son and a dutiful one. He would never oppose my wish—which is that you and Edda should marry and change nothing."

She had put the same proposition to Edda's former suitors and they had scorned it, but Alwyn said, "I would do that, if Pauli agreed."

"Pauli has much intake land and strong sons ... Stay here tonight, Alwyn, and tomorrow that man, Fergus, will unite you and Edda in holy matrimony—marry you."

Alwyn, a dullard but strong, solid and rather handsome, said, "That would suit me," and looked at Edda. Edda, with the hatred draining away and only awe and admiration left, felt weak and tearful, but she had never at any time seen her mother give way to such weaknesses; so she controlled herself and said simply, "Thank you, Mother."

Then the old woman, propped against the pillows, said an extraordinary thing. "We are the playthings of the gods, or they are ours. Yesterday I sacrificed a bull to Mithras. Today I celebrated Thor's day, and now something strange in me feels that Christ, too, should have his chance." She could have explained that something strange, but who would have understood her nostalgia for civilisation as she understood it? For more than fifty years she had lived with the barbarians and they had treated her far better than her Christianised Latin-speaking master and mistress had done, though, in his careless and limited way, Pollio had been kind enough. Yet the hankering for some aspect of her former life had always been there, and some sure instinct led her to associate Christ with a gentler, less raucous way of life, and she meant to support Fergus to the full extent of her power.

She lived to exert it for another three years, and if there was anything inconsistent with using threats to invoke some nameless power in order to force people to pay at least a lip service to Christ, she was unaware of it. She was putting into practice the theory she had expressed about making use of what one had. And Fergus was of the same mind. He was a useful man with his hands, and soon converted the spare stable into a church—primitive, but recognisable as a place of worship. There was an altar, draped with a silk bedcover which, had he known it, had once been part of the furnishing of a brothel. Had he known, he would probably not have minded, for he believed that when he elevated the Host, the wine became the blood and the bread the flesh of Christ. If one could accept so great a transformation, smaller changes were trivial.

Above the altar hung the crucifix, carved from pinewood—easier to work than oak—and into it Fergus put the whole force of his frustrated artistic nature. The crucified figure writhed in agony—and caused a good deal of questioning in the minds of those who came to look at it out of mere curiosity. Why should a god submit to such treatment? Had he no power? No followers to come to his aid?

Fergus explained patiently, repetitively, often obliged to fall back upon the folk-lore concerning Paulus, with which he was by now well acquainted and occasionally rather bored. Paulus, he explained, could have gone downriver on that famous occasion and done no damage, pretended to be a friend of the enemy, saying truthfully that he was not a man of Beofric's tribe.

"So he could have saved his life. And who would then remember him now? Paulus gave his life, a willing sacrifice. And Jesus Christ, our Saviour, did the same."

They listened and were puzzled rather than convinced or converted. But, very gradually and slowly, something seeped through.

A kind of magic played its part. Gilda's daughter, Edda, and Alwyn had been married in the strange new fashion, according to the old woman's whim, and Edda, though well past child-bearing age by common reckoning, was almost immediately pregnant, and, in the month of harvest, delivered of a fine boy, to be followed, incredibly, by another boy and then a girl.

Then there was this curious ceremony of baptism. The man Fergus had rigged up, inside the little building which he—and a few others—called a church, a wooden bowl containing water, which he blessed and therefore regarded as holy, and babies given their names there seemed to flourish in a rather exceptional way. (Nobody bothered to observe that only strong babies were carried to Mallow.) Adult converts, should any come along, would be baptised by total immersion in the river at Beofricsworth.

Fergus came to be accepted, at first by Gilda's command and presently for himself, as a handy man to have around. He did not despise manual labour, and in busy seasons would throw off his habit and do a day's work with the hardiest. And although his own habits were ascetic, he was not—at least to begin with—critical of gluttony or drunkenness. If invited to a feast, he mixed in well, only insisting on asking a blessing on the food before the eating began, and on rendering thanks afterwards. To the flock, which did not yet regard him as their shepherd, this was no more than an amiable eccentricity. He accepted the three main feasts of the year while giving them different names and interpretations. Yule he called Christmas and said that it celebrated, not the near-death and revival of the sun, but the birth of the Christ-child; the springtime fertility rites he twisted into a commemoration of Christ's death and resurrection; and the jollifications that marked the end of harvest he called a thanksgiving to God the Father for the kindly fruits of the earth. From the sacrificial offerings made at this season the little church at Mallow received only a meagre share—the crumbs, as it were, that fell from the old god's table; but Fergus accepted small offerings gratefully and graciously, and used them to feed himself, so that he should not be entirely dependent upon Gilda and her family.

His patroness puzzled him. She had saved his life; given him the stable, allowed him to build a little hut for himself abutting its southern side; she fed him at her own table and always seemed delighted to talk to him in the tongue they shared. Yet she was not pious in the accepted sense of the word, and certainly not in the manner of women converts he had known. It had taken a great deal of persuasion to coax her into being baptised—not in the river, she was too old and frail for that, but like a child, at the font.

"Why do you hesitate?" he asked her. "You befriended me, and through me, Our Lord. You are plainly a brave woman; are you not brave enough to declare openly on the side of Christ?"

Again and again she would brush the question aside, just as, in the past, she had brushed aside Sweyn's arguments and protests; but one day, when her end was near, though neither of them guessed it, and indeed it seemed as though, fragile but carefully tended and indomitable of spirit, she was good for many years yet, she said, "Something has always deterred me. To be honest I feared the loss of power, all gods being jealous of each other."

"What power, Madam?" Gilda saw that this was not an idle question, but one from the heart. So she smiled, shifting the innumerable small creases, fine as cobwebs in her still-fair skin. "That I cannot tell you. But you saw for yourself on that first evening. I challenged that horde of drunken oafs to harm you at the risk of my displeasure. They fear me, and not—not without cause. That is what I mean by power, and it is something you would not understand. It is a singular thing," she said, the planes of her face shifting again, "except as child-bearers and hand-maidens, women seem of such small importance where the gods are concerned. Of Mithras I know little; Paulus never spoke of him to me, except to give me instructions, but he was the god of soldiers—and no woman can be a soldier. Woden, Thor and the rest of that hierarchy promise immortality only to fighting *men*. Your creed is more lenient, but one thing worries me . . . I should not be happy in heaven without the company of the one I loved on this earth."

He imagined, reasonably, that she was referring to her husband, and was ready with the reassurance. All good men who had lived before Christ came or, since His coming, had not been fortunate enough to have heard of Him, would survive death and be recognisable. He spoke of the Transfiguration, with Moses and Elijah appearing in recognisable form. And he seized this opportunity to persuade her that her own baptism and her prayers as a professed Christian would do much to help the souls of the departed into the unity of Christ's kingdom. She thought for a little and then said, "Very well. I will take the step."

The conversion, openly admitted, of such a powerful member of the family, of the tribe, would be in itself a triumph, he thought, unaware that Gilda intended to make use of the secret power which she had inherited from Ethelreda to ensure that, when she had passed from this earth, Fergus's position should not be undermined. At the moment, even with her support and his personal popularity, the Church at Mallow-with-Beofricsworth was small and weak.

The new faith—still new after more than three years—appealed mainly to women and a few men who, through age or disability, did not feel sure of Woden's favour. Fergus had emphasised the gentler, more feminine side of his creed by making and setting up, just inside the church door, a statue of Mary, Mother of God, with the Christ-child in her arms. He had deliberately made it pretty. Mary's hair was yellow; her eyes, her gown and the child's eyes were bright blue. And below this pretty statue was a ledge upon which women placed floral offerings and sometimes a trinket. Even to the hardy Anglian women this carved thing was more attractive than the stark plain wooden representation of the tortured figure which the pretty, pink-cheeked baby had become in the end. Fergus was aware of that and in a way deplored it; but if Mariology helped, took one step towards Christianity, it was not to be despised. One must make the best use of what one had.

Fergus always attributed the rush of new converts which followed Gilda's baptism to the good example she had set, and he chose to disregard what she had herself said about the power which she had not explained. Of that power she retained enough to serve her for the remaining days of her life and on her deathbed. How, after such long feebleness of body, she could tell that her end was near, nobody bothered to wonder, but her family took her orders seriously.

"I shall have Christian burial," she announced, and her family understood what that meant: interment in the earth. This was not entirely unknown in their tribe, though more generally the corpse was incinerated and the ashes enclosed in a pottery urn before burial. In either case, some small possessions of the dead person were buried with him, together with food and drink to sustain the soul on its long, dark journey. In fact, when Beofric died he had been buried with the long ship which had brought the first settlers to Britain and then made another journey to bring back the rest of the tribe. He had been buried wearing his best clothes and his golden collar, the symbol of his chieftain status, with his silver-rimmed drinking-horn and a few other things for which his eldest son, Osric, could have found good use but which he dared not grudge.

Gilda said she wanted no such burial gifts. She said that everything she owned was to become the property of the little church. Actually, she was making an enormous assumption, for what indeed did she own? Or what, allowing that she owned it, should not, when she died, be divided amongst her sons? Her voice was weakening but she still spoke lucidly, saying, "This is my wish..." Fergus, and any successor of his, was to remain in possession of the little church and the priest's dwelling attached to it. She also wanted him to have enough of the old garden to be able to support himself.

Her only valuable trinket, a necklace made of lumps of amber strung together with links of gold, was to be placed over the head of the Virgin in the church. Pauli's wife, Hilda, who had long coveted that necklace, could hardly complain, since had her own mother-in-law remained a heathen and gone to her death as one, the amber beads would have gone into the fire with her.

In the three and a half years of Fergus's ministry, he had not been called upon to bury anyone; so he made the most of it, and when he said, "Go forth, Christian soul," all those present, even the unconverted, felt the impact. And Fergus himself, logical and hard-headed, had made an extraordinary concession, quite out of keeping with his creed, which claimed that the body, once the soul had left it, was an inert, unfeeling thing. He remembered how Gilda had shrunk from the cold, always seeking the seat by the fire in winter, demanding to be carried out to sit in the sun on fine days in summer.

By this time he had, working hard, covered the floor of his stable-church with planks of pine. The only stone available in his area of clay and chalk was flint, and he had never had time or energy enough to spare to split the egg-shaped stones. But, remembering how Gilda had hated the cold, he took up three planks—she was very small in life, and even smaller in death—and made a grave for her, midway between the statue of Mary and the altar. Into the central plank, after it was replaced, he carved a cross, the name "Gilda," and the letters R.I.P.

5 Cerdic

A.D. 834

"NEVER MIND ABOUT ME. I AM A DEAD MAN," BROTHER DUN-
stan said, speaking through bloody bubbles. "Save yourselves.
Take to the woods...Aaah." The sound, half scream, half
groan, was wrenched out of him by Brother Matthew's efforts
to lift him down from the back of the foundering pony.

After Brother Dunstan, who had chosen to go to battle with
the other men, Matthew was the youngest and strongest of the
little group gathered there in the twilight of dawn, but he could
not do what he wished to do: lift the boy down, lay him flat
in the church porch where there was some elbow-room, let old
Brother Benedict probe the wound, apply a salve, administer
some palliative for pain, and then call upon Brother Thomas
to perform the last rites.

"He is tied on," said Brother Benedict, whose sight was
failing in an unusal way. Most people grew long-sighted with
age, but Benedict, bat-blind to anything two arms' length away,
saw within a narrow scope with exceptional clarity, and now
saw what everyone else had missed, the rather complicated ar-
rangment of rope which had kept a badly wounded, but still
conscious, man in position on the pony's back.

Somebody produced a knife, but Benedict said, "Let be! I
can untie him and it will be quicker." His hands were tremulous
and mottled but nimble, and after a minute he said, "Take him.
I think he is dead. God receive his soul."

They all crossed themselves. Later they would pray for his
soul, guiltless though it might be, for before going out to fight,
as he had said, "For Christ against the heathen," he had confessed and been absolved.

There had been a little argument before he went. Men dedicated to the religious life were not supposed to engage in armed combat. A monk, renouncing the pleasures of the world, in a sense renounced the responsibility. He became a neuter, emasculated by his own wish. But it had been useless to remind Dunstan that Christ had told his disciples that, if somebody smote them on one cheek, they should turn the other for a similar blow.

Dunstan said, "Yes, but He also said He had come not to bring peace, but the sword. And this war against the Danes is in the nature of a crusade. I shall go and I shall fight for you, for women and children and Christians everywhere. I ask your blessing. And if you withhold it," he said, smiling, "I shall still go."

So he had gone when Cerdic, who liked to think of himself as king of Anglia, disputed though the title might be, had called out the fyrd. Every able-bodied man between the ages of sixteen and sixty. And he had come back in this fashion, to warn them. Literally with his last breath.

"Dear, dear," said Brother Benedict mournfully. "An arrow struck his chest, and someone without skill hacked it out, doing more damage than the arrow itself."

"And his warning," Brother Thomas said. "Do we heed it?" He looked and sounded nervous, ready to take to the woods at once. Nobody gave an immediate answer.

"They may pass us by," Matthew said, not very hopefully. "We have nothing worth stealing."

It was true. There were no silver vessels or ornaments on the altar, and the Virgin's only trinket was a string of amber beads. It was all too clear that nobody in the rather isolated area which the church at Mallow served had been inspired to buy his way into heaven by endowing the place and the six monks. At rare intervals, someone would pay, in cash or kind, for Masses to be said for a soul lingering in purgatory, but such slight income was all consumed in keeping the brothers fed and clothed, and the church in repair.

"It is so. We have nothing," Brother Benedict agreed. "But they are savages. They might wreak vengeance on us for being so poor and thus disappointing their greatest lust. They might enslave us."

Of all the unworldly things to say, Brother Matthew thought. Who would bother to enslave a man purblind, tremulous and forgetful from age?

"They would *kill* us," Thomas said. "It is not only for wealth that they attack religious houses. They hate us for being Christians. This poor boy spoke of a crusade, and so it is. Christianity has stiffened the resistance. I think we should flee. At once."

"Each man must decide for himself," Matthew said. And that was as true a statement as the one about their poverty. There was no titular head of this small poor house, which was neither an abbey with an abbot, nor a priory. Merely six men who had renounced the world, kept canonical hours, and made the best of what was available. But so far as they had a leader, it was Matthew, who was neither too young nor too old, who could read and write, and be trusted always to see both sides—or more—to any question.

"No," Brother Benedict said with decision. "I am too old. I cannot walk far. Or fast enough to keep warm. I shall stay."

"I would lend you my arm," Thomas said, and immediately regretted the offer and amended it. "To the nearest charcoal-burner's hut or some such shelter."

Brother Lawrence looked at Matthew for guidance, received none; looked down at the dead man.

"Someone should give him a decent burial. I shall stay. There are times when the pains in my face make the prospect of death not entirely unwelcome." He suffered from neuralgia, which none of Benedict's potions or plasters would relieve.

"I shall go," Brother Peter said, also looking down. "It was his wish. Not lightly to be disregarded."

"Very well," Matthew said. "Take blankets and what food you can carry." Thus he made plain his own intention. "God keep you both."

The day brightened. In the yard of the tavern which stood between the church and the road, a cock crowed. It was morning. The requiem Mass could be said. And poor young Brother Dunstan be buried.

There was no need to dig a grave in the small plot of what had once been waste land. The little church still had a floor of pine planks, and Brother Benedict remembered a story told him by a monk of the preceding generation. Somewhere between the statue of the Madonna and the altar there had once been a plank with some marks scored on, marks made indecipherable by the wear of footprints. One day a certain brother, on his way to the altar, had felt the marked plank and the two adjoining it collapse under his feet. Only the grace of God had prevented him breaking a leg. The rotted wood was as soft as new cheese, and the hole below it was thigh deep. At the bottom of it was a skeleton wrapped in silk, rotted and brittle. The bones of the hands were crossed on the bones of the breast, in Christian style, and there was a wealth of pale yellow hair. The old man who had told Brother Benedict this story, with all the emphasis lying on his own escape from injury, had said that the bones were not moved, nor was the hole filled in. New planks had been laid. So there was a grave all ready for Brother Dunstan, and since the savages might come storming up the road from the south at any moment, the three remaining monks were glad to use it.

When all was done, Matthew hurried across the intervening space between the church and the tavern. Ever since old Benedict had mentioned enslavement, half his mind had been with the alewife, a woman named Gilda, and her three pretty daughters, aged between fourteen and eleven. He understood that, although the Danes were not much given to keeping slaves themselves, they often regarded captive females as a marketable commodity, and he felt that Gilda and her children should take to the woods, at least for the time being.

Gilda—it was a name which recurred in this family—was a tall, angular woman with a hard, bleak face. She looked older than her age, the early thirties, for she had had a hard life. She'd married young a man who'd never had much about him, even when he appeared to be in sound health. Brother Matthew often wondered whether the lung-rot of which he had died, just before the birth of the youngest child, had been latent in him long before it showed itself, and had made him seem idle and feckless. He also wondered whether the extreme fairness and delicacy of the little girls—especially the youngest—which gave them the appearance of being creatures from another world, might not be due to ill-health.

This morning, when he entered the kitchen, Gilda was stirring something in a large vat which stood near the hearth. The mash for a new brew of ale. She whirled around as he entered, made the perfunctory little bob, and said,

"You have news?"

"Yes. And bad."

"Mark?"

Her only son, her eldest, her standby, who had gone off

when the fyrd was called out, though he was not yet sixteen and therefore not eligible.

"Nothing about Mark particularly. But our men were over-run." He told her in what fashion he had heard the news. She said, "God rest him. God rest them all."

"Amen to that. Brother Dunstan suggested that we should seek refuge in the woods. Brother Thomas and Brother Peter have already started out. I think, my daughter, that you should go, too."

"I can't. Listen!"

From the inner room came the sound of muffled coughing. "Mary?"

"And Emma. Edith is the only one on her feet."

Not for the first time Matthew suffered bewilderment about the ways of God, who allowed one affliction after another to befall the worthy and good, almost as if He were deliberately testing them to see how much they could bear without breaking. Sometimes, as now, facing this poor woman, the bewilderment was tinged with anger, instantly repented, of course.

"If only Bosworth were safe, or Wiptun, or Triver, Brother Lawrence and I could carry . . ." But he knew as he spoke that he was wasting breath. The three little townships which had once been called Beofricsworth, Wippedtun and Other River, could offer no refuge. They were stripped of men, left only with women, children, the old and the infirm. And they were all clogged with people—women and children and old men and cripples from smaller places like Mallow.

"Perhaps we are safer here," Gilda said. "All the Danes want at the moment is wealth. And in a humble ale-house they can hope for nothing but ale." As she said that, something flashed in her eyes and was gone. As Brother Matthew remembered her, she had never been beautiful or even pretty, but her eyes had always been noticeable, greenish blue rather than simply blue, or greyish blue, or grey. And the worry, the work and anxiety which stripped her face to the bone had not affected her eyes.

He said, a trifle awkwardly because he felt that now he was adding to her troubles, "If they come—and I fear they will, perhaps the girls . . . I think that Mary and Emma and Edith should be kept out of sight, if possible. I wish with all my heart that I could offer you sanctuary in the church. But these Danes are heathen; they would not respect such sanctuary."

"Nor you. Would it not be wise if you look to the woods?"

She had more than once shown a slight tendency to treat them all as ordinary men. Nothing disrespectful or offensive: in fact, to the contrary. Kindly. Before her husband died and some obscure wrangle over the land that went with the tavern had reduced her to dire poverty, she had made a particularly tasty sweet cake of oats and honey, and would send some across, saying that she knew all men liked sweet things. She had also said that some of her brews were better than those of Brother Benedict, blessed as his might be. There had been other instances, and now here she was, suggesting flight to him, who had come to suggest flight to her.

"No," he said. "I did not go to the battle. I hope not because I was more fearful than Dunstan or any other man, but a monk, unskilled in arms... Difficult to explain. Now it is different. Here I stand and shall stand, before the altar that I have served for hard on twenty years, and the heathen will see..."

Gilda thought: Yes, all men are vain, and he is no exception. She said, "I have a hiding-place for the children. Sometimes the defeated flee before the victors, and if Mark comes, two jumps ahead, I shall hide him, too. For the victors there will be ale for the taking. And cider. And wine."

For years, ever since her husband gave up all pretence of tending his few acres, she had supported the family by her skill at making brews of every kind, far superior to the ordinary run of such stuff. What she knew had been handed straight down, mother to daughter, for a long time, and even in prosperous times, when there had been no need to *sell* what was produced at Mallow, at a house called for some forgotten reason the One Bull, its hospitality had been famous. And the place itself was worth a look. Pictures on the walls, a picture made of coloured tiles on the floor.

"You will offer the enemy hospitality?" Brother Matthew asked, bewildered again.

"Why not? In any case they will take what they want... It occurs to me! Only the cross on the tower shows that there is a church behind this tavern. Would it be wise to remove it?"

Somebody had built a little wooden tower at the east end of the stable which had been made into a church, long ago— so long ago that nothing remained but legend. And on top of the little tower a cross stood, strong and resolute, a declaration of faith. Inside the tower hung a bell, flawed in the making and rejected by some larger and more prosperous community, but gladly welcomed at Mallow.

Apart from the tower and the bell, an extension of the little south-facing cells on the south side, and the porch to the west, which served the tiny community as communal room, nothing much had changed in the four hundred years that had elapsed since another woman named Gilda had given a missionary named Fergus a stable in which to establish his church. Neither that Gilda nor Fergus was remembered now.

Something lived on. Brother Matthew said, "I cannot do that. It would be like lowering one's standard in the face of the enemy . . . Where do you propose to hide the girls?"

She would have been glad of his help in the hiding, but she said, "It is better that you should not know. The heathen do not shrink from torture . . ."

Some terrible tales were told of how the Danes set about extracting information from those they suspected of having knowledge of hidden wealth.

"We must have faith in God," he said, holding to the rules, though in view of what had happened to English Christians in the north towards Brancaster, and in the south towards Walton, faith was difficult to sustain. "And if you need us . . ." That sounded ridiculous. What could three men, one very feeble, do to help others when they could not help themselves?

"God bless and keep you."

"And you," she said.

When he had gone, Gilda set about getting the girls to their hiding-place. Next to the kitchen there was a room always called the store. In it was a door which gave upon a space divided into three small rooms.

The two younger girls, coughing and flushed with fever, were laid in one bed. Edith would occupy the one next to them. The little rooms had no doors, and the partitions between them were flimsy. They were all lighted from one small window in the wall opposite the doorless openings.

Into the third cubicle, Gilda and Edith carried food and medicines.

"Let them cough," Gilda said, "until you hear voices. What they are bringing up is better out than in. But if you hear a sound that means I am not alone in the house, give them this, in measured doses. This is for pain. Let them not suffer. And this . . ." Gilda produced an axe of the kind used for splitting wood. "This is in case the worst happens and I am killed or taken away. With it you could enlarge that window-space or hack down the door. Death by starvation is not as easy as it sounds. And it would be a very evil man who would not treat you kindly."

It was the first indication which Gilda had ever given of her awareness of her eldest daughter's beauty. All her girls were pretty, but Edith was now at the stage where even plain girls acquired a bloom, and the pretty became beautiful—for a season. Edith had been born beautiful and was now very lovely indeed.

"I shall now close the door and block it," Gilda said. "Do your best for them."

They, Mary and Emma, were blood of her blood and bone of her bone, her children, but in a way she had relinquished her relationship to them when what they coughed up began to have bloody streaks. They were suffering from their father's disease, and with him she had learned the hopelessness of clinging on to one upon whom death had set his brand as clearly as men made their mark on cattle before letting them run in the common grazing-field. She had battled for his life for three years and had been defeated.

In the store she set herself to the enormous task of obscuring the door to the hiding-place. First the cross-legged trestle—easy to move. Then a full barrel of ripe ale and the vat of raw mash had to be lifted. She'd always been a strong woman. Once in the past, when the old ox dropped dead in the middle of the ploughing, she'd hitched herself to the plough and heaved and strained, leaning so far forward that she was practically on all fours. Nobody remembered that, when her husband died and his brother claimed the land because it had been pledged in return for various loans!

To conceal the top of the door she hung up a side of bacon, a skein of onions, a bunch of dried herbs. Standing back, she gave her camouflage a critical look, and was satisfied. Then she left the store, and in the kitchen, in the drinking-room of the tavern, completed her preparation for guests, welcome and unwelcome.

Her most urgent hope through that long day was that Mark would come home. She had never seen a battle or had speech with anyone who had taken part in one, for this area had been peaceful and settled for at least two generations, but she was familiar with the sagas and the folklore, and by exercising her imagination she could visualise how opposing forces were drawn up. In the centre of the English line would be Cerdic, well armed and well armoured, and around him would stand the pick of the hastily assembled English force—the biggest, the tallest, the most formidable-looking, those with some sort of armour, long swords or battle-axes. Nobody would place a boy not yet sixteen, his bones not yet set into manhood's shape, wearing a sheepskin jerkin and armed only with a bow and arrows, near the centre where the fiercest fighting would be. Nobody with any sense. And Cerdic was renowned for his good sense. He was known as Cerdic the Wise.

She imagined Mark, perhaps bearing a standard or—far, far better—stationed out on the extreme left or right of centre, so that when the Danes broke and began to flee, his paltry weapon could inflict the maximum of damage on their unarmoured backs.

But the Danes had not broken.

The English had broken, and Brother Dunstan had come to warn his brothers-in-God to take to the woods.

Brother Dunstan had been tied on the back of a pony, and had arrived at Mallow just as light was breaking. A boy like Mark, light of weight and long in the leg, could almost match a laden pony's pace, and, at least within ten miles of his home, he knew all the short cuts through the woods. If, in the clash and clatter of battle, the English line broke in the way that she imagined, like a string of beads, scattering—then there was a chance, merely a chance—but she was a woman who, almost from the day of her marriage, had been forced to cling to chance—that Mark would be here by sunset.

Once or twice, three times, several times, made restless by anxiety, she went to the front door of the tavern and looked out. The old road, at this point straight as a taut thread, ran from north to south. On one side of it stood the tavern and behind it the church, and beyond these the village. On the other side, scooped out of the forest and seeming to grow out of it, were houses, none of them large though one of them, known as Sweynshall, was fairly substantial and well thatched. It belonged to the avaricious brother-in-law of Gilda's who had loaned, so he said, so much to Gilda's husband that he had a right to land that Gilda's husband had so ineffectually tilled.

But what did it matter now? Eric, greedy and unjust as he had been, had turned out with the fyrd and gone to fight. His house, his acres would all be forfeit; he himself might be dead.

His house and all the others were deserted. The men had gone out to fight; the women and children and the old had gone to Bosworth.

"Why didn't I go, too?" Gilda asked herself, and answered herself. A simple answer. She had too much to take with her, and she had no faith in Bosworth being a safer place than Mallow. And, be honest: with all the good women of Mallow, Bosworth, Wiptun and Triver, she was in disfavour and had no real friend.

She blamed the men rather than the women. Men came and drank her ale, her cider, her wine—she could make wine from almost anything, even the flowers of the ubiquitous dandelion; men went home and praised her liquors, comparing them with the brews their wives made. So she was hated. But she could bear the disapproval of wives and mothers so long as men kept coming to the One Bull—for liquor only. She had made that clear from the start and it partly accounted for her bleak, repellent expression.

Mark did not come. Nobody came that day. Darkness fell. Mark might travel by night, but the Danes would not take the risk of moving in unknown country in darkness. Gilda made up the fire, left the black pot of broth just a-simmer, and lit a candle, so that Mark, if he came, would not think the place deserted; then, straining her back again, she pulled out the laden trestle and went in to see the girls.

The two younger ones were asleep, but Edith was alert.

"Has anything happened, Mother?"

"Not yet."

"Mark has not come?"

"No. But we must not lose hope." Gilda was aware of a strong bond between Mark and Edith, forged by shared hardships and similarity of nature. Holding the candle low, Gilda looked at Mary and Emma. "How has it been with them?"

"Bad. They have coughed all the time. Emma could eat nothing. Mary drank some milk and ate a crumb of bread and then she was sick."

"What medicine?"

"Only a tiny dose to soothe, about an hour ago. They were so exhausted."

Before speaking of time, Edith glanced at the candle. Its stout tallow body was scored lightly at intervals, each segment supposed to burn for an hour, more or less. It was a method of time-keeping learned from the monks, and, inaccurate as it was, better than nothing.

"Poor children," Gilda said. She spoke with feeling, but with detachment. The worst moment for her had come—and gone—when she realised that the ordinary winter cold and following cough could not be eased by a mixture of horehound and honey and blackberry wine. Then the blood streaks had appeared, confirming all her worst fears. She had known then that they were lost to her.

Now her real feeling, all that could be spared from concern about Mark, was for Edith, shut away here with two dying sisters. She said, rather harshly because life *was* harsh, "Perhaps it is as well for them. They were never strong, and to survive in this world a woman needs strength. They would have had no dowry. And now, with things as they are . . ." Her voice trailed off; she took a breath and began again, looking towards the small window over which Edith, as instructed, had hung a dark cloth before lighting the marked candle. "If you need me, Edith, I mean if . . . you know what I mean . . . hang a white rag in the window. Whatever happens, I will try to come."

"Take no risk," Edith said. Throughout the long day, the silence broken only by the sound of the flawed bell, Edith had been thinking, gravely, realistically, dispassionately. Never before in her life, since the time when she had been an unthinking child, had she had enough leisure for thinking. Always, always there had been work to do, and at night she had fallen asleep as soon as her head touched the pillow. Today, with nothing more to do than tend the two hopelessly sick little girls, locked in because the Danes were coming to kill, to rape, or enslave, she had fingered many thoughts, some of them curiously akin to Brother Matthew's in his most questioning, rebellious mood. And now her mother had summed up the whole situation: "Perhaps it is as well for them."

"Try to sleep," Gilda said.

"If Mark comes," and here was Edith giving direction to the mother who had always in the past directed her, "throw a small stone at the window. I would like to be the first—no, the second—to know."

"But if he comes, Edith, I intend to hide him here, with you and . . . them. Until we know how things go."

"Mark might not agree to that. He may come to assure you that he is alive—and to gather supplies. Then he may take to the woods, as an outlaw."

Curiously, that thought had not occurred to Gilda. Her mind and much of her day's activities had been directed to another end.

She went out, stooping low so as not to disturb the things that hung from the top of the door; for the third time she strained every muscle in her body to put the trestle-table and its burden into place, and, still partially crippled by the effort, reminded of those days when she had done the work of an ox on the plough-land, she went into the kitchen. There at the table, shovelling into his mouth the mixture of meat and onions and oatmeal, kept warm all day long and intended for Mark, was a man. Not Mark, not a Dane. Her husband's brother, Eric, the enemy who had applied for the judgement of the Hundred of Mallow, and by them been given possession of the tavern's small fields and the pasture. Her enemy rather more than the Danes, who had, so far, done her no injury, except that they had, in a way, taken Mark from her.

Arrogantly, she ignored the facts that they had not spoken for almost twelve years and that he was now eating her food.

"You bring news of my son?"

"No. I saw nothing of him, after the men from Triver joined ours." He shovelled in another mouthful. Gilda said nothing, but when he spoke it was as though he were defending himself against a charge. "The young cluster together. At the rear. I had rather hoped to find him here."

A lie. He had never given Mark a thought until this minute.

"Are you the only survivor?" She could put into a simple question a contempt for the survivor and her opinion that only the worthless survived.

"Oh, no. We were scattered. The line broke when the centre gave and the king was taken. It was a massacre! I climbed into a tree. Some lay and pretended to be dead. When it was dark I dropped down from the tree, skirted their camp and ran."

"And now?"

"There is talk of an amnesty for all who did not take up arms. In fact, just before the battle began a Dane, their spokesman, offered peace to all who would surrender without striking a blow."

"I wonder you did not accept," she said cruelly.

"A few did," he said simply. "And were immediately felled by arrows from our own bowmen."

"I hope to God that Mark's hand sped one!"

"It is possible. He always had a good eye and, for his age, a strong arm." He spooned up the last drops of gravy. "We fought on empty bellies," he said, almost apologetically. "I was making for Bosworth when I saw your light and remembered that you had stayed here. I came to beg a crust; but the smell from the pot..."

"It was meant for Mark."

She considered herself a good Christian, but, since the quarrel and the alienation of the little holding, she had found the order about forgiving enemies and doing good to those who had despitefully used her hard to accept. And the fact that this man had escaped, apparently unscathed, and was here (while Mark was God knew where), and had just eaten, if not all, the greater portion of food she had intended for her son, did nothing to assuage the bitterness of her spirit.

"So now you go to Bosworth to take shelter with women and children, and pretend that you never fought."

"If I can hide this," he said and thrust his left arm into the candlelight, showing a four-inch-long-gash, the two lips of it held together with clotted blood.

"A sleeve will hide it," she said, but her voice was no longer contemptuous. He was still her enemy, but he had been wounded, albeit but trivially, in the fight with the enemy of them all. She moved to a shelf, out of the full range of candle and firelight, and from a number of jugs selected one, poured from it, handed the cup to him. "This will hearten you for the rest of the journey." It was her very best cowslip wine, perhaps of all wines the most bothersome to make, since gathering the flowers just at the right time, not a day too early or too late, and stripping the petals free—not one scrap of green must be included—was time-consuming, and of all wines cowslip was the most likely to fail and turn into a sour brew, useful only as a purge.

"That was meant for Mark, too," she said. "But I have more."

Eric felt that she had, after all, relented towards him and

come at last to understand that all he had sought was simple justice. And two sips of the almost colourless but extremely heady wine made him relent towards her.

"You would be wise to come with me, Gilda. To Bosworth. The amnesty may hold good where many people are concerned. But every net has a hole in it. A woman alone would be easy prey for a few drunken ruffians. And you have the girls to think of."

"As I said at the time when others left, what I own cannot be driven or carried. Casks, vats, flagons. I have a new mash of barley-brew which must be stirred every fourth hour. I have ripe ale and young wines that would not travel well. I must stay with what I have, little as it is." Rancour swelled again. "As for the girls, of whose welfare you think, though belatedly, rest assured they are as safe as any can be in such troubled times." Not by a glance or the flicker of an eye did she betray where their perilous safety lay. "How many, do you think, will come here?"

"I cannot say. They will fan out, scouring the country for what they can steal. Having broken us, some may fall back to Walton, where they are well established. Some must raid Triver, Wiptun, Bosworth. Here is the crossroads. If fifty come this way, it would take no more than a dozen to sack Mallow." He swallowed the last of his wine at a gulp and said, "I must go." The wine went to his head. "Gilda, I promise you, if this blows over, as it may—we in the south and those in the north have been overrun, but the Middle Angles may stand—then I promise you I will return that disputed land. In return for this." He indicated the empty platter, the well-licked spoon and the empty wine-cup.

"May we both live to see that promise kept," Gilda said.

He slithered away into the starlit darkness, taking the road towards Bosworth, a road not deliberately made, like the straight one—a road casually made by the traffic of men's feet and animals' hooves over the long years.

When he had gone she stirred the mash in the vat again; lit a new candle; replenished the fire and added meat to the stew. Mark might still come.

He did not, yet the night was busy with comings and goings. The defeated men were drawn to their homes; some to pretend, like Eric, that they had never left them, others prepared to take to the woods, and preferring the woods that they knew.

They were all desperately hungry, and some bore wounds more serious than a gash on the arm. All but one told the same tale, and only one had news of Mark: not very positive, not very hopeful, but news.

"It was a madcap scheme," the man said, "such as only the young undertake. It was to release the king. After the slaughter, the Danes moved on a mile or two and then camped in a hall to celebrate the victory. You will understand, lady, that we who had saved our lives by this means or that—myself, I lay in a ditch and looked dead—were making little groups, for safety's sake, according to our destination. We kept to the woods. When we were about level with the hall and moving very stealthily, a boy said, 'The king is there, and presently his captors will all be drunk. Even a little fire could cause a panic, and a few determined men could make a rescue. Who is with me?' Four or five said, 'We are.' All young. The rest of us were too broken from wounds and hunger. Of the young, Cerdic was ever careful. I saw him give his dinner to a stripling, saying that the boy had growth to make."

"You think my son was one of that small number?"

"I cannot tell, not knowing your son by name or by face."

In her mind Gilda took leave of Mark much as she had done of Mary and Emma, but with far more grief, he being her son and her firstborn. Yet she felt a certain pride, too. It was so like her boy to suggest—or if not suggesting, joining in such a desperate, foredoomed enterprise. One could be proud, and at the same time wish that Mark had come in with the others, to be fed, bandaged or salved, and then hidden, with a chance of living on, if the Middle Angles put up a more successful resistance. And alongside these thoughts ran the strictly practical one—there was now no crumb of bread left in the house, and tomorrow she must bake.

By some agreement, immemorially old, the One Bull had always provided the brothers with bread, since they had no oven. They were, in fact, singularly ill-supplied with any domestic equipment. They slept in narrow cells attached to the south wall of the little church, and the porch at the west end, only two hundred years old, served them as common room and dining-room.

Mallow was part of the diocese of the bishop of Bywater, and he was supposed to make one visitation a year to all religious houses. Within Gilda's memory, His Grace had come once and been supremely dissatisfied with what he found. There was no lodging for him except at the tavern and, though Gilda's mother had done her best, sending Gilda, then as nimble and long-legged as Mark now was, speeding down to Bosworth for fresh-caught fish, the bishop's attitude of deep disapproval had not softened. He had called the little religious house at Mallow, 'a paltry, poor place, serving little purpose.' He had proposed that the six monks should be transferred to a larger and more orthodox establishment, and that the religious life of the region should be handed over to a secular priest. He had also de-plored—despite the close and well-working arrangements be-tween the tavern and the church—the relationship between them. It was unseemly, he said. Even the secular clergy, to whom many concessions—including that of marriage—were made, were not supposed to frequent taverns.

But His Grace had not provided the six monks with an oven or a kitchen in which food could be prepared, nor with any endowment. Grumbling and scornful, he had gone away and never guessed that the time would come when Bywater would be forgotten and Mallow remembered.

Brother Thomas and Brother Peter had plodded steadily on, knowing what they were escaping from but with not the vaguest idea of where they were making for. They had no known destination, safety being an abstract term. They had intended to go westward, but the woods defeated them; there were pools which must be skirted and, more dangerous than the pools, here and there, in clearings, patches of marsh, at this season of the year glazed over with the dead vegetation that had flour-ished there in spring—the marsh buttercups and water lilies, now joined by the fallen autumn leaves. Into one such hidden quagmire Brother Thomas had stepped, and had been almost immediately engulfed to waist height. There was so much suc-tion in the hidden mud that Brother Peter, trying to pull his fellow out, was almost drawn in, too.

Neither of them had much innate sense of direction, and the avoidance of obstacles deflected their path, so that they ended by walking towards the very enemy they had fled from. They saw no one of whom they could ask directions, and in the course of a whole day's walking had not seen the hut of a charcoal burner, the refuge they most hoped for.

Dusk fell early in the woods, and since the pools and the

quagmires made walking in the dark impossible, they halted, glad of the respite, thankful for the blankets which they carried, rolled, over their shoulders, and resigned to spending the night in the open, a thing neither had done before in his life.

On firm, leaf-thick ground they spread one blanket and on it knelt and prayed the usual Evensong prayers. Then they sat down and began to eat. At midday they had gnawed a crust as they walked. Now they sat, backs against a massive old oak, and the smoked bacon sweet on their tongues.

Suddenly Brother Thomas said, with food in his mouth— a breaking of the rule for mannerliness at table—"Wolves!"

"What wolves?" The long day's walk and the exertion of pulling Thomas free had temporarily dulled Peter's senses. "Oh, yes, wolves. Would they attack two grown men?"

As the settlement at Mallow had spread, more trees being cut down for building and for firewood, more fires lighted and more people about, the wolves had retreated, but there were stories about attacks on ill-guarded young animals in hard winters, and once a little girl, straying from a number gathering primroses, had disappeared. Her clothes and a few bones had eventually been found.

"Anything that moves," Brother Thomas said, beginning to move, with speed and purpose, pushing his food-bag into his satchel, rolling up the blanket, eyeing the oak, its trunk too thick, its lowest branch too high. "We must find a tree into which we can climb," he said, tugging at that portion of the blanket on which Peter still sat, prey to inertia. "Come," he said.

Oaks, similar to that under which they had been sitting; beeches, less bulky but smooth-barked, and high-branched; useless saplings; and then, perhaps in answer to Brother Peter's prayer to St. Antony, on the edge of another possibly treacherous clearing, a tree which had been struck by lightning and severed. A third of its trunk leaned down so that its dead branches touched the ground; the remainder merely leaned, as easily mountable as a stairway. The men climbed, breathless, hurried to the first forks, and there installed themselves, safe enough but not comfortably.

Each woke several times during the night, cautiously shifted position, asked, "Are you awake, my brother?" The wakings never coincided, and when Brother Thomas wakened to the light of morning, Brother Peter was still asleep, wedged into his niche, wrapped in the brown blanket, almost invisible. Thomas was about to speak when he realised that this time he had been awakened by something. Craning his neck, looking sidewards and downward, he saw that the clearing was now alive with men, soldiers, and a few horses.

Afterwards, in a tale that lost nothing in the telling, Thomas said he would never know exactly what warned him that the men were Danes. He had never seen a Dane, and in shape, size, colouring, even in armour, they differed very little from the English. He had seen the men of the fyrd march out, with young Brother Dunstan among them, and perhaps now he was struck by the fact that all the men in the clearing were fully armed—those of the fyrd had not been so well equipped. Or there could have been something about the decoration of the tunics they wore under their armour, or about their leggings. Something, thanks be to God!

The clearing was too wide to allow him to hear their speech very clearly, but he was very careful about waking Peter, whispering, "Be quiet," before the wakening was complete. Then he said, "Danes!" and pointed.

Two men lifted from the back of one of the horses a stool, neither three-legged nor four-legged, but solid, a cube of red leather. They placed it under a tree, and another man, a veritable giant, walked forward and took his seat on it. Other men jostled into position, forming a semicircle.

Then, from the small group still gathered with the horses, a man came out, stumbling slightly at first as though he had been pushed, but he recovered his balance and his dignity and, when he was immediately before the giant on the stool, stood straight and still. He wore no armour—simply a white tunic and breeches, and his head was bare.

There seemed to be a conversation between the man on the stool and the man in the white tunic. It was maddening to see and to hear just enough to know that words were being exchanged, and yet not to hear the words, to be able only to guess. The man in the white tunic seemed either to be refusing to do something or to agree with what was being said. He shook his head, spread his hands.

Then from the men with the horses another man came forward and placed on the bared, golden head a circlet of gold, a broad band which, at its upper edges, seemed at intervals to sprout leaves, also of gold. The crowned man appeared to accept that as of right, but when yet another man came forward, carrying sword and shield and chain mail, he indicated by a gesture that he repudiated them.

"It is the king!" Brother Thomas whispered. "Cerdic himself."

What happened next was horrible, because it was so long-drawn-out. Cerdic made one last gesture of refusal, and the giant made one of patience exhausted. A man ran towards an oak—not yet full grown—and threw a rope around it; two men took Cerdic, unresisting, to the same tree and lashed him firmly. Then the bowmen moved in, not to kill, but to display their exquisite skill, and to torture. The arrows, in this still clearing, sped by expert hands, nailed Cerdic's body to the tree by transfixing only his fleshly parts to it. Even his ears were pinned. He would die, of course, Brother Thomas knew, from sheer loss of blood—even the most trivial of the wounds ran red—but it would take time, and all the time this good man, this just man, Cerdic the Wise, would suffer, suffer, suffer.

God-the-Holy-Father-Maker-Of-Heaven-And-Earth, Jesus-Christ - Our - Lord - Who - Suffered - For - The - Sins - Of - The - World; Holy-Mary, Mother-Of-God, twitch one elbow, misdirect one aim so that one arrow, just one, it needs only one, goes through his heart. Let him *die. Let him die.*

But the sport lasted until the giant lost patience and interest, and gave another order. A swordsman came forward and with a single slash severed Cerdic's head from his body. The head, held to the oak-tree only by the ears, frail holds against such stress, since to the weight of the head was added that of the crown, broke away and rolled, while for the space of a few heartbeats the neck spouted a red fountain then the body, an empty sack, sagged against the ropes, and all seemed over.

But it was not. From the group around the horses, three boys were pushed forward, and beheaded without ceremony. A fourth waved back; he was carrying a harp and actually dared to strike a few funeral notes, not unlike human voices chanting for the dead, before he was hustled away.

Then the giant stood up and stretched himself. The two men who had set the stool in place took it up and carried it towards one of the horses. Some of the archers, to whom this had been mere sport, recovered their arrows.

They all departed through an opening in the clearing, and the horses' hooves, sounding loud on the paving, informed the two hidden listeners that the giant and his minions were on the old road, going north to Mallow, to Bosworth, to Triver.

When the silence had lasted a long time, the two monks mustered courage to descend, to advance, keeping wary eyes on the opening through which the Danes had gone. The clearing stank of blood.

"Not Mark. Nor this. Nor this," Brother Thomas said, inspecting, one by one, the severed heads of the dead boys.

Again slow to understand, Peter said, "Did you expect to find the ale-wife's son?"

Thomas had feared to, but he could not explain why.

They reached the headless corpse, sagging against its bonds. The angle of the torso had set free to dangle a heavy, intricately worked silver cross on a chain.

"I saw him touch it," Peter said with awe. "During the questioning."

"Bargaining. I think myself that the man on the stool was bargaining. Offering the king's life, if he would abandon his faith."

"About that we shall never know with surety," Peter said. "But Cerdic, though his claim was disputed, was crowned and anointed. He must be given Christian burial."

"After this danger has passed," Thomas agreed.

Then, as they loosened the ropes and freed the body, something extraordinary happened to them both. They were timid men; they had taken flight, but now courage flowed into them. It was as though this limp, ensanguined body had by a touch wrought magic, making them bold.

"We will take him to Mallow and bury him there," Brother Thomas said. And Peter agreed, only saying in his cantankerous way, "What of the boys?"

"We cannot carry them, or bury them. We are not certain who they are. But we will commit them to the infinite mercy of God. More than that we cannot do. We do not know their names. But all men are known unto God."

Together the two monks performed the necessary committal service, and then turned their full attention to Cerdic, king and martyr.

Wrap his body with its multiple wounds in one brown blanket; knot the corners of the other to make a sling which two men could carry.

But, and for a moment, in the blood-stinking clearing, it

sounded ludicrously like some game children played. Where was his head?

There were the three dead boys, each with his head so close to the body; in one case not even totally detached. There could be no mistake. Nor could it be denied that Cerdic's head, upon which the crown had been set—and they both knew that that had been a mocking gesture, not dissimilar to the crowning of Christ with thorns—was now lost.

"I admit," Brother Thomas said, "at the last moment I closed my eyes and did not see what happened to his head."

"And I was being sick," Brother Peter said. "Quietly."

"So, since neither of us saw, we must assume that the heathen took it, for the sake of the crown. But _we_ know, do we not, that this is Cerdic's body and that on the day of the Second Coming, when the dead rise from their graves, his head will be united to his body, by God's providence."

It was, indeed, an article of faith, for in the beginning Christians had been torn limb from limb by hungry lions in Roman arenas; pious men had been drowned at sea and their bodies eaten by fish; in orthodox, blessed graves, bodies had rotted and often bones had been disturbed. But at the great day of Resurrection, God who had made all, would unite all, and every man would stand, whole as he had once been, to be judged.

Carrying their burden and it was heavy—the two monks set out to retrace their steps. They were, after all, only one day's journey from their church, and they knew how not to trust those patches of greensward or level, leaf-strewn patches which had been deceptive yesterday. Yet their progress was slower. They were burdened, and yesterday's exhaustion, added to the morning's emotional stress, defeated them.

"I have gone at the knees, like an old nag," Brother Peter said. "I can no more."

6 Ingwar

AT MALLOW, IN THE LULL BETWEEN THE LAST REFUGEES AND the first invaders, who were said to be hard on their heels, Gilda made dough for a fresh batch of bread and, waiting for it to rise, went hastily to the hiding-place. The trestle moved more easily now, since the cask on it was almost drained.

At first sight all three girls looked dead, Mary and Emma curled up together and Edith kneeling on the floor, her arms spread across the foot of the bed and her head, turned sideways, resting on the fur cover. On the stool by the bed stood the flagon which had contained the poppy juice which brought sleep even to those racked by coughs or writhing in pain. It was empty.

Controlled woman as she was, Gilda cried, "Oh God! No! Not Edith!"

Edith, for all that she looked so fragile, had never ailed, never coughed or seemed listless: she'd passed from childhood to womanhood without the aching back or aching head that often accompanied such transition. It was her spirit that had failed.

I put too much upon her, Gilda thought with remorse; she was still at an age to be sheltered from harsh facts. Now, and by her own hand... My fault, my most grievous fault. I as good as told her that those two poor little things would be better dead. She applied it to herself.

Holy Church—and Gilda had lived all her life in close contact with one little branch of it—was very harsh upon suicides, harsher than with murderers. A murderer might have any number of reasons for what he did, a suicide but one: despair, that sin deadly because it showed complete lack of faith in God, was a defiance, and allowed no time for repentance.

If the brothers knew what had happened in this small room, they would not give Edith Christian burial in the little churchyard. They must never know!

With that thought, Gilda put her big, work-roughened hand to her daughter's face. It was warm!

Her next actions were anything but fond. She reached for the jug of water which stood nearby, and emptied it over Edith's head, held upright by the hair. Then she smacked her face, palm on the left cheek, back of the hand to the right. She shook her until finally, after a lifetime, the girl opened her eyes, blinked, said, "Mother," in a bewildered way, and began to cry.

"This is no time for tears," Gilda said, her relief, remorse and pity all voicing themselves in something as astringent as wort juice.

"They both died—happily. And I..."

"I know. I *know*. We have no time. I left the door open. Edith, get into another room; eat, drink, restore yourself."

"And Mark?" Edith asked, her consciousness expanding.

"No news so far." This was a girl-child, not to be pressed upon any further. "If he were dead somebody would have seen and told me. We must hope."

There was no time for more.

The Danes arrived at the crossroads soon after midday. Their leader, the giant Ingwar, recognised a strategic position when he saw one. He also knew that a house with ale to sell announced the fact by exhibiting a bush on a pole above the door.

"I stay here," he said. And he named those who should stay with him. These intimates and chosen ones were not actually the subject of envy from the others, who must go on to a place called Triver, or turn off to a place called Bosworth. To be closely associated with Ingwar—cousin to the king of Denmark, and as a leader, unsurpassed—was an honour, but it had grave disadvantages. He disapproved of private looting and had fanatical ideas about rape. The punishment for a man proved to have violated a woman was simple, logical, but terrible.

Also Ingwar was given to what those associated with him knew as black moods, when nothing and nobody pleased him; when he would decry even a victory—such as yesterday's—

counting and naming the dead, not exultantly but with melancholy. In the depths of such a mood he would fret even over the enemy dead, and would say, "For every man slain, on whichever side, some woman weeps."

His treatment of Cerdic, who claimed sovereignty over part of what was beginning to be known as Suffolk, had been in a way typical of Ingwar's waywardness of mood. Immediately after the battle, he had behaved most courteously to the prisoner, actually pointing out the advantages of a treaty which would leave Cerdic some shadow of authority. Cerdic had chosen to be defiant and say that it was impossible for a Christian to make any kind of a bargain with heathen. Ingwar had then, with enormous patience, tried to persuade Cerdic to renounce Christianity—"The religion for women, children and dotards." Cerdic, misjudging Ingwar's sincerity, and remembering how the Danes had played false with other prisoners, thought he had nothing to lose, and answered hotly. Even so, he might have escaped with his life had not a few reckless English boys made that futile attempt to rescue their king. Ingwar then misjudged Cerdic, and thought that his defiance stemmed from a knowledge of the plot and his certainty of its success. The result had been the scene witnessed by Brother Thomas and Brother Peter. A further result was the black mood in which Ingwar arrived at the One Bull in Mallow.

When Ingwar was so low in spirit that even a victory seemed valueless, he could escape by two means—by getting very drunk, or by listening to sweet music. Unlike many Danes, he was as a rule somewhat abstemious and inclined to be critical of sots. The fact that the Danes were less drunk than the boys had imagined they would be had been one of the causes of the failure of the overnight plot. But today Ingwar intended to become a sot himself.

Of the youthful plotters, some had died in the fire they had kindled, or in the resulting scuffle, or in the clearing with their king. One had been spared because he played the harp very well indeed. And that boy was Mark, Gilda's son. (It was proof of the unimportance and general ineffectualness of her husband that it was her name, not his, which identified the family.)

It was a singular irony that Mark had been spared because he could make music. There'd been so little time to spare when he was young, the time when such skills were acquired. The land which went with the tavern had still belonged to them then, and there were too many jobs which even a six-year-old could do. And Gilda, who could play a little, and to whom the harp belonged, had been too busy to teach her son much. Also there was growing up everywhere the notion that playing the harp was, like needlework and cooking, a feminine rather than a masculine occupation. However, there was the harp, and there was the boy with his inborn talent, and there close at hand were the monks who provided encouragement. As God was said to love a cheerful giver, so He was said to love sweet music. Mark had often played in the tiny church.

When the foolish boys were taken, Ingwar had been willing to spare the life of any one of them if only some excuse, acceptable to all, could be found. A boy who could shoe horses might have been spared, but during the four centuries after the English had been settled, skills had become specialised, and ordinary people did only ordinary things. Mark, questioned about any special ability, said that he played the harp a little, and Ingwar said, "Give him a harp!" had listened, nodding his head to the rhythm, felt some slight relief from the oncoming mood of despair, and had then been distracted. So Mark had been hustled away by those who deplored their leader's softness, and had come face to face with death in that clearing. But Ingwar had noticed—he was known as Ingwar Hawkeye—and had said, "Take that one away!"

Of this Gilda knew nothing.

She saw the Danes arrive. Saw the huge man who was the leader halt, give orders which split the force into three, and then turn, with the smallest of the three forces, into the forecourt of the tavern. Careful of his own as well as of others, Ingwar had chosen not only the privileged ones but also such of the lightly wounded as had managed to walk this far.

She met them at the door and said, without humility, with bitter parody of welcome, "All that I have is yours," and stood aside. Ingwar said, courteous even to those about to be robbed, "I thank you, lady." Then he himself stood aside and said, "Wounded first."

In the battle at a place which had no name but was later to be known as Daneley, the English, though so abruptly defeated, had managed to strike some telling blows. Those who had received a blow and survived and struggled on were all wounded above the belt; men wounded in the legs were being taken care of in the hall, slightly damaged by fire, where Ingwar had spent the night.

As the wounded men came in, and then the giant leader and his entourage, Gilda saw Mark, well to the rear among the servants and the horses. He had left carrying his bow and some arrows; he now carried a harp, and his beautiful curling yellow hair was all gone. But she knew him, and almost cried out. But Mark put his finger to his lips.

She understood that he had been made a prisoner. She did not know that he had been involved in a plot which made his life doubly forfeit and which might rebound upon her and his sisters. She thought: I must find some way of letting Edith know.

The house, built by a Roman in Roman style, was far more suitable than any English hall, however spacious and grand, for the purpose it was now called upon to serve. It offered some privacy. There were adjoining rooms, with beds in them. There the walking wounded could rest and lie quiet while the others caroused on what the ale-wife had made ready. There was fresh-baked bread and plenty of meat, all smoked: pig-ham, mutton-ham and, as might be expected in an ale-house, plenty of liquor. "Here is ale; here cider," Gilda said, indicating the casks. "These are wines."

Language presented small but not insurmountable difficulties, since the people who now called themselves English sprang from the same stock as the Danes, and used many of the same words, though differently pronounced. The English knew more words, because for many generations they had been in touch with Christianity, and even the most ignorant priest knew a little dog Latin. Ingwar understood Gilda when she pointed out the jugs and said, "These are wines," and she understood him when he said, "Bring me wine," but she made no move to serve him. Let him choose his own; let his servants do the pouring; let God judge! She had used what she had to the best advantage, aiming to do the most damage to the greatest number—and some of the wine was harmless for the simple reason that she had run short of the deadly stuff.

Ingwar chose wine because it worked more quickly than ale. He was surprised to find it in this poor little wayside tavern. He associated it with monks, or with churchmen who were not monks. He had enjoyed a blissful, swift easement of melancholy in the palace of the bishop of Bywater. Red wine, he remembered, and now called for red, and lifted his cup and said, "To all brave men, here or in Valhalla." And that brought the memory of Cerdic—a brave man if ever there was one—to the forefront of his mind, and the melancholy which he had been fighting off since early morning took a step nearer. He said to the nearest person he had for friend in this group, the two others having gone as leaders to Triver and Bosworth.

"Harold! For what would *you* die, inch by inch, as that so-called king did this morning?"

"For you, my lord," the man said. A shade too promptly? That was one of the worst things about this state of mind: the suspicion of everybody. Ingwar knew that of the fifty-odd men under this roof, thirty at least would die for him should such sacrifice be required; yet now he doubted the one whose devotion and loyalty had been many times tested and proved.

He did not answer. He held out his cup for more wine, and drew down the corners of his mouth, and Harold, a simple man, thought: The black mood is on Ingwar again; before I can draw ten breaths he'll be forbidding all pillage, and offering to pay that grim woman for what we have eaten.

To forestall such incredible yet likely action, Harold said, "While the light lasts, may the men make a search of the houses across the road?"

"In orderly fashion," Ingwar said, gulping down the red wine of oblivion—let it work, and soon, soon!

Orderly fashion meant fair shares for all—for the wounded who could not take part in any sacking, for those whose duties forced them to be elsewhere, and, let truth be faced, for leaders like Ingwar, too lordly and proud to go foraging for a few coins hidden under a straw mattress in a humble dwelling, silver or even silver-gilt cups and jewels in more prosperous houses and in churches, and, of course, marketable slaves.

Under some commanders the rush for plunder could become a riot, often resulting in the destruction of the covetable thing, and even more often in rancorous disputes between men who were supposed to be blood brothers. Ingwar's way was better and was beginning to be copied by those who had the strength of body and will to exact obedience.

"I doubt if this place will yield much," Ingwar said. "The houses looked to be deserted, and the people had ample warning."

"What about this house? Judging by the fare, it does a busy

trade." To Harold, that held out hope of coined money. No man called at a tavern and bought ale with a pigeon.

"We have accepted the hospitality of this house," Ingwar said dampingly. "Now, where is that boy with the harp?"

Gilda answered, "I think he stepped into the yard."

She had sent him. Under cover of the jostling, the eating and drinking, she had managed to whisper that he should go and strike a few notes under the window of the disused part of the house, so that Edith should know that he was alive. She had also ordered, in a more urgent whisper, that he should drink nothing. For now the hurly-burly was such that she herself could not tell the harmless liquor from the other.

When the deadly additions worked, it was essential that Mark should not be involved; so she said, "I will call him," and going to the yard door, shouted roughly, "You there, with the harp! Your master calls for you."

Hurrying past her, Mark said, "She saw me!"

In the late afternoon four of the walking wounded died. There was nothing unusual about that; a blow to the head, which could sever an ear or dislodge an eye, often did more damage than was seen at first. Soothed by the wine and the music, Ingwar took these deaths philosophically. Part of the price of victory, and now they were in Valhalla, guests of the gods forever. To the men who had not gone looting because they were too drunk or too idle, or were tending the wounded in rough-handed fashion, or staying close to Ingwar with an eye to self-advancement, he said, "Bury them while the light lasts. We may move tomorrow."

Then there were worse tidings. A man hurried in and said, "My lord! Harold . . ."

"What of him?"

The man doubled over, clutching his belly. "Dead," he said through his teeth, and then committed an offence, emptying his bowel, noisily, into his trousers. Even to pass wind in the presence of an equal was an insult. Unless . . . There was an affliction known as gut-rip. It occurred in camps too long occupied and not well-enough ordered; it occurred on ships too long at sea and not well-ordered. It could be passed from man to man, and it could, within a few hours reduce a strong warrior to a weakling. In no camp, in no ship commanded by Ingwar, had there been an occurrence. He had always been as fanatical about burning or burying or swabbing down as he was against rape and private plundering. Even now, getting up from the red-covered stool and setting out to see for himself what had happened to Harold, Ingwar was sufficiently in command to say, "Take him out. Into a shed or something."

But, crossing the road and making his way towards the cluster of houses which the English had apparently deserted and which his own men were now supposedly sacking, Ingwar's self-distrust rose to the surface and he thought: Harold dead! My fault. I did not think about the possibility of ambush! He took his sword-hilt in his hand and moved warily.

The first house he reached seemed to be deserted, but there were three men in it—his own, and all afflicted in the same humiliating, stinking way. They knew nothing of what had happened to Harold, and showed an infuriating indifference to all but their own woes. They managed, however, to assure him that there had been no ambush.

Between the first house and the second, two of his men ran past him, leaping in the air, tearing off their clothes, screaming, scratching themselves. In swampy places, in warm weather, very small, humming flies would come out in the evening, and swarm about men, driving them mad in somewhat similar fashion. But here was no swamp; it was cold weather, and he could see no flies. He knew both men by name and called to them sharply. They ran on, laughing.

Another house: several men squatting and groaning and stinking, and one apparently asleep. The little pile of plunder lay on the table. Nothing of worth. And no information about Harold except, "He went on, my lord," and a hand moved from clutching the racked belly, to indicate the direction in which Harold had gone.

Ingwar found him in a house better furnished than those he had seen so far, and he had died as old men did, if in youth they had been fearless. One stroke from Thor's hammer! After death in battle, it was the best death that could befall a man. But Harold was *young*, Ingwar thought, pushing through a group of men not afflicted by the gut-rip or the fly-madness. Some of them had already placed the body on a bearskin, preparatory to carrying it to wherever Ingwar, once informed, should direct.

"What happened? Tell me exactly."

"The chest," a man said and, elbowing aside some of his fellows, enabled Ingwar to see a chest built into the wall against which it stood and into the floor on which it stood. It was banded with iron, and there were locks. Not a thing that could be taken whenever its owner fled.

"Lord Harold," the man who had chosen or been elected as spokesman said, giving Harold a sudden promotion, because of the dead only praise was demanded, and because Harold had been Ingwar's friend, "he wrenched the locks away, lifted the lid . . . And died. Struck dead, my lord."

"As I see. What was in the chest?"

"Nothing. It was empty."

At this final irony, Ingwar's lurking depression gave way to fury. He looked at the chest with hatred. Turning to one of the men, he said, "Run across to the tavern. Some of the wounded died and I ordered burial. I have changed my mind. Tell them to bring all the dead here. They shall have a funeral pyre. You and you, run to the other houses. Tell everybody to muster here and to bring something from each house. Something that will burn."

This was an Ingwar more to their taste than the one who sat brooding, even after a victory.

There was no particular ritual about the disposal of what remained of a man after his spirit had gone to Valhalla or to Hel, which was an undefined place, not of punishment, but reserved for those not fit for the company of the gods. A sacrifice, however, was always acceptable, and, looking down at the dead man whose protestation of devotion he had received so coldly so short a time ago, Ingwar wondered what living thing could be ceremonially sacrificed. Not a horse: they had too few, and they were needed to carry the plunder, or for riding. Of hounds they had none, since they had come to England on serious business, not for sport. They had one prisoner—technically a slave—but he was the boy with the harp. And in all the settlement no living thing bleated or mooed or grunted.

Cats! Cats showed a strange fondness for places rather than people, and in his time Ingwar had seen settlements, far larger than this, deserted by all but cats who had remained behind—whereas even stupid sheep would follow—or had returned, if taken away in sacks.

"You and you," he said, "go hunt a cat. If you fail to find one, fetch the cock from the tavern." A cat would be preferable; cats, because they so often escaped from dangerous situations, were said to have nine lives, which hinted at some kind of immortality; also they were very clever at getting into places, and since all the dead wished to go into Valhalla, there was a shadowy connection.

Presently Ingwar realised, with mounting dismay, that Harold would make his passage through the fire and the unknown into the hoped-for place, well attended, for the men coming back with stools and benches and hastily chopped-up bedsteads, with window-shutters and bales of straw, brought more dead. The man who had seemed to be asleep in the first house that Ingwar searched was found to be dead—and there were two more like him. Three others had been struck by Thor's hammer; one smitten with the itching, dancing madness had declared that he was on fire, and thrown himself into a pond dug for the watering of oxen, and two, in separate places, had suddenly vomited, throwing up, not the good food and liquor of their midday meal, but blood. A fatal bleeding.

Thirteen men dead in the course of a single, peaceful afternoon, and even more suffering from the gut-rip, which here had taken an unusual course. Ordinarily, it began with one man and spread, step by step. This had fallen like a curse. And the usual cause of all disorders of the bowel or belly—something bad eaten or drunk—was obscured by the fact that some men, like Ingwar himself, were unaffected, and that the dead men had died from diverse causes. Bad food did not invite a blow from Thor's hammer, or set their flesh on fire and drive them mad, or make them fall into a sleep from which there was no waking. More and more Ingwar inclined to think of spells, curses, and the spiteful aspect of Freya, the goddess who, womanlike, concerned herself with little things. Freya was the giver of good crops, fruitful breeding, even of such small things as luck in churning. Such blessings fell from her right hand. If annoyed, she opened her left, and scattered miseries, but seldom in such variety as had fallen upon Mallow this afternoon.

One of Ingwar's difficulties was that he was an orthodox man with a wayward mind. He believed that Thor gave victory to the brave, but only if the swords and axes were sharp; the archers in practice. He believed that Freya could send the gut-rip, but he also believed that it came from unwholesome conditions.

Even the brave blaze of the wooden house, the sound of the

horns, and the screams of the cat as it was thrown into the flames could not lighten the black mood, for which there was now ample cause, and which was now shared by everyone.

Mallow stood higher than Bosworth, and, down in the lower village Icel the Short, who was in charge of the raiding party, saw the red glow, and thought that Ingwar was allowing some of his more riotous followers a free hand for once. Not to be outdone, he allowed his own to burn three houses.

Still mixed in mind, believing that he—or possibly the place—was cursed, Ingwar did what he could, in a practical way, to keep the complaint from spreading. Gut-rip sufferers were not to be allowed in the house; they must lie in the barn, the stable or some other outbuilding, and preferably in straw. They should take only water, no milk being available. Ingwar noticed that the ale-wife was very co-operative, warming the water in her kitchen and even helping to carry it out. The young harpist was equally helpful, prisoner though he was.

The sound men needed food, and Gilda provided it, with an off-hand kind of apology, and making a tiny slip.

"We never had more than would see us through the worst of the winter," she said.

"We? Your husband turned out with the levy?"

"I have been a widow for many years. I had two daughters. Both are dead." Her son bent over his harp. During the water-fetching and the heating of it for the comfort of racked bellies, they had exchanged more hurried words, and there was understanding between them.

"You have been unfortunate," Ingwar said.

"Most unfortunate," Gilda agreed, thinking of the alienation of her property. But fortunate, too. She had Edith, safe in hiding, and Mark who, if only Mary, Mother of God, would heed prayers and send the blessed opportunity, might yet escape. And there was still hope. To the north and to the south the Danes had been triumphant. But the Middle Angles were preparing to stand, and might prevail. To that end Gilda had contributed. Thirteen dead! Given more time, she could have worked more havoc. But her resources had been limited, and she had done her best with what she had. All things which, used in responsible fashion, worked for the good of whoever swallowed them. Even that scanty grey dust collected with endless patience from the blades of rye in a damp season—a pinch of it could ease a difficult birth, and a larger dose could rid a woman of an unwanted pregnancy. "Eight," they said, "or nine, is enough; I can no more!" But an overdose of it, so the stories told, could produce an ailment known as St. Antony's Fire, an inflammation of mind and body that sent people mad. The same could be said of the poppy syrup: in moderation good, in excess—and how nearly Edith had escaped!—fatal. As for the purge, again and again a small dose had cleared a clogged bowel, and Gilda had put into one ale-cask all she had. For the other deaths, men in good health one minute and stone-dead the next, she could not account or feel wholly responsible, except that such deaths did occasionally come to big, heavy men who had eaten and drunk and then exerted themselves to work or to hunt. But it was just possible that the few who had died in this way had taken a little of all the brews, and that the effects, warring against each other, had resulted in the desired end.

"I wish nothing to eat," Ingwar said, "but the red wine. If any is left . . ."

"I think, a little."

Earlier he had, she knew, having kept a sharp eye on such things before the general muddle began, drunk two jugsful, one at least tainted. And taken no harm. Why? Because he was so big?

When she looked at his size, considering him not as an enemy but as a man, something in her long-deprived body stirred. Her husband had been in every way a small man, and since his death she had been so busy, making a living for them all, making ends meet, worrying about the health of the two little girls, that lust had lain quiescent in her. A blush of shame, red as the wine she handed to him, momentarily softened her bleak face, and Ingwar, on the fringe of his troubled mind, thought that perhaps as a girl she had been comely.

Gilda had no idea whether this wine had been tampered with or not. She hoped so, all the more fiercely for her lapse. But no harm came to Ingwar, who proceeded to drink himself to near insensibility.

It was raining in the morning, a steady downpour from a low grey sky. Ingwar went his rounds. No more men had died, but they were in sorry condition and low in spirit. The whole yard reeked of the illness, with now and again the acrid whiff of smouldering embers quenched by water. The men needed milk now; tomorrow they would need fresh, lightly-cooked red meat. Even with such sustenance they were unlikely to be fit to march next morning, as had been arranged.

"Take a horse," Ingwar said, "and go to Bosworth. I want a cow in milk, a bullock, two years old. And a pig for the ale-wife."

He also wanted news, but that would already be on its way; leaders were expected to report daily.

He was ashamed of his hope that some kind of misfortune had struck Icel in Bosworth and Thorkill in Triver, something that would mean that the delay was not entirely due to what had happened at Mallow. None of it was his fault, but it reflected on his leadership. He could hardly be deposed, having been appointed by his cousin the king, but it was all too easy to get the nickname Unlucky. No longer Ingwar Hawkeye but Ingwar the Unlucky.

Icel's messenger from Bosworth arrived first. Nothing but good to report; no resistance and much plunder. The messenger from Thorkill at Triver, arriving rather later, having had a slightly longer distance to travel, told the same story. These little riverside communities were richer than might be expected. They did a certain amount of trade with other coastal or riverside places, even occasionally with the Continent. Coined money and even a few rare luxuries, spices from the Far East, had been found.

Inwardly beating his breast, Ingwar said, "Good, good!" and then, choking on the words, told what had been happening here: thirteen men dead and a greater number so stricken that tomorrow's march must be delayed, until the next day, at earliest, and even then it could be slow.

"A pity," the man from Triver said. "Cerdic and his muster were taken by surprise and ill prepared. In that central plain the Middle Angles will be gathering men every hour, and making their positions stronger."

"I do not need you to teach me my trade," Ingwar said, coldly hostile. "Get you back and tell my lord Thorkill that I and mine hope to be ready to march at sunrise on the day after tomorrow."

Icel's messenger, the man from Bosworth, was more sympathetic—but who wanted sympathy? More understanding?

"So many ills, my lord. All different, but in the same place, at the same time..." He hesitated. The Danes believed that all men were free and, to a degree, equal, but on sea and on land there must be leaders, and Ingwar was a formidable one. "Could it be," he framed a rebuke as a question, "the curse of the cross?"

"What cross?"

"The one under which they fight. The sign of their god. They say he died . . ."

"I heard enough about *that* from Cerdic," Ingwar said irritably. "At Bywater I counted more than twenty crosses. They did them no good, and us no harm."

"We took them all down, my lord. The one here stands proud and high."

"Here?"

"Behind the tavern. Perhaps only visible from the by-road."

"I'll see to it," Ingwar said, starting up. "Get you back to your lord and carry my greetings. Say nothing to alarm. Tell facts, not talk of curses." But the man knew by the tone of his voice and the look on his face that the shaft had gone home.

Ingwar went into the yard again and called to the sick that the milk and the good red meat they needed was on its way. Then he looked about for the symbol of the god of whom his own gods might be jealous. He saw that unless you were searching for it, it was easily overlooked, but it was there, almost lost amongst the jumble of humped thatch and gable-ends of barns, sheds, stables.

Such a poor, paltry thing, he thought, and had one of those thoughts which his black mood threw up: if Freya could be so jealous over such a trivial thing as to heap such misfortune on him because he had not seen and destroyed it, then she was as small-minded as—though more powerful than—any ordinary woman. (Ingwar was married to a querulous, fault-finding woman, whose company he avoided as much as possible, whom it was a positive pleasure to leave behind in Copenhagen.)

The poor little wooden cross surmounted a poor little wooden building, no different from and rather smaller than the one in which his horses were now lodged. He advanced towards it vengefully.

Brother Thomas and Brother Peter, though unaccustomed to comfort, woke stiff-jointed from a night spent on the forest floor, under a leafless tree that offered small shelter from the rain. The excitement of the previous day had worn off.

"I think," Peter said, "that this is a fool's errand. Why not bury him here, with as much respect as we can show?"

"He should have Christian burial," Brother Thomas said, "and only Brother Matthew is ordained."

"And he may now be dead."

"That we must ascertain."

It was the habit of contradiction rather than anything else which made Thomas take the opposite view.

They said their prayers, ate some of the food they carried, and took up their burden, heavier now because the blankets were sodden. Once moving, they felt better, more certain that they were doing the right, in fact, the only thing. Even if the Danes had slain all the brothers, the church was still consecrated.

"I wish we could have found his head," Brother Peter said, presently.

"Its disappearance was a mystery. But it would have been that much more to carry. I must halt for a minute."

Somewhere a wolf howled. A night sound and rather uncanny. They laid down their burden, eased their backs, took deep breaths.

"We may be running into a nest of hornets," Brother Thomas said. "The very thing we fled from."

"Does it matter so much? A man can only die once. And from what we have seen of the forest, we could have died of starvation."

At intervals the wolf howled a solitary cry, never answered, never shared. One lone wolf would be unlikely to attack two grown men, in daylight. They both had their knives, not weapons of offence or defence, eating implements but kept sharp, since most meat was tough and some bread stale, and often a sandal must be mended with a bit of rawhide.

The wolf's cry came from no particular direction; its sound echoed and bounced back from the trees, and to Brother Peter's ear it seemed, after the fourth or fifth call, to sound appealing rather than menacing. They were now nearing that part of the forest, near Mallow, which wolves avoided because for many years they had been hunted or trapped.

"I think it is in a wolf-pit, poor thing," Brother Peter said.

"About that we can do nothing," Brother Thomas said with a touch of asperity.

"Except kill it and spare it a slow death from starvation."

Brother Thomas thought, uncharitably: Food matters so much to him that even a hungry wolf evokes pity.

"And how would you manage that? If you reached down into the pit, it'd have your hand off."

"Not as I should do it," Peter said. Sensing Thomas's lack of sympathy, he did not bother to explain.

They reached the first of the pools which, on their outward journey, had made them diverge. Very near home now. A new thought struck Thomas.

"Will our brothers believe that this is indeed the king? A headless body . . ."

"How would the head help? None of us ever saw him—I mean until we did, yesterday. And in any case, even Brother Matthew must concede that only a Christian would wear . . ."

Then they both stopped, for on the far side of the pool they saw the wolf, sitting on its haunches and with something between its paws.

The first to see what was to be commemorated for so long in song and story, in sculpture and in painting, they were at first incredulous. The wolf looked so like a dog, and its attitude was so like that of a dog waiting for its master, protecting something that it had been left to guard. But, as though to banish all doubt from their minds, it threw back its head and howled again. Then, certain that it had drawn their attention, it rose and trotted away with the air of one who had done a duty and done it well.

"The head!" Brother Thomas said when he could speak. "A miracle, no less."

"A miracle," Brother Peter agreed. Then, raising his voice, he shouted into the thicket, "Thank you, Brother Wolf."

There was not, as was sometimes reported, and commonly believed, a miraculous union between the head and body. There was wonder enough without that. That the wolf should have carried the head so far, and not a toothmark on it; that he should have delivered it, at the right moment, in the right place, to the right people. And that the golden crown was still on the yellow hair.

When Ingwar threw open the door and strode into the little church, Brother Matthew was on his knees, praying for forgiveness for cowardice. He had stayed, when others had fled; he had not chopped down the cross, but he had not allowed the bell to be sounded, and he had not ventured forth, as a brave man would have done, to see what had happened to Gilda and her children. He'd been, in fact, lukewarm. As bad as being faithless, if you looked at it in one way. But always, always there was another way.

Look at St. Peter, for instance. One moment defending Christ with a sword, and the next denying all knowledge of Him. Suppose in that courtyard Peter had been bolder and said, "Yes, I am one of His followers. One of the chosen twelve." Somebody in that mad moment could have run him through with a sword, and then where would the Church be? Was it not possible that there were times when God Himself forced discretion upon the would-be courageous?

And what use were prayers uttered in such a muddled state of mind? Begin again...

"Stand up," Ingwar said.

Brother Matthew knew that his moment had come. But he took his time, adding another little prayer. "God give me courage. For the sake of Our Lord, Jesus Christ, Thy son." He crossed himself, and stood up. The giant Dane looked very large in the doorway. He wore no armour, except the highly-decorated belt with the sword on the left, the dagger on the right. Close-fitting trousers of soft, well-beaten leather fitted close to his legs, and his tunic was of fine wool, dyed scarlet, and wonderfully embroidered around the hem and shoulders. Around his neck gleamed the golden torque, and matching bracelets, each three inches wide, shone on his wrists.

"Are you the man in charge here?"

"I am a monk. And a priest."

"A poor place," Ingwar said, taking a comprehensive glance. He'd seen small churches, but never so small as this, and never one which did not boast at least a pair of silver candlesticks.

"Yes. We have always been poor," Matthew said, not without dignity.

Ingwar entertained another thought of the kind which came in his black moods. He knew that his men resented his rule about pooling all plunder, and would evade it if they thought it safe to do so.

"Or you have been stripped already?" That would account for the fact that no one had mentioned this tucked-away church.

"We have been spared."

"What lies hidden there?" Ingwar eyed the place where the

planks had been recently disturbed. Elsewhere dirt filled the spaces between the boards.

"The bones of a woman, dead long since. And the body of one of the brothers who died yesterday."

"Take them up. And when you speak to me, say, 'My lord,' or 'Jarl.'"

Matthew knelt again, glad to do so for, despite his calm manner, fear had him by the knees. He began to prise up the end of one plank with his knife. It gave, and he raised it three inches; the scent of soil and of blood and the dried rosemary which Brother Benedict had laid in the form of a cross on Brother Dunstan's breast seeped through the aperture. There had been no spare blanket in which to wrap the body. This terrible man would see the blood on the habit, and guess.

His fingers went cold and sweat-slippery on the plank's end, and it fell back into place. To Ingwar—suspicious of everybody—this looked like a delaying trick.

"Try again and do better," he said in a voice like a snarl.

Brother Matthew tried again; did better. He had one plank lifted and laid aside when he was disturbed again, this time not by an inner thought but by a babel of voices, high and shrill with excitement, and then, cutting through it, his own name, shouted and repeated.

"You may answer, if that is your name," Ingwar said loftily.

"They know where to find me." But Matthew edged past the giant towards the door. Restricted as they were for accommodation, the brothers had always made a careful distinction between church and secular business. The latter, whatever it was, must be discussed in the porch.

There Brother Thomas and Brother Peter lowered their burden reverently and talked disjointedly, interrupting each other. Cerdic. Martyred. His head cut off. His head lost. Christian burial. The wolf. Brother Lawrence kept saying, "A miracle! A miracle!" and Brother Benedict's short-sighted eyes were spilling the easy tears of senility.

"Brother Thomas, as the elder, will speak first," Brother Matthew said.

So, for the first time, simply and starkly, the tale was told, while Peter unwrapped the rain-blackened blanket and displayed the body and the head. Ingwar, standing behind Brother Thomas, was so tall that he could see, without craning, over his head. He could also see, at a little distance, three of his own men, the healthy ones, drawn hither by the hubbub. And watching.

Cerdic's head, though placed in position, had moved with the jolting, and now lay by his right shoulder. It did not look dead—no staring eyes, no sagging jaw. It could have been a face carved from marble, serene, invulnerable. Ingwar thought: A good man and brave, but stubborn. His depression reached nadir. Brother Thomas finished his story and Brother Peter felt that he had rather underestimated the part played by the wolf; so when it was his turn to speak, he said,

"The wolf called us, again and again, with such appeal that I thought it was trapped. And look! It had carried the head for miles, and not a mark. And no mud, either. And the crown in place."

"My lord," Brother Matthew said, somehow managing to sound the reverse of humble, "have we your leave to bury this man in a manner appropriate to the faith in which he lived and for which he died?" That was bold talking, but he felt reckless.

"Go through your antics," Ingwar said roughly. He was angry now, because he was again being torn between two sides of his nature. One side said, "If ever a man deserved to go to his grave wearing what ornaments he wore in life, this is the man!" The other side knew that he was being watched, and that leniency was easily mistaken for weakness. So he reached out a long arm and laid a hand on the crown. "Not with this. A waste of good gold."

The crown was firmly wedged; in order to remove it, his fingers became entangled with the yellow hair, and he was obliged to use his thumb as a lever, pressing against the skull.

Later, when the simple story had been embellished and twisted, it told that Ingwar, the Hawkeye, the Dane had been instantly converted. This was untrue. What happened was known only to himself, though that was miracle enough. The depression lifted, as though a dark cloak thrown over him had been whisked away; as though his spirit had been a songbird, closely caged, and somebody had set it free. He knew what ailed him, and he knew how to cure it. He was his own man again.

Brother Matthew said, "Brother Lawrence, toll the passing bell." Not much could be asked now of Thomas and Peter, who had walked carrying a burden, and who had undergone, if not a miraculous, certainly an emotional experience. "Brother

Benedict, prepare the body for burial. I will myself widen the grave."

Within his own limited sphere of authority he was operating well, with that lucidity of mind that a prospect of near-death induced, and the big Dane's use of the word "antics" had held little promise. What must be done must be done without delay.

Ingwar, holding Cerdic's disputed crown, a pretty thing, but unsubstantial, weighing no more than one of his own bracelets, strode back through the yard of the tavern, past the barns and stables and shed to which he had banished the gut-rip victims. The stench seemed to be less, and more men were on their feet, swilling out their soiled trousers, washing themselves. The process of recovery, which he had reckoned would take at least two milk-fed, beef-fed days, had begun, and seemed to be moving fast. Some were already demanding food. He realised then that his messages cancelling tomorrow's march had been sent too soon, and were the result of his own despondency.

He held the crown aloft for all to see, and shouted cheerfully. Inside the tavern, where the sound men were housed, he picked one, known to be a good horseman, to ride to Triver and tell Thorkill that the muster would be held tomorrow after all; that men were to bring in the plunder and what food they could find, but no livestock. None of the other men present was a horseman; never mind, a runner would do, Bosworth being nearer. He was looking around for one, young, light-footed and lithe, when the ale-wife stepped forward and said, "Why not send that idle boy who plays the harp? He has long legs. He is familiar with the road."

It was the opportunity for which Gilda had been praying and planning. She wanted Mark to disappear and escape, but not from this house. The resultant search might reveal the secret hiding-place.

Dawn seemed to come earlier next day, for the weather had cleared; the morning was sunny, and what wind there was blew from the south. Very early, men came carrying all portable treasure: stuff to be loaded onto horses and, at a time which Ingwar chose, divided as fairly as was possible. Amongst it was the string of amber beads which the Virgin at Mallow had worn for as long as men could remember, and before that. Ingwar, however, did not give the order to start loading, and he had his red stool carried out into the forecourt of the tavern and placed between the doorway and the well.

Those who disliked his rule about pooling all plunder, and who had seen him emerge from the little church with a golden crown in his hands, muttered among themselves, for the crown, undoubtedly the most valuable single thing that had been seen since the sacking of Bywater, did not appear on the growing heap of silver-rimmed drinking horns, silver spoons, bracelets and belts and necklaces, knives with fine handles, and similar things. Those who muttered that Ingwar was breaking his own rule were quickly quelled by those in whose eyes the giant leader could do no wrong. There were a few scuffles, but no outright fighting, for that was another thing of which Ingwar Hawkeye disapproved.

Finally they were all mustered and stood in roughly concentric rings between the well and the road, and on the road itself. Then Ingwar came out and did not sit, but stood on the red stool, and the horns blew for silence. Wasted breath, for all were silent, thinking that Ingwar, who was always unpredictable, was about to conduct one of his curious lotteries.

Such divisions of loot, though often annoying, could also be amusing and were in a way fair enough. "Come forward any man with a wound in the left leg, or the right; take your choice. Any man with a scar to show on the right arm, or the left, the head, neck or chest. Come forward any man who uses his left hand rather than his right; take your pick. Married men. Men pledged. Men who'd lost an ear, an eye, a finger. Take your pick." Once, at Bywater, he had actually said, "Any man with six toes?" Amidst the great gale of laughter, one man stepped out and Ingwar said, "Show me." True enough, the man had six toes and footwear wide enough to hold them comfortably.

It was a rough-and-ready method, but it worked, in a way, offering something almost as impartial and haphazard as the judgement of the gods, who decreed that this man should fall, this man live to fight on; this man make a happy marriage, another an unhappy one; this man keep his wits and his teeth; this end as a mumbling, stumbling dotard before he was even old by man's measure.

"I have called you together," Ingwar said, in a voice he did not need to raise in order to be heard, "first of all to release you from the oaths of allegiance which you took to me when this expedition sailed. Every man here is a free man, fit to decide for himself. I will tell you what I have decided for myself. Some may know already that I never much favoured this expedition against the English, kin to us. Against Byzantium I should have moved far more willingly. But I had sworn allegiance to my cousin, the king, an allegiance which I now withdraw in the sight of you all. You are equally free to withdraw yours from me. Or, if you wish, to renew it in different form. I propose to stay here. To settle and to rule in my own fashion. To the south and to the north, the English, in a war forced upon them, defended themselves and their land bravely, but they were defeated here and they have no leader now. If we move against the Middle Angles, they will be between the hammer and the anvil; if we do not move, we shall have good neighbours to the north of us." He broke off and gave a great laugh, self-mocking, but hearty. "Us! I speak as though you were all of the same mind. I know only my own." He stopped speaking, awed by the thought that what he now knew of his mind had been there for many years, something to be ignored, or turned to another channel. Ever since he had come to full growth, he had known that he was more fitting for kingship than the weak, vacillating, unmanly man who, by an accident of birth, was king of Denmark, but this knowledge he had refused to face, even when offered—as he had twice been—the crown of Denmark by would-be rebels. And perhaps, behind his smooth, secretive face, his cousin the king had known more than he showed, always seeing to it that Ingwar was sent on petty little errands, like this one to England, testing the English resistance, preparatory to an invasion which might not happen at all, or, if it did, would by some trick be entrusted to some other man. Ingwar's valour, his talent for organisation, his keen sense of justice and personal popularity had been exploited, but always on trivial things. He'd been reduced to a kind of pirate, always destroying, never allowed to build. Now he was free; he had conquered a kingdom, admittedly a small one, but his own.

And he was not prepared to bribe men to stay with him; those who did, with no other persuasion than loyalty to himself, would be given land, the real source of all wealth, and honourable titles. All through this campaign he had noted how rich the soil was, capable of supporting a far larger population than it now did, and the climate, though variable, was on the whole clement. A Land of Promise.

Thorkill said, having thought things over, "Ingwar, this is a dangerous decision. When the king hears of it he will call for your head!"

"Then let him send a man to fetch it. I shall be ready."

"Not one man, my friend. An army."

"I can match it. By the time the king, my cousin, has received the news, made up his wavering mind, chosen a commander—will you be the one, Thorkill?—I shall be ready for that, too. You doubt me? Then go."

Icel said, "Ingwar, I have my family to consider. My mother, whom I respect; a wife whom I left with some reluctance; two children whose future is my care . . ."

"Then you must go, too. Join Olfkell, as we were all supposed to do, and fight the Middle Angles, or take to the ships—they are still at Bywater. I said every man must decide for himself."

"It is a hard decision."

"All decisions are hard," Ingwar said, though his, from the moment that he had taken Cerdic's crown in his hand, had been easy. No family to consider, only a querulous, barren wife.

The clear sun was making its low, winter circle of the sky. Ingwar pointed to a tree and said, "Think, men, and let no man be swayed by another. I want only volunteers with me. When the sun touches that tree I shall ask for a show of hands."

It was, as Icel had said, a hard decision. The men most inclined to stay with Ingwar were those who had reached the age when settling down was not unattractive, yet they were the ones who generally had wives already, or were pledged. Some had come on what had sounded to be an undangerous invasion for the sake of easy plunder, in order to gain a bride-price. Some who would have stayed feared the king's vengeance, for what Ingwar was doing was treachery, no less, and the king had a long arm. Curiously, none of those who were tempted to stay doubted that Ingwar had the power to hold down and rule the territory that he had chosen for his own; however, few men stayed. Everybody knew that one Dane was as good as ten Englishmen.

They gathered into little groups, muttered, spoke more loudly, threw their arms about in wild gestures, suffered from indecision, gnawed their thumbs, but gradually a shifting began, those who intended to stay with Ingwar coming towards him, the rest moving towards Thorkill and Icel, and carefully avoiding Ingwar's eyes, as though they were conscious of being disloyal. There was no need for a show of hands, but he asked for it none the less, because even such a break with custom as this must be handled in the customary manner. His party was far the smaller—only thirty-seven, but he was content. He had not actually put it into words, but he knew what he was asking—that men should give up their very nationality, their homeland, their Danishness, for the sake of a personal loyalty.

There on the ground lay the heaped plunder, and neither Thorkill nor Icel, taken unawares by Ingwar's action, felt sure enough of himself to enforce the fair division of spoil as Ingwar had done. It was one of his crack-brained ideas; let him deal with it, for the last time, Henceforth, what a man took, he should keep.

"My lord," Thorkill said, "should the spoil not be divided now?"

"As you wish," Ingwar said, very amiably. He had stepped down from the red stool as soon as he had finished speaking, and now he took a step or two to where metal glittered, and the rare jewel shone. He looked at it contemplatively for a second or two, and then nudged it, with gentle contempt, with his foot.

"Divide it among your own, my lords. Mine have no need of such trinkets. Every man with me shall have an English village—and be a thane."

It was the kind of dramatic gesture which enraged some people and enthralled others, and which, above all, attracted the singers of songs and the makers of stories, and thus ensured a precarious immortality. When history became something made of ink and paper, a monkish record, Ingwar and his brief but extremely successful reign were ignored or treated as myth; in songs he was remembered.

Not far away another and very different form of immortality was on the brew.

Just before Cerdic, king and martyr, was lowered into his grave, alongside some unknown woman and Brother Dunstan who had died in battle (the interment was of necessity somewhat hasty, for who knew how long the giant Dane's permission to perform antics might last?), Brother Benedict, who now at close range saw only with his fingers, took hold of the silver cross, on a chain which had, rather strangely, held to Cerdic's body, as the crown had held to his head.

"Should this be buried with him? In a pagan way? I always believed that a Christian went out as he came into the world, naked but for his winding-sheet. Would not this pretty thing be better employed on the altar?"

"To be taken by robbers?" Matthew asked. For as he dug, as he had been given permission to do, the heathen, who had seen their leader emerge with a golden crown, had come in and snatched from the Virgin the only ornament she owned— the necklace of amber.

"I could set it into this board," Benedict said, and he indicated one of the planks, which were to be laid in place. "Silver blackens," he said, "but it does not corrode. It would in time be indistinguishable."

None of the others immediately understood the significance of that speech. For years Benedict had been going blind in his peculiar way, capable of saying that the woods across the road were turning green with the coming of spring, or were gilded by autumn, but having to have his meat cut for him, and stumbling over a threshold.

"I could inlay it," Benedict said. "I had some skill as a carver when I was young. Lately . . . the truth is, my sight for things near me, long absent, has returned. Yes, indeed. I could count the very hairs on his head." He looked down at Cerdic's head, now, by means of firm wrapping apparently re-united with his body. "One hesitates," Benedict said, "to proclaim a miracle, but it happened as soon as I touched him. Like the lifting of a mist. And what with the strange behaviour of the wolf . . ."

II

Anna, Brother John and a Pilgrim

1348

IN A BUSY INN THERE WERE MANY WAYS IN WHICH AN OLD GREAT-grandmother could be useful, and Anna Gilderson so hated Marian, her grandson's wife, that the thought of being obliged to her, to owe her a crumb of gratitude for her meagre lodging and such food as a woman of seventy-two could chumble, was loathsome to her; so she often undertook more than she could really manage, especially as she was almost always encumbered with the great-grandchildren.

She often told them stories which had been told to her by *her* grandmother, who had had them from *hers*. Some were straightforward tales, the language very simple; some were told in crude verse, often obscure, partly because the verses had originally been made as a kind of protest against circumstance, which, stated plainly, would have led to trouble, and partly because in such verses everything had been sacrificed to rhyme. In these the old woman took particular pleasure, because they afforded her amusement, and were sly, as she was herself, after all, when everything began to fail, all looks gone, joints growing creaky, every defiant action busy and worth your keep more and more of an effort, and even appetite gone—what was left, except a secret laugh?

Marian did not like her to show herself at the front of the house. Understandable in a way, yet hurtful. She knew what she looked like, old, lop-sided, almost toothless, but she was *clean*, and although she had not had a penny to spend on clothes since her husband died, she was not yet in rags, though mending became more infuriating; sometimes stuff was so rotten from wearing and washing that stitches broke away. In cold weather her nose developed what she called a dewdrop at the tip of it, and she carried a cloth with which to wipe it away. But some-

129

times, busy with this or that, she forgot, and Marian said, "Disgusting!"

A softer or weaker woman would have broken under such treatment; Anna merely grew angry and muttered under her breath. And even that was rebuked. Marian said, "Talk to yourself, talk to the devil!" or, "Be careful; people'll say you're a witch!" There was always some slight danger of that, when a woman grew old and developed a wart or two, and had almost as much hair on her face as on her scalp. But such accusations were usually brought against old crones who lived alone and did not attend Mass with regularity. Anna lived in a place always full of people and bustle, and she went to church every Sunday and every saint's day. It was easy for her, even in the worst of weather; she had only to walk across the yard and slip into that part which was the most sacred and yet the most public part of the great abbey which, with its many buildings, its gardens, orchards and vineyards, covered so much ground that it almost united the prosperous, growing town of Mallow with the dwindling, decaying village of Bosworth which, in Anna's grandmother's day, had still been a port of some consequence—or at least so Anna's grandmother had claimed, but Anna was now finding from her own experience that what you remembered first-hand and what you were told as a child had a tendency to become blurred.

As she told it to the children, it was a highly dramatic story.

"Everything shifted," she said. "There's always floods *and* high tides in the springtime, but the year my granny talked about, it was like Noah's Flood in the Bible. Three high tides running and the snow melting into the river. Lots of people drowned that time. Then, when it was all over, so much land had come down with the river and so much sand and gravel brought in by the tide that the river went shallow and no ships could come up it any more, only little flat boats. Now that was a calamity because Bosworth folk had lived by trading. My granny said they'd got so they couldn't grow a cabbage. They'd lost the knack, and they'd have starved but for the fact that our abbey was a-building at Mallow then, and there was work for all and food for men—and women and jackasses who could carry stone in from Bywater, the nearest the ships could bring it after that."

She was not aware of it, but she was covering, in a few words, as worn as the beads on a well-used rosary, far more than the span covered by an old woman's memories, however long and accurate. She was recounting history as it happened, not as it was recorded. She did not know that a man called Ingwar had given orders that Cerdic's grave must be regarded as a shrine, and that the tiny church in which his body lay should be rebuilt in flint, the only stone available in this area of chalk. Nor did she know that after Ingwar—never a Christian and honouring Cerdic through a mere whim—had come Canute, another Dane, but a convert who had authorised, indeed ordered, what he considered a suitable building.

Anna knew all about the miracles—blind men led up to the shrine and walking away, their sight restored; lame men hobbling on sticks and crutches, striding away, often dancing with joy; even men carried in on mattresses, being able to stand up after St. Cerdic had had a word with God on their behalf.

"The monks like the crutches and sticks left behind to hang on the walls," she said, "but the mattresses they can't do with, because of the fleas."

She believed in the miracles—she had witnessed several—and the children believed, because the lame-aids hung there on the plain white wall behind the tomb, which now resembled a treasure-chest, covered with ornaments of gold and silver, glittering with precious stones. The belief had grown up that unless a miracle were properly acknowledged, the blessing of a miracle might be withdrawn.

"I've known it to happen," Anna said. "There was a man over Triver way, lame as a tree, and he was cured. But he wouldn't give, or couldn't; he said it'd be robbing his family. In less than a fortnight he was lame again, and worse than he was before."

The eldest of her great-grandchildren was rising seven, getting a touch too old for children's talk, and one day he said, "Granny, you're lame and a bit lop-sided. Did you ever ask?"

"I'm too old," she said, managing, by an effort of self-control, to say it in exactly the same manner as she did when asked to take part in games that demanded physical agility. Behind the calm explanation, the acceptance, lay a deep bitterness. When the stiffness began in her knees and hips—that was back in her son's time, and he could see that it was to his advantage to keep her spry—she'd begged a silver shilling for an offering, and made her visit to touch the shrine. She had not been cured. Later, when she became conscious of her bent back, she'd tried again, with no result. She had then cast her mental eye back and realised that none of the miracles she had witnessed, and few that she had heard tell about, had concerned the old. St. Cerdic seemed not to care much for anybody over forty. But then who did?

Well, she had the children now, but Edman was nearing the age when he would be expected to make himself useful about the place, and as soon as he felt that he was useful, he'd despise her. Exactly the same thing had happened with her son. Money, whether you could earn it and hold on to it, seemed to be all that mattered nowadays.

However, on this sunny June afternoon, Anna was relatively happy. She was being busy, could be seen to be busy if that bitch Marian cared to spy on her, as she sometimes did. She was sitting down, shelling peas and cleaning bright young carrots, making ready for supper, when the inn would be full, this being the peak of the season for pilgrimage.

Edman and Hilda, a bare year his junior, and Simon, soon to be five, could, thanks to Anna, count a little, and pea-shelling gave good practice. "Only four; very bad." "I've got six!" Or five. Very, very occasionally a split pod would reveal seven, and eight was not unknown. The shelled peas went into a bowl, empty pods into a basket which Simon, too young to be expected to do one thing for long at a time, carried every now and then and gave to the pigs.

The pigstye was tucked away because, though everybody enjoyed a joint of roast pork or a fine ham or sausages or a good dish of brawn, nobody in particular wanted to see or smell a pigstye, any more than they wanted to see an old, decrepit, bent woman doing anything but cleaning floors and lighting fires or carrying hot water.

The inn, known as the One Bull, had grown alongside the abbey without being quite absorbed by it. And nobody but Anna and a monk, recognised as a good planner and architect, and called Brother John, knew how the separation between the two establishments had been preserved.

When Anna told her great-grandson that she was too old for a miracle to loosen her limbs and straighten her back, she had been telling only a half-truth. In her youth she had sinned, done something that she could not possibly confess and be absolved from, because to have done so would have involved John, who had shared the sin.

Leaving the pea-shelling to the children, she turned her attention to the carrots, and Edman said, "Tell us about the wolf."

It was a favourite with children who had never seen a live wolf but whose blood carried an inherent fear, and to whom the story of a wolf behaving like a tame beast or a Christian was a kind of consolation.

"Oh yes, the wolf," Anna said. She glanced at the cradle in which her latest great-grandchild, a little girl called Bertha, lay, placid, undemanding. She thought: By the time she is of an age to hear this story, I shall not be here to tell it, but Edman, Hilda, perhaps even Simon, will remember it.

"Once upon a time, a long while ago," she began. She had told the story so often, to her son, her grandson and sometimes to adults, at feasts, that she was obliged to give it no attention. The words, the pictures the words called up glided across her mind like a dragonfly over a pond. Her real thoughts went on undisturbed, below.

She thought of other Junes, not fingering the memories lovingly, not thinking, Ah, I was happy then! Rather scorning herself, and thinking that warm weather bred disturbing thoughts in old minds just as it bred maggots in carcasses.

There was the June when she was married, but not to the man of her choice. Up to the very end she had hoped and prayed that the marriage between Anna Gilderson and Edman Gilderson would be forbidden by the priest, after he had consulted the kinbook. They were related, and had a grandfather in common, a fact that should have made marriage impossible. But the grandfather had been twice married, and their fathers born of different wives, and that somehow made it all right. And the young Anna had often feared that, even had it not been all right, her powerful old grandfather would manage some trick or contrivance. He was a great one for keeping the family together. He was never one for much talking, and what stories he knew were nothing like so fascinating as the grandmother's had been, but he always held that, though the Gildersons were mere innkeepers, somewhere in their ancestry was a king who was also a giant, seven foot tall. Anna's grandmother made mock of such claims—never to his face, though, and it was true that he himself was much above ordinary height. So were his son and his grandson, whom Anna wished not to marry.

There was something so gloomy about him, and she had been so gay-hearted, such a one for a laugh!

Still, give him his due, he'd been kind enough, and if in this world you couldn't have what you wanted, you had to make the best of what you had.

She was thirty—mother of a son and old enough to know better—when the abbot, a great builder, wished to make St. Cerdic's church larger and more worthy of the shrine it held. Those before him had built, he considered, in a sorry, haphazard fashion, not even attempting to incorporate the original building into the vast, soaring abbey church, leaving it, low and small, looking tacked on, as it were. The only way in which an improvement could be made was, all agreed, by extending the small church over the space occupied by the yard, the barn, the stables of the One Bull inn.

Two monks, one old and plainly important, and one young and handsome, who, without the tonsure and the habit, would have been a most attractive man, came to discuss the business with Anna's husband who, disliking the idea, made only the feeblest of protests; any inn, he said, needed its stabling for travellers' horses, and where there were horses there must be barns for hay and corn. He was hemmed in. On one side of the One Bull, the buttressed wall of the abbey stood grey and solid, and on the other, separated from the inn by a mere entrance giving access to the yard, was a smithy. Next to the smithy was a cookshop which did a thriving trade, especially with a kind of cake called Cerdic bread, which was made to a secret formula so that it never deteriorated. It was true. With a sufficient supply of Cerdic bread you could travel, well fed, to Walsingham or Canterbury—or Rome. And beyond the cookshop was another shop, very prosperous, selling relics, some of finely carved wood, some coarser and less long lasting, made of clay.

And beyond, all space was occupied, even crowded. "Nobody hereabouts," Anna's husband said gloomily, "would sell or lease me space. I'd be ruined overnight."

The elder monk said, "There would be ample compensation." There would indeed. A pilgrim, cured some years ago of paralysis, had left his whole estate to the abbey of St. Cerdic. "You could move, retire, or set up an inn elsewhere."

The gloomy man said, "Oh, I couldn't do that, unless I was

forced. We've always been here. The freehold handed down from time immemorial."

It was a serious conversation about serious things between the owner of the inn and the abbot's representative, but on a different level something else going on, never to be explained; perhaps never to be forgiven. Just what, when you came to think about it after forty years, was no more than a meeting of the eyes as the younger monk, having spread his proposed plan on the table, looked up and Anna looked down. Love at first sight? Lust? Lechery? Sin without a word spoken or a touch exchanged. She turned red as a poppy, he white as chalk.

Noticing nothing, the elder monk said, "Father Abbot has set his mind upon this, Adam Gilderson, and wished work to begin after harvest. It would be . . . unwise to oppose him."

When they had gone, Anna's husband said with great bitterness, "Go or be shoved! That is what he meant. After being here generation after generation, back to the giant king's time. As for the compensation! The way prices are going, whatever my lord abbot thinks sufficient today would be useless by this time next year. It's ruin, my girl, no less."

He fell into dumb melancholy, as was his way.

She was pretty in those days and had kept her looks through childbirth and years of hard work. She had a dress the colour of a dove's neck and a head-dress rather too fine for wear by an ale-keeper's wife, but her presence in the yard, the stables, the barn, did not attract much attention; she was always busy and nosy and interfering. Her husband, always a low-spirited man, was inclined to seek comfort in the consumption of his own wares, especially towards evening, and both the inn-servants and the servants of guests were thinking about their supper.

That had been in June, too, the old woman cleaning carrots remembered. A June evening, heady with the scents of summer, especially of fresh hay in one of the barns. And she'd been as sure that the young monk would come as she was that the sun, now sinking in the west, would rise again tomorrow. He came, carrying his measuring-rod and looking very businesslike.

So, on a bed of sweet hay, she committed adultery, and he broke the vows of celibacy which he had taken in ignorance of what he was forgoing. It was all hurried and secret and sinful and all the more delicious, like the apple in Eden. There were moments, usually before the consummation, when she could think of nothing but the joy to come. Afterwards it was different, and hard sense took over. In one of these afterwards she said bluntly, "I have betrayed Edman, and you, my love, have cuckolded him. Think! Do we not owe him something?"

"Were I rich, and free, I'd give him all I had—and then take you away!"

"I was thinking of the possible."

"And what is possible?"

"That he should be left with his tavern just as he inherited it. He is much attached to it. Could you not draw *different* lines on those papers of yours?"

He had the sudden, most un-manning and quite unjustified suspicion that she had deliberately seduced him with this end in mind. The thought eased his infatuation, but left him still with a heavy burden of guilt towards God, and certainly some obligation towards the innkeeper. But what could he do? As regards God . . . Impose extra fast-days upon himself; sleep on the floor instead of the straw-stuffed palliasse; mortify the erring flesh in every possible way, bear toothache without complaint and without resort to known palliatives. Oh yes, all these and more. Not enough! But, and it came to him in a flash, he had something of far more value than mere flesh to offer up: he had his talent and his craft, his growing reputation as an architect.

Monks built well, that was acknowledged fact; they had endless time and patience and were inspired by the belief that they were building to the glory of God. But the vast majority of them were just ordinary men, no more gifted than men outside the walls of religious houses. Within the religious orders, as outside them, any man with a special talent was rare and valued. Brother John was such a one. He was a Benedictine monk, but not a member of the St. Cerdic community; he'd been *lent* to do the job which now, out of consideration for Edman Gilderson, innkeeper, he was not prepared to do.

But how to avoid it? He had already determined to sacrifice his talent and lose his reputation by saying, "I cannot do it," but such defection would not save the yard of the inn, for the abbot would simply engage another architect.

He carried his problem into the little side chapel with which it was concerned. There was the altar, draped in white velvet, heavily embroidered with gold and silver thread; between silver-gilt candlesticks was the silver and ivory monstrance with the little light glimmering. All very rich and costly, but it paled when compared with the shrine which lay slightly to the left of it, all a-glitter, or even with the statue of the Virgin, old but freshly painted, with genuine gems on the yellow head and about the slender white neck.

Did saints long dead sometimes condescend to speak into the ears, into the minds of mortal and sinful men? That was a question that Brother John could never answer with any certainty; all that he knew was that, as he stood there, the answer to "How can I do this?" came, as perfect and whole as a circle drawn with a pair of compasses.

In a short time, admitted to the august presence without delay because he was the expert, and privileged—some people waited weeks for an audience with the abbot—John stood, seemingly humble, inwardly sure, and said that any attempt to enlarge or alter in any way the little chapel of St. Cerdic would be not merely a desecration but also an error of taste.

"My lord, perfection cannot be improved upon, and as it stands the small chapel is perfect, except perhaps in the matter of lighting. The proportions could not be bettered, and any extension, either of length or width, would reduce the significance of the tomb. What is needed, in my humble opinion, is a large window on the northern side."

"The north? Why not the south?" The abbot was not accustomed to being told what to do.

"There again, my lord, I was thinking of the tomb as a focal point. It—and the statue of Blessed Mary—enlivens the southern side; the northern side is blank, and a window of good coloured glass—perhaps depicting the saint's martyrdom, and incorporating the story of the wolf—would be a great embellishment."

The abbot thought: There is little sense in engaging an expert and then disregarding his advice. And he visualised a glorious window, coloured with sapphire and topaz, with ruby and emerald.

"Expense need be no object," he said. "Where, in your *humble* opinion, is the best coloured glass obtainable?"

"Undoubtedly Nevers in France," Brother John said. And he knew that he had won the day.

Later he crossed the disputed yard to tell the innkeeper that his property had been reprieved, and to say good-bye to Anna in the safe presence of her husband. Suspecting her as he did of pretending love with an ulterior motive in mind, he had no notion of the heartbreak which she concealed behind warm expressions of gratitude. He went on to his self-imposed penance, laying aside his skill and his instruments, becoming just an ordinary monk again. Nobody wondered at the change in him; it was well known that in most cases the shining promise of genius in youth faded and died as a man reached maturity.

Anna was left to face her own punishment, hard at first but easing with the years. She reared her son, nursed her husband when he was taken with what was called a graveyard cough, and buried him. Her son, less gloomy than his father, proved to be mean in small matters, but there was some excuse for him. He was enlarging the inn, building upwards, since there was no room elsewhere. Anna understood the necessity—as did his wife—and worked well and willingly for no pay.

When the joint-evil struck and St. Cerdic did nothing for her, she could think that he only cared for the young, and she did not immediately associate her ailment and the lack of a cure with the sin committed more than a lifetime ago. And the fact that she was remembering now plainly showed that she was in her dotage. And that was a little frightening because after dotage came death, and now that unmerciful memories assailed her she saw herself defenceless before the judgement of God, who had judged and punished her, surely, enough already—taking away her husband and her son, leaving her to the merciless treatment of her grandson and his hateful wife, Marian.

The peas were all shelled, the carrots all cleaned, and her story—the only one which nowadays could hold Edman's attention—was done, too. The yard was filling up with horses and mules and humble donkeys, and with people. Time to go; to give the children their supper and to have her own in the room, always cool and damp-seeming, even at the height of summer, and then to see them in bed in the little rooms, no bigger than cupboards, which adjoined. For guests at inns had as much objection to children as they had to very old, very ugly women. Everybody liked to pretend that, apart from the sick seeking cures at St. Cerdic's shrine, everybody was between the ages of twelve and forty-five, and all hearty and sprightly.

Much of her heavier work was done after all the guests and even the servants were abed. Stiff-jointed and bent as she was, she could wash up, scouring greasy plates with fine wood-ash.

She could polish pewter and what silver there was, and rub knives to a fine brightness on a board sprinkled with brick-dust. She could no longer scrub, as she had for so many years, because once down on her stiff knees she could not rise without aid; she could, however, moving slowly and painfully, use a broom, not gathering up what she swept but pushing it either towards the hearth which somebody who *could* kneel dealt with each morning, or out of the door.

She was doing that on this midnight of St. Peter and St. Paul's day, and stopping to breathe the sweet night air and looking up at the stars and the moon, when she became aware of something moving to her left, seeming to lean and grope at the whitewashed wall. It was a man, and had he been walking in ordinary fashion she would have gone in, shut and bolted the door and roused her grandson. Inns were apt to be robbed when the pilgrim season was in full swing, for pilgrims carried not only money for their journey but also gifts for whichever shrine they were making for.

A man who looked unable to walk without support and who, becoming aware of her, said, "Help me!" constituted no threat, however, and, lame herself, she was in instant sympathy with him.

"What ails you?" She took a few tottery steps towards him. Leaning on the wall, he limped towards her, and she saw with some slight surprise that he was well dressed and young, and, except for the fact that he looked so ill, would have been handsome.

"My servants deserted me. I was wounded—and lamed at Calais. Two years ago, madam, and since the physicians . . . St. Cerdic . . . last hope . . . and now I feel ill all over. And my servants ran away. I need help. Are you prepared to aid me? I promise . . . Well rewarded. Please forgive me if that . . . mercenary, offensive . . . I am alone."

He was talking disjointedly, as she herself sometimes did when her mind was on the present, not on the past. And he was lame, as she was; alone, as she was.

She said, "Come in. It is hard on midnight. I will give you a potion which will ease the worst of your woes, and then I will take you to St. Cerdic. He lies only just across the yard."

She offered her gnarled, brown-speckled hands, and the young man clutched them with his smooth, white, bejewelled ones; together, swaying, rather like the three-legged race which children delighted in, they made their way into the kitchen, and there she gave him a drink of what, in his right mind and in his own place, he would have spurned, as she would have done in those happier days when good ale and even wine were available. And for years after that she had made brews as her grandmother had told her—good herbal brews which worked for, admittedly, trivial ailments. But of late years she could not walk far enough to collect what she wanted; the woods had retreated as Mallow had grown, and she'd had so little time, and Marian had said, "mucky, messy," and again mentioned witchcraft. So she had given up, and now relied entirely upon dregs, what was left in tankards or winecups and not drunk by servants more active than she was. Sometimes she was very unfortunate and had to be content with rinsings, a very little water swilled round in the discarded drinking-vessel. Tonight she had been lucky, and had collected almost a mugful of what would bring a temporary easement to her joints and to her resentful mind, and finally bring sleep, which she craved above all things.

She shared the muddy stuff with this extraordinary visitor, and although it worked for her, and for him, in a way, in another way, it did him little good. His voice gained strength and she was obliged to say, "Hush. You will rouse the house. And the innkeeper, my grandson, is extremely strict. Anything that hints of fever—any spot, even a sneeze—bodes ill for him. And his wife is worse."

She was only too well aware that, in admitting a man whose fever was worse than his lameness, she had done an unforgivable thing.

"Come," she said to this unnamed, unknown man, "I will guide you to St. Cerdic."

"Yes," he said. "That was my destination, because of my leg. But all my servants ran away . . ."

"You can lean on me," she said. They moved, uncertainly yet with purpose, across the yard, rounded the last building, and came upon the full glory of what in her mind she always called John's window. Softly lighted from within by the glow of many candles, the colours were muted.

"Beautiful. As I expected," he said. "I was being carried in a litter, you see. We stopped to rest and then they all ran away."

"Never mind," she said, "you got here." He was young, the

kind who most benefited from a visit to this shrine. Almost certainly his lameness would be cured, but the fever, evident in his hot flesh, foetid breath and rambling talk—what of that? She had known and made good febrifuges in her day, but that day was done.

There was always a monk keeping watch over St. Cerdic's shrine—not as a guard against thievery for, bad as things were, nobody would dare rob a shrine, and if somebody was mad enough and bad enough to try, one unarmed monk could not have stopped it—but to see that things were done in order, and a record kept.

Candles burned on the altar and before the statue of the Virgin, and on a candlestand between the tomb and the wall on which hung the sticks and the crutches and leather strappings which told of cures. The stone floor around the tomb had at some time been covered with black marble, and the whole shrine enclosed by a low railing of finely-wrought iron, touched here and there with real gold.

"There you are," Anna whispered and released her hold. The man stumbled forward. The monk ceremoniously opened the little gate in the railing and indicated the spot, bare of treasure and no larger than a brick, which the hopeful pilgrim should touch. It was already beginning to be hollowed out. No hopeful hand could take anything from the solid stone, but touch after touch through the uncounted years had worked minute but cumulative erosion.

The monk recognised the old woman from the inn, and for a moment thought that she had brought a pilgrim with no time or patience to wait for tomorrow and the crowd. He noted that the would-be supplicant was young and rich . . . But he stank! Not of unwashed flesh or clothes or too close contact with animals. What Anna had scented when she was in contact with the young man, out in the open air, in the kitchen with the width of a table between them, and then in the open air again, hit the monk full blast as he opened the little gate and held it while the pilgrim passed through. The charnel-house stench of plague!

The monk moved away hastily, and by the light of the candles which burned in a semicircle about the Virgin's statue he hastily scribbled the required record: time of visit, sex and condition of supplicant, and gift. Cures were no longer recorded as once they had been. A sceptical bishop of Bywater, on one of his annual visitations, had asked too many questions, and even suggested that cases of miraculous healing should be investigated after, say, a year.

"Two golden chains, four rings, a jewelled belt and purse," the monk wrote, seeing the young man—condition lame and fevered—place these things on the shrine before he even knelt or touched the small space of exposed stone. Then he slipped away, through the door which connected the small chapel with the great church.

Anna knelt by the altar and did not pray for a miracle, but for death. An end to weariness, dear Lord. All day, everything, even telling a story to the children, even remembering, had seemed more and more of an effort, and getting that poor young man across the yard had taken the last even of the false strength derived from the mixture of dregs. Heaven she could not aspire to; hell she hoped to be spared; purgatory, less defined, sounded restful. "God spare me the shame of being useless and left to Marian's care. Mary, Mother of God, intercede for me. Let me go to my rest. I can no more."

Church was the one place where she could kneel and be sure of being given assistance to rise, and since, after a time, her prayer for death appeared to be as fruitless as her earlier prayers for a miracle, rise she must. She raised her head and looked about for the monk or for the young man. Her head came up on a straighter spine than she had known for many years, and the locked joints, as she tried to raise herself, being alone and with no help forthcoming, moved with the ease of axles suddenly greased.

The miracle had happened. Thirty years dropped away as she stood up and took in the wonder of it, with no one to tell.

She thought, dispassionately because the miracle had restored her spirit as well as her body, that all along her trouble had been that there was nobody to tell. Never able to tell Edman how she had saved his yard for him; never able to tell John that he had been wrong in thinking she had played the whore for half an acre of ground. Even smaller things must remain untold; she could never for pride's sake tell anyone that she had raised a miserly son, and after his death, suffered miseries from her grandson's wife.

Still, whether shared or not, the miracle had happened, and she could begin to think about plans for the future—away from the One Bull at Mallow. There must be many people who, while unwilling to employ or give houseroom to a lame, bent old woman, would welcome the services of one miraculously restored to sprightliness, ugly though she might be. And was it, in fact, necessary to be quite so ugly? Men shaved; so could she. And with some better clothes and a clean linen head-dress . . . Still, first things first! She turned towards the shining shrine and whispered, "St. Cerdic, I will remember my debt to you."

She hoped that the young man had had his miracle. And she thought that the monk, seeing that he was ill as well as lame, had led him away to the infirmary.

This had not happened. In the morning a groom, rising early, came upon a corpse of what he took to be either an inn-guest who had walked out for purposes of his own, leaving his valuable things in his bedchamber, taken a fit and died, or a man who had been set upon and robbed. No gentleman wore such fine clothes without a belt and a purse hanging from it, and few men with such white, well-cared-for hands lacked a ring to wear.

The groom roused the landlord, who denied all knowledge of the man, and was moreover angry that a possible victim of robbery should be found upon his premises. It was the kind of thing which gave an inn a bad name. Many innkeepers were suspected of being in league with thieves, passing on information about wealthy guests and their destinations. Edman Gilderson, though avaricious, was strictly honest, and it seemed utterly unjust that people should be able to say that a man who looked as though he had been strangled—his face was the same dusky colour as that of a man who had died on the gibbet—and then robbed, had been found in the yard of the One Bull.

It was still very early in the morning with few people about.

"Would you like to earn an honest fourpence? Very well, take or drag this man and lay him by the abbey gate. And say nothing. My inn is full of people who seek healing; to hear of a death so close would distress them. You understand?"

For fourpence—a week's wage for even a nobleman's trusted groom—the man was willing to understand, to act and be silent.

The abbey wall was heavily buttressed, and the main gate projected at least twelve feet into the roadway. Between the last buttress and the side of the gateway was a space like a cave. Having deposited the body there, the groom looked down at it and pondered. A plum-coloured tunic of silk was not a thing that he himself could wear, but it was saleable, and in London there was a market for such things. So he removed it, folded it small, and tucked it inside his own homespun one.

The first to view the body after that was a washer-woman taking a bundle of linen to the pool called the Wolfpit. She was a poor ignorant woman and could not know that this pool was what had made possible the building of the great abbey and the growth of the town. Long ago, when it had seemed desirable and politic to exploit St. Cerdic in the cause of Christianity, the problem had been lack of water. Mallow had no river and was dependent upon wells, like the very ancient one in front of the tavern, or upon ponds where clay had been dug out for the building of houses.

An Italian monk, carrying within his narrow dark head all the inherited talent of ancestors who had set fountains playing and aqueducts striding through many arid places, had prowled about and found the Wolfpit pool, and observed that it never changed its level whether the season was wet or dry. Therefore he deduced that it was fed from a spring and, having no easy outlet, seeped its surplus into marshes and quagmire. Given enough labour and enough stone, he said, he could divert its surplus and give Mallow a stream, if not a river. He had been as good as his word. For two centuries Mallow had had its flow of water, called because of its slowness the Ooze. The few who needed to put the name in writing spelt it as Ouse.

Because the Wolfpit was now, except for its outlet, lined with stone, it was a favourite place for the washing of clothes which could be cleansed by hard beating.

The washer-woman, having spied the body and judged it to be dead, not intoxicated, ran for the parish priest whose life was so much more closely interwoven with that of the townsfolk than was the abbey. Father Ambrose, a man of experience, recognised with sorrow and alarm the sign of the plague—the swollen glands under the arms and in the neck. His alarm was not for himself; he had survived the pestilence in his London seminary, but so far as records went no case had been known in Mallow, which made everyone vulnerable. He said nothing, however, for he was a believer in the theory that for every person the plague killed, fear slaughtered five. He gave the body hasty but decent burial and hoped for the best.

At the One Bull Anna spent the day with the children.

Inside the monastery the monk who had scented plague, and retreated, said nothing, not wishing to be avoided by his fellows. When he sickened—as he was sure he must—he wanted to be cared for in the infirmary, not banished like a leper. Fear certainly attacked him and produced some curious symptoms, but he did not die. Many others did. The source of contagion lay there, on St. Cerdic's shrine: a pouch of velvet, embroidered with pearls, a belt of leather studded and clasped with gold.

At the One Bull, it was not old Anna left to the untender mercies of Marian. It was Marian saying, spiteful to the last, "I always knew that your grandmother hobbled and bent sideways in order to avoid...Oh, my head! My head!" Marian died, and her husband soon afterwards. The most dedicated nursing by their great-grandmother failed to save the younger children. Young Edman was untouched, and moved abruptly from childhood to adult, in responsibility and gravity and anxiety. Years later he would tell of that terrible time when his great fear was that he would be the only person left alive.

In the confusion he hardly had time to notice the change in his great-grandmother, of whom he had been fond but never respected much. During that disastrous summer, with the harvest ungathered in the fields just beyond the town's boundary, and people being buried in common graves, sometimes with no ceremony, since Father Ambrose died of exhaustion and his three successors of the pestilence, Eddy's great-grandmother was always there, and that was enough for him. Once he said, plaintively, "You won't die, Granny, will you? Promise me, promise me, not to die."

"Not until you are a man, my dear. How could I die with so much to do?" He believed her. And when the pest, having killed half the population of the area and a third of the monks, passed on, and she said, "Now is the time to buy land," he believed that, too.

III

8 Andrew and Katharine

1540

THE LAST OF THE LEAD RAN INTO THE OILED WOODEN MOULD and began to cool. Presently the man in charge applied the wooden stamp and removed it. On a depressed panel the letters HR stood out in bold relief: the property of Henry, King of England.

The man in charge had some imagination. Most people called such a carefully-measured, easily-carried lump of lead "a pig" because its colour and its slightly rounded shape faintly resembled the body of a pig, devoid of head, legs and tail. Andrew Mason used the word, too, but now he looked at the wooden mould which, having served its purpose at Mallow, would go on to be used in other places, and thought that it looked like a cradle without rockers. And out of a cradle new life should come! The mould had brought death to St. Cerdic's abbey at Mallow. For without the lead guttering on its roofs the building would not last long.

He did not regret the dismantling of the abbey on religious grounds; he was all for the Reformed Church, and shared with many people the feeling that the monks had grown too rich, too fat and idle, and too far away from the ordinary people. What he did mourn over was the destruction of beautiful things, designed with skill and made by patient craftsmanship. He was a craftsman himself and greatly preferred making to unmaking. At the same time he was proud that he had been trusted enough to overlook this particular part of the demolition process. Lead was very valuable, and the amount of it that could be reclaimed from any one set of buildings was quite incalculable, and so dishonest men—many with more resounding titles than master-mason—cheated, sent in false returns, and lined their own pockets. That he had never done, and never would.

All around him was the clatter and bustle, the holiday feeling of one job completed, the next not yet begun. Laden carts began to move, with shouts and the crack of whips accompanying the sound of shod hooves on stones. The precious lead was being carried away to London, and might even be used in the fabulous, fairy-tale palace of Nonsuch which the king was building at Cuddington, near Ewell in Surrey. Other carts carrying tools—the moulds, the balances for weighing—things concerned with the destructive, lead-strippers' trade, and the personal belongings of men who carried all they owned with them and could make a camp or a lodge anywhere—were being loaded on, and the sheriff's men, grand and superior, were moving in to auction off such dispensable things as so many yards of wall-panelling or floor-planking or window-glass.

The more valuable things had gone months before: all the wall-hangings and the pictures, the glass and silver. The king, though his life had been something of a muddle, had a sense of order, and realised that, before the rain was allowed to seep in because the lead guttering had gone, everything valuable should be removed.

The abbey itself had been offered for sale as it stood, but the market was now glutted and no one had come forward to offer a good price down in order to be able to call himself Lord of the Manor of Mallow. That had happened already, in rather too many places. So what was left of Mallow, including the best of the stone, was to be offered to the highest bidder. Andrew Mason, saying to his youngest apprentice, "Simon, see my gear packed," saw the landlord of the inn, the One Bull, pushing forward with the intent, as everybody knew, of buying some panelling.

Andrew, who knew the inn and its owner well, having lodged there for a month, guessed that Ed Gilderson would get what he wanted cheaply, for few men would bid against him. He was known to be rich, owning not only a prosperous inn, but also parcels of land here and there. He could therefore outbid the ordinary fellow and, being cautious, would not attempt to buy anything likely to be wanted by men richer than himself. Two fine new houses were being built within an easy ride of Mallow, both on land that had belonged to the abbey. Sir Francis Colman called his Abbot's Hall, Sir Robert Thickthorn's was the New House. Andrew, who had his own saddlehorse, had visited them both, seen things he yearned to correct, and wished again that he were creating rather than destroying.

When the last cart had rumbled away, Andrew stood, a lonely man, aware of his loneliness. He'd called cheerily enough

to his own workmen, "See you on Monday at Bywater, lads,"
and they'd called back, but he sensed that they were glad to
be travelling and camping without him. In these days of change,
the gap between master-craftsman and men seemed to be widening. There was less solidarity than he could remember in his
own days as an apprentice. No man, except when roaring drunk,
would refuse to obey an order, or behave insolently, but there
was now a kind of restriction. They'd be talking and laughing
together, and then go silent at his approach, even when he had
merely looked in to see that they were comfortably lodged.
During the job at Mallow they had accommodated themselves
very comfortably in what had been the abbot's parlor; he had
lodged at the inn. And he had deliberately arranged not to make
the journey with them. The cart would head for Bywater, where
a smallish priory awaited the stripping, and he intended to make
a tour of several new houses going up in the neighbourhood
of Colchester.

He thought that he was probably more aware of this isolation
than most masters were because he had so little private life.
He'd married as soon as he was in a position to support a wife,
and had then for a time accepted only jobs within easy distance
of his home. His wife had been pretty, lively and frivolous and
he had adored her, but she and the baby had died on the same
hateful day. After that, the house in which they had been so
happy became intolerable, and he'd sold it, become a completely mobile man. He'd never felt the desire to marry again,
or to settle.

This way of life had prevented him from attaching himself to
any place or any particular group of people. Such loneliness
carried the compensation of independence; so long as he did
his work, nobody required him to be at any particular place at
any particular time, and now, having seen his men off, he had
time to spend as he chose. He decided to pay another visit to
the little chapel of St. Cerdic and to take one more look at the
wonderful north window.

He could view it without that submerged feeling of regret,
for the chapel was to be preserved and to continue to serve as
a parish church. The innkeeper had told him that it had been
touch-and-go between St. Cerdic's and the larger, far less ancient chapel of Our Lady, which stood on the far side of the
main abbey church. The king's commissioners and the bishop

of Bywater had met and talked and argued and, in Ed Gilderson's opinion, made the wrong decision.

"Nobody gave a thought to my convenience, or the convenience of . . . worshippers," he said, having almost said "pilgrims" in the old-fashioned way, saints and their shrines being gone out of fashion. "People have to go through my yard, and I have to put up with them. If they'd fixed on the Lady Chapel and left the gate, down there, by the bridge, it'd have been better for everybody. Let me fill your glass. Not to mention that the Lady Chapel is bigger and better built."

And not to mention, Andrew Mason reflected, that if the little chapel across the inn-yard were dismantled and left to ruin, the innkeeper would gain space and a solid stone-built structure to use as a stable or barn or pigstye. Andrew had not spent his working life in his particular trade without learning to recognise self-interest when he saw it. And perhaps this man credited him with power that he did not possess, hoped at this last moment that a word here or there might be effective.

The irony was that it could, just could, have been so. In the overall scheme of things a mere master-mason did not count for much, but as an expert—yes, he was listened to. It was then, a mere three weeks ago, that he could have said, if he had wanted to, or had he been bribable, that of the two debatable structures, the Lady Chapel had the firmer foundation. And those who never thought about foundations or balance or stress might well have listened. For the truth was that the more men moved away from the concept of beauty as a thing apart from everything else, the more they fell prey to utilitarianism, and therefore to the experts.

However, even had Andrew been tempted to exercise persuasion and speak up for the Lady Chapel, that impulse would have vanished as soon as he saw the great window of St. Cerdic's. No such glass was made nowadays; one colour, a rose-pink, had been lost forever, and all the others had become harsher.

The window was, of course, too big, completely out of proportion with the chapel itself, but it was so beautiful that that didn't matter.

The shrine, which Andrew had never seen, but had heard tell of, was gone. There remained only a plain slab of stone with a cross carved into its surface. To Andrew's eye it looked as though a cross of metal had once been inset there, and rather roughly prised out. The black marble of which the innkeeper had spoken had also been removed. The stripping had been very thorough. Behind the tomb, on the plain whitewashed wall, were the hooks and nails upon which the cast-off aids to the lame had hung. Andrew, no believer in the worship of saints and their shrines, which smacked of idolatry, spared a moment to wonder whether Cerdic's bones had been left in peace. Probably, because such things had little marketable value in England now; the days of relics were done.

But his main concern was for the window and the almost incredible skill which had gone to its making. How could men, working with something as tricky as glass, have managed to make two monks look genuinely astonished, and a wolf benevolent, and the face of a man, his body bristling with arrows, wear the expression, both agonised and patient, like that of Christ on the cross? It was a mystery, and how right skilled men had been in former days to refer to a craft, however practical, as a mystery!

Then his practical side took over. The window was extremely old; it was very large and it faced north; it was vulnerable to strong winds, to rain and snow, and each little segment was jointed to its neighbour by a narrow setting of lead. Lead was subject to wear and tear and to the ageing process; it could actually crumble.

Standing there, he thought; I would like to do something to preserve it. I *will* do something!

He was not very rich, but he had money saved and not a relative in the world. He could leave what he owned to the parish church of St. Cerdic at Mallow for the upkeep of the north window.

He went outside, and at a corner of the window, low down, tested the lead with the tip of his knife. It was already crumbling. He thought: I'm healthy, I may well live another twenty years, and then it will be too late. I must act now.

He remembered the landlord's dislike of people using his yard as a passage to and from the church, and so he went out by the way by which he had entered. And there, lying overlooked and forgotten, was that last pig of lead. The property of the king. It was stuff which was going to be in short supply in the near future, with all the new building going on. And even if he were provided with money, would a mere parish priest have the knowledge or the influence to obtain something rare?

Am I, at my age, with my reputation for honesty, going to steal from my king? Yes. If it can be called stealing. I'll work extra hours, without charge.

He decided that he would confide, not in the landlord, but in his wife. Ed Gilderson was more garrulous, more convivial, but those very qualities made him less suitable than his wife, who was a silent woman and one with a dignity out of place in one in her position. Andrew had noticed from the first that, whereas Ed regarded the people who used the inn as possible cronies, his wife treated them as guests—not very welcome ones, but people who must be treated with civility. There was about her something of the lady of the house giving hospitality, rather than selling it. Most important of all, Andrew judged from her attitude towards himself that she strongly disapproved of the work upon which he was engaged. He returned to the inn with the intention of requesting a private talk with her.

The inn was a curious building; its narrow, low frontage, tiled with small red tiles, was backed by two wings, both with an upper floor; one wing was half-timbered, the other of dressed flint. The low, tiled portion looked as though it might be merely a porch, but in fact it covered the main room of the inn, a larger room than the frontage indicated. The walls of the room were whitewashed, and in rather poor condition; some of the whitewash, and in places some of the plaster, was peeling off. In other places, faint flecks of colour showed. The floor, not rush-strewn as many still were, was similarly variegated, with areas of brick and of large floor tiles, red, primrose-coloured and bluish, interspersed with patches of very small, multicoloured tiles. It had amused him, as he took his meals at one of the white-scrubbed tables, to stare at the small tiles and try to discern some sort of pattern, but, had there ever been one, it was too much broken, and too frequently interrupted by the plain surfaces.

A maid-servant was ladling freshly scraped salt into the wooden bowls in the tables, and when he asked if Mistress Gilderson could spare him five minutes, she came rustling out from a side room and said, "Yes?" civilly enough, but without that slight shifting of the planes of her face which was her smile. Just then two men entered, sat down and called for ale.

"It is," Andrew said, "a rather private matter."

"Very well. Come this way."

One glance around this very private sanctum assured him that he had been right in his assessment of her feelings, and right in choosing her as his confidante. This was the room of a very pious woman—pious in the old style. There was a prie-dieu, a very beautiful little statuette of the Madonna with a few primroses in a small silver bowl on the bracket by her feet; there was a large crucifix on one otherwise bare wall. In a window embrasure—a new addition, he imagined—was a flat-topped table bearing papers and books in orderly alignment. The other furniture in the room consisted of a chair with cushions, a stool and a high-backed settle, a plain chair behind the table, and—strangely out of place—an oak cradle.

Mistress Gilderson indicated that he should take the cushioned chair, and went to the one behind the table, so that her back was to the light.

"Well?" Not exactly impatient but very positively saying: I-am-a-busy-woman-with-no-time-to-waste.

Normally he was short-spoken though more articulate than most of his kind—he'd had some schooling—but now he found himself hesitating and back-tracking in his anxiety to explain his feeling for that north window, and his purloining of a pig of lead, an act which broke a lifetime's habit of honesty. The woman's face was so shadowed that he could not judge what impression his words were making. All he could really see of her was the glint of yellow hair left uncovered by her head-dress and caught by the light from behind her.

"The value of the lead I cannot judge exactly," he said, "since it varies from day to day, always rising. But I can assure you that the king, his grace, shall not lose by this. I could offer to pay in money, but that would draw attention. I shall pay in labour, uncharged for. You understand?"

She said, "Yes." And she moved, her right arm in its close-fitting, tawny-coloured sleeve, reaching out, her hand plucking a quill from the stand, dipping it into the inkstand and writing very quickly on a piece of paper. "You wish to entrust me . . ." And she read out the terms of the trust.

"Yes. You have it exactly. And you will undertake it?"

"Most willingly," she said, with the first hint of feeling she had shown. "This is very curious; I always looked upon you as one of the destroyers."

"Hired, because I knew my job and was regarded as honest."

"How strange! Judas was so regarded. He kept the bag, the communal purse. But thirty pieces of silver suborned him."

The tone of voice and the comparison stung.

"Living in this quiet place," he said, "you do not understand the climate of opinion in the outside world. Had I refused this work, I should have been instantly suspected."

"Of what?"

"Of disapproving. Being against what the king wants."

"Does he know? Has he ever known? For a sincere Protestant one must have some respect, but the king is not that. He desired the Church of which he now calls himself the head to remain virtually unchanged, yet in order to enrich himself he attacks and destroys the very bastions of Catholicism—the religious houses. It is not unlike throwing a man from a high window and ordering him to stop halfway from the ground!"

"Madam, in some company such talk would be held to be treasonable."

"I know. I also know that had I any courage I should say such things on the market-place. I lack courage."

"Many who had it came to no good," Andrew said mildly.

"Ah, yes. Sir Thomas More, Bishop Fisher. More lately, poor Robert Aske."

"He was a rebel. He led thirty-thousand armed men against his anointed king."

"Whom the pope had excommunicated," she retorted sharply.

Almost against his will, Andrew was becoming fascinated by this woman, so unlike any other he had known. His mother, a simple, kindly woman whose one positive act had been to insist that he should have a little schooling; his wife, another simple, very pretty, light-hearted creature whom he had mourned and missed and about whom he had felt some guilt because it was in bearing his child—the fruit of love . . . but the years had silted up—twenty years of gathering oblivion; and women hired here and there, when the rare itch took him. He had never before had any kind of contact with a woman who used words like "suborned" and whose talk was not confined to things—what to eat, what to wear, and such. Speaking now as he would have spoken to another man—had he ever met him—who was handy with words, set in opinions and willing to talk, he said, "But surely, even you must admit that some reform was needed." In that belief he had operated for four years.

"Reform? Oh, most certainly. But surely you, as a mason,

can distinguish between the need to mend and the need to destroy. If thine eye offend thee, pluck it out—not sever the head in which the offending eye sits. Perhaps," she said, and her voice softened, "I feel somewhat too vehemently upon this subject because it affected my whole life."

"In what way, madam?"

"I was convent-bred. Otterly, a poor, small house, one of the first to fall. Almost ten years ago. For the professed nuns places were found in other houses. A brief reprieve! Three of us, not yet even novices, were sent home. Having *known* no other home. It was infamous!"

"Young enough to adjust," he said, as though speaking to himself. And how very well she had done it!

"Adjust! To what? A house ruled by my oldest sister who had rid herself of me when I was three. Two others for whom my father was desperately striving to provide some sort of dowry. Incidentally, I had had mine—twenty pounds down when the nuns took me. It was not returned! My father hires his land from the man who is now my husband, and I was singularly fortunate in that he asked no dowry. I repay him to the best of my ability. I keep a clean kitchen, clean beds. I see to the business side." She tapped some of the papers with a delicate finger. "I have failed in one respect. The cradle remains empty."

Andrew did a rough-and-ready mason's reckoning in his head. Too young to be a novice, say fifteen, sixteen. Ten years ago.

"There is time yet," he said.

"Maybe," she said and he saw her shoulders move in a gesture which might mean anything: resignation, don't care, God's will. "If things go on as they are doing, I foresee a time when all the rules break down and a man will be able to divorce his wife with far less reason than childlessness. The king's first wife, the good old queen, gave him no son, and that was, to his mind, being childless. So he put her away and married Nan Bullen, who gave him another daughter. For that, and not for the reasons bruited about, since no man of sense could believe them for a moment, she died a shameful death. And now gossip says—and I assure you, Mr. Mason, even living in this *quiet* place one hears news—the Princess of Cleves is not to his taste; her nose is too blunt or her mouth too large. With such an example being set by the most important man in the realm, what hope is there of order and security? You yourself admitted that had you refused to help with the demolition, you could have lost your ears and been made destitute. That is tyranny, Mr. Mason, and always, always, the Church of Rome has tried to hold tyranny at bay. Not always successfully, or with immediate results. But, given time . . . So, I contradict myself. What I mean is that things will grow worse; there will be more chaos. But eventually things will improve and the Church will then restore order."

Not as she hoped, he thought. The monasteries and abbeys and priories could never be rebuilt, because their lands had been sequestrated. Rightly, Andrew believed, because too much land had been owned by too few people, and often people to whom good husbandry was not of first importance. This thought he did not put into words; he had no wish to lose her goodwill. Yet her next words were in accord with his reflection about land.

She lifted a paper and laid it down again. "There is another result of all this upheaval for which we shall all pay dearly—and soon. The religious may not have been invariably good landlords, but the new men are worse. Acres of good tillage being turned into sheep-runs. Wool means wealth, of course, and *some* mutton is edible. But the price of bread must rise when wheat is no longer grown, and since one man can tend sheep on an acreage that twenty men tilled, there will be great unemployment."

"But the turning over of land to sheep is no new thing, madam. Did not Sir Thomas More complain of sheep eating men?"

"True. But it is now being done on a vaster scale, and involves men who, simply because their holdings were small, could not make sheep-runs. I have here a letter from Sir Robert Thickthorn who received from the king nine hundred and fifty acres of St. Cerdic's land. Not enough. He wishes to purchase from my husband one of the last of his little holdings, leased to a man who cultivates every inch. 'To round off proposed sheep-run,' he says blatantly."

"And your husband will sell?"

"He would. Did he know. Fortunately he reads with such difficulty that I deal with such things. Like this!" She tore the sheet of paper across and across and again. Very neatly. She put the eight resulting pieces in a neat pile. "I use such scraps for writing reminders to myself," she said.

Convent-bred, indeed. Where the rules of the Order, whatever Order, were *kept*; nothing was untidy and nothing was wasted. And Andrew Mason realised that one of the reasons why the One Bull at Mallow was one of the best-run hostelries he had ever known was that it was run by a woman who would have been, in ordinary times, a nun. He entertained for a moment the idea of such women, thousands of them, cast out upon the world—for, as this woman had said, the reprieve had been brief for those sent from small, poor houses to larger ones. Some of the young would marry; older ones would live by plying their skills, as spinsters, sempstresses, embroiderers, nurses. He had been marvellously lucky in finding such a trained, intelligent—though rather misguided—woman to conspire with him in his project of saving that beautiful window.

Again, before he could speak, changing the subject and bringing it down to practicalities, she forestalled him.

"This ingot of lead: where is it? How much does it weigh?"

"It lies in the space where the carts assembled, just inside the main gate. And it weighs a pound or two short of seven hundredweight. Seven hundredweight is the average, but this, being the last, may fall a little short."

"More than you and I could manage between us? I am very strong."

"Far more. It would take at least three men, and strong ones. Mine are all on their way to Bywater. But I am here. Do you know of two men, either ignorant or bribable?"

The sun had moved as they talked, and now shone its low, February light in at the window in such a way that one side of her face and head was gilded, the other still shadowed. A face much too stern and high-nosed to be pretty, but completely reliable.

"I think the priest of the parish, who will know and appreciate what we are trying to achieve, and two men of his choosing, too drunk to know what they are doing. Leave it to me. Is it covered?"

"Yes, I flung a cloak over it."

"I will send on the cloak. To Bywater, is it not?"

"Yes. And from there I will arrange to send you money so that the labour can be paid for."

She said, "You may not be a good Catholic, but you are a

good man. God go with you even though you are, perforce, bound on the devil's work."

Despite that stab, he wished her well, too, hoping that what she obviously needed—a baby, preferably a boy—might be granted. He knew that, given time and opportunity, he could have loved her, not only with his body, but also with his mind. But he was an honest man and she was another man's wife.

She led the way, carrying a lantern which cast a good light because its panels were not of thinly-pared horn, but of glass, and the candle which burned within it was a thick one. Father Alban, a great ox of a man, and the two men who, elated with drink, each thought himself as strong as seven, lifted the pig of lead and slid it into a sack and hoisted it on to the two-wheeled barrow used for the transport of barrels. He had previously sworn them to secrecy on the Bible which, for the last two years, had by the king's order, been chained to the altar in St. Cerdic's. It must be a secret, he said, because, if the news got about, every parish church in the land would be clamouring for a similar favour. "And that," he said to Mistress Gilderson, "is true, as far as it goes."

She had a place for it: under her writing table. There, covered first by a rug, then with a fitted velvet case which she had already started to make, it would masquerade as a footstool until it was needed. Father Alban took a far less anxious view of the state of the north window than Andrew Mason had done, and when the promised money arrived he had every intention of putting it to a more useful purpose.

The money never came. Andrew's horse, young and always inclined to friskiness, had stood in the One Bull's well-provendered stable for three weeks, with only two short outings, and was prepared to be very frisky indeed, pretending to be greatly alarmed by sights familiar to every horse on a country road—an old woman leading a goat, a pheasant flying low, a dog chasing a bitch, a man carrying a hod of bricks. Accustomed to his steed's antics, and knowing that they would wear off before he reached Wipton, Andrew rode with carelessness, his mind on other things: the beautiful window which he hoped his efforts had preserved; the innkeeper's wife who had insisted upon giving him a noon-piece to eat on the road—a meat pasty wrapped in a napkin, and some ale in a bottle.

It was well after noon when he stopped to eat, dismounting to stretch his legs and allow his horse to drink from a wayside stream. The napkin was of fine linen, beautifully embroidered. Nun's work. A waste in a way. He thought of her story and of the unsentimental way in which she had mentioned the empty cradle. Well, God send her a child, soon. He imagined her yellow head bent over more rewarding needlework. He folded the napkin carefully and placed it in his pouch.

He was in the act of mounting his foot in the stirrup, his other leg flexed for the jump, when some deer came, as was their habit, to drink from the stream. A splendid excuse for the horse to rear and swivel sideways, and then, for half-a-mile run in genuine panic because its rider was not in the saddle but dragging heavily on one side and bumping...

He had thought his relationship with his men left something to be desired but, when at last they knew, what they said would have pleased him. They'd lost the best master in the world; they'd never look on his like again. Generous, they said, and just, and honest in all his dealings.

Katharine Gilderson, having that strangely intimate talk with a stranger, and mentioning the empty cradle, hearing him say, kindly, that there was yet time, had not thought it necessary to tell him that in almost ten years of marriage she had suffered four miscarriages and was at the moment pregnant again.

This time she seemed to be carrying well; two most dangerous periods safely past; three months, four, five. So it could not be true that Edman—give him his full name for once—was to blame for the miscarriages, just as, it was whispered, the king was for his first wife's many miscarriages and his second wife's three. A new and terrible disease, which learned people called syphilis and the unlearned called the French pox. Nobody knew anything about it; there was no known cure and the whole thing, being of a sexual nature, was too shameful to be openly discussed.

But, in her logical way, as this baby held, Katharine felt that she had wronged Edman in her thoughts, and she became again the sweet-tempered, rather all-at-sea girl with whom he had fallen in love, the girl who had turned into something different after two miscarriages, slightly scornful and superior, he thought, because she could read and write.

When, well into the sixth month, she suffered yet another miscarriage, more serious than the others, more like a premature birth, and died of it, Ed Gilderson could truly say that he had lost the best wife a man ever had.

He mourned her sincerely for a month and then, mending up his life as a man must do, began wooing a likely girl who bore his own name, though she was no relation within the third or even the fourth degree.

The new bride could not read or write, but little was required in that way of an innkeeper's wife. Especially now when he was selling off his scattered holdings.

With the proceeds of his outlying land, Ed Gilderson was able to buy out the smithy which for so long had stood beside the inn. The narrow entrance, formerly shared by inn, smithy and church, could now be divided, and, thanks to the amount of stone, sometimes free for the taking, sometimes sold very cheaply, Ed Gilderson was able to make two imposing arches, one giving access to the greatly expanded inn yard, the further one to a path which skirted the yard, made a right-angled turn, and ended at the church door.

During the following years trade became brisk. The monks had exercised some kind of toll on the market-place; with this abolished the market expanded rapidly. The increase in the wool trade helped too, as did the annual sheep fair. The north-south road was busier than it had ever been before, and so was the inn.

A few people who had known the place in Katharine's day complained that standards had fallen, but the One Bull was still fairly good, and there was no competition. Travellers were becoming rather fanciful, and though some were still content to bed down in a room with three or four other men, more and more were demanding separate bedrooms.

The second Mrs. Gilderson, though she could neither read nor write, was sharp-witted where money was concerned, and could add sums in her head with swift accuracy. One attendance at church on Sunday satisfied her religious needs, and so Katharine's room was never used. In 1542 Ed decided to turn it into a bedroom. The prie-dieu, the crucifix and the statuette of the Virgin—things for which there was no longer any demand—were stored away in an attick, low, dark and window-less, which had been made by lowering the ceiling of one of the upper rooms in the flint-built wing. It served a dual purpose: a dumping-place for things which were unwanted at the moment but which might be used some day, and a bedchamber for maid-servants.

In Katharine's room the table was to remain in the window embrasure and serve as a wash-stand, holding basin and ewer. The footstool, in an ideal position for a woman sitting with her back to the window, might prove awkward for a guest standing to wash, shave, arrange his hair on the other side, facing the light. "Move it," Ed Gilderson said to the men who had already brought in a bed and a night-table for a candlestick. "We can't," they said, having tried. Ed made a sound of scorn and exasperation, strode over, pushed them aside and tried himself. Something to boast about, having single-handed something that two sturdy men couldn't shift. He couldn't shift it, either.

"Leave it for the time being," he said. "It must be made of lead." Curious choice of material for a footstool, but then, his first wife had been an unusual woman. He was worse served, but on the whole happier with his second, a more easy-going creature, already the mother of a likely boy, and pregnant again.

Where and when the notion that the room had something uncanny about it started, nobody knew. Probably with some silly maid, as such stories usually did. The second Mistress Gilderson, a woman of good sense, had a theory about it. Maids, she said, were almost always girls from large families squeezed into small cottages. "It's the space scares them, Ed. That and being alone in a room for the first time in their lives." She spoke of what she knew, for she, member of a large, noisy family, reared not exactly in a cottage but in a smallish farmhouse, had felt something the same during her early days at the One Bull. Only after dark, and only occasionally, for instance when she was obliged to go, for some reason, into the room adjoining the kitchen where the barrels and wine-bottles were kept—the inn having no cellar. There, once or twice, she had felt that, though alone, she was not alone, and could have sworn she'd heard tapping on the door which now led from the barrel-store into the passage serving what was still known as the New Wing.

Such fanciful notions she had kept to herself and resolutely quelled, because she had a standard to live up to. Ed's first wife had been by all accounts a very clever woman, and Alice knew that she was not at all clever, in that way. She had not wanted, at that time, Ed to think her silly as well as unlearned.

And now the feeling had worn off entirely. But the memory of it made her tolerant of such feelings in other less fortunate, less sensible females.

She said things such as, "Mollie, go with Kate to make the Garden Room ready. Many hands make light work." Or, "Kate, I will come and help you to turn the bed in the Garden Room." The decline in standards at the inn was in no way due to sloth or carelessness on the part of the new wife; it was simply that her standards were those of a farmhouse, not of a convent with its pernickety ways.

Katharine's room was known as the Garden Room because, with the expansion onto the smithy ground, the making of a little garden had become possible, with a few rose-trees, red, white, and the true Tudor rose, red and white; daffodils, gilly-flowers, marigolds; a bush of rosemary and another of lavender, a few common herbs.

The Garden Room was reserved for privileged guests or for those who, through age, disability or mere obesity wished to avoid stairs. It was not in general use because, since by now no chambermaid would go in alone to make the bed and empty slops, it was rather a nuisance.

A belief in ghosts was as old as time, though the truly Catholic Church had been somewhat sceptical. Stories of hauntings had survived, however, and been handed around. Usually the stories were associated with some crime: sometimes the victim was earthbound, which seemed unfair, sometimes the perpetrator of the crime, who should by rights have been in hell. It was all a confusion which sensible people chose to ignore, or to enjoy only in a strictly make-believe way.

Ed Gilderson could never be quite certain whether a reputation for having one haunted room did an inn good or harm. Trade showed no sign of decline, though now and again a traveller would ask *not* to be given accommodation in the room with the ghost. On the other hand, many people were frankly curious, and every now and then somebody would ask to see the room, and sometimes gay young gentlemen staying at Abbot's Hall or the New House would dare one another to spend a night there. Ed, like an amiable host, tempered his own response to what he imagined a guest wished to hear. A sturdy, "It's all nonsense. I've lived here all my life and never seen or heard anything out of the way," or "Well, odd things do happen. But I know nothing to account for it here." By that he meant that there was no known story, like the prevalent ones about the king's second and fourth wives—both beheaded—who walked, as the saying went, at Blickling and Hever and Salle and Hampton Court, or about the pedlar, murdered for his small wealth on a lonely stretch of road near Daneley, whose ghost accosted certain travellers, offering spectral wares at exceptionally low prices.

On the afternoon of a day late in January 1547 it began to snow, a few huge flakes sauntering down, and then a full-scale blizzard, a howling wind straight from the north. Travellers who might, in ordinary circumstances, have pushed on decided to be safe rather than foolhardy, and the One Bull was crowded in an unseasonable way.

Amongst the guests was a youngish man, lame in one leg. He wore what was called a built-up shoe, its sole a good three inches thick and the heel at least six inches. He was on his way to take up a position as tutor to the sons of Sir Robert Thickthorn at the New House. Not the career he would have chosen had he been fully able-bodied, but it would serve. For a time. It was his ultimate desire to become a writer of poetry, plays, pamphlets, and he felt that a more adventurous life would have provided material. As it was, he must make do with what offered itself.

Unexpectedly, in view of his shabby clothes and scrawny mule, he demanded a room to himself, extra candles and his supper served privately. Ed Gilderson thought of the Garden Room and then had doubts; yet one could hardly, without giving offence, say, "Show me first your money." Abruptly, he remembered his first wife; whe would have dealt with the situation in her own peculiar way with no embarrassment to herself or to the young man.

The young man said, rather unpleasantly, "You doubt my ability to pay for luxury. How right you are! Expecting to reach the New House this evening, I spent my last penny at midday, but Sir Robert Thickthorn guaranteed my travelling expenses, and, I am sure, will honour his word. You need not worry."

He went straight to his room and stayed there, with the jug and ewer pushed aside to make place for papers and writing-stuff, reported the maid who carried in his supper. So he had taken no share in the talk which began after supper in the main room. It was on this kind of night, with the wind howling and the snow blowing or the rain lashing, that people snug indoors by a fire in good company, enjoyed talking about frightening things, earthly and unearthly. One traveller, only two and a half days' travel from London, had brought word that the king was dying, and that began the talk. About what would come once the breath left the now gross and already rotting body of the man who had ruled with absolute authority—defying even the pope—for thirty-six years and, though married six times, had begotten only one son, a pale frail boy, and two daughters, both of whom he had himself dubbed bastards. And it was said that, in his declining days, the king had been horribly haunted, not only by the ghosts of his two executed wives, but by others whom he had sacrificed on his way to absolute power—Sir Thomas More, Cardinal Wolsey.

The mention of the king's one son, pale and frail, touched Ed Gilderson, for that was exactly what two marriages had given him. Alice's second pregnancy had ended in a miscarriage, and so had her third. After that, no more. And whether young Edman would live or, living, ever have vigour and health enough to run the One Bull in proper fashion was a constant worry to a doting father. Now, to divert his mind, he steered the talk into a discussion about ghosts in general. The subject was eagerly taken up.

The shabby young man in the Garden Room was comfortable and happy. He sat where Katharine had once sat—back to the window which rattled and shook in the gale. He'd moved the basin and ewer to one end of the very solid table, set the extra candles in position, and spread his papers. When his supper came, brought by a comely, fresh-faced maid, he said, "Put it there," and indicated the other end of the table. He fed himself with his left hand and scribbled rather frenziedly with his right, sensing that such a God-given opportunity might not come his way again. Sir Robert had two sons, a gap of three years between them, and so one lesson would not serve for both, and a tutor's work did not begin and end in the schoolroom. He was indeed a kind of superior servant, expected to turn his hand to anything.

Leisure might be short at the New House; even the candle supply might be limited, but, thought the young man, "Tonight is mine!" And he scribbled assiduously. He was annoyed when, in response to the feeling that he was being watched, he looked up and found that he was not alone.

The woman must have come in very quietly. He took her for the landlady; her dress, very modest in design, was of excellent material, dark blue with white lace at the neck and wrists, and her head-dress was of fine linen, starched to a gloss. He imagined that she had looked in to see if he had all he needed for the night.

He said, "Good evening, madam," but he did not rise, and he held on to his quill, indicating that he had no time for talk. She did not answer, but simply stood and stared. He took her silence as a rebuke, judging her to be one of those haughty new middle-class women who thought they should be treated as great ladies. Unwillingly he got to his feet and bowed and, with the intent of putting her in her place, said, "Thank you, I have all I need." Even then she did not answer, or smile, or move, and he became aware of the silence, not merely hers, but all around; the silence of a house in the dead of night, the last tipsy reveller gone to bed. And a quick glance at the candles, burned low, informed him that it was indeed late.

He had always wished to be a poet and a playwright; he knew that he had talent and insight and imagination, yet now, at what he later realised was the crucial, the testing moment, he still thought in strictly practical terms, and imagined that he was being confronted by a dumb woman, a conscientious landlady come to see why he was burning candles so late.

Then why didn't she gesture or gibber, make some attempt to communicate? Dumbness was not such a rare affliction; there were people born dumb, people made dumb by some shock, people—usually older—who had had a fit and recovered, but with the power of speech lost; but they all *tried*. This woman did not. She simply stood there and stared, and he, guilt already planted in him because travelling expenses, as guaranteed by Sir Robert, did not necessarily include extra candles burning down to their roots, said, "Very well, I understand. I have done now." As he had; the wonderful flow of inspiration had broken off. To be recaptured? Who could tell? Irritably—and he was an irritable fellow, as those he taught, those he was to teach, well knew—he leaned to left and to right and blew out all the candles but the one to which everybody was entitled until he was into bed. In performing this ordinary action, he had of necessity taken his eye from his unwelcome visitor and when he straightened up she had gone away as quietly as she had come.

Being dedicated, self-approving, and to a measure self-satisfied, he would in ordinary circumstances have resumed work, but the room was very cold, the fire having died down and all but one candle being extinguished. So he gave up and hurried into bed, where the maid, fetching away his supper-tray, had placed a flannel-wrapped brick, still exuding a welcome heat.

And he would have gone on his way next morning, with the wind appeased and shifted and the snow beginning to turn to slush, without giving the night's experience, a visit from a dumb landlady, careful of candles, another thought, except for one thing . . .

When interrupted, he had been writing in modern terms, as so many would-be poets did, an ancient story, culled from an old neglected book. He knew that he was not being original in writing about Helen of Troy, but he was doing it differently. He had just written, "And Helen, unchanged, unchangeable, from the highest tower in Troy looked down . . ." The next, he thought immortal, line was still-born, because a dumb and insolent woman, careful of candles, had dared to intrude upon the privacy which, with Sir Robert's guarantee, he had secured for himself.

He wrote in the new, much more easily acquired and more easily passed on, Italianate hand. Now, below his last line, and in an older, more monkish script, and very conspicuous in the middle of what remained blank of his page were the words—

North Window

He stared unbelievingly and, lacking the credulity which would have fertilised his imagination and made him the poet he though he already was, sought some rational explanation. He'd left Helen looking down from Troy's highest tower; had he in fact visualised her at a window? A north window? Had he, interrupted, scribbled the two words absent-mindedly as a reminder? Even, perhaps, thought of the window and its aspect when half asleep, and made the necessary note? The different style in writing he could account for easily. He had written so in early youth at the monks' school. But the position of the words puzzled him; paper was precious and expensive, and to write two words in the centre of a sizable blank space would have been against his nature even when half asleep.

He exonerated his overnight visitor for, except when she entered and when she left, she had been in full view and never near the table at which he sat.

He packed his few belongings carefully and went out to breakfast in the big panelled room where, over bread and cold bacon and ale, men were talking of a disturbance in the night. A terrible crash to the rear of the inn. He said he had heard nothing, occupying as he had done a side room.

Breakfast was being supervised by a woman, obviously the innkeeper's wife, who bore not the slightest resemblance to the woman who, by haughty silence, had rebuked him—he thought—for extravagance with candles. Of her there was no sign. The landlady seemed to be perturbed by guests complaining about a disturbance in the night, and after a visit to the kitchen came back with an explanation which freed the inn of all blame. "Sirs, I have just heard. The church window blew in during the night." She added, not being handy with words, a remark which only the pedantic young tutor thought quaint, "It was overlarge for its size."

One guest, familiar with the inn and the church, said, "A pity. It was an admirable window."

"And its loss will be felt, if the wind blows from the north," the landlady said.

North. Window. North window. Very curious.

What he lacked in some ways the young tutor made up for in others; he had a lively curiosity. Before mounting his mule and proceeding to the New House, he limped over to the church. In some places the snow had turned to slush; in others it still lay white, making the morning light clearer than the grey sky warranted, but clear in glum fashion.

It was so small a church, and the window had plainly been overlarge. He understood the landlady's remark. Bits of glass, and the lead that had bonded them lay scattered all over the floor, and dismally surveying the ruin was the parish priest. He had once been, the sharp observer of detail noticed, a man of some size; now he was shrunken and grown downward, as old men did. His soutane was not only too wide for him, but also too long, so that, picking his way through the wreckage, he was obliged to hold it up in order not to trip over it.

The young tutor could not know that only seven years earlier, Father Alban had been "a great ox of a man," and not only strong in body but also lively in mind. He had contracted some kind of fever which came and went and which had reduced his body and, partially, his mind. Often, weak but lucid, Father Alban most heartily thanked God that his work was routine, once learned never forgotten. What he knew when he was twenty, he still knew at thirty-seven, but in other areas he was liable to confusion. His priestly duties he performed faithfully; called upon to deal with the unexpected, he lapsed into premature senility and could often be incoherent.

"A calamity, young sir. No less than a calamity. And all my fault, my most grievous fault. God may forgive me. I can never forgive myself. And how can I explain to *them*?"

"I fail to see why you should blame yourself, Father. It was the wind." The young man spoke absent-mindedly, his attention on a sizable piece of the window depicting a wolf wearing a most unwolflike expression.

"Neglect," Father Alban said. "And the money never came. The man was dead. It was such a *beautiful* window."

The young tutor had come simply to glance, not to get involved with an old man's lugubrious talk. His gaze moved to a section the size of a dish. A head of Christ, but without the halo or the crown of thorns which were usual.

"Possibly enough could be salvaged to make a smaller window," he said, less from a desire to comfort—he was not a particularly tender-hearted man, except where imaginary woes were concerned—but rather as a means of ending this conversation. Speaking, he looked towards the huge space in the wall, and saw, framed by a few remaining fragments of glass and lead, a man, a carpenter or mason, judging from the apron and the hair-protecting cap. "And here is the man to help you."

"Where?"

"Looking in at the window."

"There is no man at the window."

"Perhaps your sight, Father . . ."

"My sight is excellent. Excellent." It was a well-known habit of old men to ignore the damage the years had done.

"A man," the young tutor said firmly. "By his dress a mason, or . . ."

"God have mercy! Christ deliver us!" Father Alban said in so agitated a manner that the young man turned to see what ailed him. There had been nothing threatening or hostile about the man at the window. "The *thought* has haunted me off and on for seven years. Am I now to be haunted indeed? God forbid!" Stumbling through the pieces and splinters of glass, he made his way to a bench by the further wall, placed there for the benefit of the old and infirm. He was trembling, and despite the chill, sweating. He looked like a man on the verge of collapse.

The mason had gone from the window and the young tutor half-hoped he would come in through the door and set him free to leave. But nobody came.

The priest fought his way out of shock by remembering his function. Souls, not promises broken under duress, or windows blown in by gales, should be his care.

"My son," he said, his voice quavering, "you have a rare gift—and a dangerous one. You must never exploit it. I speak now with the authority of my office. Keep silence about what you see. Remember Our Lord's injunction to those who saw Moses and Elias at the Transfiguration. 'Tell the vision to no man.'"

Somewhat bewildered, the young tutor said, "But the mason . . ."

"In Mallow," Father Alban said in a firmer voice, "there are two masons and three carpenters. All are at Triver, working on a new house. My first thought when I saw this calamity was: Who can ever board up the gap? The man you saw, Mason by name and by trade, died seven years ago, suddenly, unconfessed, unabsolved. Even his burial was incomplete, since none knew his name at the time. The only other person who knew of his—one might say—*devotion* to that window, the innkeeper's first wife, a most pious woman, had other things to think of, and was herself dead within half a year. I alone bore the burden of the secret."

"What secret?" The young man had forgotten his desire to get away.

"Allow me a moment to compose my mind. Sit here."

Father Alban moved a little. The young tutor accepted the invitation gratefully, for his lame leg was weak as well as short, and standing long in one position was a strain.

"Have a care! That is St. Cerdic's resting-place. We try not to tread . . . There again I have perhaps been negligent. It should be railed. There was never any money, alas, and even iron in short supply, since so many people are rearing impressive gateways. Andrew Mason showed great foresight in providing the lead."

He told his story badly, with asides and diversions and self-accusations. "I am in no position to judge any man; I assume that Andrew Mason was ordered to destroy. Perhaps against his will. And his end was terrible. When he did not join his workmen in Bywater, they waited for two or three days and then searched, but in the wrong place, so that he was buried as a stranger. Still, all men are known unto God. His horse was recognised . . . I forget how the news reached me, but I broke it to Katharine Gilderson and that I shall never forget. Just for a moment—no longer—she looked heart-broken, as though in a manner he had been very dear to her. Yet I am sure she had never entertained an unchaste thought. But for the changes, she would have been a nun, you understand. Probably an abbess. She had the learning and the sense of order. Her room was like . . . and her clothes. Always very fine, but giving a nun-like impression."

Enlightened at last, the young man said, "I think I saw *her*, too. She carried her hands folded, thus."

"As a nun would."

"I took her to be the landlady, careful of candles."

"Ah, yes. Did not one of the first to see Our Risen Lord suppose Him to be the gardener?"

"You think," the young man said slowly, "that the woman last night and the man, there, were ghosts?"

"I know it. Poor souls! Earth-bound because I failed. As I said, the *thought* has haunted me. How lightly we use words of grave import! Haunted, we say, with no conception of the real horror. A soul without a habitation! We who know, my son, must pray for their release."

The young tutor had learned the ineffectuality of prayer, years and years of it, praying that his leg would grow. There had been faith once, the certainty that when he woke he would be as other boys. Then doubt. Then disillusion souring into scepticism and a growing self-engrossment and belief in his talent. Many things he could not do; one thing he could.

Even now, made aware that he possessed another gift denied to the ordinary man, that of second sight, he was able to dismiss it as of comparatively little importance. Already something, not yet fully recognised, was at work within him.

IV

9 Marguerite

1620

"YOU'D BETTER GO TO BED, JIMMY," MARGUERITE GILDER-
son said when the clock showed eleven. "I'll wait up."

"If he's . . . I mean, can you manage, miss?"

Every bone in his body ached for bed; he'd been on his feet
since five in the morning, being pot-boy, stable-boy, waiter,
odd-job man. He was only eighteen and had grown four inches
in the last year, sappy growth that had not yet had time to
harden. He was also suffering the absurd yet intense pangs of
calf-love, in itself a debilitating thing.

"If I can't, I must learn," the girl said crisply. "If we lose
the inn, I shall probably have harder things to do than putting
a tipsy man to bed."

There! she had herself used one of the forbidden words, the
nicest—tipsy.

"Trouble," the boy said, "takes different people different
ways."

"I know! Now go to bed. That is an *order*, Jimmy."

"All right," he said. And then, "Where'll you wait?"

"Here."

He went out without so much as a good night. Offended,
she thought, by her emphasis on the word *order*. But somebody
must give orders and somebody must accept them. And, as
Jimmy said, trouble affected people differently. She knew how
it had affected her. Made her hard and cold and bitter and quite
capable of dealing with her father, drunk or sober.

Suddenly she heard some bumping. People said that, in
some haunted places, the supernatural manifestations took the
form of sounds like furniture being moved, and the One Bull
had for many years been said to be haunted, by what and in
what fashion, nobody could say. And Marguerite had never
been credulous or afraid of anything that could not be seen or
handled—or, and that only lately, afraid of being poor and
degraded.

175

She had been right in ignoring the bumping, for, within a minute or two, there was Jimmy, dragging in her very own chair from her very own room.

"I thought, if you must wait up, you might as well sit comfortable," he said. "Good night, miss. I hope... I hope it'll all work out right."

He did not wait to be thanked, but darted away to the back stairs and the servants' quarters, where only a few months earlier there had been four men, each with his own duty and place. Now, except for one ageing woman, growing deaf, but still a superb cook—when there was anything to cook—who still, even in the changed circumstances, went to bed the moment the evening meal had been served, and who snored—he was alone. He dropped on to his bed without undressing. Aware, within himself, of failure. The spirit was willing, but the flesh was weak.

His last thought, before complete exhaustion hit him a hammer blow, was that, despite all her bold talk, Miss Marguerite was the last person to be called upon to bear what she had been called upon to bear. She was so frail-looking, so like the flower after which she had been named, all white and gold. And she'd led such a sheltered life...

Before sitting down in the comfortable chair, Marguerite opened the door into the yard. The kitchen was stuffy, though the fire was out. Somewhere, in the trees in the abbey grounds a nightingale was singing, a waterfall of pure, melancholy sound, dropping through the warm May night. Inevitably, she was reminded of Mrs. Houghton's establishment at Highgate; the musical evenings, with Lucinda playing the harp, and herself at the spinet. All lost and gone forever, for even if Father had succeeded in borrowing enough to stave off immediate disaster, he would never again be able to afford to pay, not the fees (the word smacked of something that Mrs. Houghton strenuously avoided), but the contribution to that unusual, elegant household, in which, after some initial awkwardness, the landlord's daughter had settled so well and been so happy. And—this was the shrewdest cut of all—had a chance of making a decent marriage. For in addition to providing a background, some training, even some tenuous relationship with herself, Mrs. Houghton found husbands for girls whose fathers could provide dowries. Only in November, Mrs. Houghton had said, with Augusta safely engaged, "Well, Marguerite, dear, your turn next."

And look what she'd come to when she made her annual Christmas visit! It just didn't bear thinking about.

She heard the horse's hooves, sharp under the archway, muted in the yard, and, a few minutes later, her father's heavy steps. Reasonably steady. He came in, seemed surprised to see her; said, "My dearie, you shouldn't have waited," and sank down on the bench that flanked the table. It was obvious that he had been unsuccessful in his last desperate attempt to raise a loan.

He was not a man built for failure. He was some inches above average height, well-muscled and very handsome; well, even expensively dressed. Months of hard drinking had blurred his features and put some flabby flesh on him, but even now, just below the dejection of his expression and posture, the geniality, frankness, confidence, ability to be happy, things he had been born with and which forty-three years of good living had fostered, remained, only just submerged, ready to break through again at the slightest encouragement.

Of that the outer world had given him none; could Marguerite? She fumbled about in her mind for something of cheer to offer. Feeling, and sounding, idiotic, she said, "I saved your supper."

"I'm not hungry." And there was pathos there, too. He'd always been a hearty eater, kept what was known as a good table, not only for guests who paid, but also for servants.

"What I need is brandy," he said, and half rose. He'd never expected his daughter to wait upon him. But he sank back. "Tired," he said apologetically. He who had never been tired!

"I'll fetch it," she said. For what did it matter now, with the end of their world in sight, whether he went to bed half sober or dead drunk?

After a few gulps he said, "It's *you* I fret about. I can get some sort of job, and Edman's all right; the school'll look after him. But you, my dearie . . ."

Again she hunted for something cheerful to say.

"Father, I shall be all right. I can earn a living."

"Doing what?"

"I can do many things, a little." All things destined for use in a private, fairly well-to-do household.

She could cook a *little*, partly because, up to the age of

eleven, banned from the public rooms and the yard, she had been allowed into the kitchen, where old Becky, then ably assisted by two sturdy maids, had been willing to let little miss watch and help; and partly because at Mrs. Houghton's it was understood that young ladies should, without doing anything ruinous to the hands, acquire a certain amount of culinary skill. But to think of doing it day after day...

She could play the harp and the spinet a *little*; but how could a female, even one with outstanding talent, make a living by that?

She could sew and embroider a *little*, but she hated needle-work, and Mrs. Houghton believed that too close an application to it was bad for the eyes.

Read a *little*. That Marguerite had enjoyed, but Mrs. Houghton thought that too much reading was as bad as too much sewing.

Write a *little*. All Mrs. Houghton's young relatives, cousins to the third degree of herself or her deceased husband, could write a letter of invitation, congratulation or condolence, and copy a recipe.

Count a *little*; enough to deal with household accounts and see that they were not cheated.

The only one of her accomplishments which seemed worthy of mention was the needlework. She knew that she should say, boldly, cheerfully, "Father, there is no need to worry about me. I can always..."

The words just would not be said. Bent over, stitching away on other people's clothes forever and ever!

The brandy, combined with whatever else he had drunk earlier, loosened his tongue. Addressing her, not as his dearie, his darling daughter, but as though defending himself from some unworded accusation, he said,

"It was the law ruined me. Away back, there was a law, one alehouse to a village. The One Bull was an alehouse then, and Mallow a village. So we grew and did nicely. Then they say Mallow is a town, and up goes the King's Head to catch all the trade coming in from the south, and the Green Man from the north. Too much competition!" He drank angrily. "And as if that wasn't enough, they must move the sale yard! Right back to the old monks' time, Holywater Meadow was good enough and big enough for sales and fairs. Then some bloody bastards"—he broke off, appalled at himself. It was to protect her from such language that he'd banned her from the public rooms and the yard—"shifted it to next door to the Green Man, so dealers can bid out of the windows! They do. I've seen them do it. Then, to cap all, there's this law about labourers only allowed in taverns for an hour at noon. They don't get an hour at noon. Their time was at the end of the day. Not big money, but regular. Kept the moss from growing on the doorstep..." He tipped the bottle over his glass and watched the last drops run. "And that's the last of the brandy-wine!"

Suddenly tears came into his eyes. Not to fall, but to stay there, magnifying the red veins. "I've failed you, my sweet girl. You that I love. That I meant to do so well by...Simply made things worse...Better I'd let you toughen up from the first...Blasted rotten world."

Now she should say, Oh, no; that he'd conferred great advantages upon her; that she was grateful. Then go on to say that *because* she had lived with Mrs. Houghton, she was equipped to earn a living. But again the words would not be spoken. And indeed she agreed with him that, if they were now to be poor, it would have been better had she started emptying bedroom slops as soon as she could carry a bucket.

She looked at him sitting there, broken, maudlin, on the verge of tears, and felt some pity, but more revulsion, the greater because she had once admired him so much, regarded him as omniscient and omnipotent.

She said, as though to an enemy, "You'd better get to bed. Do you need help with your boots?"

"Not yet," he said. He pressed both hands against the tabletop and stood up; stood as though trying to remember or to decide something. "I know. Clean forgot the horse. Didn't even unsaddle the poor brute."

A loving, a dutiful, a compassionate daughter would have offered to go with him, offered to hold the lantern, found something hopeful, even if false, to say. She stood dumb, locked in her own stony misery, and when he said, "Good night," and stooped from his greater height to kiss her, she turned from the watery red eyes, the smell of brandy and other liquor. His kiss fell on her hair.

Horses first, Jimmy thought, waking from one of the crazy, indescribable dreams which had lately afflicted him. The thought of all he must do before he saw his bed again settled like heavy

armour on his body. But take things in order, and it was wonderful what a man could get through.

Running low on forage. Next thing we know we'll have
overnight horses and no fodder. Well, that was something for
the master to worry about. Poor man, he did worry and he did
scheme, going all the way to Colchester to borrow.

And what silly sod had gone and left the stable door open?
Easier for him, of course, with a great truss of hay under one
arm, and a skep of oats in his other hand; he would not have
to lift the catch with his elbow.

It was dawn-bright in the yard and dim in the stable, and
he walked straight into it, sagging, swaying. Dear God!

Dropping the hay and the oats, backing away and being sick
in an impossible fashion since his stomach was empty as a
drum, Jimmy, retching, producing nothing but spit, remembered something he'd heard a sailor say about sea-sickness.
Retching, the man had said, could go on for days, and if you
could force yourself to eat or drink something it gave your
stomach something to throw up. So, still retching, he made
his way to the barrel of water, drawn from the well overnight
and intended for the horses. Cupping his hands, he drank. Inside
him the water bounced, and he was sick again. Then restored.

Who was going to tell *her*?

Breaking calamitous news was woman's work, but the only
woman, aside from *her*, was old Becky who, if she chose to
hear and chose to understand, would be concerned for herself,
dreading the poorhouse.

Not old Becky. Me!

His demented imagination presented him with a picture:
Miss Marguerite, stricken to the heart, would turn to him for
comfort, throw herself into his arms, weep on his shoulder,
and he would come into his own, as in the dreams, and say,
"Leave everything to me." Simply by being male, by being
there, he would establish himself.

In reality it worked out quite differently, but not unsatis-
factorily. She, always lily-white, turned the colour of ashes,
and her eyes darkened with shock. Her pale lips parted, but
made no sound. Then she found her voice, found some kind
of strength.

"Who knows?"

"Nobody. I came . . ."

She nodded approbation. "I'll come. Wait outside."

In less than a minute she joined him in the passage that led to the kitchen. She was tying the sash of her robe very tightly as though to hold herself together.

"Have you a knife? Get one."

As they crossed the yard it occurred to him that she shouldn't see quite what he had seen. "Better let me go first," he said, intending to cut the dangling figure down, stretch it out so that it looked more ordinary, more like a dead man should look. But his hand was unsteady, and the rope of the halter tough. With two strands still unsevered, he found the knife taken from him.

"Hold him," Marguerite said. Jimmy did his best, but it was an impossible order; master and man collapsed together on the stable floor. As Jimmy struggled up, Marguerite said, "You must help me, Jimmy. We don't want a burial at the cross-roads, do we?"

That unhallowed burial ground, a rough triangle, lay at the opening of the Bosworth road, avoided by people, even in daylight, avoided, curiously, even by animals, though the grass grew lush over the unmarked humps. Criminals, suicides and, it was said, a witch, lay there.

"No. But I don't see . . ."

"You need know nothing. Just help me. Leave the thinking to me."

Just outside the stable door stood the sack-barrow, or barrel-barrow, rather like a bit of a ladder, its staves slightly concave. At one end was a ledge to prevent sack or barrel slipping. It was mounted on two small wheels and had handles at the upper end. Jimmy used it several times every day to fetch water for the household, for the stables. It saved many journeys with buckets, for the One Bull was still dependent upon the well which stood between its front door and the highway.

Jolting, steadied by his daughter, pushed by his servant, Ed Gilderson made his last-but-one journey. His bedroom adjoined Marguerite's, on the ground floor of the old thatched wing, whose upper rooms were now uninhabitable through decay and damp.

"*Across* the bed . . . as a man in a fit might fall," Marguerite said. "And head down." She hoped that the position would account for the peculiar appearance of her father's face. She had seen only one dead person in her life, her mother, in this very bed; Mother had ailed, more or less, since Edman's birth.

She'd been peevish and complaining and always inclined to favour her son at the expense of her daughter. "You must give way to Edman. You are the older and he is a boy." No loss to an eight-year-old, sure of her father. In death, Mother, her face the colour of tallow and her eyes closed, had looked very peaceful. Father, his face swollen and purplish, eyes staring and bulging, did not. (Drunk, acting on impulse, Ed Gilderson had bungled his own execution, allowing no sudden drop that would have broken his neck. He died of strangulation.)

By one of those chance circumstances known as coincidences, one of the four guests at the One Bull was a doctor, come all the way from London to tend Sir Richard Colman at Abbot's Hall, who was suffering from jaundice. Doctor Lee could easily have pushed on and been fed and lodged at his patient's home, but he was a touchy fellow and hated the way in which professional men were treated in great houses—a kind of grudging acknowledgement of a skill which placed them between family and steward or butler, and invariably meant a hard straw mattress and bad food. So, when he could—and he could afford to pamper himself—he chose to lodge at an inn.

By nature he was puritanical; he agreed with his king that the smoking of tobacco was detestable and harmful; he believed that most people drank and ate too much. Confronted by the dead body of a middle-aged man, gross, congested about the face and neck, Doctor Lee had no hesitation in reaching his verdict; an apoplectic fit. And secretly he thought the man fortunate; all men stricken in this fashion did not die; some lingered on, half paralysed, or with speech and sight impaired. The man's daughter, very frail-looking, but mercifully unhysterical, seemed able to take charge, and said she had a brother. So, satisfied, Doctor Lee rode on to Abbot's Hall where he was to prescribe for Sir Richard a diet of the most savage deprivation: no alcohol in any form, no cream, no butter; a little lean meat once a day, one egg a week. It had invariably proved to be effective.

So there was an absolutely ordinary and conventional funeral, and Ed Gilderson was laid to rest with his ancestors in St. Cerdic's churchyard.

I failed him, Marguerite thought again and again. Recalling that last evening when she had not said any of the things she *should*, she felt guilty. But the guilt was partially expunged because she had managed and contrived: deceived everybody.

Edman was granted two days' leave. His school was a bare half-mile from his home, but casual visits were not allowed. To a large extent the monkish tradition had survived, aptly, for the school was built on the site of the old monastery and incorporated one intact cloister.

Brother and sister had never been close; the age difference, four years, was just wrong, and their mother's unashamed partiality for her son had done nothing to lessen the elder child's inevitable jealousy. Even a common grief did nothing to bring them together, and everything that Edman said sounded callous, cold, self-interested. At thirteen he was already a lawyer in embryo, taking a great deal for granted, assuming that he was heir, and aggrieved that his inheritance should be so poor a thing.

"As an inn, it is worthless. Father must have realised. But the site must have some value. Two, possible three, houses could be built on it. And so near the centre of the town."

Up to that moment Marguerite would have denied—and with truth—that she had any feeling for her home. Father's strict rule about keeping the family rooms and the public ones apart had resulted in a feeling of restriction. She'd left for Mrs. Houghton's without regret in the first place, and subsequently, at the end of each Christmas visit, with positive pleasure. But now something, probably no more than a wish to oppose Edman, made her say, "It is one of the oldest buildings in Mallow, and Gildersons have always lived here."

"This Gilderson does not propose to do so. And if Father had intended me to, he would not have sent me to school."

"He went to school himself."

"Only for two years. *I* shall proceed to Cambridge and take my degree in law." He switched his attention from himself for a second and said, "You, of course, will get married. If we can sell the site for a hundred pounds, you shall have ten as a dowry."

"Open-handedness will be your downfall," the ungrateful girl said.

Mr. Hutton, Mallow's one lawyer, called upon his gentleman clients, but received ordinary ones in his office. However, out of feeling for two children so recently bereaved and left in such sorry circumstances, he conceded a point and went to the One Bull. As well as performing an act of kindness, he was considering the interests of another client. He wanted to make an off-the-cuff assessment of what the inn, its contents and the ground it stood upon were likely to fetch.

Both the young Gildersons, he thought, were curiously unyouthful—not in looks, in manner. Mr. Hutton's business brought him into contact with many bereaved persons, and he had reached the cynical conclusion that, with adults, what a deceased person had to leave, and how he had disposed of it, was of paramount importance. (Or, of course, there was the kindlier view—a busy concern with material things did distract the mind from bereavement.) Children, however, tended to be more emotional. These were not. After a thought, wistful and unfounded, that his own two, about the ages of these but in reverse order, would seem more grieved, if he, their father, fell dead of a fit, Mr. Hutton was relieved to be dealing with such controlled young people, for what he had to tell them was bad.

Astonishing, too. Who would have believed, short of seeing it in black and white, that Sir Richard Colman of Abbot's Hall had lent Edman Gilderson, of the One Bull in Mallow, a hundred pounds at 10 per cent interest—and with the inn as security?

The boy said, obviously understanding the wording if not the implication, "Sir Richard has lien on the property until the debt is paid back?"

"That is so. There are other debts, of course, all trivial in comparison. Sir Richard has first claim."

Not his to criticise the law, but he had more than once thought it harsh that a secured loan took precedence over a mere debt to people who had provided goods or services and had received no interest. Of a hundred pounds, loaned five years ago, Sir Richard had already received fifty.

Marguerite said, "So whether the inn stays open or is sold depends upon Sir Richard?"

"That is so."

"If it is sold, I shall be homeless. And without occupation." A statement of fact, as though she had made some remark about the weather.

"You have no relatives?"

"None."

Mr. Hutton thought: A pity! He spared a second to wonder

what became of such girls. Less than a hundred years ago—incredible to think what had happened in such a relatively short time—there would have been some sort of nunnery.

"The inn has been your occupation?"

"Since Christmas I have run it with some help from an old woman and a boy. My father had not been completely well for some time."

A kind way of putting it. A man's debts, his lack of relatives, and the fact that he had made a completely idiotic will—but legal, in that it was properly signed and witnessed—might be concealed until his death, but a man drunk well before noon, albeit on his own premises, drew attention.

"So I understand," Mr. Hutton said, and without thinking, he glanced at the girl's hands. White as milk, narrow, with exceptionally long fingers. He doubted if she had ever done a real day's work in her life. She had supervised. And the boy who had helped was certainly not this rather precocious brother. He wore the uniform of the grammar school: a simple somewhat monkish garment, grey, buttoned all down the front with wooden buttons, carved with what St. Cerdic's symbols had dwindled down to—just a crown with upsticking points and two arrows transfixing it. Anybody handy with a knife could carve such an emblem, but it took more skill to make the wolf's head, so it had been quietly abandoned.

Oh dear, oh dear, I must control my thoughts, fix my mind!

Edman said, "Sir, what is the site of the inn worth?"

"I cannot say. It depends upon the demand. And possibly some part of the building could be converted into a dwelling house or shop. I should like to look over it."

A curious, rambling irregular building, partly in fair repair, partly decayed. The upper-floor rooms on one side were damp and rotten under the sagging thatch—and it was merely a matter of time before the rooms below would show patches where the rain had seeped through. The flint-built wing was in better condition, but plainly built to serve a special purpose—housing people for a night or two. Not suitable for use by a family of such substance as to afford, or desire, so much space. The most attractive room in the place was in the centre. It was panelled, and the surrounds and overmantel of the wide hearth were of black marble. The most demanding of newly-rich wives would consider it a suitable parlour, except for one glaring disadvantage: it opened straight onto the street. Perhaps a porch,

Mr. Hutton thought. But then, this admirable living-room would be separated from the habitable bedrooms and the stairway that led to them by a long passage which skirted the kitchen and the room which served as a cellar.

It was highly improbable, he thought, that the kind of person he had in mind, moneyed, but not rich, would consider setting up house here.

But there was space; there were a yard and outbuildings; there was a garden. Knock the whole thing down, and it would be possible to build three moderately-sized houses between what remained of the abbey wall and the road that led to the church and the graveyard. Proximity to a burial ground was not an advantage. Shops, then. And immediately the planning mind faced another obstacle. All those sound, rain-proof rooms were only accessible through the main house.

Quite hopeless. It would be his unwelcome task to report to Sir Richard Colman that the One Bull seemed to have been one of the less lucky investments. Still, he had his interest, and, standing or dismantled, the inn should fetch around a hundred pounds. This information he would, he thought, defer conveying for a day or two, since Sir Richard had suffered from jaundice severe enough to warrant sending to London for a doctor. Even easy-going men, suffering from this ailment, turned liverish of humour, and in the best health, Sir Richard had never been good humoured...

Marguerite, face to face with Sir Richard, thought: If I can get round *him*, I can get round anybody. Sir Richard's face was still yellowish, but the stern regime prescribed by Doctor Lee had abolished one horrible sympton—seeing everything yellow. All day he had gone around seeing blue as blue, red as red. And he saw her as she was, young, charming and pretty, and beautifully mannered. Her curtsy, as she entered, was as graceful as a flower bowing before a gust of wind and then straightening up. With a wife and two daughters, all clumsily built and still awkward, though the girls had tuition from one of the best dancing-masters, Sir Richard appreciated this girl's grace and the way, when asked to be seated, she sat, back straight, feet together, hands folded in her lap.

Despite all this, when she said, "Sir Richard, I have come to ask a great favour of you," he was not disposed to grant whatever she might be about to ask. And when, in a quiet, most pleasing voice, she explained what she wanted, his wrath exploded.

"Great God!" he said. "Never in my life have I heard anything so ridiculous. So outrageous!" Then he remembered that Doctor Lee had drawn some connection between loss of temper and the liverish humour. Trying to control his temper made him still more angry. "In a weak moment I made a loan to your father. For a specific purpose, mark you! He planned to rebuild that tumbledown eyesore. I've seen no evidence of such work! In fact, the place is worth far less now than when I lent money on it. And now you have the audacity to come here . . . to come here and ask me to transfer the loan to you. A minor in the eyes of the law. And a woman!"

"But I would pay the interest. And the security—the inn—would still be there. I hope, more prosperous. I could practise certain economies."

On the night of his death, Father had done most of his drinking elsewhere; but for months, perhaps years, he had drunk at home, and had been given at times to a drunkard's lavish hospitality. Free drinks because somebody had a birthday or somebody's wife had had a baby, or it was Christmas, Lady Day, Easter, May Day. Any excuse.

I'll stop all that! As Jimmy had said, trouble took different people in different ways; Father had run away from it, soaking his wits in a barrel or a bottle, trying to cover the real situation with a fine show of open-handedness.

"Economise till you are black in the face—an ailing business is a failing business and will grow worse."

"An ailing business is not necessarily a failing one, sir. My father suffered several setbacks and lately was not in good health. I have ideas which I am anxious to try—but of course, while he lived, I could not interfere. But I am so sure that I could improve things that I promise to pay, not merely the interest, but five pounds off the debt each year."

He thought that over and rejected it.

"That would be to place an unwarrantable burden upon yourself and an increased risk upon me. I see no future for the building, but the ground is worth about a hundred pounds."

"So your loan would be recovered." He nodded. She said, almost dreamily, "The various smaller debts—the brewer, the wine merchant, the miller and the forage merchant, amount in total to about twenty pounds. My home is demolished, the ground is sold. Your loan, Sir Richard, is safe. The small debts must die with the man who incurred them. Will not that give rise to ill-feeling?"

She asked the question innocently enough, but Sir Richard, staring at her, saw that her eyes were not, as he had at first thought, blue, but green. Grass-snake green!

"Mr. Hutton handles my business affairs. And he is very discreet."

After a tiny pause, she said, "I am not! I should feel it my bounden duty to explain to all those poor little men, with their poor little debts, that, though there had been a sale, they could not be paid, because you . . ."

He looked at her with something near horror. It was not in nature for a girl, so young a girl, to have dealt such a telling blow, to have named four men with votes to cast.

"Are you repeating, like a parrot, words Mr. Hutton put into your mouth?"

"Mr. Hutton only explained the situation. And looked over the inn—thinking little of it."

"Did he suggest that you should come here? With your proposal? And the argument about ill-feeling?"

"How could he? I only decided to come late this afternoon. Nobody knows. As for the ill-feeling, that occurred to me just now, when you refused, and I could foresee the result of that refusal."

"Hmm! You appear to be a young woman of remarkable foresight. Tell me this. Foreseeing, as surely you must, that what you propose would not be acceptable to any reasonable man, what alternative would you?"

"None. I hoped that you would think my plan reasonable. But . . . Well, yes. There has been talk about Sir Robert Thickthorn building some new almshouses . . ."

He jumped as though he had been stung. For eighty years Colmans and Thickthorns had been rivals, competing for power, prestige, public esteem, public office. In the neck-to-neck race the Colmans had always been handicapped by being careful with their money. The Thickthorns were downright extravagant. Sir Robert Thickthorn had been one of the first men to buy the new and hereditary title of baronet. Sir Richard Colman, naturally, must have one, too, and it had cost him one thousand and ninety-five pounds. Ten years ago, but he could still feel the wrench. Now his inherited paranoia assured him that behind all this was a deep-laid plot to make him look mean and grasping and Sir Robert open-handed and benign. Such feelings must be concealed.

"Oh. And how much did he offer?"

She looked so genuinely puzzled that either she must be innocent—or the best actress ever born.

"Sir Robert? Why, nothing! How could he? I only this moment thought of it myself. But it would be the perfect solution. If Sir Robert would consider it. I am not well-informed about money, but I think that a hundred pounds for a building already standing might be cheaper for him. Then I could repay your loan to my father. Twelve deserving old people could move in immediately. I should still have some space left. And possibly Sir Robert would add to his consideration for the poor by paying a trivial sum for the left-overs which no inn can avoid."

He thought, A she-devil, inspired by the devil. Nothing else could account for such dead accuracy. But, feeling that, he kept his head and in his turn was cunning.

"You are young, lacking in experience. Problems solved on impulse beget others. Let us think." He spoke at some length and with considerable feeling about the deserving poor being likely to receive not only left-overs from the kitchen but also lees of wine, dregs from barrels, and getting tipsy and therefore becoming undeserving poor. And if custom at the One Bull were slack already, how much more so would it be when jibes could be spoken: Are you putting up at the Almshouse? He mentioned lice and uncleanly habits, so prevalent even among the deserving. And . . . "Old people die," he said, "and there is nothing more conducive to melancholy, the very opposite of what a good inn's atmosphere should be, than a death in the house. No, indeed. Now that I have time to consider your original proposition, I regard it as preferable to this hare-brained scheme."

Rattling back towards Mallow in the small, two-wheeled cart, used for all purposes of fetching and carrying, and pulled by a thickset, strong pony, Marguerite thought, I have won! But only the first round. I shall not be homeless; Jimmy and Becky will not be homeless, but we still have a long way to go.

Entering Mallow from the north, she passed the Green Man with its yard all a-bustle, many windows lighted. Her victory over Sir Richard suddenly paled and lost substance. Over the archway at the One Bull the gay sign creaked. She looked up at it and saw for the first time with seeing eyes. Not a mere oblong board painted, but the silhouette of a bull about to charge, cut from metal and enamelled. It never faded or cracked; a rain shower could wash it clean and bright again. The little strip of grass beneath the white animal's feet was starred with small flowers. Somebody in the past had had money to fling about!

Behind the gallant sign the yard was quiet, and in the stable with its ten stalls there were three horses— one of them Father's.

Ridiculous! Outrageous! Well might Sir Richard use such words. The weight and size of her undertaking almost cowed her. But she straightened her shoulders and composed her face before entering the kitchen, and she was able to say, with quiet triumph, "The inn will not be sold—at least for a year."

She had confided in neither Jimmy nor Becky, and now she explained nothing. As she settled down to the supper that had been kept waiting for her, one aspect of inn-life in most desperate need of economy was there on the table, clamouring for attention: a joint of roast beef from which only two portions had been cut.

It was one of the most damnable of travellers' fancies that at an inn they always expected a roast, and that roast to be beef, the most expensive of meats. Offer the relatively inexpensive mutton or pork, offer fowl or fish, however fresh, and the discontent was plain. They would go away and say that beds at the One Bull were clean and comfortable, but the food was below standard.

Of course, most travellers had been on the road all day, had had little or no dinner, and felt they had a right to expect... And, of course, Becky couldn't possibly know that tonight there would be only two guests. And, of course, now three of them were eating—two heartily, Marguerite with little appetite.

"I can well remember," Becky said, as though sensing what was in Marguerite's mind, "when labouring men was allowed, they'd come in and eat anything that was handy. Eat it standing, too, right there in the tap-room. Slice of any cold meat between two slabs of bread, and a pint, or mebbe a half, and they looked on it as a treat."

Jimmy thought that anybody who ate standing up would be heartily welcome. Two guests, seated and very demanding, had kept him very busy. One had declared the mustard was stale. "Bring some fresh." "I like horse-radish sauce with my beef." One thought that salad should be eaten before meat, the other took his after, and wanted a little more oil on it.

But as soon as the kitchen meal was finished he set about the washing up. It was thanks to him that Marguerite's hands remained smooth and white.

The idea of having a few permanent guests, paying something but not enough to make them fussy, recurred to Marguerite several times during the next few weeks. She visualised elderly people, without settled homes or families, not so old as to be sickly or half-witted or bothersome in any way. Of such ideal people there seemed to be a great dearth. She mentioned the matter to Mr. Hutton in a tentative way when he looked in, agog with curiosity. Sir Richard had told him nothing, except that the One Bull was to continue as before. And the girl was little more communicative. Yes, she said, Sir Richard had been extremely kind and agreed not to press for payment. Mr. Hutton, who had a strong puritan streak and who knew Sir Richard pretty well, thought it an odd arrangement. He was glad that the girl was not to be rendered homeless, but one couldn't help feeling a slight suspicion.

When Marguerite said, "Mr. Hutton, you know many people," and mentioned her scheme he said, after a little thought, "But people such as you would welcome—I mean with a little money and no...er...disability or handicap—are never at lack for a home. I know of only one family who would gladly rid themselves...But the unfortunate lady is quite mad. You find custom still slack?"

"It always improves slightly in summer," she said, trying to be brave. "But not enough."

"I will," he said, "put in a good word for the One Bull whenever I can."

"Thank you." A good word, she thought, something to focus people's attention on this inn and make them pass...Another brilliant idea flowered, and with help from Jimmy was put into action. It worked for a week. Then Mr. Hutton re-appeared, looking sorrowful.

"I wish you had consulted me. It is the wording which is

offensive, possibly even libellous. You see, to display a public sign saying that the One Bull is the best inn in Mallow is derogatory to the King's Head and the Green Man. It may be true—but that makes it even more offensive."

"So I must take them down?"

"That has been done already. Nothing less would content Mr. Hoskins and Mr. Bragg."

She had spent a long time preparing the signs; she painted rather well, and each bore the sign of the One Bull copied from the one over the archway; white bull on green grass, blue sky behind him, and then in thick black lettering the offensive words.

"If I changed what they object to, to 'Stay at the One Bull,' would that be permissible, Mr. Hutton?"

"Permissible, but unwise. It would invite retaliation. Neither Mr. Hoskins nor Mr. Bragg is . . . er . . . a long-suffering man, and though I would be the last person in the world to wish to offend you, your . . . er . . . position renders you exceptionally vulnerable."

"To scandal?"

"Yes. The slightest whisper . . ."

"The slightest whisper and *I* shall come running to you crying 'Slander!'"

How in the world was she able to make the distinction?

"That would be totally unwise. By far your best plan would be—with the busy season approaching—to reach some kind of agreement with the other landlords. Possibly they would prefer, and their guests certainly would, not to be so over-crowded at certain times. I know that a certain antagonism was engendered some years ago. Perhaps it is time for the olive-branch. I have already tried, to an extent, to prepare the way."

"Thank you. I will think about it. Do you know where my signs are now?"

"Yes. In my office."

"I'll send Jimmy to collect them."

"They must not be displayed in their present form."

"I understand that."

Mr. Hutton thought, almost angrily, that people who looked and indeed were so vulnerable, should be more willing to be guided. It was not, really, for him to say that both Hoskins and Bragg were uncouth and ruthless characters. And he had no wish to mention that, in addition to spreading scandal and blackening her name, they could and probably would act against the horses in her stables, against the guests in her dining-room.

A layer of thick black paint over the libellous words. Let it dry. Then, brilliant white on black, paint the amendments. Once again go with Jimmy under cover of darkness, to plant one, firm on its pointed post, into the grass verge about a quarter of a mile north of Sheepgate, the other the same distance south of Rivergate. The maddening thing was that people did notice, and for several nights the One Bull was full to capacity.

But a sign on a pointed post was as easily plucked out as it was planted. After the fourth removal, she gave in.

10 Marguerite and the Shearers

THEN, ON A HOT MORNING IN MIDSUMMER, THE SHEARERS arrived.

Long ago the owners of sheep-runs had realised that though one man, helped perhaps by a dog or an active child, could manage vast numbers of sheep on wide acres, shearing was another matter, needing many hands, all at work at the same time; and they must be skilled hands, too. So the gangs of men, each with his own shears, had come into being and formed, if not a guild, a craft.

Ordinary country people regarded the shearing gangs with aversion, thought them little better than outlaws, locked up their hen-houses, counted their geese, issued grave warning to their daughters. The shearers, though they lived rough, fed on the whole badly, and worked themselves to death every day while the season lasted, thought of themselves as the élite among labourers, free, independent and extremely well paid.

This particular gang, twenty of them, marched into the One Bull as though they owned it. Their spokesman asked, "Where's the landlord?"

"My father? He is dead."

"I'm sorry. A fair man . . ."

"I can get you anything you wish."

"A proper dinner. We've starved for a fortnight and walked from Daneley this morning."

"It is a little early for dinner."

"We know. We'll drink first. Not beer. Wine, if you please." She looked dubious and he laughed. "No need to worry your pretty head; we can pay."

Becky, hastily consulted, confirmed this. They were the scum of the earth, but each man earned more in a day than regular labourers earned in a week.

They were not ill-behaved, though their table-manners were uncouth. They ate hurriedly when the food came, but they ate with appreciation. It was evident that the spokesman, always addressed as Captain, had them well in hand. When he said, "Drink up, boys. We're on our way," they obeyed as one man. This discipline emboldened Marguerite who, aided by Jimmy, had served the meal and the beer to which the drinkers had moved after the wine, and had been fingering another idea.

"What did you mean about having starved for a fortnight?"

He explained, curbing his language, but allowing resentment to show. In some places the work contract included board. "Generally bad," he said. "Stuff nobody else'd eat." Sometimes they found their own food; and that was difficult. "At the end of the day we're dead weary—except Tar-boy. And the shops, the inns'll fob him off with anything."

"I wouldn't," Marguerite said. "I would bring you a good meal—cold of course, but good. And beer as cool as I could manage."

Once or twice, in the summer, Mrs. Houghton had organised little outings with what she called alfresco meals. Everybody had enjoyed them very much, and declared that even a hard-boiled egg tasted better when eaten in the open air.

Captain described to her their well-planned working route, assuming that she knew her own neighbourhood. She did not, but as he talked his big, brown, scarred hand drew a map on the air. Roughly a shape like a fan, with Mallow where the handle would be.

"I can manage that," she said.

"We'd pay and pay well," Captain promised.

"Your father—God rest him—would turn in his grave. Mixing with scum!" Becky was horrified.

"I mixed with them yesterday and took no harm."

"If you can't see the difference, I can. Yesterday you was under your own roof, with Jimmy going in and out. *And me here!*" The very essence of chaperonage summed up in three words. The presence of another, and senior, female was a magic safeguard. It was rather surprising to hear old Becky echoing Mrs. Houghton's beliefs.

"It's a way of making money out of left-overs." Marguerite spoke all the more defiantly because, waking in the night, she had entertained some nervous qualms.

"It's a way of getting yourself robbed—or worse. The roads ain't safe for anybody after dark these days, leave alone a young woman. And ask yourself what the men'll think of you. They work half naked. At least take Jimmy."

"How can I? Guests might arrive with heavy bags and horses. Could you deal with them? If I took you with me, could Jimmy deal with the horses, the bags *and* whatever food was needed? If I send Jimmy, I'm left to deal with heavy bags and horses."

"Better that than going amongst a lot of wild men alone, and driving home in the dark. Better still give up the whole idea."

"Becky, I *can't*. I've paid a few shillings here and a few there; I've promised further payments next month. Do you realise that yesterday every one of those wild men had a two-shilling ordinary, with wine and then ale? If they pay half as much for a cold supper, and for the ale extra, and stay in the district for a fortnight, I can keep my promises and show that I am in earnest. It's a God-sent chance."

"God send it may be so," Becky said, giving in at the mention of God, the only refuge and protector the poor and the desperate knew. God had, on the whole, been very good to her. Born one of a large poor family she'd thought herself blessed to be taken into the One Bull as soon as she was able to be useful: plenty of food; a chance to learn things; a kind master, and another, and another. She was now older than her first master had been when he died; she had outlived his son and his son. She reckoned that she must now be well over seventy, but her place was secure—in fact, as the fortunes of the inn declined, her value and power had increased. And she was still going, a bit forgetful now and then, tiring easily but otherwise sound. And having exerted herself to argue with Marguerite, said all that it was her duty to say, and been confounded, Becky placed her faith in God and busied her hands with the making of the nice little loaves of bread which Marguerite had asked for—and thus started the argument. The most anybody could do was the best they could and leave the rest to God. Though sometimes the saints . . . Out of fashion now, but when you could remember seventy years, so must be three or four years more than that, you had lived through so many changing fashions that you could no longer be worried about fashion. Becky still marked loaves with a cross and believed that the saints would often give attention to little things when God was too busy.

So, when Jimmy, scowling and glum, announced that the cart was ready, Becky put a hand to her neck and hauled on a piece of string. "Take St. Christopher with you. He's the one to look after travellers." Suspended from the string was a little medallion, made of base metal, and so worn by use that its design was difficult to see. Marguerite stooped so that the old woman could slip it over her curls, gently pull them free, and then tuck the little charm into the top of her bodice.

Becky had all day been undecided about her young mistress's hair; it was largely that which made her look pretty, and perhaps it would be wiser to cover it with a white mob-cap such as servants wore. On the other hand, perhaps the rough company into which she was venturing would have more respect for a lady.

Longacre, well to the south of the town, was ideal sheep country, touching the river at one end of its narrow length, then rising to land easily drained but not treeless. It was not land attached to any great house, or even a farmhouse. Only the shepherd and his family lived there in a clod cottage. Except for the girl's promise to bring supper, the men would have been dependent upon their own resources, which meant what Tar-boy could find on a hasty dash into Mallow, late in the day. And their drink would certainly have been river water.

They worked, as Becky had warned, half naked and, moving

away from the stinking shearing-pen, had thrown themselves down in attitudes of exhaustion in the shade of a group of hawthorn trees. On the sheep-nibbled, thymy grass the pony's hooves and the iron-bound wheels of the little cart were almost soundless. Marguerite was quite near before they were aware of her presence. Then somebody said, "She's here, Captain." He rose at once and came to meet her. He was filthy, his face and torso covered with dust through which sweat had channelled. And she had never known that men had mats of hair on their chests.

He was totally at ease. He said, "So you came. I was beginning to wonder."

"It was rather farther than I expected, and I had to stop twice to ask my way."

They were all on their feet now, and crowding round. One last lingering light from the sun, going down in a splendour of crimson and scarlet, illuminated them all, dirty, near-naked men. But so grateful!

Marguerite had prepared this alfresco meal somewhat on Mrs. Houghton's lines, but more substantial, since it was intended for men. All the same it was a meal that had cost very little; the meat enclosed in the nice little loaves, which Becky had made so unwillingly, was left-over meat; the lettuces and radishes in the washbowl of salad were home grown, and at this time of year, hens laid so well that eggs were almost valueless.

To the shearers, however, this was a feast, something unknown in their experience.

The two small casks of beer, lowered last night by Jimmy— as disapproving as Becky, but less articulate—into the well to cool, and then hauled out and covered with wet cloths to retain the coolness, presented a problem. A cask, in order to yield its contents, must stand upon something, and here there was nothing but the cart's tail, which meant that she must wait until the last drop was drawn, and light in the west faded and dusk fell. She had hoped to deliver the sundown meal and be off. Tomorrow she must remember to bring one of the cross-legged trestles.

But the journey home, the braving of the darkness, and all the disapproval from Becky and Jimmy was well worthwhile, for Captain said, "Such a feast, and brought to us, is over and beyond the worth of the two-shilling ordinary that we had yesterday. I told you we'd pay, and so we will."

It was like having twenty guests sitting down at one time in the dining room—and infinitely more profitable.

She took pains to make the makeshift meals as palatable and as varied as possible: meat patties, sausages, liver. She took onions, both fresh and pickled, mince-pies, gingerbread, saffron buns. Even when the men moved on to a place where food was provided, they begged her to continue her visits. "What Mrs. Bettison calls board you could put in your eye and see no worse for," Captain said.

Presently she began to do little errands for the men; they wanted tobacco, new clay pipes to replace broken ones, new belts. They were always punctilious in proffering such requests. "If it ain't too much trouble, lady." "If it ain't imposing," and their thanks were fervent.

On the second night Captain met her, wearing a shirt; on the third, others had copied him, and by the fourth almost every man gave this sign of respect. It was probably true that Father would indeed turn in his grave if he could see her alone with twenty men of the kind from whom he had tried to shelter her, and Mrs. Houghton, if she could know, would certainly swoon, but Marguerite was enjoying something which had started from a mercenary motive and turned into something else. From the moment in the morning when she began planning what would please and surprise them until the moment when, having been pleased and surprised, they wished her good night, she thought about them—always as two entities, Captain and the others.

Such a way of thinking seemed ordinary, inevitable. In every way he stood apart. The men themselves paid tribute to whatever it was that made him different, although he worked, slept, ate alongside them. He was not the biggest or the oldest—size and age were both qualities which commanded respect—yet his authority seemed to be absolute, and the men trusted him even with their hard-earned money.

Marguerite Gilderson had spent much of her life in an atmosphere so class-conscious that any mention of the fact that her father kept an inn was absolutely forbidden, and her reading had been restricted to stories suitable for young ladies; the prince might fall in love with the goose-girl, but she was a princess in disguise—or the roles might be reversed. So she toyed sometimes with the notion that Captain's ascendancy was due to the fact that he was actually of superior class; that there was a mystery about him; he was a gentleman come down in the world. Yet there was not the slightest shred of evidence to support this romantic fancy. His speech was as homely as that of the men, and once, when he was angry and unaware of her presence, the expressions he used were distinctly coarse.

Yet the power which he exercised over the gang began to spread towards her; it was *his* look of welcome, *his* word of thanks, *his* good night which mattered.

For her age (now just seventeen, for she had had her birthday early in June), and considering her background, she was an exceptionally clear-sighted, competent and self-willed girl. She could have said with complete honesty that she had determined to save the inn because she did not want to be homeless—or see Jimmy and Becky homeless. In the same good cause she had faced and to an extent outwitted Sir Richard Colman. She had taken on the task of feeding the shearers because it meant ready money and a chance to reduce her debts sufficiently to show that she was in earnest and therefore deserving of further credit. Then the men's gratitude had fed her vanity, and the providing of nice things for them, very cheaply, had confirmed her opinion that she was a good manager. It had also convinced her that the world was less dangerous a place than people said, or than she had imagined. After the first evening she had not felt that venturing alone among so many men was any challenge to courage; after the second, driving home alone in the gathering darkness lost its terrors.

Becky still worried and grumbled, and always asked, "Have you got St. Christopher?" Marguerite could now think how amusing it was that an old woman, whose most venturesome journey was to go on foot to St. Cerdic's church, should have acquired and attached such importance to the saint who was the travellers' friend.

Jimmy still seemed silent and sulky, but that Marguerite attributed to the fact that, while she was absent, he had to be active inside the inn and in the yard. Becky prepared food, but did not serve it, and Jimmy was certainly overworked. And although the inn was never comfortably full, it was never completely empty, either. Two guests; four; one night, six: too much work for Jimmy to handle. "If only we could be *sure* of six every night, Jimmy, I'd look around for a boy to help you in the yard, or a girl to wait at table. But we can't be sure, can we?"

"I can muddle on," Jimmy said. "After all, this can't last. Three weeks is as long as *they* ever stay in one place."

So it was Jimmy, who would, he assured himself, gladly have died for her—even the slow death by overwork—who struck the first warning note.

It was true. Time sped when you were busy and happy, and she had not realised that work on a sheep-run called the Grindle was the last job the shearers would have in this area. In four days' time they'd move north.

She told herself resolutely that it was the cessation of regular income which caused the depression which attacked her. But that was nonsense, because when she first began taking over the alfresco meals and gloated at selling left-overs for such a high price, her mind had leaped over the next weeks and fastened on the wool sales with optimism. The sales must bring custom to the inn, and after them would come the Bartholomew Fair, and after that the cattle sales. Feeding the shearers then had seemed merely a stop-gap, a means of paying off parts of her debts and proving that she was credit-worthy. Now, at the thought of their imminent departure, something dropped like a fog between her and the future.

She told herself that gloom was the result of over-tiredness—a valid excuse, for she had never neglected a routine duty in order to prepare her pleasant surprises for the men or to run their little errands. She'd laid tables well in advance, ready for the influx of customers which never came, made beds, aired and dusted rooms, checked on stores, planned meals, looked after the garden, exerted herself to be pleasant to creditors and to guests.

It was true that Becky had done the actual extra cooking, but she'd done it unwillingly and had needed to be cajoled. She had actually said that she had forgotten how to make saffron buns—there'd been so little call for them lately.

It was true that, when the baskets of food were ready, Jimmy carried them out and helped haul out and wrap the casks of chilled beer, but where anything else to do with the shearers was concerned he'd shown a kind of lethargy which had demanded something of her spirit to dispel and get into action. Often enough, when she got into the little cart and sat down on the hard plank that served it for a seat, it was the first time she had sat down all day. Then came the driving, all on rough, jolting roads, and some over mere tracks. And the truth was that she was not built for hard physical work; she was too fine-boned and had none of the wiry resilience that could compensate for lack of sturdiness.

But always, always, as she approached the place where the men were waiting, strength and spirit would revive. She was never vivacious or talkative, partly because it was not in her nature to be so, and partly because, even when she was liking the men best and basking in their gratitude, she was aware of the gap between them. But she smiled and said gracious things: "I hoped you'd enjoy sausages for a change" even, "And now, what would you like tomorrow?" They never proffered a suggestion.

They! An anonymous mob of brown faces. Men out of whom she was making good money, men whom it pleased her to please.

Captain was a different matter, though he was just as anonymous since she did not know his given name. But now she was face to face with the fact that all the rest could go north without causing her a real pang, whereas the thought of not seeing him again blotted out the light of the sun.

The idea that she was in love with him dawned very slowly, and was entirely unacceptable, as incredible as a blue rose or a green moon. She was innocent and ignorant and class-conscious. Mrs. Houghton had seen to that. There were the poems, the plays, the masques and the stories in which love, being in love, falling in love were prevalent themes, but nothing to do with reality. To regard them as real would be as silly as thinking that you could have a rainbow for breakfast. It was, of course, desirable that girls should be married, have homes and families of their own, and Mrs. Houghton worked hard to bring this desirable end about. A girl not positively repellent in appearance, and with a reasonable dowry, with the sponsorship of Mrs. Houghton could be sure of a husband, whom, in due time she would love because he would give her his name, provide for her, father her children. (How exactly this would come about was one of the mysteries. There were whispers, of course. The general belief was that it was done by a certain kind of kiss given by a man in no way related. There were other theories, too bizarre to be credited, though one of Mrs. Houghton's girls, coming back after marriage, had confided to her best friend that there was nothing enviable about the married state. It was just like being poked with a stick.)

However, little of this had any relevance to Marguerite's feelings now—the sheer desolation at the thought of Captain going, the knowledge that only four more evenings remained. After that he would not come forward with a smile to greet her, give her a hand down from the cart, lift out the baskets and hand them to underlings, help her to set up the two casks on the cart-tail, and say, "Line up, boys; don't push."

At the same time it seemed to her impossible that she, Marguerite Gilderson, a member of an old and respected Mallow family and one-time member of Mrs. Houghton's "family," could be in love with a foot-loose shearer.

On the evening of the day after Jimmy's remark had alerted her, she examined Captain carefully and critically, trying to be objective in her assessment of him. As usual he smiled briefly as he greeted her—but then, so did they all, and some with heartier, more long-lasting smiles than his. As usual he helped her alight from the cart, but in a businesslike way, immediately turning his attention to the baskets, setting up the casks.

Against the deep tan of his skin, his bleached hair, his pale grey eyes and his teeth seemed extraordinarily light: an attractive contrast, but it could be matched by half the company. The others were dark-eyed and dark-haired. There were several in the gang with more claim to good looks. He was shapely and muscular, light on his feet, but these were common qualities. So why? Why, when she said, "Are you moving on Friday?" did her throat hurt, and her voice sound small and plaintive?

"Yes," he said. "Norfolk next week."

Another man said, "And we shan't half miss you, ma'am."

"I shall miss you, too. You've been my best customers!"

But it was Captain and him alone she would miss.

On impulse, she asked, "And after Norfolk?"

"Yorkshire. Then we're done for the year."

Even now, when she was struggling with an unfamiliar emotion, the question of ways and means, the business of earning, the money morass into which she had been so abruptly catapulted, stayed with her, and her next question was very practical. "Do you earn enough during the summer to last through the winter?"

"Oh, no. We do other, different things. I go out with the herring fleet. Some of the others, too."

They did different things. A few of them were not the rootless nomads they appeared to be, and after the late shearing in Yorkshire would hurry home to help with the harvest and the ploughing. Others found work for a time in the mass slaughter of animals which took place every autumn, or worked on the coal cobs, bringing coal from the north to the south as colder weather increased the demand for fuel. There were other jobs which could only be done in winter: ice-cutting, snow-clearing. But Captain did not elaborate upon these occupations. No business of his; no business of hers. He went herring fishing.

"It sounds—rather hard," Marguerite said. "Have you never thought about settling down?"

"I'll settle down when I'm dead," Captain said, dealing a deathblow to what, had the answer been different, she was poised to propose. Which was, to put it bluntly, that the One Bull needed a man-about-the-place.

Driving home, she told herself, You are an idiot! You have had a lucky escape. You could have made a fool of yourself.

So the four days ran out and it was Friday.

A fine hot day, but with thunder clouds piling up. The gloom matched her mood as she drove to keep her last rendezvous with the shearers. To mark the occasion she had brought a special treat for them—the best beef. The joint, not cut into when it was hot, had sealed with all its flavour and juices inside it. She had gooseberry tarts and a big basket of ripe cherries.

The shearers had finished work earlier than usual and had spent time shearing each other, washing off the accumulated grime, even washing some clothes. They faced the long trudge into Norfolk and another spell of hard, gruelling toil, yet the camp had an almost festive air. The little break from work and the prospect of a move exhilarated them.

This evening they all stayed closer to the cart than usual, even when the food had been passed about and all the cool ale was drunk. They were waiting—waiting to say good-bye. People could say what they liked about them, call them scum, rough and uncivilised; the truth was that they had natural good manners and behaved well to anyone who treated them properly. The hurt feeling climbed into her throat again, but she fought it down, determined that, when the moment came, she would say that she hoped to see them all again next year and wished them the best of luck until their next meeting. She'd say it to them all—though the words would be meant only for Captain.

He said, "Well," and jerked his shorn head. Tar-boy, happily combining shyness with perky importance, came forward, holding a paper-wrapped parcel as though it were red-hot.

"Ma'am, we ask you to accept this token of appreciation. From us all." He'd learned the words by heart and, having handed her the parcel, looked at Captain for approbation.

Marguerite opened the paper and saw an exquisite thing. It was a little scent-bottle, made in the shape of a dove, of milky-white glass except for the darker ring around its neck and the tiny coral-pink feet. Almost every girl at Mrs. Houghton's had owned such a trinket, but she had never had one.

"It's beautiful," she said. "Quite the prettiest . . . And I do not possess one. Thank you. Thank you all."

She looked first at Captain, whose face remained impassive, then at the crowd of sunburnt faces, most of them grinning, pleased with the success of their surprise.

"Take a sniff," someone said. She fumbled. The makers of such delightful toys were very ingenious.

"The head unscrews," Captain said with his usual brevity.

A scent unknown to her, sweet, heavy, powerful enough to override for a moment the odour of sheep, of men, of tar and the harsh lye soap with which the washing had been done, but troubling too, like some kinds of music, some lines of poetry.

She said, almost brokenly, "There was no need. You have paid and paid well . . . for anything I did. And I . . . I have enjoyed doing it." She swallowed and said the words she had prepared, very near to tears, quite foreign to her nature. They said they wished her the same; she could count on their being here next year, they wished her all the good luck in the world.

Captain said, "Better be on your way. There's rain about. Good-bye. And thanks again."

Actually, though thunder could be heard rumbling in the far distance, the purple clouds had moved on without spilling a drop, and, with the moon rising, her homeward journey would be made in as good a light as her outward one had been. The pony could see in dim light and always made a sharp distinction between a trot that took him away from his stable and one which took him home, the lightened cart almost bouncing.

About a quarter of a mile short of the main road there was

a belt of trees, but even there it was not completely dark. It was an avenue of stripes, black and white—black where a tree obscured the moonlight, white where the moonlight penetrated.

Her mind was far away from the robbers who were said to set upon travellers. Resolutely, in order to forget her absurd, inner misery, and attempting to face the bleak future bravely, she was thinking about paint. Thinking that now that she had a little money to spare, and the shearers had gone, she could set Jimmy to painting the front of the One Bull in time for the wool sales, while she did some of the work he ordinarily did. She had, actually, little faith in the trimming-up process: what the One Bull needed was not a freshly-painted face but a different situation. However, for such guests as did move into the centre of the town, ignoring the King's Head and the Green Man, the One Bull should present a shining face.

One of the trees, or its shadow, moved. The pony shied away and the shadow made a lurch for the bridle. A man's voice said, "All right. All right. Good evening, ma'am." The pony calmed, he stepped into the light: one of the shearers. She knew his face, but not his name. In fact, the men to her were largely nameless. She knew Captain and Tar-boy, Sammy who played the fiddle and Jack who had the tiresome summer cough. (She'd taken him a mixture of honey, horehound and vinegar which had worked, and she'd charged threepence.)

"I wondered if you'd saved me a bite."

"How could I? I did not know that you were not there. Probably one of your friends saved your share."

"Likely!" he said in a way that denied any such likelihood. He said he'd been obliged to go into Mallow; he had an old granny there in an almshouse; he couldn't move away without just looking in.

"Ain't there so little as a few dregs?" he asked.

Tar-boy had said, "From us all," so probably this man had made his contribution towards the price of the pretty thing which now lay in her lap. And of course there were always dregs in every cask, about a cupful of cloudy stuff which could be obtained by tipping the cask forward, and although every shearer carried his own drinking vessel, she always took a few, because some of theirs were always broken or mislaid.

"It will be nothing but dregs," she said. "Help yourself." He must have passed by the very door of the Green Man, she reflected, and that stupid law forbade him to go in and buy a pint. Twisting on the seat she said, "There is a mug in one of the baskets. Let the cart-tail down, pull the cask to the edge, then tilt it towards you." The pony fidgeted and she turned back and spoke to it.

After a minute the man said, "Can't be done. You need three hands." She saw the truth of that. She jumped down and went round to the back of the cart. He had his hands on her instantly.

She screamed. There was nobody, nothing within earshot except the pony which, startled, set off at a gallop. She kicked and clawed, tried to bite, but the young man knew what he was about; all you had to do with an unwilling girl was to get her skirt and petticoat up over her head, then her cries were muffled, her arms impeded by her own clothing. There was a special satisfaction in raping the unwilling, and when the victim happened to be a virgin it was like a bonus.

She lay, completely shattered, for some while after he had run off. She wished she could die there beside the road under the trees, die and be forever free of this soiled and humiliated body. But death came when it chose, not when it was wished for. She must get up, get home, concoct some tale, and wash, wash, wash. Not that any amount of washing would ever make her clean again.

She stood up and immediately the world swung about her. Leaning against the nearest tree she was horribly sick. When the last spasm passed, the world steadied and she set out to walk.

She had never walked any distance in her life; journeys to and from Highgate had been made by stage-wagon, and for the rare outings Mrs. Houghton had borrowed or hired a coach. In Mallow, Marguerite had walked around or across the market-place; no more. Now she was stumbling, in her dainty, unsuitable shoes, along a rough-surfaced lane. A mile and a half, perhaps even two miles before she reached the smoother main road, and after that a mile to Sheepgate. And near it the Green Man. There the windows would be lighted, and she must remember to cross the road, lest the light should shine on her and she be seen. She felt that the unspeakable thing which had happened to her was written all over her.

She arranged what she must tell Jimmy, who would be waiting up for her. And then, still in the lane, she stopped short and made a whimpering sound. For now she knew everything! Not with kisses, but by this terrible performance, were babies made! A baby and no husband. Like a maid abruptly dismissed from Mrs. Houghton's. There'd been whispers; Peggy was going to have a baby. And the believers in the begetting-by-kisses had wondered how anybody could have kissed Peggy, who was so remarkably ugly. Oh God, oh God, what did I ever do to deserve such punishment? And what can I do now?

She set herself in motion again, a sleep-walker's gait, and still some distance from the main road heard galloping hooves, a voice calling, a slapping rein being vigorously applied. A patch of darkness under some trees, then into the moonlight—Jimmy!

Anything less like the knight in armour riding to the rescue of a maiden in distress could hardly be imagined than this gangling boy in his shirt sleeves, mounted upon the bare back of the thickset pony, especially as, having managed to gasp, "Are you all right?" he burst into tears.

As though from a great distance she thought: *I* am the one who should be crying! She said, "Oh Jimmy. I was never so glad . . . Don't cry. I'm all right. Something was rattling. I got out to see. And the silly pony ran away."

By comparison, his own experience sounded more harrowing. He spoke of it with an occasional gasp and sob. He'd been so busy. Five people had arrived late, and he was so busy serving them he hadn't been able to run straight out when he heard the pony return. Then she didn't come in. So he thought perhaps she had, and gone to her room. So he'd hunted and called all over the house. Then he'd realised. He'd thought he'd die . . .

"Every night I've been worried to death," he said, with a final gulp.

"I'm so glad you brought the pony. My shoes are in shreds. My feet, too." That was the right line to adopt, she thought; concentrate upon trivialities, upon the immediate things. Try not to think. Or to remember.

He hoisted her on to the pony, a painful business, for though the pony was plump and well fed, its backbone seemed sharp as a saw. Think about something else. Think about marrying Jimmy with all possible speed. He'd never think of it himself, of course. She must do it all. Something of the *flavour* of the future reached her then, a hint of things to come. Always,

always, she would have to do it all. She would have a kind, devoted, respectful husband, but...

The vicar of St. Cerdic's had accepted the rather poor living offered him by his Cambridge college, into whose hands it had fallen, because it offered the kind of life for which he thought himself best fitted. He was scholarly, physically slothful, ascetic by habit. Born into an earlier age, he would have been happy in a cloister; born rich he would have been a studious gentleman in a well-stocked library. But because he knew that he had chosen the easy way, every now and then he'd allow his conscience to prod him into an activity that smacked of the fussy.

He was very worried because Jimmy had no name but Jimmy. It was understandable, since Jimmy was a foundling, dumped at the doorway of the little orphanage which some charitable lady of the Thickthorn family had endowed long ago. Children left there were better off than those who fell into the keeping of the Poor Law authorities; better fed, better clothed and, when of an age at which they could be expected to earn their keep, sent, as far as possible, to kindly masters, and to jobs within their poor little capacities. But they were not given names—beyond those necessary to distinguish one child from another. Jimmy was Jimmy.

So, once married, what would the girl's name be? Her own name was old and well-established. Gilderson, quite definitely a derivation and contraction of Gilda's son, reached back and back. The parish records were meagre, but they showed that the Gildersons and the One Bull were part of Mallow's history.

And they were both so young! The vicar judged the girl to be the elder, the blushing, stammering boy younger by two years. Did either of them know what they were about? Averse to marriage himself, the vicar looked upon them as children about to venture upon a dangerous enterprise. He was inclined to advise caution, delay. Taking Jimmy aside he asked rather sternly was there any *reason* for this hasty marriage. Had Jimmy *done*—well, anything which rendered marriage necessary? Jimmy turned as white as he had formerly been scarlet and his eyes sparkled.

"No. I ain't, and if anybody but a parson even thought such a thing I'd knock his teeth down his throat. I been worshipping the ground she walk on for years and when... when she said about getting married, I all but died. Then I...I kissed her hand." There could be no doubting his sincerity, but with the one sound reason for marrying in haste ruled out, the vicar still thought, and said, that they would be well advised to wait until Jimmy was eighteen.

"But I am. I'm nearly nineteen. And maybe more. You see, sir, they reckoned foundlings' birthdays from the time they was took in. Nothing else to go by. I could've been two. Who'd know?"

Mr. Hutton, the nearest thing to a crony that the vicar had in Mallow, took an entirely opposite view. A fatherless girl—and a pretty girl to boot—needed a male protector, and who else was likely to marry Marguerite Gilderson? The five-hundred-pound dowry which her father had left her in his silly will existed only in words written on paper. As for the boy being nameless, what did that weigh against the fact that he was a good worker and apparently devoted not only to the girl but also to the inn?

"I've kept an eye on things there," he said, "and one or two people whom I have recommended have spoken well of him, remarking upon his versatility. Probably he is not overburdened with brain—but she has enough for two. Between them they might somehow contrive to keep the One Bull going."

As they well might, now that things were changing so fast, and coaches were becoming quite common. Undoubtedly the One Bull offered the best accommodation, having the biggest yard. And though the precocious schoolboy was the indisputable heir, he could not, even had he wanted to, do anything about the inn until he had paid his sister that non-existent, mythical five hundred pounds. And that could never come about.

"As for Jimmy's lack of a surname," Mr. Hutton said, "it is far from unusual. Most surnames are a mere matter of usage. Smith, Baker, Brewster, Woodman, Sawyer, all derived from an occupation. Nothing so sacrosanct about them. And I could tell you of many instances when men have actually changed their surnames, especially when a proud family ended with a female anxious to preserve her name. An easy, and not costly process, but demanding, of course, due formality."

Informed of this, Jimmy said with a shyness which masked something very different, "Then, if there's no objection...I mean, the old master was good to me, and the One Bull and

name seemed to go together. I'll choose Gilderson and be proud
to."

So Marguerite Gilderson and Jimmy Gilderson were married.

St. Cerdic's had changed a little over the years. Edward VI,
pious in his own Protestant Way, had probably felt a little guilt
about the money his father had derived from the destruction
of the religious houses; to make up for it he had established
grammar schools and allocated some funds for the improvement
of parish churches. The money was not to be spent on fripperies
or on anything which savoured of popery. The creaking, rotting
floor of St. Cerdic's had been paved with stone, and the church
had been given a pulpit from which the interminable sermons
associated with Protestantism could be preached. The pulpit
stood slightly in front of and to the south of the altar, between
it and the window which, though smaller than it had been, was
still large for a church of its size. In the centre of the window
was the head of a man. Some people said it was Christ's, others
believed it was St. Cerdic's. There, too, was the head of the
wolf, looking like a kindly dog. The rest of the window was
plain, except for a border of coloured glass, small pieces arranged in no particular fashion.

Edward VI had had but a short reign, poor soul, and his
half-sister, Mary, who succeeded him, being a Catholic, had
restored the crucifixes, the altar ornaments, the statues; had
given—or encouraged other people to give—gorgeous altar
cloths and robes for priests. Mary's reign had been short, too,
and she had been followed by Elizabeth, who had tried in vain
to pull England back into the half-way position favoured by
her father. But the tide of Protestantism was running too strongly
and, by the end of her reign, St. Cerdic's looked very much
as it was to look for the next three hundred years. The new
king, James I, was a firm Protestant, and the rites by which
Marguerite and Jimmy were married were as plain as the bride's
dress, which was greyish blue. She had worn black for her
father, good black, but she had bought it before she fully
realised the desperate situation of the One Bull's finances, and
now she had nothing—not even the wish—to waste upon
wedding finery. Yet one could not wear black for one's wedding; so she had compromised.

The vicar's doubts about the suitability of this marriage were confirmed by the bridegroom's behaviour. A silly, clumsy boy, not even standing in the right place.

"Move over," he said in a hissing whisper. "The bride will stand to your *left*."

Jimmy moved from the place where he had been standing. Under his feet there was a stone slab and, under the stone, rotted planking, and under that the bones of three people. About them Jimmy knew nothing—nor indeed did anybody else. But something happened to him, something perfectly ordinary in the circumstances. Here he was, the boy who until a few days ago had been just Jimmy, but was now James Gilderson. He was about to be married to the most beautiful, the most desirable girl in the world. He was prepared to work himself to the bone in her service and in the service of the inn which, being in part her property, would in a few minutes' time be his.

And a man should be master in his own house.

11 Adam

1725

THE MAN WHO HAD WALKED THAT MORNING FROM DANELEY—and before that from Colchester, and before that from London—stepped out of the traffic on to a triangular piece of waste land, knee-deep in poppies and wild scabious, and stood there, staring across the road at the inn, the One Bull which had so unexpectedly, yet so rightly, become his.

A right pretty place, he thought, and laughed softly to himself. Then, moving further back to obtain a better view, he almost fell over a hump in the flower-and-grass-covered patch, and spared a moment to wonder why, in the very centre of an apparently thriving market town, so much ground, and a corner site at that, should be allowed to run to waste. He'd spent his life in the densely overcrowded part of London between Aldermanbury Postern and Moorfields where, on a bit of land this size, somebody would have run up a narrow four-storeyed building and let out rooms, two or three families to each.

The Gildersons had never been reduced to quite that level, but they had always been poor and short of space. They had also always been oddly out of tune with their surroundings, holding themselves aloof, regarding themselves as superior. Which they were, all being honest in a neighbourhood where crime was prevalent and far more rewarding than hard work; they'd all been married in church, and had their children baptised. And for four generations they had held a grudge against the world.

This Adam Gilderson had never known his great-grandfather, but he knew the story by heart: how he'd never got on with his father, the innkeeper, and had finally left home to find his mother's brother, a lawyer well established in London, who'd done little for him except apprentice him to a cabinetmaker and given him a meal once a week—Sunday dinner, not at his own table, but in the kitchen, with the servants. "Not that there's any shame in hard work," Adam's grandfather,

himself a carpenter, had said, "but my father felt ill-done-by.
And when his father died, he *was* ill-done-by and no mistake.
Everything left to the second son, always his father's favourite.
So you see, there's no justice in this world, but that's no excuse
for not minding your manners and mixing with riff-raff. Bear
that in mind."

It was borne in mind, with a variety of other things. The
rarity of the name Gilderson; the fact that the uncle who had
treated great-grandfather so shabbily had attained some high
office under Cromwell; that all Gildersons were at least two
inches taller than other men, and all had a little learning, passed
down from great-grandfather Gilderson.

And probably, thought the man standing amongst the weeds
of what was called Pottersfield Corner, the other, the usurping
line of Gildersons here in Mallow, had been equally careful to
cherish myths. For the last of them, a woman, very old and
perhaps by now dead, had set the lawyers to work and they'd
found him with little difficulty. So here he was.

Stepping, this time more cautiously, over the hump beneath
which a suicide lay, Adam Gilderson crossed the road and
entered the place which was to be his own.

He had little experience of taverns. Now and again he'd
dropped in at the Weavers' Arms, a decent little beerhouse
near his own home. On a carpenter's wage, with a crippled
mother and a sister to support, he could not afford to drink
much. Family legend had made him expect that the One Bull
was superior to the Weavers' Arms, but it had hardly prepared
him for what he now confronted: an oak-panelled room with
a marble-surrounded hearth; various doors, all labelled—Coffee-Room, Dining-Room, Tap and Private. There were other
doors, too, and from one of them a young woman emerged,
gave him an assessing look then, judging by his clothes, assigned him, with a gesture, to the back regions.

"My name's Gilderson," he said, and enjoyed the flurry, the
hasty little bob, the servile, "If you would come this way, sir."

The old woman, his distant relative, lay in a vast, curtained
bed, propped upon many pillows. A white shawl covered her
shoulders; a scarf of white lace muffled her head. The whiteness
made her tiny shrivelled face look yellowish. Dead. Only the
green eyes were lively. And her voice when she spoke was
astoundingly strong and vibrant.

"So you got here at last. I was beginning to wonder."

"I had things to settle. And I wa..."

"Go away, Lizzie."

A woman rose from the place where she had been sitting, half-hidden by the bed curtains, and went softly out.

"Walked? I sent money to that rogue in London. Coach-fare and clothes."

"I know. But I have a mother and sister. I left it with them."

"Stand nearer the window, so I can take a look at you."

The lengthy scrutiny would have embarrassed most people, but he bore it calmly, staring back, thinking that she was the oldest person he had ever seen. Over eighty. Ninety, perhaps.

"You'll do," she said at last, almost grudgingly. "A Gilderson all right. Something must be done about clothes. And don't say you walked from London in any servant's hearing. Servants are the greatest snobs in the world."

"I know that. I'm a carpenter."

"I know *that*. Thirty-five years old. Unmarried. Now that I've seen you I wonder how you managed that. Still, I managed it myself. I never intended to make any man *my* master. I'd seen enough of *that*!" She brought one hand out of the shawl's shelter and with one finger tapped her teeth thoughtfully. She still had teeth, and in fair condition, but her hand was like a dried bird's claw. "In the next room, you'll find a cupboard full of clothes. My father's. They should fit. Go and change. I'll order dinner in here. I expect you're hungry."

The clothes were all good, the clothes of a solid burgher; nothing was showy, nothing had been so much in the latest fashion as to be out of date in the month. They had been well guarded against moth, and they fitted him well. He had a queer feeling, an out-of-character feeling, that the fine linen and the good broadcloth had been waiting for him. That the inn had been waiting.

A table spread with a glossy white cloth had been set up for him midway between the bed and a writing-table in the bow window, and Lizzie was waiting to serve up the food brought by another maid. A tray had been placed across the old woman's knees and she lay a little higher. Every dish contained enough for two, and both the maid and mistress kept up the pretence that the meal was being shared. Actually, the old woman ate almost nothing—a mouthful of this, a mouthful of that. But she drank a good deal, brandy slightly diluted with water. Adam drank, far more cautiously, a glass of pale wine. It was as well to be careful of unknown things.

"I sleep now for half an hour, Cousin Adam. Walk around. Have a look at everything. Then we must have a talk."

Lizzie lowered the pillows and Cousin Margaret—after all, she had acknowledged the relationship, distant though it was— lay back and closed her eyes and looked very dead indeed.

But when he returned in half an hour, she was again propped up and drinking tea. Tea he was fairly familiar with; it was taxed and very expensive, but servants in big houses saved the tea-leaves and made a second brew; now and again he'd been offered a cup—insipid stuff. Now and again, as a treat for his womenfolk, he'd bought a two-ounce packet, and that had been different. Comforting. Invigorating. He had always thought it iniquitous that tea, beer and ale should be taxed, and gin should be tax-free. Wine and brandy were also taxed, but they were rich men's drinks and so did not concern him.

"Well?" Cousin Margeret demanded. "What do you think of the place?"

He'd thought several things, the most outstanding being that there seemed to be rather more servants than necessary. But he could hardly say that. He fell back on his craft. "It all seems to be in excellent repair."

"Spoken like a true carpenter!" she said, malice in her voice and in her glance.

"That's what I am," he said, unperturbed. "We learn what to look out for. Dry rot, woodworm, death-watch beetle."

"You and the vicar will have most illuminating talks on such subjects. You and I have other things to discuss. The past and the future. I suppose you know nothing of the family history."

"Of my branch, I know what is to be known. I can trace my descent from my great-grandfather who was born here, but left home because his father made life intolerable for him."

Nothing specific had been handed down; sons not getting on with fathers generally hinted at physical violence, but the short time he had spent with Cousin Margaret had indicated that unkindness could take other forms than clouts over the ear. She was, after all, nearer to that ancestor by one generation, and could have inherited or imitated his scornful manner, his barbed tongue. Both hinted at some kind of social superiority.

"He made life intolerable for everybody," she said. "My wretched grandmother, both his sons, me until I could defend myself. He was an abominable man. My grandmother made the gravest possible mistake—she married a pot-boy. God knows why. Love, I suppose. She was a woman with a very lively imagination."

He was a man accustomed to doing sums in his head; accustomed also in the art of dovetailing, and he saw that, unless Cousin Margaret was almost older than she looked she could not have been very old when her grandfather was making her grandmother's life wretched. And marrying a pot-boy was hardly the kind of thing which would be remembered and handed down like a cherished relic.

"She kept a journal," Cousin Margaret said. "There on the table; the black book. No, don't bother now; you can read it at your leisure. I will just explain. I think that somewhere in the Bible there is mention of the confusion that takes place when a servant is promoted. That promoted servant—a man without a name, even—bullied everybody. His wife, poor woman, was allowed no say at all in the running of this inn which, after certain liabilities were discharged, was indisputably hers. But his, through her. She was young, she liked people, yet he confined her here, as strictly kept as a nun. She had two boys. The elder, less pliable, ran away—the story of her heartbreak is there in that book. His name was Edman. But you are Adam. Were you named by mistake?"

"No. My mother thought the name had been over-used, and started again. With Adam, a good Biblical name."

"It smacks," she said, "of Puritanism, but let it go. The second son stayed here and was amenable—Yes, Father; No, Father; As you say, Father. It was going to be, 'Yes, Father, Margaret shall marry the man you choose' . . . But that I could not allow. He died."

Often enough he'd seen a fog creeping in, coming in with the tide, striking cold through the clothes a man wore for labour on a reasonably warm day, blinding a man's eyes so that he could lose his way even in familiar, well-trodden streets. Something of the feeling of being chilled and blinded came to him now, and he was almost as certain as he had ever been of anything that the bully's death had not been entirely natural. The old woman put such venom into two simple words.

"After that," she went on—and the jubilation in her voice confirmed his fanciful thought, "everything became very different here. So much unhappiness to make up for. We were all very gay. Unfortunately," her voice changed, "my poor father, who had been so down-trodden, allowed no say in any matter, even his affectionate nature constantly jeered at, was really not fitted . . ." She broke off, feeling no need to explain that he'd drunk too much, spent money, lent money, gone to the races at Newmarket far too often, and left the management of the inn to her. Yet there was the need to explain why the fortunes of the One Bull had declined again and forced her to take a certain action, beginning something which her heir would be obliged to continue if the inn were to continue to prosper. And why she should fear his opinion puzzled her and angered her. She'd been the sole judge of her actions for a long time.

"I daresay," she said, scornful again, "that walking in as you did, you had leisure to observe a rival hostelry on the verge of the town."

"The King's Head? I noted it, yes. But only in passing."

"There was a time when it and its fellow, the Green Man on the other side of town, stole our custom and almost ruined us. That was when my grandmother was a girl. Coaches saved the situation—for a time. We have, as you have probably already observed, a wide entry, and stand where the road is wide. For a clumsy coach drawn by several horses, that was an inestimable advantage, and gave us for a while a monopoly. My grandfather, naturally, took all the credit for the new prosperity. And I believe that as a pot-boy he *had* been industrious, and that as master he did much to put the fabric of the building into the good repair which you, as a carpenter, observed and admired."

Harmless words, but with such a sting to them! He had never encountered anyone in the least like her. There were female servants in big houses, sometimes insolent, sometimes kindly, occasionally managing to be both at once; there were the rough, degraded, gin-drinking women of the slums, beggars, hawkers, prostitutes; the decent women like his mother and sister. His mother, before she became crippled, had helped in a cook-shop; his sister did plain sewing, but the wages were pitiable and they'd both realised that a man, sober and home-loving and unmarried, was a thing to be cherished and looked up to.

"Tea is all very well, but it does not sustain me as brandy does," the old woman said. "Be so good as to hand me that glass." Lizzie, knowing her mistress's habits, had placed it ready to hand.

"Until you are accustomed to it," she said, "go carefully with this stuff and with whisky. For me, it no longer matters." She sipped, swallowed, sipped again. "Very curious," she said in yet another voice. "When first I heard that you had been found, I said to myself, *Nunc dimittis* and prepared myself to die... Tell me, do you fear death?"

"It is not a matter to which I have given much consideration. But yes, I suppose so. In the way every man does."

"Then take comfort in the thought that eventually, when the time comes, the idea of going to sleep forever has its own singular attraction. One becomes very weary... But I realised that, if I died, weakly giving in, before I had seen you and instructed you, I should have failed in my duty. There is much that I must tell you."

Noise interrupted her: clattering hooves, rattling wheels, a horn blowing, a babble of voices.

"The mail coach," she said. "*Our* monopoly! Charles, the man in charge of the yard, knows all about the horses; the kitchen is under control. Just mingle, be welcoming, assume that you are host and the people your guests. Get along, now."

Jerked out of his element, a fish out of water, indeed, he did his best.

Next morning he was informed by Lizzie that Madam always woke early, took tea, issued orders, did whatever writing was to be done, and then rested. "She will be ready for you, sir, at ten."

He had slept until eight, and somehow Cousin Margaret's early-morning activity seemed to rebuke him, and when at ten o'clock he presented himself, she said, "I trust you slept well," with that same edge of malice. She went on to say that it was time to talk business. She proceeded to ask him questions, all of which he felt had been asked and answered by somebody else that morning. Still, he felt that he came out of the inquisition well; he had noticed how many people had taken a full meal in the dining-room; how many horses had been stabled; roughly how many people had called in the evening or this morning, so far, to collect or despatch letters or parcels.

"Not," she said sourly, "that we gain by such traffic. We do the public a service. But I suppose we derive some benefit from being known as *the* coaching-inn in Mallow. Though I have known people to alight from a coach and walk to the King's Head to save a few pennies on their supper. Supper!" she said, even more sourly. "You might as well call it dinner and have done. For travellers it is the main meal of the day. Of course, you must do as you think fit, but I have always been careful of the One Bull's reputation for good food and sound liquor. Have you any head for figures?"

"I reckon fairly well."

"Then you can, perhaps, understand me." She began to pour facts and figures before him. With a different kind of old woman he might perhaps have suspected some failure of mind, for everything, every figure she quoted seemed to prove that he had inherited, or was about to inherit, something of little worth. And then she changed completely. She said:

"There is the question of servants. All are needed on certain days—like yesterday. But it is not their fault that there are idle intervals, and indeed, to a large extent, the good repair upon which you so kindly remarked is largely due to idle hands being usefully employed. I know how others do, but I would never stoop to asking a man or a maid to work part-time, just when they were needed. Nor have I ever used what is virtually slave labour—orphans, paupers, some mere children, eager to work for their keep. Some wage, however trivial, I have always paid. And I have been repaid..."

That he could not contradict even had he wanted to. She had been, he had learned, too weak to leave her bed for six weeks, yet everything within the inn and in the yard had worked like clockwork.

"I have also had a care for the horses," she said. "It may sound ridiculous to you, but no coach-horse, or indeed any horse on my premises, has been fed chaff which gives no energy. And no lame horse has ever left my stables. I have always kept two strong animals in reserve. And I may tell you, anybody who brought one of my good horses back in a sorry state had the rough edge of my tongue, and then a free drink—which gave small comfort next day."

Sorting the figures and everything else out in his head, Adam said, "Yet you live well, Cousin Margaret."

She said, "Yes. I smuggle. Oh, I assure you, in the most safe and discreet way. That is what I have braced myself, kept alive for, to tell you. If you disapprove of it, go your way. If you also wish to live well, listen to me."

She explained in great detail. Easy enough to get contraband goods, French wine, brandy, tea and tobacco into the country; little boats in little creeks and inlets served smugglers well. But once the stuff was ashore, that was when trouble began. The everlasting problem of distribution.

"But how easy," she said, "when given a little thought. Ale, or call it beer if you like, benefits from being rocked. So, down at Bywater, barrels go aboard all the time, and get a good shaking to Amsterdam or Calais, some as far as the Sugar Islands. Some, of course, are sold at their destination; some are lost at sea, but a sufficient number comes back . . . Now, I wonder . . ." Once again the teeth that looked about thirty years old were tapped by the finger of a hand that could have been a hundred; the old eyes sparkled green. "A test case," she said. "You're a carpenter! Go into the store-room—we have no cellar here. Pretend that you are an excise man. See what you can discover."

He'd glanced in at the store-room during his brief inspection of the place yesterday, and noted that it, like every other part of the inn, was clean and tidy. Full casks stood on end, three deep, along one wall; those in use were ranged along a solid table; empty ones lay on their sides, ready to be trundled out through the door which gave upon a passage leading to a side entrance. They all looked innocent enough. The casks in use were plainly labelled by strips of metal laid upon their tops: strong beer, small beer, cider; smaller casks said sherry, port wine, Rhenish, Canary, whisky, rum.

Adam stood there, embarrassed by his ignorance. Small beer—cheaper than strong—was what he had drunk in his rare visits to the Weavers' Arms; he had a vague idea that port wine was red. The wine he'd had yesterday was pale; would that be Rhenish or Canary? Not that it mattered. Nothing that was contraband, nothing smuggled, would stand here in open display. You're a carpenter! Carpenters knew about wood; so did the coopers who made barrels, though theirs was a specialised and more highly-paid trade. So the secret lay in the barrels themselves. False bottoms? Inside partitions?

He eyed the empty barrels, imagining them full of what they were supposed to be full of, but within that fullness a secret, watertight compartment containing whatever somebody wanted hidden there. The container would be of oak, the most water-resistant wood; therefore a cask that had been tampered with should be slightly heavier when *empty*. Not when full, if the hiding-place was packed with tea or tobacco, both light-weight, compared with liquid.

One by one he lifted the empty casks and, so far as he could judge without scales, they all weighed the same. They all looked the same: the legal measurement-mark branded into their sides, and B.B. in large letters. The brewer's initials, he guessed. None of them rattled when shaken—he imagined that the secret compartment, lightened of its contents, might swing loose. But wait! There was one slight difference. The double B was not always in the same position on the barrel's side. It was either high or low, just above the bunghole. Possibly accident, possibly very significant to those in the know. But in order to make certain, he would have to break into two barrels, one marked high, one low. Casks cost money and hacking into two would be a noisy business and attract attention here. In fact, a man in a green baize apron had already looked in and asked if he could help in any way and Adam had said no; he was just taking stock.

Having taken stock and made what, if not a discovery, was something near enough to it to convince Cousin Margaret that he was observant, Adam made his way back to the private part of the house. He was eager to show, to prove, to establish himself in her eyes. Lizzie was on guard. "Madam is sleeping," she said. "The little naps keep her going. I will call you, sir, when she wakes."

She did not wake. The everlasting rest of which she had spoken was now hers. So imperceptibly that Lizzie had not noticed, the little nap had slithered over into death.

Adam had known her for almost exactly twenty-four hours and her obvious dislike of him made it impossible for him to like her. Yet he felt bereft.

The vicar said, "A most remarkable woman. So generous but without ostentation. Not a regular attendant at church, I regret to say, but of high moral character for all that. Her death is a loss to St. Cerdic's—and indeed to the whole of Mallow." He looked at Adam hopefully. And indeed when Adam had leisure to look into things, he found amongst the meticulously-kept books a small one labelled "Personal expenditure," and saw that Cousin Margaret had been extremely charitable—and in her earlier years extravagant about clothes.

He found the little book when he was hunting for anything

which would offer the slightest clue about the smuggling. He found none. Except for this lack, everything was recorded with the utmost fidelity; every penny taken, every penny spent accounted for, and at the end of each year just enough profit to make the whole exercise worth while. No more. Certainly not sufficient to allow the inn's owner to be so lavish to the church, the foundlings, the inhabitants of almshouses, shipwrecked sailors, and such vague recipients as "Poor woman; sixpence." The vicar had said, "Without ostentation," and Adam wondered whether Cousin Margaret who, during her last hours of life, had struck him as being intelligent beyond ordinary, had been unostentatious because she was cautious and might have felt that somebody would wonder how the owner of an only-just-prosperous establishment could afford to be so generous.

During his first week at the One Bull, Adam was not unmindful of his mother and sister; in fact, he thought about them a good deal, happily envisaging them settled in on the ground-floor family rooms, being waited on, eating better than they had ever done in their lives, and enjoying the garden during what remained of the summer, and, after that, huge fires. He was fond of them both; he half suspected that his mother's disability, a gross distortion of joints and near immobility, was largely the result of having worked as a laundress, either going out by the day or washing at home, in order to eke out the meagre family resources. She deserved the best, and so did his sister Kate, who had for so long combined conflicting duties, looking after the invalid, doing plain but beautiful sewing, and keeping the home together, always some kind of meal awaiting Father and Adam, and then Adam only.

It was useless to write them a letter. The thin line of literacy had been extended from father to son. So, Cousin Margaret's funeral over and done with, but her influence still strong, knitting the place together into a fabric solid as a board, Adam took the coach to London, that life-line coach which ran, carrying mail, between London and Norwich.

Late August. At no time of the year was the contrast between the town slums and the country so appalling. Stenches to which from long usage his nose had become accustomed now offended it.

His mother, rigid in every joint and her hands so distorted as to look like something carved out of wood by somebody out of his mind, said, "Adam, I am glad for you. It all sounds very nice, but I should not feel at home there."

In one way he himself did not yet feel at home there, and in another way he had felt the feeling of home-coming, a kinship, a rightness; this for me; me for this. Confused, baffled, he said, turning to Kate, "How do you feel? All depends on you now, Kate."

It was now too late for Kate to express an opinion differing from her mother's and, although Adam made the inn sound very comfortable, it also sounded rather grand. By Kate's humble standards, Adam now looked grand, wearing the kind of shirt which Mother, in the old days, had washed for other people, and which Kate herself now stitched for heart-breakingly small pay.

"I leave it to Mother," she said.

"I'm Aldermanbury born and bred," their mother said. "The Gildersons—well, even them that was born here—never really belonged. Somehow. I mean not the way I do." She looked back over the years of married life. A good husband, a steady husband she'd had, and a good son too, but never really fitting in, never seeing that, if you were poor, if you lived in Aldermanbury you'd be happier fitting in and taking the good side of slum life with the bad. Setting up to be different simply made things harder.

So if Adam could afford to pay the rent and send enough money so that Kate didn't have to do so much sewing... She did not mention the cost of the brown medicine which sometimes dulled the pain, or of the gin which sometimes made her feel almost light-hearted.

Adam said, "You shall have enough to keep you both in comfort." He was relieved, and slightly ashamed of his relief, to be going back to Mallow alone. He had a great deal to think about, a great deal to do, and a family would only complicate things. Also he was aware that the kind of people with whom his mother and sister had become rather friendly since his father's death were not the kind of people he wanted about him in his new life.

So far he placed no orders for liquor, the inn being so well stocked, but on the day after his return to Mallow the brewer's dray—a low cart drawn by two thickset horses—arrived in the yard.

"Is that all for us?" Adam asked as, with the usual smoothness, unloading and storing began. "It seems rather a lot."

"Usual mid-August delivery, sir," the drayman said cheerfully. "Hot weather *and* harvest. And not all for you, in a manner of speaking. The old lady—sorry to hear she'd gone, by the way, sir—was very obliging. Served as a sort of clearing-house."

No great lucidity of mind or speech was required of a drayman, and this one had already guarded against thirst on his journey from Bosworth, but he explained as well as he could. It suited Mr. Brewster, the brewer at Bosworth, to send in one good load; and it suited some people to collect. "S'matter of fact, sir, there's places around here where the dray couldn't go, roads too narrow." Big houses, he said rather vaguely, generally had fair decent roads leading to them, but take farms . . .

He accepted Adam's offer of a drink. "I don't mind if I do, sir. But not beer, if it's all the same to you. When you work with it, you sorta lose the taste . . ." Adam thought this rather a misstatement, since the man reeked of it, but, willing to take the charitable view, thought that perhaps the reek might come from his clothes, not his breath. "What I fancy is a nice drop of port. I gotta sweet tooth."

He drank his wine and went blithely away, some underling having heaved the empty barrels on to the dray.

Almost immediately the vicar appeared, accompanied by a boy with a wheelbarrow. He explained at some length that he had revived the custom of the Church Ale. "An innocent revelry," he said, "which brings people, not regular church-goers, into the—how can I describe it? The ambience . . . an awareness of the church. We must move with the times. Of course, I know that in the past the ale was home-made, and I believe there was a great deal of competition between good women anxious to provide the best. But we cannot revert to the Middle Ages, can we? And having the liquor limited and under control, as it were, prevents excess. I think it was the widespread drunkenness, which brought the old Church Ale ceremony into disfavour."

The vicar's barrel was trundled away in the wheelbarrow. Later in the same day a farm cart came and took away two barrels for Sir Francis Colman at Abbot's Hall, and on the following day—Wednesday, market day—several farmers collected what they called harvest beer. Some paid on the nail;

some said they always settled up when they sold their barley or wheat, and Adam, consulting Cousin Margaret's books, saw that all was in order.

Then, one evening, on what Adam, rapidly adapting to the rhythm of inn life, knew was going to be busy, because the coach from London was due, there was a slight interruption of the régime which had been honed to such perfection that he sometimes felt that his presence, his surveillance, were completely redundant.

"It's Sir Francis, sir," the rather flustered maid-servant said. "He wants to see you, sir. Very particular, he said. In the oak room, sir."

It was called the oak room, but it was now no more than an entry hall from which other rooms opened off. The panelling, as Adam had observed during the first few minutes of his arrival, was fine, made long ago when panelling was made in imitation of wall-hangings—linen-fold it was called. And the fireplace of black marble was very grand indeed. But the room was ill-lighted even on a sunny day, having only two small windows, and with so many doors it was draughty. It had a curious floor, too, made up partly of what local people called "pamments," large square unglazed tiles, partly of smaller ones, coloured differently. An uncomfortable room and one affording little privacy.

"Ha," Sir Francis said, adopting the aggressive stance and attitude made necessary to him when confronted by a well-grown man, however lowly born. In the Civil War the Colman of the day had taken what seemed to be the right side, which had proved not to be so, after the Restoration in 1660, and it had been a little difficult for Colman young to find mates outside a very limited circle. Sir Francis, the unhappy result of a marriage between near relatives, was of average height, but misshapen, with one shoulder higher than the other, a head too heavy for his neck, a protruding jaw too heavy for his face. He was also afflicted with a stammer which ill-humour exacerbated. A real rage rendered him speechless.

"I know you're a n-new to the j-job," he said. "But you sent me the wrong b-barrels."

A clue at last!

"In what way wrong, sir?"

"You know."

"But I don't. As a matter of fact, I had nothing to do with

the selection. Your man called for two barrels and my man helped him out with them. Harvest beer, I understood. Full strength. Did you wish the other?"

Sir Francis stared, goggled a little. Was it possible that the man did not know? Then he must be informed. He looked cautiously round; doors stood open; there were voices from the dining-room and from the coffee-room.

"When I had occasion to visit your aunt," he said, "we talked in her parlour."

Adam opened the door marked "Private," and stood aside to allow Sir Francis to go ahead of him. After the semi-gloom of the oak room, this part of the house, with its white-painted walls and wide windows overlooking the garden, seemed very bright.

Sir Francis's manner had undergone a subtle change. He had imagined that the old woman would have explained everything, and that her heir had blundered—or, worse, was being cunning and avaricious, breaking a long-standing contract in order to make a new one, more advantageous to himself. It was what he, in the new landlord's position, would have done.

"I hope now, Gilderson, that you are going to be reasonable."

"About what?"

"Come now! I think you know." Sir Francis waited, willing the man to know, willing him to admit his knowledge. If not, it was going to be most embarrassing. A justice of the peace being obliged to explain what, looked at dispassionately, was a sordid bit of lawbreaking. "Surely," he said, almost coaxingly, "your aunt must have explained, informed you of what she..." His stammer was getting the upper hand, and now he was all but speechless.

"She was not my aunt, sir. The relationship was far less close. She wanted to see me, and I came as soon as I could. She died before I had been here twenty-four hours—and much of that time she was asleep. I'd be grateful if you could tell me what I am supposed to know."

Adam did not feel disposed to help the man; he knew the type. He was not going to say that Cousin Margaret had mentioned smuggling, and almost with her last breath had sent him, mockingly, to test the powers of observation, and then died, leaving him with only the certainty that the secret involved barrels. He sensed that he was about to be let into that secret, and although he gave no sign of it, he felt a thrill of excitement.

With the air of a man at home in his own house, he said: "May I offer you a drink?"

"Yes. Brandy . . . if you please."

Adam turned to a side-table where the brandy, untouched since Cousin Margaret's death, stood. He now knew enough about it to know that it was not to be poured out like water or beer, and Cousin Margaret, he remembered, had drunk hers diluted. There was a carafe of water on the table, renewed every day, because the One Bull was still running on the lines which Margaret Gilderson had laid down long ago. He managed, with a gesture, to ask Sir Francis whether he wished for water, and Sir Francis, with a shake of his too-heavy head, indicated that he did not. And then, speaking as though he were the anxious host and Adam the rather difficult guest, he said, "Will you not drink with me?"

"Better not. My drink so far has been small beer, and maybe I'm a bit old to change now. But never mind me. You were about to say . . ."

Sir Francis took a gulp and then another, and felt better. He swirled the good liquor around in the glass, savoured the scent of it, gulped again. He knew only too well that to drink noisily, to sloop as they called it, was a sign of ill-breeding, but with one's lower jaw so far protruding from the upper, how else could one drink? Sloop, sloop, sloop, and the inevitable, most desirable result. He was able to say, "Look here, my good man. Bear in mind that I am a justice of the peace and that the Brewster Sessions issue licences. Whether you wish to continue the . . . the game which your . . . close relative played so long and so successfully, is, of course, for you to decide. But I warn you, one incautious word out of you and you'll find things made very difficult. You understand me?"

"Perfectly."

Thus guarded, Sir Francis explained what was actually a very simple method of tax evasion. Inside certain barrels, all marked with the B.B. low down near the bunghole, were brackets which held smaller casks suspended in such a way that they were completely surrounded by beer. A suspicious customs officer could tap a barrel, and nothing but beer would flow from the bunghole; he could attack a barrel from the top and see nothing but beer. "To justify his suspicion he would be obliged to smash a barrel, and to destroy property merely on suspicion would be outside his mandate. You see?"

"I see. Very clever. I should have thought, though, that the double casks would weigh heavier."

"They don't. The staves of those barrels are planed very fine, and the inner containers are positively fragile."

Adam, careful to betray nothing but lively interest, asked a number of questions. Some Sir Francis could answer; many he could not. "One thing I can tell you: being involved in this needs a certain liveliness of mind and, as in my case, hard work. The fewer people in the know the better. I, for instance, trust no one. That means that in the dead of night I must steal down to my own cellar, remove the barrel top, take out the container and replace the top, *with my own hands*. So you can imagine my chagrin . . ." He accepted more brandy, and became almost confidential, telling Adam how he made up for the deficiency in the beer-barrel's contents by adding water. "And even then it is better than small beer."

He also explained the method of payment. "Your . . . close relative always allowed three months' credit. I—and doubtless all her other *special* customers—paid what was ostensibly owing and then, person-to-person, settled the other debt. She was a most discreet woman. She never spoke of one of us to another. But I am sure that I am not the only person in the district to hope . . . that you will, er, emulate, I mean keep to the old ways."

"I shall think about it, sir. Very seriously, I assure you. Tax on brandy has never affected me; that on tea I have reason to resent." He thought of his mother and Kate, now able to afford the taxed tea every day. He thought also of his own position, proprietor of a well-run, over-staffed inn, not very profitable. He thought of Cousin Margaret, sitting here all those years, an elegant spider in the centre of a complicated web, making money which enabled her to extend charity even to lame horses.

He was, in fact, almost decided; nothing much to lose and a lot to gain, and another consideration bearing down. One day, and not in the too-distant future, he'd need to take a wife, beget a son.

"To begin with," Adam said, "I'll send a cart, first thing tomorrow morning, to collect the two unsatisfactory barrels and deliver the ones you expected."

"That might not be wise. No. I think the better way would be for my man to come again—the weather is hot and the harvest work exceptionally heavy. I'll send in, and now that you know—see that I get the right ones."

There was clatter of feet in the passage, a knock on the door. The vicar's ugly, saddle-nosed, buck-toothed boy.

"Oh, sir," and he did not mean Sir Francis. "There's a young lady took ill. In the church. The vicar, sir, Mr. Fison, sir, he say can you help. She come off the coach, sir."

"I'll come," Adam said, accepting the responsibility, though not all those who came by that coach were guests and therefore his concern. Church and inn were, however, close neighbours; and he was glad to leave Sir Francis.

12 Adam and Isabel

THE YOUNG LADY LOOKED DEAD. MR. FISON HAD PLAINLY done his best for her, lifted her on to the front pew and put his wadded cassock under her head. All around were the odours of smelling-salts and brandy.

"I did what I could," Mr. Fison said. "There are occasions . . . I keep a few restoratives . . . but, poor thing, poor thing, no response at all. I greatly fear that it is not merely a swoon."

"We'll see," Adam said. He lifted the girl and bent her forward so that her head touched her knees. The phrase, a mere bag of bones, shot through his mind. In and around Aldermanbury he'd seen plenty of people to whom the same description applied, and plenty with the same waxen pallor. But they did not wear silk, or travel by coach.

"How did you know that she came by coach?"

"She told me," the vicar said. "It was really most disconcerting. She just . . ."

The girl made a little sound, moved, lifted her head and looked at them blankly for a second, and then with a kind of fear.

"It's all right," Adam said quickly. "You're all right. Don't move for a bit." To Mr. Fison he said, "Where's the brandy?"

"I can't exactly . . ."

"S'in your pocket, sir," said the boy. "And the salts is there on the pew." The vicar produced a rather handsome hunting-flask, unscrewed its silver top, and poured out a few drops into it. "I wasted a good deal," he said, apologetically.

And swigged rather more, Adam thought, holding the minute cup to the girl. She sipped. The boy retrieved the smelling-salts bottle and waved it vaguely about.

"I'm extremely sorry to have given you all so much trouble," the girl said. Her voice, soft and musical, accorded well with the silk dress, but was contradictory to Adam's near certainty that what ailed her was hunger. It needed a little effort to ask the vital question and, when he did, it sounded gruff.

"When did you last have anything to eat?"

"I . . . oh, perhaps yesterday or . . . really, I cannot remember. I'll go now. Thank you all very much." With a rustle of silk she swung her feet to the floor, stood up, and swayed, grasped at the carved pew-end, steadied herself. "Oh, dear," she said with the hollowest possible assumption of a light manner, "perhaps I need air."

"I know what you need. Come along. Hang on to me. It isn't far."

"I know what you're thinking," she said when she had eaten enough, yet with daintiness, to take the sharpest edge from her hunger. "I eat like a starving dog. And that is what I am—a runaway, starving bitch. But I've been living on water. All the way from Bristol." She ate another mouthful and added, "Sleeping in churches. Do you suppose I should have died in that one if the parson hadn't found me?"

"I should think it very likely."

"And that might not have been such a bad thing." Her face darkened. "I shall not get a very warm welcome when I get to

Norwich. How strange, I don't think I can eat any more, delicious as it is."

"Drink the milk," he said. "I've heard say that it's better not to eat too much after a long fast. I'll see that something is put in your room, so if you wake in the night . . ."

"You mean I can sleep here? How extraordinarily kind! And you know nothing about me. If I told you, you wouldn't believe me. I wouldn't believe it myself if I read it in a book. I don't think Father will believe me—he's very unworldly. I doubt if he knows what a brothel is."

"And you do?"

"I lived in one for a month. Not that I . . ." She did not colour, but she looked away, staring at the window, against which the soft darkness pressed. "That is what is going to be so *very* difficult . . . Either people will not believe that it was a brothel, or they will believe it, and then *not* believe that I had no part in it. But I assure you, Mrs. Plumber never made a penny out of me. On the contrary, indeed. This fine dress, these shoes, and the coach fare—I *stole*. Yes, I'm a thief. But better that than the other thing. At least to me. And in a way I'd earned it. Look!" She pushed back the full, lace-cuffed sleeve and revealed on her thin upper arm some fading bruises, yellowish, purplish.

To the physical violence which the strong inflicted upon the weak, Adam was no stranger. Men beat their wives, their children; costermongers beat their donkeys. Now and then a woman would turn the tables and strike back—often with fatal results. Adam's grandfather and father had both told him, when he was young and shocked by the cruelty all around him, that it was useless to worry over what you couldn't help. Nevertheless, at the sight of the bruises, anger and compassion filled him.

"I think I could tell you," the girl said, "to see how it sounds! My name is Isabel Prentice and my father is a poor parson in Norwich. Completely unworldly, devoted to books. My mother died years ago, and I kept house and helped with the parish as well as I could. Calves'-foot jelly for the poor, made out of chicken bones. That kind of thing." Her mouth moved in a bitter-sweet smile. "Then Father re-married, or rather was married by a large, strong-minded woman with some private means. This is not a stepmother story; we never quarrelled. It was just that there was no need, no place for me any more. And one day my stepmother heard through a friend who had heard through a friend of an old lady in Bristol who was lonely and needed a companion, one who could read.

"Messages went back and forth, and a decent-seeming man, who said he was the old lady's son, came to interview me. He thought I was very suitable, engaged me and gave me my coach-fare. I went on the right day, and to the right address only to find..." Remembered horror darkened her face; her voice changed. "I must say for Mrs. Plumber, she was not one to give up easily, but then neither am I. She tried everything— cajolery, flattery, pretty clothes—as you see. Then came the rough treatment: shouts and blows, solitary confinement, bread and water. Always with the promise that if I would behave... I almost reached the point."

She shuddered, but her gaze remained steady. "In fact, Mrs. Plumber had underestimated two things—my resilience, for which I can claim no credit, since it was not inexhaustible. One often hears people say 'I would sooner die than do such and such a thing.' I'd said it; I'd thought it, but... The other thing was that, even in the most debased of women, there can be some spark of kindness. A poor painted creature called Carrie deliberately left the door open one evening, after bring- ing me my bread. I waited until the house was quiet. I knew where Mrs. Plumber kept what she called petty cash. I knew exactly what the coach-fare was. I took it to the exact penny and came away. And now... I must confess that, when I went to that church this evening, I was very low indeed. I sat down. Then the parson came and I tried to explain my presence. I stood up and he began to tell me about the antiquity... and down I fell. What a long dreary story! I felt I must explain. If I have been tedious, please forgive me."

The carpenter in Aldermanbury, with a disabled mother and a sister only partially employed to support, had never seriously contemplated matrimony, and had thought himself fortunate never to have been attracted to any woman. He had pitied rather than envied the various men he knew who had either married or taken up with a woman, and spawned, adding child after child to the miserable multitude who, without work, starved or, with work, slaved for a pittance. Yet he was not entirely without sexual experience—years ago, when he was young and callow—both experiences vibrant at the time and then easily put away. The possibility of making a little extra money by picking strawberries at Fulham, in the last of the long summer's daylight, and the husky girl whom a day's picking had not exhausted. There was that. And then a bought woman in Bishopsgate, smelling not of strawberries, but of musk. Neither experience had he wished to repeat and, in fact, in later years he had been positively glad that the family, the Gildersons, come down in the world, yearning for past glories, would not be perpetuated. Since coming to Mallow he had slightly changed his mind about that, but had had little time to think. It was just that he felt, at the back of his mind, that one day he would marry a sensible, amiable woman and beget a son who, in due time, would become landlord of the One Bull.

Now, listening to the girl's story, hearing that musical voice, watching the small graceful gestures, he felt something new to him. Not the lust of the eye; she was far too thin and pale to inspire merely carnal thoughts. He was familiar with the desire to protect and provide; he had felt that towards his mother and sister, but always with an accompanying feeling of duty. To protect and provide for somebody to whom he owed nothing would be a delight. He pitied her—all the more so because she had told her story without self-pity, indeed with something approaching detachment, tinged with a wryness that was almost humour.

"Your father," he asked tentatively, "has he shown no concern for you? You said that you had been in . . . in Bristol for two months."

"He cannot be judged by ordinary standards. He is writing a book. A valiant attempt to synchronise the Synoptists—Matthew, Mark and Luke, you know. He may miss my help with that; I always tried to keep his pages in order. And he will certainly miss me in the running of the Ragged School. But such concern would be very glancing. I can well imagine him saying, 'And where is Isabel?' My stepmother will say, 'Surely you remember,' and tell him, for the fortieth time that I am in Bristol—and very happy. He'll believe it." She looked distressed again. "Oh, dear, when I arrive . . . Such confusion, he not understanding a word I say, and she calling me a liar."

"Tomorrow will be soon enough to think about that," Adam said. "You should go to bed now."

"In a real bed, thanks to your kindness! My bones yearn! Church pews are very hard."

He conducted her to what had been Cousin Margaret's room.

In accordance with his orders it had been made ready: fresh, lavender-scented sheets on the bed, a thick, slow-burning candle, a jug of milk, a plate of sweet cakes on the night-table. "You will find all you need there, I think," he said, indicating the chest of drawers. He had, so far, done nothing about the disposal of Cousin Margaret's clothes. At first he had imagined his mother and Kate moving to Mallow and using or getting rid of things as they chose. Since their decision to stay in London he had, almost every day, planned to pack a couple of bags with the most useful and practical garments and send them by coach, but he had not yet done so.

He would not have admitted that he felt an aversion to this particular room, yet he tended to avoid it, simply moving all the books and papers into the next-door room, which had been his ever since his arrival in Mallow. Even his cursory and uninformed glance at the dead woman's things had confirmed what her list of personal expenditure had hinted at—a fondness for fine clothing at some time in the past. Everything of fine quality; nothing very new.

In fact—and the thought struck him only now as he lighted the bedside candle—while the inn had been a prosperous concern, Cousin Margaret had spent lavishly on herself; then she had taken to smuggling and lavished the money on charity. Ill-gotten gains. Tainted money. Had she felt that?

The girl, with a remarkable lack of self-consciousness and with unfailing instinct, had pulled out the right drawer and now stood, in the gathering light of the big candle, holding up a white garment, long, voluminous, yet of stuff so fine as to seem unsubstantial. She said in awed voice, "How very beautiful! It's almost . . . almost as though I were expected."

As soon as she was in bed she fell into the deep sleep of exhaustion. After a while she woke, hungry again, and realised with a pang of guilt that she had forgotten to extinguish the thick candle, now very low in its holder, but bright. She ate several of the small cakes and drank some milk, revelling in the softness of the bed, and the pillows stuffed with down, the fine linen of the sheets, the more-than-fine lawn of the night-dress.

To find that she was not alone in the room did not surprise or alarm her. Travelling from Norwich to Bristol in the orthodox way, she had learned a little about inns. Often, with a sudden influx of guests, innkeepers put two, even three people in a room. The sharer of this room was a woman, busy at the table in the bow window. Reading? Writing? Completely engrossed. One hesitated to disturb such concentration, but some civility was demanded. The girl said, softly, "I hope you do not mind sharing your bed with me. It is very wide." The woman took no notice at all, but that did not seem strange to the girl, who had grown up in the ambience of a man who could similarly absent himself and be deaf to anything except a call to food. And really, why should she bother? Give way to the wonderful feeling of floating, away and away . . . She made one last effort. "The candle," she said, "will not last long." The woman at the table ignored that warning. Possibly deaf. No matter. Turn over, go to sleep again.

On the other side of the dividing wall Adam Gilderson was shadow-boxing with things he could name—all uncomfortable—and others which he could not name, and none of them, curiously, concerned with the girl, the waif, sleeping in the next room. A man must sort himself out.

All the old family traditions must be remembered now. Gildersons were poor, but honest. No Gilderson ever scamped a job, or got into bad company, or got on the wrong side of the law. Gildersons contracted legal marriages. Gildersons kept their word, even if it meant working half through the night to get work done in time. On and on and on, all adding up to the fact that, despite being poor and done out of their rights, the Gildersons were superior people.

Was Adam Gilderson now to turn smuggler?

Cousin Margaret had done so—and she was a Gilderson. Ah, but of the other, the usurping branch.

He considered the process of breaking free. How many people would resent his withdrawal? And of those, how many were in a position to do him harm? 'Bear in mind that I am a justice of the peace . . .' There seemed no obvious risk in carrying on the clearing station; after all, Cousin Margaret had done it for years, and for an innkeeper to fall foul of men in position could be dangerous.

Had he committed himself? No, he had said he would think about it. He had, however, promised two of the secret barrels. And he had been thinking about it when called to the church. In fact, had he not disliked Sir Francis Colman's manner, he would probably have given a more positive answer, for he was against import taxes which, while hitting the rich to whom they were merely fleabites, deprived poor women of the comfort of tea, poor men of the comfort of tobacco.

Why so dubious about the whole thing, now?

(He did not know, and, if told, would have thought the whole thing fanciful nonsense, that, in the church, his decision not quite wholly made and his mind diverted by the need to help the girl—not really his responsibility—he had stood on a flagstone, indistinguishable from any other, which covered the bones of a man who, in the days when people believed in miracles, had been a renowned miracle-worker. The whole great abbey, Mallow itself, had grown up, rooted and nourished by what lay forgotten, lost—the splendid shrine demolished, the miracles regarded as superstitious myths.)

When, in the darkness of that warm August night, Adam Gilderson made up his mind, he believed that he decided against carrying on with the game because that seemed the harder thing to do, and he had been reared to believe that the harder course was the right one.

The decision made, he was ready to sleep at last. Then he remembered the girl. He must see that she had a good breakfast. Give her a little money so that she could pay for food and a bed at Thetford or Wymondham.

In the morning she looked better, vastly better. It was incredible—and to a thinking man, pitiable—what a difference a little food and a good night's sleep could make. Especially to the young.

He had sent her a message by the chambermaid: would she breakfast in the public room or prefer a tray in private? In private, she said, and having seen a well-laden tray carried in, and allowed her time to get started on the meal, he tapped at the door and entered. The light from the window caught her hair, densely black and looking as if it had just been polished. Of course it has, he thought. Poor girl, sleeping in churches, with not even a brush for her hair.

"I took advantage of everything, even the scent," she said. "Quite irresistible!" This morning her melodious voice had a new quality, almost a gaiety which it had lacked last evening. Adam looked at the little scent-bottle, a white dove with tiny pink feet. A toy, useless to him.

"If you like, you can keep it. In fact, take anything you like or can use. Everything in this room belonged to a distant cousin of mine. She is dead. The stuff is useless to me. I'll find a valise for you."

"Oh, how very . . . No, that would be most unwise. Who would believe my story if I went home laden with what is so obviously *not* the reward of virtue?"

"I didn't think of that."

"I'm glad I did." She chewed a mouthful thoughtfully. "I woke quite early and lay thinking . . . Truly, I have been running around like a hen with its head off. I'm under no *compulsion* to go home, am I? I could find work of some kind. I'm quite well educated and in the domestic line well trained in making bricks without straw. I was *lured* to Bristol under false pretences, but surely somewhere a lonely old lady needs a companion. Or some family could do with a governess. Or a cook."

"Well, yes, I suppose," he began.

Afterwards he could reflect that he had been given no time to think, to weigh things in his mind. In the house the predeparture clamour began. A lordly voice shouted, "Landlord!" and a subservient one said, "Sir, you're wanted."

"The coach . . ." Adam said, and saw her change before his eyes. All the restored youth and animation drained out of her face, leaving it as pale and sunken as it had been overnight.

"I'll be back," he said quickly and ran out into the yard. There were, he knew by this time, customers who liked to be seen off properly and given a chance to say a few words of compliment or complaint.

"I shall give my age as twenty. So much more responsible, don't you think, than seventeen and a half?"

"You look even less than that."

"Wait until I am wearing this," she said, stitching away at a grey linsey dress, the only one in Cousin Margaret's wardrobe which lent itself to the role of companion, governess or even—a last resort—cook. (Last resort because, as she said, cooks were all middle-aged and stout, and were, or pretended to be, Mrs.)

She said, "Your distant cousin must have been a very elegant woman, Mr. Gilderson. All her shoes pinch my feet which I never, until now, thought over-large."

And of course nobody could go looking for a decent post wearing a pair of satin slippers, meant for indoor wear and already suffering from hard usage. So shoes to fit her must be made.

"I can never, never repay you. I can only hope that God will."

He was unable, just then, to give her his full attention, for she had come, with her airs and graces, her pathos and talent to amuse, at the wrong time for him. He was too busy extricating himself from the net which Cousin Margaret had woven and left as part of her legacy to him. She'd been such a secretive old woman that he could only move, now, by the process of trial and error. He often thought that nobody had been so completely befuddled as he was in the last weeks of August and all through September. By the mere law of averages, some people received the right barrels and were content, and came in and said, "This for the beer, Mr. Gilderson. This for the other." When he tried to explain, some said: Well they'd always known it was too good to last; others, like Sir Francis Colman, were angry and made threats; a few whined—and that was worst of all, hitting a sensitive nerve. "Look at me," said a cadaverous man wearing a peculiar waistcoat under a shabby jacket. "About this time of the year I go up to the Grindle, and the shepherd there fills all these little pockets. With tea. Maybe you, Mr. Gilderson, coming from London, don't understand what a bit of tea, cheap and untaxed, means to a lot of poor women, with winter setting in."

And once a thin dark man, with a face that could have been hacked out of hard wood with a blunt hatchet, slithered in and argued and, finding Adam obdurate, went away saying, "You'll be sorry for this, Mr. bloody self-righteous Mr. Gilderson!"

The money for "the other," Adam kept separately, waiting in blind ignorance for someone to collect or demand it. The thin dark man had not asked for it; in fact he had hardly mentioned money at all, except to say that Adam was breaking up a very profitable organisation.

In the midst of all this confusion the girl called Isabel slipped into place so quietly and naturally that he was hardly aware of her growing importance in his life. He found himself looking forward to the end of the day when, everything in order, he could settle down with a pint and his pipe and let her entertain him. He had never before enjoyed the company of anyone who could talk easily and gaily and make a story out of almost nothing. When the grey linsey dress was made to fit and the shoes had been delivered, she could walk out, and within a day or two knew more about Mallow than Adam did. A fact she would report, saying, "Isn't it interesting?" Or she'd begin, "Wouldn't it be fascinating to imagine..."

She was anxious to find a post, and with this in view called upon the vicar. "Not that my father was useful about such things, but many parsons are. And Mr. Fison said he would bear me in mind. I was obliged to deceive him slightly." Her voice regretted the deceit, her eyes danced. A parsonage background, she said, was desirable, a guarantee of respectability and an explanation of education. Also, in this case, a kind of claim on a class solidarity. "But it is quite extraordinary how they know one another. Even my father, so unworldly. They went to school or college together; or they met at a convention. So I said my name was Smith, that my father was dead, years ago; that I had lived with an aunt in London. I explained my plight on that calamitous evening as due to shock—the shock of learning that another aunt, in Brancaster, had died, too. I was quite ruthless, dealing out death right and left." She laughed, and Adam laughed with her. Then she said, "Mr. Fison also said something to which I do hope you will not take exception. He thought this inn an unsuitable address, the more particularly as we are both unmarried. Any correspondence with a potential employer, any interview, should involve the vicarage. Not that his parlour looks as though any competent female would occupy it for ten minutes without wielding a duster."

"He is probably right."

"I am so glad that you are not offended. Oh, and then he told me a most fascinating thing. He thinks our sign is wrong and that the words One Bull should not refer to an animal, but to a papal communication. Had you ever heard that?"

"No. I'm sorry, I don't see the connection."

"I am not myself very clear. I would not commit myself, but I have a vague idea that papal communications bore leaden seals. Bulla. Bullion. A possible connection. But nothing like so pretty as the present sign."

Prettiness had hitherto meant little to Adam Gilderson, but he was not colour-blind and he saw, and more important, felt that dead grey, with demure little white collar and cuffs didn't suit a girl with black hair, near amber eyes and no other colour in her face except lips almost the exact shade of the scent-bottle dove's feet. He suggested making another dress to fit.

"And surely my cousin had some trinkets. Er—ear-bobs or some such thing."

"Oh, yes. In the table drawer, but I thought it would look presumptuous."

"I like you to have pretty things," he said. So, keeping the grey linsey for day wear, she wore tawny or deep rose—both of velvet—in the evenings, and below the smooth sweep of her hair the golden ear-rings danced and flashed.

It was like a game played by two people whose childhoods had been bleak.

She persisted in her search for employment. "Shopkeepers often hear of such things. And dressmakers," she said. She cultivated their acquaintance and made him laugh with a recountal of failures. "If I ever achieve the dignity of a tombstone, I will order it carved 'Just too late!' Everybody knows of somebody in urgent need of a companion or a governess only a short time ago, but now well-suited."

However, Mr. Fison's inquiries bore fruit. An elderly parishioner, left alone because her daughter had married (incidentally a most unsuitable marriage—to a tenant farmer). Mrs. Bastion needed a companion. No rough work—there was a maid to do that. A very comfortable house on the Bosworth Road. Mrs. Bastion had been singularly unfortunate—four companions in a year—and every one completely unsatisfactory.

Kind man, he trotted along with this news, pleased as a dog laying a game-bird or a rabbit or a slipper at his master's feet. He, like Adam, had fallen victim to Isabel Smith's charm, and had he been a marrying man . . . but he was not. And too old to change now. And many parishioners preferred an unmarried priest. "I am reasonably sure, Miss Smith, that if you go along . . . You can hardly mistake the house—white, with green shutters."

"I don't like the sound of it," Adam said. "Four in a year." He had only his own experience to go upon, but in Aldermanbury and similar places an employer was judged by whether his men stuck to him or not, and an employee was similarly assessed. Good masters very seldom lost good workmen, and good workmen seldom joined the drifting unemployed.

"I'll go and mix a bit, and see if anybody knows this Mrs. Bastion."

All the time he had been aware of the fact that he had been

rather neglectful of his customers. He was not, by nature, a convivial man and, having seen that all was going smoothly, had been rather distantly civil, had been glad enough to retire to the private side of the house.

This evening he went into the Coffee Room, where the drinks served were not restricted to coffee, and where certain substantial citizens spent some of their evenings talking business and parish-pump politics. He was not yet accepted by them as a crony and sometimes, when he had looked in and said, "Everything to your satisfaction, gentlemen?" talk had ceased with an abruptness that indicated that he had been the subject under discussion.

This evening, however, as soon as he had mentioned Mrs. Bastion's name, everybody became garrulous, capping each other's examples of a meanness outstanding even in a thrifty community. She was a widow, well-to-do; she's treated her family abominably; she starved her maids—one, a charity child had actually run back to the foundling place, begging to be taken in there. As for those poor creatures she called companions...

"I can't possibly let you go there," Adam told Isabel.

For the first time he saw her colour and look embarrassed.

"But how can I tell Mr. Fison, after all the trouble he has taken? The tales are probably grossly exaggerated. Gossip usually is. And she may be less well-to-do than people think. To shun the interview without explanation would show lack of courtesy."

Adam made a sound of impatience, looked at his watch, and went out.

The vicarage stood in a street parallel to the Bosworth Road; so to reach it Adam walked into the teeth of the wind from the east. Autumn was here; winter would follow. Mrs. Bastion would almost certainly be as sparing of fuel as she was of food. The poor girl would be cold...

When he had explained, Mr. Fison's manner chilled.

"Mrs. Bastion has certainly been unfortunate in her companions. One drank, one was impertinent, the others... I forget, but certainly unsatisfactory. And in view of the fact that she employed two of them on my recommendation, I had some difficulty in persuading her that Miss Smith was a charming and superior person. It was all the more difficult since Mrs. Bastion was already in correspondence with a young lady in

Colchester. And disappointing, too. Miss Smith seemed so genuinely anxious for employment."

"That may be. I'm not anxious for her to take a post where she'd be half-starved."

Mr. Fison had a waspish side to his nature, well controlled by the need for diplomacy. Very occasionally, the waspish side, denied other outlet, planted its venom into Mr. Fison himself. It did so now. He said with deceptive mildness, "It is a great pity, Mr. Gilderson, that your concern for the young lady's physical well-being does not extend to other, more important spheres."

"And what exactly do you mean by that?"

"Precisely what I say. Surely it takes no great leap of the imagination to understand what is being said. Servants—even the best of them—talk. And if you think for a moment . . . Charity," the wasp said, "seldom extends to the provision of velvet dresses and trinkets and perfume. And now a downright refusal to allow the young lady to accept a respectable post."

"I have been very blind," Adam said.

He dashed out of the house, fury mounting in him. Fury with himself for being such a stupid fool; fury with foul-tongued, filthy-minded people—his own servants among them. Who else would know about the velvet dresses? And to think that he'd never laid a finger . . . Never even thought about such a thing.

Mrs. Bloom, who most ably combined the duties of head cook and housekeeper, was in the passage outside the private parlour. Spying! "Get out!" he snarled at her.

"I just wanted to ask, sir," she began. He pushed past her, tore open the parlour door, went in, slammed it, and stood with his back against it as though barring it against the world.

Isabel looked up from her book. His manner of entry, his red face, his harsh breathing alarmed her: his manner was usually so cool and controlled.

"Has something . . . upset you?"

It then flashed upon him that this was something he could never tell her. Yet his coming in like this, and probably his appearance, demanded some explanation.

"Yes. I'm very angry. With that parson. I went . . . And it isn't gossip. That damned woman has had four slaves in a year. He sent two of them—and was prepared to send *you*! I could wring his neck!" He could only hope that he sounded convincing.

"Is that all?"

"Yes. I mean, no. I burst in like that because I'd just made up my mind to do something which doesn't come easy to me. I've got to say it before I lose my nerve. Isabel, will you marry me? I know I'm too old for you and the place isn't doing as it should, and compared with you I'm ignorant, but I'd, I mean if . . ." He ran out of words. He *had* lost his nerve.

"I think," she said, almost severely, "that *you* have been listening to gossip. Or did Mr. Fison read you a sermon about living in sin? I really can't have you marrying me just to save my reputation."

"You . . . you knew?"

"Of course. How could I not? Greasy, sly looks. Nasty little innuendos about hadn't I got a job already? Only to be expected." She said the last words with such acceptance of the world's unkindness that it cut him to the heart, but before he could speak she said, "You're far too nice and noble to understand how loathsome people can be. As to marriage, I fell upon you—literally—in the church that evening. And you have been kinder than God to me. But that is no reason why you should support me for the rest of my life."

"But that's what I want . . . all I want. Not *support*—love and cherish." Somehow, and he never knew how he got there, he was down on his knees, saying, "I love you. I love you. I did from the first moment I saw you."

It was a felicitous marriage, and one for which Mr. Fison took full credit; had he not, in effect, made the original introduction? Had he not made Mr. Gilderson see the error of his ways? How much an error was debatable, since almost two years elapsed before the birth of the first child, a boy, christened, inevitably, Edman.

In his hurried and unromantic proposal Adam had said that the place wasn't doing what it should. He had deliberately abandoned the secret trade which had made all the difference between a buoyant business and one just holding its own. At Michaelmas, that great settlement day, when Mr. Brewster came, himself, to collect "the other money," undeniably his due, the sum that Adam had put aside was far less than the debt.

"Not to be wondered at," Mr. Brewster said. "Nobody in his right senses would pay this sort of debt without a hope of future favours. Once the word got round that you'd given up . . . See. Now I'm in a different position. Granted I can't *sue* you. But I can, and I damned well will cut off your supplies. You can whistle for your beer!"

"I'll pay. And I'll whistle up another brewer." Adam spoke with defiance, but to make good the difference between what he had received in surreptitious payments and what Mr. Brewster claimed was owed to him, he had to sell most of the trinkets which Cousin Margaret and her father had owned. And Mr. Brewster's nearest competitor was at Triver, so that the charge for delivery was higher, and the beer, for some reason, was of inferior quality.

Then a horse, an animal of quality, valued by its owner at forty pounds, was stolen from the stable, and by law Adam was held responsible. The law had been passed to curb the dishonest innkeepers who were in league with horse-thieves, but it bore hard on honest men. The disappearance of the horse was—and remained—a mystery. The archway over which the One Bull sign hung, and which was the sole entry to the yard, was fitted with a stout gate, punctually closed and bolted on the inside, and two stable-hands slept over the stable. Adam and Isabel, occupying a ground-floor room, separated from the yard by only the garden, would, they thought, have heard anything there was to hear in the quiet night.

"Now," Adam said in desperation. "I have no choice but to mortgage the inn."

"Oh dear! History repeating itself." Isabel had been reading with fascination the journal kept by a Marguerite Gilderson between the years 1618 and 1645. It was sad reading, except for entries made at Highgate where Mrs. Houghton's establishment sounded happy. After that, financial difficulties, debts, and a long record of domestic tyranny. "How could I ever have been so deceived by Jimmy? Why did I ever marry him? So ignorant and so frightened. I must bring up my boys to be brave. Thank God I have as yet no daughter!" "Terrible scene between Edman and his father this evening. I feared they would come to blows. E. threatened to leave. Would that I could! Yet I loved this place and I saved it. J. forgets this."

"Once before when the inn was in low water somebody borrowed and had to pay interest and then had to borrow more to pay the interest. Darling, think! Have you no friends who, between them, could muster forty pounds and ask for no interest?"

"The few friends I had in London were all poor, and here I have made none . . ." He stopped short, thinking: I have made only enemies . . . He remembered the dark, harsh-featured man who had said, "You will be sorry for this." Plainly a man at the very heart of the illicit trading. And near to him, Mr. Brewster, doubly offended because he had lost a safe distribution centre and a regular customer. Put the two together!

"Wait here, and don't worry," Adam said and went out into the yard, where the owner of the lost horse was standing in the midst of a little circle, some of them gentlemen who had not lost their horses and should by now have been on their way. The younger of the stable-boys was crying, the older uttering oaths and offering to fight anybody who dared doubt his word that he and Billy here had slept within reach of the horses and never heard a sound.

The owner of the stolen horse was not far from tears himself. He'd lost, he said, not just a mount, but his best friend. "Best friend I ever had, bar none."

Adam shouldered his way in, and said with the dignity and authority that was his from ancestors he had never heard about. "Sir, you would recognise your horse? Would he recognise you? And would you be prepared to take a great gamble? And ride in a jolting cart?"

He was, he knew, taking a great risk himself. And he was no gambler. The dispossessed Gildersons had never had money to squander, and as the old rickety cart jolted towards Bosworth, Adam underwent yet another new experience: an emptiness between his collar-bone and his belly, with his heart, labouring in loneliness, going thump, thump, thump, not as it had done after healthy, physical exertion in the past. This *hurt*. But he ignored it, just as he had ignored a cut finger when a chisel slipped, a bruised foot when a plank fell.

And he had been right to come; right to ignore the pain and the difficulty of drawing breath, and the feeling of despair. For there the stolen horse was, in Mr. Brewster's stable, wedged between two of the great amber-coloured dray-horses. His owner cried, "Caesar," and the animal's response left no doubt in the minds of the witnesses—those few gentlemen curious enough to accompany the slow cart down to Bosworth.

Mr. Brewster waddled out to investigate the uproar, and denied all knowledge of the horse. It must just have wandered in; why should he steal a horse? He had two of his own. He could buy anything he needed. He'd lived in Bosworth all his life, aye and his father before him, and nobody had ever accused him of any dishonesty before.

The fact that the horse was wearing a halter which, like most other portable things around the inn bore the One Bull mark—a much-simplified version of the sign over the arch-way—did not embarrass Mr. Brewster at all. Obviously then, he said, somebody with a grudge against him—and he looked straight at Adam as he spoke—had placed the horse there with a view to getting him into trouble. "And I ask you to ask yourselves, gentlemen, what put it into anybody's mind to look here—five miles away?"

What indeed?

The incident did the One Bull considerable damage.

Adam made the inevitable economies. Isabel would have made more. "I can cook. I like cooking. And I should be far less wasteful than Mrs. Bloom is."

"I don't want you in the kitchen. Besides, you have never cooked for any number—and we still have the coach twice a week." Sometimes he regarded this twice-weekly visitation as a mixed blessing. It lent a kind of prestige, but it meant keeping staff capable of dealing adequately with a number of people on two evenings of the week—and idling about for the other five. It meant reserving a room called the Post Office long before such a term was officially recognised. But with the King's Head to the south and the Green Man to the north taking the cream of the trade, without the regular coach the One Bull would have become a mere drinking-place with a few beds for those who could not find accommodation elsewhere. He understood only too well why the woman he thought of as Cousin Margaret had turned smuggler. And yet he never regretted his decision. It was only that sometimes—not always, but often enough to disturb him, when he thought of the only-just-solvent present and the not-very-promising future—he'd know that dropping-away feeling in his very vitals, his heart trying to fill the space, and the pain.

13 The Oak Room

ISABEL SAID, "MY DEAR, I HAVE BEEN THINKING. IN MALLOW and for miles around there is no place of public entertainment. Nowhere where people can listen to music, or give a ball."

Such things were completely out of his narrow experience, and for a moment he gaped at her, uncomprehending. She said, quickly, "Oh, I mean perfectly respectable places. As in Norwich and in Bristol. Places where ordinary people could enjoy themselves, at moderate cost. With refreshments," she said, warming to the subject. "Little pasties and cakes and winecup for ladies. I think the Oak Room would lend itself splendidly. It would need a platform, but that you could easily construct."

There had been a time when what was now called the Oak Room had seemed small and, with its low ceiling, cramped, to the builders of new houses intended for communal living and open to the rafters. But over the years fashions and ideas had changed, and inside a town's boundaries space had become precious. Most of the remaining big old houses had been divided and divided again. Very rich men, in the country, still built mansions with ballrooms and music rooms, but at the time when Isabel made the suggestion of turning to entertainment as a subsidiary source of income, the Oak Room at the One Bull was the biggest single apartment in Mallow.

That it was unique in other ways remained a secret.

When Adam pondered the suggestion and confessed total ignorance of public pleasure-places, Isabel was ready with information. Speaking of the past as though it were in another age, she said, "Once, long ago, in Norwich, I went to a concert. Somebody had given Father a ticket. It was *wonderful*. And then, before Mrs. Plumber despaired of me, she took me and another girl to a place, called, I think, the Floral Hall. There was dancing. Quite sedate. As it would be here, I assure you."

"Well, I know nothing about such things. But if you want a platform, I can make one. You must tell me how high and how wide."

He knew about wood, and he was not surprised to find some of the solid-looking panels so riddled with worm as to be like dry sponge, quite incapable of holding the rear of the platform which, in his meticulous way, he had visualised as being supported by outsize brackets as well as legs. The only dancing he had ever seen had been boisterous, and he didn't want his platform to shift if bumped into. Wondering what the wall behind the panelling was like, he removed a section, and was startled to be confronted by a picture.

His Cousin Margaret had called him a puritan, and perhaps he was, for after surprise came shock. The section of the mural made visible was not very wide, but it showed enough—a female, almost naked, reclining upon a low couch. It did not strike him that the female was beautiful or that great skill had gone into the portrayal. He just thought it was highly indecent.

The removal of two more rotten panels confirmed his verdict, for she was not alone; men with rather more clothing, but still very lightly clad, lolled on either side of her, and over the naked shoulder of one man another female, wearing, it seemed, nothing at all, was pouring something into a stemmed cup. He had chanced upon one of the best-preserved sections of the painted wall; it was neither flaked nor faded.

Adam was not curious about how the wall-pictures had ever come to be painted, by whom, or when. What he understood perfectly was the motive of somebody who had thought fit to hide them—as he must do, as soon as he had ascertained the state of the wall itself. It was made of some substance which he had never encountered before, so rock-hard that even his brace-and-bit made little impression upon it.

He stood back, seething with frustration; wood as rotten as a pear, backed by a wall, not of stone, but of some substance equally hard. So, after all, his platform would be no more than a solid table—he'd make it very solid indeed!

And what to do about that indecent display of fleshliness? Given time, he could have made new panels, almost indistinguishable from the old, but he had no time, for Isabel, his dear one, his darling, was already busy with plans and arrangements.

The Oak Room, she said, must start off as they intended it to go on—a place of innocent pleasure, and she had enlisted the aid of Mr. Fison. "Dear, I know," she said. "My father, so vague as not to know Sunday from Monday and with a very *poor* living, yet exercised a certain authority. When he chose to exert it. I could tell you of many instances. And since Mr. Fison is willing to countenance us and hold his fund-raising effort here, I think it would be advantageous. Putting the stamp of respectability, as it were . . ."

Mr. Fison had, in fact, moved in so smartly, so eager to put his fund-raising effort into effect, that Adam was now short of time.

Short of breath, too, and afflicted with the thumping and the pain. This time worse, lasting longer, and invading his left arm. But he survived, and made what he recognised with regret as a makeshift job. Good enough, for the oak panelling had never been attached to the hard plaster wall, but to what he called battens—upright posts of pine, less vulnerable than oak to worm, and spaced out between the panelling and the offensive wall. To two of these stout stanchions he fixed his platform, and the disgusting picture he obliterated, not with plain limewash, which would have stood out so starkly, but with a nicely-mixed bucketful of whitewash and walnut-husk dye.

The opening event was a great success. Many people, seen all too seldom in church, came to drink tea or lemonade and eat wafer-thin biscuits. The entrance price, sixpence, included refreshments. Mr. Fison made a graceful speech, pointing out that, in opening the Oak Room in aid of a good cause, Mr. and Mrs. Gilderson were doing a public service and providing an amenity which Mallow had long lacked. He hoped the room would see many equally happy occasions. He did not specify exactly what good cause was about to benefit, knowing from experience that people had wildly varying ideas of where charity should begin—and end. He also knew that St. Cerdic's could well do with one of the new "enclosed" stoves.

Adam, not a good mixer, stood about, looking, as shy people often did, aloof and haughty, but Isabel was in her element, her parsonage training very much in evidence, affable to one and all.

From that venture the One Bull did not profit by a penny. But something had germinated. Before the afternoon ended, the corn-chandler's wife, who had never before set foot in licensed premises, had decided this would be the ideal place for the wedding feast which she wanted to give her only child, a well-beloved daughter. Like most people living in the centre of the town, the corn-chandler lived above his business premises, in narrow rooms, all inter-communicating. And how lovely it would be to hire not only space but also service! And so near the church, too!

The One Bull's position was now positively an advantage. It was within easy walking distance of every part of the town: a great consideration for citizens who did not own carriages. And presently Adam introduced yet another innovation—the first sedan chair to be seen in Mallow. It was regarded with suspicion at first. What would happen if one of the chairmen was careless and let go of his two shafts? Well, nothing very damaging, since the chair had its own short sturdy legs. And hadn't Mrs. Gilderson been the first to use it, with her baby on her lap, taking his first airing?

Very soon the inn owned two sedan chairs, and, although they were mainly employed in the transport of patrons to the many and varied functions in the Oak Room, they could be hired during the morning or afternoon by those who wished to go shopping or to make calls.

The conversion of the Oak Room into a place of entertainment gave Adam a great deal of work. The main entry to the inn was still, as it always had been, into this room. By chance comers, people alighting from the one regular coach, or men on horseback, this entry was not much used; most such people used the yard door, but some still regarded the front door as the main entry, and it was, to say the least, a little embarrassing when total strangers blundered in upon a private party. Also, when the wind blew from the east, as it so often did, the opening of the door caused a great draught.

"I shall have to twist the whole thing round," Adam said. "Make the yard door the main door. Trim up that entry a bit. And outside there," he nodded towards the door by which he had first entered the inn, "I'll build a porch. Open only to the south."

"With a lot of glass. And shelves for plants," Isabel said, eagerly.

He had always been anxious to please her, and lately had felt the need to do so, since he was no longer any good in bed. It was not that he'd been stricken with impotence; far from it. As soon as the baby—a boy name Edman—was born and Isabel was quite well again, they'd come together with all the old joy and desire. Then in the moment of culmination the pain struck. Worse than ever. It was minutes before he had breath enough to say, "Don't worry. I'm all right. It's passing."

She looked so extremely frightened that he felt obliged to tell her that the same thing—more or less—had happened before. He did not explain in what circumstances—when he was worried or upset about something. She put her hand to his chest. "Darling, your heart is banging like a drum."

He made one of his rare jokes: "Time enough to worry when it doesn't." But she had been badly scared, and he had been humiliated.

She had been sick-visiting since she was old enough to carry some small delicacy to an ailing parishioner, and the recipients of things like egg-custard were vocal, not only about their own ailments but also about those of their families and friends. She'd heard several stories of people who'd dropped dead in the middle of a meal, in the middle of a job. Heart failure, it was called. Of a heart affliction that came and went, as Adam's apparently did, she had never heard.

And Doctor Allsop, whom Adam, under pressure, unwillingly consulted, was little wiser, though he owned a wooden stethoscope and used it diligently. He also knew a remedy for what was called a labouring heart. And he cherished a theory—resented by many patients—that there was some connection between a labouring heart and overweight. And, of course, there was always the connection with age. Hearts and other organs wore out. But the innkeeper, giving his age as thirty-seven, was lean and muscular and, in Doctor Allsop's eyes, in the prime of life. Nothing ailed him except bouts of indigestion, something from which Doctor Allsop suffered himself. He had learned to avoid onions, cabbage, radishes and—most punishing of all—new bread. And what he had learned he was willing to impart, together with good advice which applied to everybody. No over-exertion, no over-eating, no excitement. "Sound as a bell," the doctor said cheerfully, happily ignoring the fact that the one bell in Mallow was St. Cerdic's, and that flawed in the making, and that a common way of describing anything faulty was "Cracked as Cerdic's bell."

Despite this assurance, bed was never the same again. The fear remained, and Isabel was always ready with excuses; she was too tired; her head ached; was that the baby crying? She extended her solicitude for him to every sphere, begging him not to lift, not to carry this or that—particularly irksome now that he had so much work to be done. Now and again he caught her looking at him with an odd expression—too nearly akin to pity to please him. Actually she was thinking how much he had aged, and reflecting that there was one disadvantage of marrying a man so much older than oneself. You were doomed to watch your love grow old and grey. She rather annoyed him with her constant admonitions to be careful, to spare himself, to hire more help for heavy work. "After all, we can afford it," she said.

The fortunes of the One Bull had taken an upward turn. The Oak Room not only earned its keep; it also attracted custom in a variety of ways. The concert nights were particularly lucrative, bringing in people from miles around; many stayed the night. The stables were busy again, and it was a fact that people sampling the inn's hospitality for the first time found a quality about it. Never here was the landlord drunk, quarrelsome or careless, and the landlady's manners seemed quite incongruous with her station in life.

There were three immensely busy and highly profitable years, marred only by the recurrent attacks suffered by Adam. So far as he could conceal them from Isabel, he did so, and if he could not he made light of the affliction. "It's nothing lethal or I should be dead by now." To himself, however, he also counted the years and faced the prospect of dying before Edman was of an age to take over. The fact that the old relative who had made him her heir had run the inn alone for many years was no comfort; she'd been a tougher character altogether. He still could not look at his wife without feeling the desire to protect her. And the best way to do that was to save money. "I declare, you are becoming a miser," Isabel said, only half teasingly.

"I know. I'm thinking of the boy's future."

"He'll have this place."

"He may not take to innkeeping. It's not what I should have chosen for myself, had I had any choice. Would you?"

She thought before answering and then said, "Yes. I enjoy it. Short of having a huge house and entertaining friends all the time, I can think of no better way of living." (Isabel often thought of the woman called Marguerite Gilderson, the keeper of the journal, who also seemed to have enjoyed the company of people and the bustle of the inn, and had then, through the whim of her pot-boy husband, been almost imprisoned, obliged to stay in the private part of the house and take no share in the running of the place.)

But Adam was determined that when he died Isabel should have a choice as to what to do, how to live. With this in mind he set about looking for a small house, suitable for a widow with one son. He wanted something near the shops, with a manageable garden and its own water-supply. He could go about this search quite openly, saying that, when his mother died, he hoped to persuade Kate to come to Mallow and live near, but not with him. Isabel said, "I'm sorry I called you a miser, darling. I understand now. But could she not live here, with us?"

"It wouldn't work. My sister is a woman with very strict views. She'd be shocked to see you drink a glass of wine."

To the south of the One Bull, between the great gate of the abbey and the river, there was a stretch of the old wall, still solid and sound. At some time in the past an enterprising builder had built three small houses there, making use of the old wall. As dwellings in the congested town centre, they were eminently desirable, since their windows overlooked not only their own small gardens but also the space and the trees of what had formerly been the abbot's pleasure ground. The area was not too much overgrown, for various people held certain grazing rights, and the animals kept the grass down. The three houses had so often been occupied by widows that the popular name was Widows' Row. People with happy natures said that to live there was like living in a private park; the more morbid said that to live in a place built into a ruin and looking out upon others would depress them. But Isabel had always shown an interest in ancient things. So when one of the widows, said to own all three houses, died, Adam walked along, prepared to run his carpenter's eye over the fabric and estimate the amount of work needed to put the little house into tip-top condition. He would then invite Isabel to inspect it, asking, "What do you think? Would Kate be happy here?" By her answer he could judge whether *she* would be.

He felt that he was managing things rather well as he walked along in the early spring sunshine past the great gate, which nobody had bothered to demolish, and in at another gateway, punched through the thickness of the wall to give easy access to Widows' Row.

His was not exactly a happy nature, but he liked the place; the quietude after the busy street, the daffodils in the little gardens. What ruins were visible—grey stumps, a tallish pillar, half an arch, and an octagonal building which had housed the monks' doves—did not depress him, and he felt would not rouse in Isabel anything but interest.

Isabel was as near that morning to being a widow as she was ever to be.

The widow, so recently dead, had been named Bettison, and her son was already there, taking stock of this, a very minor part of his inheritance.

"I sold it," he said complacently as soon as he understood why Adam was there. "It was bespoken while my mother—God rest her—was still alive. A consortium." He brought out the word with all the satisfaction of a man whose vocabulary had increased by one word. "A consortium of gentlemen and businessmen have had their eyes on it for a long time. They want it for a public assembly room. Rooms, I should say: a ballroom, a card-room, a reading-room. They've even got the name fixed—the Athenaeum." Another unfamiliar but impressive word to be produced with smug pride.

There was no malice in the statement. Mr. Bettison was not one of those who had regarded the Oak Room at the One Bull with envy. Why should he? He had his acres and all the money saved by his thrifty ancestors.

Adam experienced the now all-too-familiar sensation of his inside falling away, leaving a cavity filled with pain and the rapid thump-thump-thump of his heart, and the feeling of strangulation. And this time he had the horrible feeling that he could have lost himself for a moment. He certainly had no memory of what had happened to him in the space of time between his saying, "I see, Mr. Bettison," and finding himself out in the sunny street, with the market-day traffic clattering past.

A very bad attack and, thank God, no witnesses. Also, thank God, time to compose himself, time to make light of it, before he must tell Isabel that competition was looming on their very doorstep.

Her latest idea had been that it would be pleasant for people who patronised the Oak Room to have the use of the garden on warm evenings. Not much contrivance was needed. Remove the door marked "Private," and rehang it a little farther along the passage; change the furniture in the room with the bay window, and make the centre of the bay into a door. She visualised little arbours covered with honeysuckle and other climbing plants.

Adam had made the alterations and was currently engaged on constructing rustic benches and tables. He gave the shed which he used as a workshop a very sour look as he passed it.

Isabel was out marketing. She still made that her responsibility, though nowadays she took a boy with her to carry her purchases. Adam hoped that news about Widows' Row had not spread. He wanted to break it to her gently. Yet how could such news be broken gently? An end to prosperity. Back to the just-making-ends-meet, the semi-weekly coach. And the poor girl would feel a loss which he would not—the company, the concerts about which she took such infinite trouble. She'd take it gallantly, he knew. She'd pretend not to care. She'd say they'd managed before, and could again, but . . .

Oh God, why didn't I stick to smuggling?

Then another thought struck. Very soon he would not be able to save anything for the future when he would not be able to look after her! That hurt worst of all, and contrary to his habit, he went into the bar and poured brandy. It had an almost instant effect, and he saw a solution to his problem. If only he could move quickly enough.

Sell the One Bull while it was still showing a healthy profit. Buy a small house in which Isabel as a widow could live; invest the surplus. Work as a carpenter, harder and longer than any carpenter ever did. The more he thought of it the more he liked this brandy-inspired idea. Busy inns found ready buyers. And this new place, with its outlandish name—Athenaeum—would take some time to build. He might well be able to get rid of the inn before it fell back into being a place expensive to keep up, and employing staff needed twice a week, standing about idle the rest of the time.

He tried the words over. "Darling, I have decided that the time has come to retire."

Would that alarm her, anxious as she already was about his health?

"Darling, how would you feel about . . . ?"

"Darling, in view of the competition which we shall be faced with in about a year's time . . ."

They brought her home on a board, one of those which, laid across trestles, made a market stall.

They explained, in great detail, with endless repetitions. There was this bull, you see, got loose, run wild, run mad, running amidst the crowded stalls. A proper shambles. And Mrs. Gilderson between a trestle, heavier than this one, and the wall. Squashed, they said, and dead by the time they got her out.

She looked no more dead than she had—and it seemed a lifetime ago—when he first looked at her in St. Cerdic's. Somebody had thrown a horse-rug over her body, concealing all damage. The hair, like black silk—how often had he run his fingers through it?—lay smooth and undisturbed. Even the little hat she wore when marketing . . .

Dozens, hundreds, no doubt thousands of men survived such bereavements, waited a decent time and then married again. But such easy comfort was not for him!

There were times when he felt an almost overwhelming impulse to go away, to leave the place where everything reminded him of his loss. A good carpenter was always welcome in the navy and he felt that, in new places, amidst strangers and with exacting work to do, the keenest sense of loss might be dulled, if only temporarily. But there was the child, *her* child! To whom could he be trusted?

And there was the One Bull. For the place, and for his position as landlord he had almost no feeling, but Isabel had been very sentimental about it, constantly referring to its long history and the fact that it had remained in one family for so long. There'd been a Gilderson at the One Bull since before anybody kept records. He'd teased her about that, saying that no nobleman with a great estate could be prouder of his family link with a family place. She'd said, "But few, if any of them, go back so far. There should be a family motto: Here we are; here we stay."

Because of this, and then because of the inertia resulting

from hard drinking, he stayed on, seeing the inn through another decline, seeing Edman grow up. He loved him, no doubt about that, and indulged him shamelessly, but there were times when he could not look at him without a piercing pang. So like his mother! Not so much in colouring as in form. In Edman, Adam's fair hair and Isabel's dense smooth black had emerged into bronzy brown and his eyes were blue, or grey, or green; one could never be sure. It was in shape that Edman resembled his mother, fine-boned, elegant, not fitted for the rough-and-tumble of life. Gildersons were, by tradition and in fact rather bigger than most men, and their long sojourn in London, where most men tended to be short, had not affected them. Edman could not be called short, but he had not the Gildersons' above-average height, and none of their brawniness. Yet when Adam presently suggested that, having done so well at school, Edman should proceed to pursue a career less physically exacting than that of innkeeper, Edman scorned the idea. "I can do anything that is required of me," he said. "And I like being my own master."

"At the beck and call of any drunken drover wanting a pot of beer and saying, 'Hurry up, there!'"

It had happened. Adam, working almost single-handed and seldom stone sober though never completely drunk, had been told to hurry up, or to look sharp. And once, when he served a pint instead of the half that had been ordered, the customer had said, "You want to sober up, mate." The behaviour of customers had declined with the inn's fortunes and with its owner's appearance. The clothes which he had inherited and which had once looked so well on him were now too large, for he had grown very thin. Being thin set another problem, too, for a face collapsed into ridges and folds and pouches was difficult to shave, especially with a drunkard's uncertain, early-morning hand.

Nothing, however, no persuasion, no warning would sway Edman from his determination to become an innkeeper. He was a brilliant scholar—even his schoolmasters, grudging with praise, admitted that. He should go far—starting with Cambridge. And there was the money, so painstakingly saved and, since Isabel's death, such a mockery. "Son, think it over. You could hold your own with the best there."

"I hope to be able to hold my own anywhere," Edman said. Yet he was, growing into adolescence, growing into manhood, what he had been in childhood—a pretty boy. Slender as a girl, mild of manner, except when provoked, and possessed of wit and charm which would, Adam felt, be totally wasted on the inn's present clientele. He was, in fact, very much his mother's son.

But what Adam recognised as irony—and bitterly resented—was that, once the One Bull became known as a lower-class place, it stole a certain amount of custom from the Green Man, which in its time had stolen so much from it. During the wool sales and the cattle sales, drovers and carters liked to get drunk out of sight of potential employers. Their custom was not to be entirely despised; they drank beer in vast quantities, and now that gin and all spirits were taxed and the licence to deal in them cost fifty pounds a year, a drover drinking beer in the tap-room was as profitable as a gentleman taking brandy in the Coffee Room. Men of the rougher sort preferred to eat where they stood, and did not demand service at tables with starched tablecloths and shining cutlery and polished glasses. And Adam, even when he felt most sour, was bound to admit that not all these humble men were rough and uncouth. But some were, and often they would become quarrelsome.

When men who were articulate had a dispute they fought with words, or, over a serious matter, with swords or pistols in a duel. The inarticulate had fist-fights which sometimes developed into a general brawl, in which furniture and crockery suffered. So did the inn's reputation.

Edman reached the age of eighteen before he really took his place as a putative innkeeper. Adam, hoping against hope that the boy would change his mind, had suggested this and that. Visits to Cambridge, where two of his contemporaries at the grammar school now were, on the one hand, submitting themselves to what was almost nursery discipline, on the other enjoying a privileged freedom. After that, London. "Everybody should see London once in his life," Adam said, and he did not mean Aldermanbury, where his own mother had died and been very decently buried. Kate, refusing all brotherly offers, had married a leather-tanner, widowed, with four children.

After London, Paris and what was known as the Grand Tour. Not an experience available to most innkeepers' sons, but made possible for Edman Gilderson because of that secret hoard which it hurt his father to think about. So sure that, all things considered—the difference in age, the fact that as a general rule women outlived men and that he had these attacks—his love would outlive him! How better to spend it than on the boy? The boy who, having seen all that Europe could offer—Florence, Rome, Naples, Venice—came home to Mallow and said, "Time I settled down. And glad to. To be *entirely* truthful, I was *homesick* all the time." He had inherited his mother's trick of emphasising certain words.

Adam said, "Well, you have had your chance."

It was autumn, the time for the cattle sales, when good breeding stock, worth coddling through the winter, fetched high prices, and the less worthy were bought for meat. After an unusually hot day for the time of year, beer was in great demand and tempers rather short. There were raised voices and then blows. Adam had learned to ignore such things, but this evening he thought with a touch of malice: Go ahead! Show the boy what he'll be up against!

The boy shouted in a voice his father had never heard before, "Get out! Settle it in the yard."

Striking out at his opponent, one man said, "Mind your own bloody business!"

Then it was like a whirlwind let loose. Like a fighting machine going into action. Two blows, delivered with utmost speed, yet with precision. Nothing hasty about them. Adam, who had seen how quickly, in this kind of thing, enmity could change targets, had time to think: Now they'll both set upon him and kill him! He moved to intervene, and then the pain struck. Through it, through the helplessness, the paralysis, the near death by strangulation, he watched, as though from a great distance and as though through a mist, Edman take both stocky men by the collars of their smocks and run them out into the yard. Fortunately, on account of the warmth of the evening, the door stood open. Had it been closed, Adam, through the pain and the breathlessness, the near loss of consciousness, thought both drovers' heads, impelled by force, would have cracked against it.

As it was, Edman came jauntily back, rather ostentatiously wiping his hands upon his handkerchief. He said, "Just for good measure, I knocked their two silly heads together." Then he turned with his sunny smile—his mother's smile—to a man who had been watching with a bovine lack of interest.

"I am sorry, *sir*. Your pint has lost its head. I will draw you a fresh one."

After that exhibition of authority backed by force, Adam felt that he could give up. Everything he had done since Isabel's death had been done for the boy and with the very vivid hope that Edman should choose some occupation unconnected with the One Bull, that unstable place. And typical of the inn's ups and downs was his own health. Good, bad, indifferent. And of no matter, anyway. Isabel had died, but the world had not stopped. Only for me. And when I die she will not even be remembered.

The management of the inn passed into Edman's hands with none of the friction inherent in the situation. "Do as you think best, boy," Adam would say. "It's all yours, Edman. I only wish I was leaving you something more worth while."

"We're holding our own," Edman said.

14 Edman and Athena

ONE MORNING—EDMAN HAD DISCOVERED THAT THE MORNING was the best time to attempt conversation with his father— Edman said, "I've been thinking about the Oak Room."

"I wish you could have seen it in the old days, before the Assembly Rooms got going." The consortium of gentlemen and businessmen, planning and building the Athenaeum on a grandiose scale, had hardly visualised it as a middle-class rendezvous, but harsh economics prevailed over snobbery. There simply were not enough gentlemen in the area to make it a viable concern—even with the subscription at two guineas a year. So although the ballroom and card-room remained a preserve of the county families, what had been planned for a reading-room was now regularly hired for wedding and christening parties and similar festivities once held at the One Bull. If the Oak Room came to life four or five times a year it was lucky.

Unlike most people who drank too much, Adam tended to be more reminiscent, more sentimental, when cold sober, and now, saying, "It was all your mother's idea," he enlarged upon the past glories of the Oak Room. But the porch, he pointed out, was his own idea. "I believe that once upon a time this was the general dining-room, but it was too draughty. Nobody thought of a porch." And he now did not particularly want to think about it, for it was one of his failures. He'd tried to keep Isabel's cherished flowers alive, but every one of them had dwindled and died.

"Full of notions, your mother was. Planning to have a tea-garden when she . . ."

Edman said hastily, "What happened here?"

"Oh," Adam said, deferring the necessary drink for a moment longer. "When I was working on that platform . . ." he explained. "The paintings," he ended, "were positively indecent."

"Old?"

"I should say so, judging by the state of the wood that hid them. I had to work fast that morning, I can tell you. I was mortally afraid she might come in and see them."

Whitewash, Edman knew, would wash off; walnut stain was a different matter.

"I wish I'd seen them," he said.

"I could take down another couple of panels if you like," Adam said quite easily. Pandering to the boy's whims was a habit too long established to be shaken off now that the boy had come to man's estate.

The painting revealed by the removal of two more worm-eaten panels was not shocking at all. No female flesh indecently exposed. All men, very quaintly dressed and in the centre a white bull, garlanded with flowers.

"Our bull," Edman said in the awed voice of one speaking of something holy. "That's how the place got its name."

"Maybe. Though I seem to remember the parson telling your mother a different tale. Something to do with the pope. You want to see more?"

Disappointing; the paint flaked, even the very hard plaster affected by damp. Then another indecency: some women, wearing very little indeed, surrounding a man upon whose head one woman was placing a wreath of laurels.

"Beautiful!" Edman said. "Beautiful!"

"Well, I differ there. But, of course, I'm old and out-of-date." And late for the first drink of the day.

He'd been more or less inebriated for almost fifteen years, and usually the effect upon him was predictable—just a dulling of misery. He never became merry or aggressive; he never fell down; he was never sick. Now and again liquor played him a trick, as it had when the Oak Room was hired for a christening party for the coal-merchant's child. Forcing himself to some show of affability, he had asked the baby's name, and when the proud mother said, "Isabel," he had almost shamed himself by crying.

Occasionally drink would make him emotionally bold; then, and only then, could he bring himself to visit her grave. Often he was ashamed that he did not tend it more regularly; he had only to walk so short a distance, and he knew people who travelled miles to visit graves on certain anniversaries: they'd bring flowers, saying that the dead person had always liked roses or pansies or whatever it was. In a way he'd envied them; they were bearing grief in the proper way. He'd never liked flowers since Isabel died; couldn't bear to go into the garden. For the same reason he had locked away everything that would remind him of her: her dresses, her books, her sewing-box. But now and again, drunk to a certain degree of insensibility, he could face a visit to the graveyard.

The day on which he had pulled down some of the old panels and seen Edman lock the Oak Room, saying, "I want nobody to see this just yet," was such a day. He felt able to go into the garden and pluck a sprig of rosemary—about the only green thing in dead winter. Then, with a bucket half full of water and a scrubbing brush, he set off.

It was not a grave which demanded much attention; Isabel lay under stone, not grass, but moss would encroach and sometimes there were bird-droppings. Always when he left the stone clean he'd think: I must do this more often, but months would pass before he was again able to.

And on this day drink played a new trick on him.

It had happened before, but only in dreams, delicious, wonderful dreams in which she was not dead at all but alive and well, talking to him in the voice he so loved, laughing, even singing. Then he would think that her death and his grief and his drunkenness were really a bad dream from which he had just awakened. The real wakening, when it came, was as cruel as the bereavement had been. Such dreams, in fact, did much to keep sorrow lively.

Today he was not asleep; he was not insensibly drunk. He was walking past the church porch on a grey winter afternoon, carrying a half-bucket of water in one hand, a scrubbing-brush in the other; he had a sprig of rosemary and a new lump of strong lye soap in his pocket. And he was capable of thought. There in the little church he had first seen her; there they had been married, and there her coffin had lain while Mr. Fison had talked, in his church voice, about resurrection and the life everlasting.

And Adam had not believed a word. He never had. He'd early come to the conclusion that to be religiously minded was something special, like being double-jointed, or able to waggle one's ears. And at the moment when belief would have served him, as he stood there by the coffin which held the body of the only person he had ever loved, Adam had thought: If I believed in God, I should be angry with him. Why couldn't an all-powerful deity let that bull knock down a stall and kill somebody old, or unhappy, or unloved?

Yet there, all at once, emerging from the shadowy porch, she *was*. Solid and real, hurrying towards him as she had done when he'd been absent for a few hours, welcoming hands outstretched. It was all so real, so ordinary, that when he put his arms round her and held her close, the rosemary in his pocket was squashed and gave off its bitter-sweet scent. And when the pain struck, she was holding him and saying, as she had done in the past when he had had an attack in her presence, "It's all right, darling. All right."

He was not immediately missed. Men who took a drop too much often toppled into bed early. And since Mr. Edman had taken over, the old master had counted less and less. When he was missed and a search mounted, he was found, his head on the overturned bucket and a scrubbing-brush clenched to his chest. Upon his face, so hollowed and furrowed, was such a look of peace and happiness that it was hardly recognisable.

And it would have been wrong to say that Edman was glad. Say—relieved, because Father would almost certainly have disapproved of the purpose to which Edman intended to put the Oak Room. He would almost certainly have protested. He would, almost as certainly, have referred to Mother, whom Edman could barely remember except as a soft voice, a sweet scent, both fading as year followed year. "Your mother would not have approved of this."

All women and many men disapproved of what became known as the Florentine Club, though nobody except its members knew what went on there. Edman shrewdly traded upon something which he had observed in boys at school, and in men during his travels—the passion for secrecy, the delight in being exclusive. The club was being talked about before it had a single member. Nameless orgies were said to take place there while Edman was still, with his own hands and behind locked doors, removing the ancient panelling, cleaning the painted part of the walls, and hanging the rest with black and scarlet cloth. The cloth was a certainty, for it had been seen to arrive; black and scarlet—the devil's own colours!

No servant was ever allowed to enter the room; so who cleaned it? Was it cleaned at all? And what went on there that demanded such secrecy? Shocking entertainments, with naked women prancing about on the stage? Political gatherings with the aim of restoring the Stuarts to the throne?

Young men of a class which the One Bull had seldom seen of late began to frequent the Smoke Room, anxious to find out, anxious to join.

"There's nothing secret about it," Edman said, managing to convey otherwise. "It's just a club, of a very private nature."

"I'd like to join."

"You would have to be approved by the committee. And be accepted by the other members." Edman was the committee, and so far there were no members.

"No club has ever black-balled me yet!"

"This is rather a special club. Members are not supposed even to know each other's names. As secretary, I must of course know, but I promise not to divulge anything. Perhaps you would like to fill in this form."

The would-be member promised on his honour to abide by the rules, respect the privacy of other members and of the club, and never to lend the key which would be entrusted to him when he became a member.

Schoolboy stuff, but it worked. When Edman had sixty

forms signed, exercising a kind of snobbishness but not too rigid, forty young or youngish men received a package containing a key, a narrow black velvet mask, called a domino, and a letter telling him that he was now a member of the Florentine Club, and that he would be known as Lorenzo or Cosimo or Giovanni.

The Florentine Club flourished because it provided something different, something lacking in everyday provincial life. And nobody, even had he not been pledged to secrecy, would have cared to admit that in the main it was somewhere where you could drink and gamble and where no woman could intrude. And sometimes Edman Gilderson, whose name in the club was Machiavelli, did provide entertainment of the highest order. Actresses brought down from London; musicians brought from God knew where; now and then a couple of prize-fighters, sadly handicapped for lack of space because, even though every member crowded onto the platform in order to be out of the way and in order to watch from an elevation, the room was really too small for the purpose.

Edman made a great deal of money. The subscription was ten guineas a year; vast quantities of liquor were consumed, all at a higher price than that charged on the other side of the house. Members helped themselves from bottles and decanters ranged on a long table under the painted wall. There was food, too—sandwiches, wedges of meat pie, slices of highly-spiced cake. The make-pretend atmosphere was preserved even over such an everyday transaction; you took what you wanted and put what you thought fair into a blue-and-white bowl. Few gentlemen carried much small change, and many of them deposited a sovereign or a guinea in exchange for five shillingsworth of provender. To cheat would have been unthinkable, and to be mean, inadvisable, for Machiavelli, usually at the gaming-table where he had the devil's own luck, seemed to have eyes at the back of his head, and another set of eyes which saw into men's hearts, recognising and being tolerant of, prepared to cater for, any taste, however odd, and able somehow to make what ordinary people decried as perversion seem normal and ordinary, and in keeping with the classical atmosphere of the Florentine Club.

Success, money made easily and quickly, and the association on rather more than equal terms with those commonly called his superiors, did not turn Edman Gilderson's head. He knew exactly where he stood and what he was doing. And while coddling the Florentine Club and exploiting it to the last penny, he had known it for what it was: a fly-by-night thing with no real roots. He knew, from his father's grudging talk, that once the One Bull had survived by smuggling, and then, more recently, in his own childhood, in fact, as a kind of public assembly place, until the Athenaeum took its custom away. While the money poured in, he had the One Bull put into such an excellent state of repair that when the lean days came he would not be worried; he dressed well, but never extravagantly; he rode a good horse, but for the most part he invested his money. And when he thought that the time was ripe for marriage, he went about the business of finding a bride in a cold-blooded manner.

Nothing to do with love! He could not remember the idyllic years of his parents' marriage, but he'd heard enough, seen enough to know what the end of it had done to his father. No woman, no person—even the children he envisaged—should ever have him in such thraldom. He wanted a wife comely enough to be lived with, amiable, sensible, domesticated, and well endowed. Such desirable creatures were rare, and in his search he was handicapped by his determination not to marry a girl who despised his calling, and by the calling itself. He was handsome, well-mannered, exceptionally well educated, but he was, after all, only an innkeeper and of a not very successful inn at that. Fathers of eligible daughters with dowries wanted something better than that!

Edman had been as secretive about the money he had made as everybody was about the club itself. It might be a paying concern; then again it might not. And how long would it last? The One Bull itself was, apart from the semi-weekly coaches that carried the mail, perilously close to being a mere beerhouse. And some very peculiar things were said about the club itself. Caught between his own demands, fathers' concern with security, and mothers' obsession with respectability, Edman's chances seemed poor.

However, his luck held, for hunting about in the matrimonial thickets was a couple who had most unaccountably bred a freak daughter. The Bettisons, both products of long-established farming families, well thought of, if regarded as mean, utterly respectable, sometimes thought that their daughter's oddity was

the result of her name—Athena. She had been born in the year
when young Mr. Bettison, as he then was, had inherited Widows' Row and sold the site for the Athenaeum. The girl's name
commemorated a successful deal.

Then she'd turned out to be both mad and bad. They'd
beaten her to within the traditional inch of her life; locked her
up on a diet of bread and water, and not too lavish at that.
Short of a death which might invoke a coroner's inquest, they'd
done all they could. She was man-mad. Several times absolutely dirty scandal had been avoided by a hair's breadth. Somewhere, down in Bywater, a seaport where bastards were the
rule rather than the exception, there was a baby, costing two
shillings and sixpence a week. All things considered, it was
lucky that there were not more.

The distracted parents had three times found possible husbands for her—the offered dowry rising all the time: four
hundred pounds; five hundred; seven. Each time something had
gone wrong, some bit of gossip, or the mad girl's own behaviour. You'd think even a mad girl, allowed out in the company
of a man about to become engaged to her, would have the
sense to behave, or at least to pretend to behave as though he
were the only man in the world. Not Athena. Let her eye light
upon a man to her more attractive than her escort, and out
came the trollop in her.

The Bettisons had reached the point where they would gladly
have betrothed her to a labourer if he seemed likely to hold
her attention in the three weeks it took to have the banns asked.
To them Edman Gilderson was an answer to prayer. Had the
One Bull been nothing but a beer-house; had his Florentine
Club been the centre for devil-worship that some people said
it was, they'd still have accepted him gladly and regarded his
meeting with Athena, his taking to her, and—far more important—her taking to him as nothing short of a miracle.

Athena was very pretty. That in itself almost justified Mrs.
Bettison's fanciful notion that she was a changeling. All Bettisons and the families associated with them by marriage were
as nearly cubical as people could be, built for work, like cart-
horses; they all had straw-coloured hair, pale eyes with lashes
so fair as to be almost invisible, and good healthy red com-
plexions. Athena's hair was bright gold, her eyes hyacinth blue,
and her complexion pale, just tinged with pink, like apple-
blossom. And she was slender, so slender, indeed that, during

that worst time of all, she was far, far gone before even her mother suspected anything.

Subsequent ill-treatment—long periods of confinement to the house, a diet well calculated to cool the blood—had further etherealised her appearance.

Edman met her by accident. Alongside the very prosperous Florentine Club, he had started another enterprise, not very profitable, but offering a service. He set aside a room marked Ladies Only for the use of women who, their shopping or errands done, must wait for their husbands. Some women drank tea or coffee while they waited, and that brought in a few pence, but there were repercussions. More light carts and wagons now used the yard at the One Bull than had done since the sale yard was moved.

Mrs. Bettison had not made use of the waiting-room before; she seldom came in to Mallow. But the whole family on a fine hot June day had attended a funeral of a relative in Daneley, and Mr. Bettison, who valued his time highly, had decided to make a round trip of it and attend to various bits of business so that he would not be obliged to visit town until the shearing was done. Mrs. Bettison's Aunt Agatha had chosen the most inconvenient time to die!

Athena must share this outing because it would be unthinkable to leave her at home—even locked in—with so many strange men about.

It was not market-day and the two women had the waiting-room to themselves. It was the dead hour in the inn's day, and when Mrs. Bettison rang the bell the sound seemed to echo through the hollowness. Edman himself answered the summons.

He saw two women, one oldish, one young, both in black. Mrs. Bettison had taken pains to make Athena look as unattractive as possible. She herself always wore black, and Athena's mourning garb had been contrived out of a dress thriftily saved. It made no attempt to fit anywhere, except at the neck, where it was buttoned close, almost to the chin, and at the wrist, where the voluminous sleeves were gathered into tight bands. The bright yellow hair was almost hidden by something not quite a bonnet and not quite a hat.

"We would like tea," Mrs. Bettison said.

Athena said, "It is so *hot*!" Her hands went to the close collar, tearing open not merely two or three buttons, but more, exposing a neck white as milk and as though by accident, just the top curves of two young shapely breasts.

Edman said, "Yes, madam." As soon as he had gone, Mrs. Bettison said with a kind of suppressed ferocity, "Cover yourself! You promised to behave."

"I only said it was hot." Athena waited breathlessly to see whether the beautiful young man would bring the tea. When he did so, serving but not servile, rather with the air of a man acting as host in his own house, Athena snatched off her bonnet and pretended to use it as a fan. The bright golden curls, released from close confinement, seemed to take on life as they tumbled free.

There was nothing else she could do, with Mother standing guard. But she managed to forget her reticule and, if the young innkeeper felt as she did, and as she hoped, almost prayed, that he did, he'd take the next step.

Comely? Rather more; she could be beautiful. Amiable? Rather more; she was ingratiating. Domesticated? Well, the first meal to which he was invited at the farmhouse, Mrs. Bettison said, was prepared by Athena herself. Sensible? That remained to be proved, but he was sensible enough for two. Well-endowed? Most emphatically, yes! Mrs. Bettison's Aunt Agatha had been far richer than her manner of life had indicated, and Mrs. Bettison had benefited. So the Bettisons were well able, and more than willing, to give a thousand pounds to get a naughty girl off their hands.

Edman was warned, of course. In the Florentine Club as in others, there was the unwritten rule—No talk about females! But one or two young gentlemen who liked Edman for himself, not as a mere purveyor of entertainment, said, "A word in your ear, old boy . . ." "In your place, I'd think again, because, damme, not wishing to offend, but I've heard . . ."

He had enough self-assurance to ignore them all. He thought he knew what ailed Athena—she was a born hunter: a characteristic tolerated in men, in women disgraceful and dangerous. And since he had no intention of ever being caught by her or any other woman, he could keep her happily hunting him until middle age doused the fires.

The difference which marriage made to a flighty girl was incredible. It was as though, standing there at the altar in St. Egbert's, looking deceptively virginal, some change had taken place in her very nature.

Excellent wife; excellent housekeeper and hostess; excellent mother of five: three sons, all sturdy; two daughters, both pretty.

The Florentine Club lasted longer than Edman had expected. Members grew older, moved away, but a new crop was always waiting. It was Edman himself who put an end to it. Too old at forty-five, he said; time to settle down and be comfortable. Life was very comfortable, for despite the expenses involved in rearing and providing for the family, his careful savings, well invested, and Athena's dowry, provided what the One Bull had so often needed and in diverse ways often found— just enough to make the difference between scraping along and living in style; "style" meaning keeping a table rather more lavish than was usual, pouring that drop more into a glass than the strict letter of the law demanded; and being able to say, "Sir, I can do without your custom in future," or, "Get your ugly phiz out of my sight. And don't come back."

Of the three boys, Adam, named for his Gilderson appearance, and in nature a true Bettison, was a farmer born, spending most of his time at his grandfather's farm and regarding his uncle Bob as his model, even in speech. His future was easily settled when the time came: three hundred acres of good arable land at ten shillings an acre, including an old but fundamentally sound house. Edman, the second son, turned out to be a bit wild. He was expelled from the grammar school in his second year there; was twice apprenticed, and twice ran away. For such an unsettled character, a sea-faring life seemed to be the answer. So it was Thomas, the home-loving, rather dreamy one who would become the innkeeper. He painted very well, but lacked the ambition that would have taken him away from home to prove his talent in a harsh world. After all, one could paint anywhere, and why not do it in comfort?

Innkeeping, as it was at the One Bull as the century aged, seemed a far from onerous business. A good staff needed the minimum of supervision; there was no bustle except on coach nights and even that was orderly bustle. Most of the customers were regulars, and either friendly or pretended to be so. The leisurely, easy life, comfortably buffered by money from outside, was no preparation for the harsh times that lay ahead. And whether the dreamy, amiable, artistic, rather indolent Thomas Gilderson was the man to deal with adversity was a question that remained to be answered.

VI

15 George

1838

"HERE'S YOUR FOOD," THE YOUNG WOMAN SAID UNGRAciously, plumping a tray on the bedside table. Unappetising to start with, the fat of the meat already congealing on the cold plate, a mound of greyish mashed potatoes and some overboiled cabbage, it had not been improved by the slopping over of the beer tankard. If she couldn't be bothered to carry that damned thing carefully, couldn't she have brought his half-pint in a pint tankard? He never drank more than a half.

And weren't there dishes, double-bottomed, which could be filled with hot water, and covered by a lid? Careless, hateful slut, he thought as he braced himself for her merciless assault. Her method of lifting him into a position in which he could deal with the tray was to seize him by the shoulder and heave.

She'd never had lumbago. And she didn't believe he had. She thought he was malingering, trying to avoid his fair share of the work. Only pride prevented him from crying out as she jerked him into a sitting position. Sweat broke out on his forehead and neck. "Where's Charlie?" he asked with a pathos that was lost upon her.

"Where would you think?" Without waiting to see whether he could reach the tray or not she flounced out of the room.

Sometimes when he considered the hatred between them, irreparable, implacable, he could see her point. She would never see his. He had made no secret of his belief that she was not good enough to marry a Gilderson; done his very best to dissuade Charlie from marrying her; said he very much doubted if the coming baby was his, and even if he was, there was no law... Pay up. Buy her off. He had insulted her breeding, questioned her integrity. And even worse. He'd wounded her vanity. While trying to dissuade Charlie, he had said an unforgivable thing. "She's pretty enough now, in a coarse way, boy. But in four or five years she'll be fat as a tub and her moustache will have got the better of her."

277

That absolutely unforgivable speech had been overheard and reported with glee by a spiteful maid. And the most dreadful thing about it was that it was true! In less than five years! She'd never recovered her figure after the birth of that first baby, and tweezering was now so necessary and painful that she was thinking about using Charlie's razor on the sly. It was almost as though the horrible old man had put a spell on her.

The horrible old man, pulled upright, but not supported by pillows, as would have been the case had his son brought his meal, groped sideways, moving as little as possible, for the slightest movement hurt; decided not to bother with the food, but managed, with caution, to get the half-pint tankard to his mouth. Drinking was more important than eating; all the stories—and to a degree he was a well-read man—proved that; in shipwrecks, in deserts, it had been proved over and over again that a man could live deprived of food for five or six times as long as he could deprived of water.

And by refusing the unappetising tray he was making a gesture. He hoped that Charlie would come in before the tray was removed. Charlie would say, "Oh dear, you have eaten nothing!" And then he would say, "Would *you*?" And thus notch up another mark against Charlie's wife, Rose. Of all the inapposite names!

Yet, when Charlie, a dear good boy with little sense, had fallen in love with her, there had been something not completely unroselike about her. A dark rose. Dark of hair and eye and skin and, it had proved, of temper too. One of the reasons why the old man hated her was that she was so detestable to Charlie. She blamed *him*, of course, for listening to his father at all, for hesitating as much as he had done, so that the baby was born within six months of the wedding.

But then, Charlie was weak; even the fond father could not be blind to that. Too much inclined to be influenced by the last person who talked with him; always wanting to run with the hare and hunt with the hounds. The result of being so nice-natured. Old George Gilderson, the reverse of nice-natured himself, appreciated amiability in others. And he hated to think of what Charlie's life would be like later on, when he wasn't here to protect him and to provide Rose with the main target for her venom.

No need to think about death yet, though. Sixty-five wasn't all that old. And nobody died of lumbago!

Nobody he'd ever heard of had three attacks of it in two months, either. In summer time, too!

Cautiously, lowering himself inch by inch, he regained the prone position which was the only bearable one. Through the open window he could hear the medley of sounds drifting up from the market-place. Market day. That was what the bitch meant about Charlie. Busy serving the eighteenpenny ordinary to such as could afford it. Fewer of them every week! Agriculture was going through a terrible slump. And, George thought, if the meal shoved at him was anything like a fair sample of what was being served in the dining-room, next week there'd be no customers at all.

Since the death of his wife, eight years earlier, he'd made himself responsible for the cooking. Not in itself, he considered, either a laborious or skill-demanding job. Just a matter of common sense and taking a little care. And in his case, being impervious to mockery. Some ignorant Suffolk clods had chosen to think that a man cooking was a subject for mirth. He'd soon put them straight on that! It had cost him a splendid steak-and-kidney pie and a customer, but it was well worth it. "Ah, a light hand with the pastry, Cookie," the fool had jibed.

"Try it first," George said. And the next second the fool sat there, meat and gravy and bits of pastry all over his face, neck and shoulders, and the pie-dish, reversed, sitting on his head like a ridiculous hat.

There was a roar of laughter—not at George Gilderson's expense. When the man had cleared his face sufficiently to be able to speak, he'd said, "I'll sue you, Gilderson."

"For an accident? Go ahead! I'm insured against accidents on my premises, to man . . . *and to beast*."

Rose, of course, couldn't cook, couldn't be expected to. The people who lived in the hovels around Sheepgate ate bread and cheese or bread and cheap jam; if they wanted a hot meal, they got it from the cook-shop. For Charlie's sake, George had been willing to teach the girl, much as he hated her, but she was unwilling to learn. Not unable. Any idiot could learn that an oven must be *hot* before meat was put into it, so that the outside formed a seal, keeping in the flavour and the juices. Any idiot . . . and Rose was far from being idiotic. She just did not care. She'd trapped Charlie, soft fool that he was, had her bastard born in wedlock, and then turned about, castigating both her father-in-law and her husband for the fact that the One

Bull was far less prosperous than she, pressing for marriage, had assumed it to be.

Disappointment made her cruel. She never missed an opportunity to complain, to deride the One Bull and everything to do with it. Charlie bore it all with stoic fortitude which left his father torn between admiration and contempt. George himself made sharp retorts. "It all looked better seen through a wedding ring, didn't it?" "Pity you didn't take an inventory before you rushed into wedlock!" "Well, they do say that three at the altar bodes no good." She was far too thick-skinned to catch the implied rebuke. It was Charlie who suffered, really, and in a way he deserved to; for it was he who, in weak-minded obstinacy, had created the whole unhappy situation, and incidentally lowered the standards of the inn and of the Gildersons' standing in the community. The One Bull had weathered many financial crises; the family had produced characters of varying ability, of varying worth, but something of respectability and superiority had always clung to the place and to the men who owned it. Charlie's marriage to Rose Webber, a girl of dubious repute, member of a family of definitely bad reputation, was a threat to something long cherished and all the more vulnerable for having so little real substance.

As for the child, poor thing . . . Even in his present low state—a near-bursting bladder added to his woes—George Gilderson was compelled to avoid the thought of the child, in the eyes of the law Charlie's son, and his grandson. Charlie hurried in. "Sorry, Dad! Sixteen today." Swiftly and with gentle competence, he did what had to be done and then reached for the bottle of liniment—horse liniment—held to be a sovereign remedy for anything short of a broken bone. It was very powerful and pungent, bringing water to the eyes of those who applied it, matching the tears produced by the pain and self-pity of those to whom it was applied.

"Let it go, Charlie," George said. "If it had any virtue, it'd have shown itself by now. And lying here for days—six days, the longest ever—I'm getting a bit sore."

"You've got so thin." Charlie looked at the untouched plate, and thought: No wonder! His face took on such a look of remorse that his father said with forced cheer, "I never did eat much in the heat of the day. Was Bettison there?" Long, long ago the Bettisons and Gildersons had been linked by marriage and, although the families were not on particularly intimate terms, it was only civil to ask, and the old man was anxious to keep Charlie talking. Aware of this, and of the fact that a liniment rub would have taken ten minutes, Charlie sat down and named all the unfortunates who had paid eighteenpence for a poor meal.

One man, much more closely related than any Bettison could be—Joe Gilderson of Curlew Farm—should have been on the list but was not. For many years the relationship between the farming Gildersons and the innkeeping Gildersons had been close and friendly and often to their mutual advantage, but the Curlew Gildersons, very prim and proper and ardent Nonconformists, had taken Charlie's marriage to Rose Webber almost as a personal affront to themselves. A disgrace to a decent family! Which it was! Which it was!

"Oh, and the Plotters are back," Charlie said, happy to have hit on a cheerful subject, a link with poor old Dad, a shared joke. And how strange it was that when almost everything else had become contaminated, all ordinary speech careful—or positively dangerous—a shared joke should act as a remedy!

"They got off the coach this morning," Charlie said, "had a bite and a drink, hired two horses and went away. But they'll be back tonight."

Into that short speech was compressed a good deal of history—the past, which both father and son knew about, and the future of which they knew nothing but had certain fears.

For many years, back to grandfather's, great-grandfather's time, the One Bull had served as an unofficial, but recognised, mail station. The regular coach between London and Norwich stopped for the night at Mallow, and this fact alone had lent the One Bull, even when its fortunes were at low ebb, a certain prestige. Then the rage for speed had begun, and the coach-routes were reorganised. The now-official mail coach merely paused in the yard, changed horses, set down and took up passengers and mailbags, and dashed on, to halt for the night at Triver during the short days of winter, in summer reaching Thetford. The change had been one of several things which had sent the One Bull into another decline.

The Plotters, as Charlie jokingly called them, had first appeared in Mallow about three months earlier. Two well-dressed men, one middle-aged, one younger, and all their actions had been mysterious. They absented themselves during the day, mostly on horseback, sometimes on foot, and the younger man always carried a bag not unlike a violin case except that it was rectangular. While they ate they talked very earnestly and in low voices, almost invariably falling silent as George and Charlie approached the table with a dish. After the supper—which was their dinner—they retired to the bigger of the two adjoining bedrooms which they occupied, and once, when Charlie carried up the whisky they had ordered as a nightcap, he saw the bed covered with maps or charts. So the men became known as the Plotters, and father and son competed with each other in inventing outrageous suggestions as to what the plot concerned.

George, remembering how heartily both Plotters had eaten—they'd even praised the food—said, "This damned thing often shifts as suddenly as it strikes. I might be in time to make a pigeon pie." He ventured an exploratory move, winced at the sudden pain and then sighed.

"We'll manage something," Charlie said.

Yes, one of Rose's frying-pan jobs! Even her frying was bad. She'd overheat the pan so that the reek of hot fat stank the place out. Enough to put anybody off. And would she crack an egg into a cup and slide it gently into the fat? She would not! Bash against the side of the pan, splutter into the fat, and if the yolk broke, who cared? She could work her evil magic even on sausages, so that they were charred black on the outside and almost raw in the middle.

Once, despairing of her, George had suggested teaching Charles a few simple cookery tricks, and Rose had laughed her nasty jeering laugh, and said, "Good God! Ain't one old maid in the family enough?" For some reason that remark had cut home to Charlie more than most of her jibes did. He'd blushed, looked absolutely confused and unmanned.

Unmanned. Old maid. George's lively, over-anxious mind had skipped about, wondering whether Rose's openly professed scorn and disappointment with the One Bull did not conceal something deeper and darker: a discontent with Charlie as a man.

Did he sleep with her? *Could* he sleep with her at the end of a day during which, at best, a grim sullenness prevailed, and at worst an active hostility?

Well, Charlie slept with her in the broader, sillier sense of the term. They shared a room, a bed. But could Charlie possibly bring him . . . ?"

The only answer to that was an indirect one. The disastrous

marriage was now three years old and there was no child except the one *said* to be Charlie's.

Charlie, duty done, ten minutes expended, said, "I'll take this away." He moved towards the tray. "And I'll bring you a bite later on. A few nice little ham sandwiches. And a pot of tea."

Suddenly George became practical.

"I'd have thought new potatoes and peas . . . It's mid-July, after all."

"So they are," Charlie said. "Rose went out and ordered. But she was hurried; so Emily took the boy to collect later on."

The boy.

Poor child! Two and a half years old and a thing to be ashamed of.

George had from the very first determined that his animosity towards Rose should not extend to an innocent child. Since Charlie had admitted responsibility and the child—christened Timothy—had been born in wedlock and there was about a fifty-fifty chance that it might be Charlie's boy, even the cynical old grandfather was prepared to make allowances, to hope that a proper upbringing might repair . . .

But it was impossible. Such a rent in the very fabric of life could never be mended.

Most new-born babies were a bit monkeyish. They grew out of it, changed colour, developed features, became, in fact, human. The poor little boy born to Rose had no bridge to his nose, just two flat nostrils above a wide, slobbery mouth. His eyes weren't right, either; very small, red-rimmed and set at a slant, and when he cut his teeth they were decidedly odd, jagged along their edges.

He was not quite idiotic; he knew his name—Timothy—and would answer to it, like a dog. And like a dog, he was, as he grew, pitiably responsive to any sign of affection.

From his mother he received none. For her he epitomised the disappointment that her marriage had proved to be. A fine healthy handsome boy, with the Gilderson nose, would have been her justification, something to fling in the face of the sneering old man whom she hated and who hated her. Left to his mother, Timothy would not have lived long. His father was always kind and gentle to him, and, curiously, even his grandfather, though unable to look at him without aversion, extended to him a pitying tolerance and an almost militant protectiveness.

The hiring of Emily to take charge of the child, at the fabulous sum of five shillings a week, a shilling more than she could have earned as waitress or chambermaid, had been George's idea. That Emily chose to combine her main duty with a certain amount of her kitchen work was proof of her good nature.

Apart from Emily, the only staff now employed at the inn was an old woman named Lucy who came in by the hour, made beds, emptied slops, did a bit of rough cleaning. She had a bedridden husband and was always anxious to get back to him; so casual work suited her and she regarded her job as a blessing, because in even the most economically-run inn there were bits and left-overs. George's discarded meal would certainly find its way into Lucy's basket tomorrow morning.

Charlie lifted the tray and George said, "I'm all right. Don't you bother about me. You've got enough on your hands."

But it wasn't overwork, the old man reflected sadly, that was making Charlie age so quickly, putting grey into his bright hair and giving all the lines of his face a downward trend. It was unhappiness. Come to that, they'd always been pretty well overworked, but they'd been merry.

Left alone, lying flat and still in enforced idleness, George thought: Well, at least Rose can be trusted to serve teas in the waiting-room. He amused himself with calculations. If sixteen men had eaten the eighteenpenny ordinary, it meant that probably ten had stabled their horses at the One Bull. A few, less considerate of their animals and mindful of their threepences, simply left them hitched to any convenient post or railing. Of that ten, perhaps six had brought their wives to market; so possibly there'd be five or six women drinking tea and exchanging gossip while they waited for their men to finish their business or their drinking. The Cackle Club, he and Charlie had named it somewhere back in the old days.

Like everything else connected with farming, the Cackle Club was in recession since the end of the Bonaparte wars had sent prices tumbling down. It had never been a very paying proposition, but it had been a service and a rather happy one, even if in the good days it was largely a showing-off place, with women gleefully exhibiting what they could afford to buy. For years now, however, the trend of talk in the Cackle Club had changed, and the emphasis was less on what one could spend than on what one could save. Women now boasted, not of the newness of their dresses, but of their antiquity. "Goodness! I've had this dress for twenty years, and it'll see me out another twenty, if I last so long." Sometimes, refreshed by tea and elated, as men were by stronger liquors, they'd exchange recipes, all aimed at economy; how to make do without this, without that.

When George's wife, a spry, gay woman, with a sense of humour, just on the wry side which matched his own, was alive and active, she'd once said, "A few more market days and I shall be able to make a sponge cake without eggs and a pancake without flour."

Dear Susie! Dead and buried and sorely missed. But he had trained himself not to brood, not to look backwards. He had Charlie to think of, and the inn. And there was a story, handed down, possibly garbled, of a Gilderson whose wife had been killed when a bull had run amok, and he'd taken to drink.

His own bereavement, equally sudden, had been different. Susie had simply said, "I'll have an early night, I think." So she'd gone to bed. Retiring some time later, he'd tip-toed about, shedding his clothes; got into bed very carefully in order not to disturb what looked like a most peaceful sleep and had proved to be the final one.

It was sad. But all men and women, once born, must die. And to Susie had been given the blessing of a death everybody might envy. No illness, no decrepitude such as was now afflicting him. And she had never had to face the worry of Charlie's disastrous marriage, never seen that pathetic grandchild.

He had spoken of the suddenness with which lumbago could strike and vanish; and now, moving a little to ease the pressure on his sore back, he found that he could move easily. Yes, gone! Wonderful. He rose, feeling a bit weak but forcing himself to speed, and began to dress. It was a quarter past three; he would be in ample time to prepare the pigeons and make the pastry for the pie. Something light to follow—one of his rightly-famous meringues.

He must, of course, shave—it was one of the things about which Gildersons were very meticulous, and though he would have been prepared to tackle a one-day's growth of beard with cold water, six was too much. He must go down to the kitchen for hot water. He had his door half open when he was arrested by the sound of his daughter-in-law's voice. No words, just her unmistakable laugh. And then a man's answering laugh.

What in the name of God was she doing up here, with a man, at this hour? This wing of the house was very seldom used—only on those all too rare occasions when the inn was crowded. The last time had been when the Mid-Suffolk Show had been held in Mallow. The rooms along this passage were in a sad state of disrepair, and had, over the years, item by item, been largely denuded of their contents. When the rooms in the other wing needed something to replace an article broken or collapsed, the rooms up here were raided.

George had moved into one of these damp, barely furnished rooms when Charlie married. That left the so-called private rooms below for family occupation.

Builders in the faraway past had not been over-concerned with straight lines and right-angles, and since this wing was erected there'd been alterations, and the door of George's room was so placed that he had to move out in order to see the top of the stairs, which led down into a kind of lobby with one door opening into the kitchen and one into the yard. He moved very softly and saw, at the end of the passage—the space between the open door of one of the disused bedrooms and the head of the stairs—Rose had a man whom he did not immediately recognise. But now he could hear very clearly.

"You go first," Rose said. "Good-bye till next week."

"It'll be a long week," the fellow said, and slapped her, familiarly, yet with a certain fondness, on the rump. Then he turned to go down the stairs. In profile he was recognisable. Joe Bettison, of all people! Fifty years old if a day; a bit wild as a young man, but settled now; a good family man and said to be weathering the slump better than most since all his forebears had been miserly.

Out of sight, at the foot of the stairs, he must have turned and made some gesture, for Rose put her coarse fingers to her coarse mouth and threw him a kiss. Then she went back into the bedroom, bundled her hair up, came out again and went downstairs after carefully closing the door.

Plain as print. Filthy bitch! No surprise, of course. He'd always known she was a whore. She'd tricked Charlie into marrying her, presented him with that caricature of a child— and might do it again! And there was Charlie, working himself to the bone to keep her. Charlie at this very minute scuttling about, doing two jobs at once, clearing up after the eighteen-penny dinner and serving in the bar.

George waited just long enough to give the vile woman time to go through the kitchen and into the ground-floor bedroom—by long tradition the connubial chamber. She'd do up her hair properly, change her dress and come flaunting out, not to serve but to dispense tea in the waiting-room.

Going down the stairs, having given the harlot time to get away, George was aware of a kind of tremor, not in his flesh but in the very marrow of his bones. Unlike lumbago, it was not disabling and he could ignore it by concentration upon the job in hand; first the shaving; then the preparation for the good meal for the Plotters, the family—and anybody else who happened to drop in.

The Plotters were, in a fashion, plotters. They were spies, experienced surveyors employed by what was not yet, but might be, a railway company. They took measurements, tested subsoil, saw where bridges would be needed and cuttings must be made. And they were obliged to work in secret, because one mention of the word railway, however vaguely, however far concerned with the future, and up jumped the price of the land. All their walks and rides were exploratory, all their reports, charts and suggestions extremely tentative. But they were working on a very promising territory. Largely flat land, no hills to be blasted through or climbed by stiff gradients; no great rivers to be bridged. Good subsoils, too; solid clay or solid chalk. A practically straight run all the way up to Lynn, that flourishing port. Ninety-nine miles, as the crow flew, but with a few diversions. And all, or almost all, running through land to be bought cheaply. Acres and acres, under the plough in the Dark Ages, then converted into sheep-runs, had, by the exigencies of a long war against the French, come under the plough again, and now, with the laws governing the import of wheat and barley from the vast, immensely fertile lands of America being relaxed, good arable land was losing value, and bad, heathy, marginal land could be had almost for the asking. Always provided, of course, that the ultimate purpose was not divulged.

Although they had hired horses, the Plotters had not ridden far that day; just in and around Mallow, the natural centre of the area. Flat as the land seemed, it undulated a little, and Mallow stood high, with the main road sloping gently southwards to Daneley and northwards to Triver. The slope to the east was more marked. Leaving Mallow to the west by the minor road known as Forest Way, one rode on the level, between remnants of the original forest, with isolated farms scooped out here and there. No towns until one reached Baildon, a town very similar in many respects to Mallow. Another old market-town grown up around another ruined abbey. Whether Baildon would eventually be linked to Mallow or become part of a separate network was a matter for the future to decide. The Plotters were today concentrating upon a possible site for a possible station.

There were arguments for and against a central site. More convenient for passengers and cheaper for the haulage of goods which the railway undertook as part of its service. Also, towns tended to be inhabited by sensible, middle-class men, who regarded the railway as a blessing, conducive to more trade. It was usually country people, notably great landlords, who deplored the railroads, and made protests, saying that the rails disfigured the countryside, and that smoke from the engines poisoned the air.

But the price of land in towns was always higher and less prone to fluctuate in value. However, in Mallow there was an area which would make an excellent site for a station and could be bought very cheaply—the grounds and the surroundings of the old abbey. It had passed by some means, no longer clearly decipherable, into the possession of a great landowner, Lord Camberwell, who owned thousands of acres in Yorkshire, in Sussex and in Shropshire, as well as a sizeable slice of London. He'd never seen the place, never wanted to, and even in the war when people were ploughing up ancient pastures, he had been given to understand that to clear the abbey grounds of the ruins, both visible and invisible, in order to make a relatively inconsiderable piece of ground fit for the plough, would cost a small fortune.

Enterprising poor men with hungry families had cultivated little pockets of soil here and there, but they seldom gained much; less industrious people stole what the little patches produced, and most of the space was a grazing-ground for donkeys, geese and goats. A hungry donkey could shoulder down even a stout fence in order to reach a cabbage; goats could literally climb; and geese, so ungainly on land, were not only graceful but also deadly accurate when on the wing.

"As I see it," said the senior Plotter, happily eating pigeon pie, "that place they call the Athenaeum is the only thing in the area with any rights at all. It does not appear to be very prosperous. I think it could be bought very reasonably."

"This would have to go, too," the junior Plotter said, glancing about the dining-room. Only one other table was occupied.

"Very poor condition, indeed. The thatched part is positively falling down. White elephants go very cheaply."

They switched to another subject as Rose brought in the pudding. She was very much the landlady, graciously performing a duty well below her dignity: even prepared to be affable about it. With the slightest encouragement she would have lingered, but she received none.

"Green satin," the younger man remarked. "Plain as an invitation card!"

"Luscious none the less?" the elder said, not without a certain wistfulness.

"The pudding?" They laughed and then resumed their serious, low-toned conversation.

"There remains the church."

It was a problem. Get rid of the wretched little plots, the unauthorised animals; buy out the Athenaeum and the One Bull; bring in the heavy equipment to flatten what remained of the old abbey walls and ruins, and there was still the little flint church of St. Cerdic's, not bang in the centre of this desirable site, but definitely on it, and astride what, with the inn and its outbuildings demolished, would be a good entry.

"A hundred years ago," the younger man said, "there'd have been no problem at all. A small, almost redundant church practically in a tavern's backyard . . . Nobody'd have noticed. Now, between the holy-holies screaming, 'This is dedicated ground,' and the antiquarians yelling, 'It's Saxon,' yes, it will be a problem. But not insurmountable."

"No. The Church Commissioners are, on the whole, reasonable men."

St. Cerdic's could, almost correctly, be described as redundant. As the town grew it had proved too small for its congregation, and it was impossible to enlarge it, for the massive ruins of the great abbey church to which it had once been a mere lady chapel, hemmed it in on one side, and the yard of the One Bull was its limit on the other. A new church, St. Mary's, had been built on the Bosworth Road on a piece of land which had fallen into the hands of the Thickthorn family almost as mysteriously as the abbey grounds had become the property of the Camberwells. The Thickthorn of the day had generously given the land and contributed five hundred pounds towards the new buildings. In style, St. Mary's was appropriately Gothic, but about it there was no faintest tinge of popery, a fact which mattered at the time. It was a comfortable church, well lighted, well heated, and the brand of religion which it dispensed was comfortably "low." It was the popular church, but some people, chiefly those with deep roots in the town, remained faithful to St. Cerdic's, and the older church had maintained some mysterious *cachet*. Cramped and inconvenient as it was, it still saw some of the most stylish weddings and christenings. Funerals, no! St. Cerdic's graveyard could take no more.

Luscious meringue, a choice of cheese and good coffee.

"In a more favourable situation, this inn would attract custom for the food alone," said the senior Plotter.

"I agree. Look, it's still light and we've never been *inside* that church. There may be some fault or flaw upon which a good argument could be based."

And a little gentle exercise between a good meal and bedtime was known to be beneficial.

In the kitchen, George Gilderson faced his problem alone. Nobody to consult; nobody to advise.

The poor little boy was asleep in the downstairs bedroom nearest the kitchen, and Emily had thoughtfully left the door into the private passage and lobby open, so that if he waked she would hear. He seldom did; that animal element in him was conducive to sound sleep. But he had been known to wake up and whimper.

Emily was thoroughly enjoying her supper. "Lovely, Mr. Gilderson. Better than my mum's, and thass saying something." Rose ate well, too, but she gave no word of appreciation. She had discarded the green satin dress, removed her corsets and donned a soiled wrapper. Slut's wear!

Well, he'd known from the beginning that she was a slut, in her personal habits, in her attitude to life. And this afternoon he had had proof . . . that slap on the rump was indicative of a long familiarity. And she'd been safe enough, with Charlie so busy on market days. She'd thought she'd been safe today, and so she would have been had his lumbago not vanished so suddenly.

Charlie was there, hastily eating his share of the remains of the pigeon-pie, but he was poised, alert, his ear cocked towards another door left ajar; for, late as it was, a few drinkers lingered in the bar; a rap with a mug would summon him. He looked very tired. But when one of the late drinkers tapped and Rose said, "I'll go," he said, "No!" and shot her a look more scathing than George had ever seen him bestow. Whatever charm she had ever held for him had worn out, George noticed, and added that fact to his thinking as carefully as he would have seasoned a dish.

"Typical," Rose said to nobody in particular. "Always on about being tired; then when I offer to help . . ."

"Dressed like that?" George asked.

"Expect me to dress up for that sort of customer?"

The running battle had been resumed. Neither contestant forbore on account of Emily's presence; she was almost like one of the family, and showed very plainly where her allegiance lay.

A decent girl and no gossip, the old man thought. Now I'd have settled for someone like that; I'm not really proud, even though we've been here, and always respected, further back than the records go.

"Talking of tired, Mr. Gilderson. *You've* done enough for the first day up. I'll do the dishes."

Rose sauntered away to the private sitting-room which silly, soft Charlie had practically refurnished in the days of his infatuation, when he was anxious to prove that Rose hadn't made such a bad bargain.

George mounted the stairs. He thought that as long as he lived he'd remember Joe Bettison going down them, so cocky, so pleased with himself. Some curious fastidiousness kept him from touching the handrail.

He went, not to his own room but into the one used for lust that afternoon. It was one of the almost empty ones, bare except for a massive bedstead on which lay a good horsehair mattress in a blue cover. If he had entertained the slightest doubt, proof lay there—a damp patch. He made a wordless sound of disgust.

Then, by the mere power of association, he thought of the state of the roof in this part of the house. Old thatch that should have been replaced years ago. You turned a blind eye. You said, "Well, we hardly ever use the rooms on that side." You said, "Maybe things'll look up next year." Tonight, weary as he was, he felt stronger than he had done when he rose from his bed, and he said to himself, something must be done.

The younger and more cynical of the Plotters took a look round the little church, and said, "It's no architectural gem, is it?"

The elder agreed. "No, the most that can be said of it is that it's old."

"That is something that puzzles me. This craze for anything old. And why only in buildings? Old horses go to the knackers; old people go to the grave; old trees are cut up for timber. Where's the logic in letting an old building stand in the way of progress?"

"Exactly." One of the reasons why, despite their difference in age and background, they made such an excellent team was that, though they could argue a thing out in a perfectly amicable fashion, fundamentally they were agreed.

Inside the church the light was dim, but outside enough late sunset remained to make the north window glow.

"Pleasant glass," the older man said, taking a backward step in order to view it better. "I'd say that was partly original . . ."

After that he was so oddly, so unusually silent as they walked back to the inn that the younger man began racking his mind for a reason. Had he, quite unwittingly, given offence? He was a young man who firmly believed that there was a reason for everything. He found the reason for his senior's behaviour. Those incautious words about age! But good God! He wouldn't have said them to anybody whom he regarded as old. How could he convey this without compounding the fault, and further offending? The forthright approach: Look here, when I said about old people going to the grave, I didn't mean you.

Fatal!

He was, however, a resourceful young man. He began to limp, to droop. He said, "I don't know about you. I'm about done, what with the coach and the riding and the walking." They were in that rather difficult stage of partnership where "Mister" sounded too formal except in front of an audience, and Christian names sounded too familiar. But the trick seemed to have worked. The elder man proffered his arm. He said, kindly, paternally, "Hang on to me. Ah, I see that the landlord is still about. There now, if you can manage the stairs . . . Would you prefer whisky or brandy?"

It was not, as the junior Plotter thought, an older man flattered into a sense of physical superiority, an unintentional wound licked over and healed. In fact, there had been no wound, for the older man was also a rational being; he knew that he was a full twenty years older than the man with whom he worked so agreeably; he knew that old horses went to the knacker's and old people to their graves. He too. One day. What had kept him silent or monosyllabic until the younger man had appealed to his sympathy, what kept him preoccupied was the fact that tomorrow he must say, and say it very firmly, that the proper site for the future Mid-Suffolk Railway station was not the old abbey grounds. When and if all these plans and surveys came to fruition, the station would be in the Forest Way area. Completely logical; trees were easier to chop down or uproot than stone ruins. His opinion had been in the balance, and now the balance had tipped over. And he knew what he was about; he knew that in the end his word carried more weight.

George Gilderson was equally sure of what he was about. He had deft hands, not only with pastry. He'd always shown a certain aptitude for carpentering, mending things. When he said, on the morning after that memorable market day, "Charlie, I'm going to have a look at that bit of roof. I'm not much of a thatcher but I could take a look at the woodwork," it caused no consternation.

The job demanded a certain amount of work indoors as well as out, but nobody took much notice of his activities. He still did the cooking. And, that done, he might be anywhere. On top of a ladder, ripping off rotten thatch; upstairs, banging and sawing. The days sped and it was market day again. With what malicious glee did George announce that he intended to spend the afternoon working upstairs. "And that should see the end of the inside work. Tomorrow I can start thatching."

Thatching was recognised as a specialist job but, working slowly and with infinite care, George was laying the new roof more tidily and evenly than could have been expected of an amateur. He wore a pair of leather knee-caps similar to those worn by horses which had fallen and broken their knees. They gave him quite a professional look. People who could spare a thought from themselves thought the old boy was making a gallant effort; estimates of his age—wildly varying—were made. And God send that I am as spry as that at his age, men thought.

When the accident happened, everybody thought it was a miracle that he was not killed or injured. It was the narrowest of escapes. He worked with two ladders lashed together; one rose almost perpendicularly to the eaves, the other lay at a sharper angle on the very edge of the newly-laid roof, and since, in laying thatch, one worked from the lower level upwards and, from a stance on the ladder, reached sideways, it was almost a miracle that he did not fall into the hole made when a rotten beam gave way. Even a rotten beam had weight, and in collapsing it brought down others, sound and weighty, not to mention slabs of plaster from the ceiling. George had taken the precaution of demolishing the bedstead, with its solid headboard, footboard and frame, which might have offered some protection to the beast with two backs, gratifying a lust all the keener for a fortnight's deprivation.

It was a very quiet accident, and any sound it made was masked by the market din and the booming clock from the tower of St. Mary's church.

Charlie must never know the truth, and there must be no scandal. With that in mind, George worked for the next fifteen minutes with the strength of ten men and with utter detachment. The main beam had fallen exactly where he had planned, literally squashing the two bodies together. He levered it up and dragged Joe Bettison's heavy body out of that fatal, most comprehensive embrace. He bundled it into a sack, dragged the sack into another room and locked the door. There would be time enough to deal with that later.

With the body of his daughter-in-law he dealt more ceremoniously, rolling it just off the mattress, straightening its skirts. Then he let the beam fall again and closed Rose's flaccid, still warm fingers around the handle of a sweeping-brush. Nearby he placed the dustpan.

It was an ironic touch—Rose had never used such humble household tools, yet the whole thing had a curious validity. What more likely than that Rose, activated by perversity, hating him and everything he did, should make an uncharacteristic show of good housewifery, ostentatiously clearing up the mess he was making? She had been very critical about the whole roof-mending operation.

He went down, and there was no need to pretend. That tremor in the very marrow of his bones had emerged and was shaking his flesh, even his mouth, as he said, "Charlie, accident. Terrible accident."

Charlie-facing-both-ways, admiring his father for his energy and skill in the re-thatching, and yet agreeing with Rose that it was all a waste of time and effort, since those upstairs rooms were never likely to be used again, said, "You're all right, Dad?"

Hasten in with the reassurance! Ignore the tremor!

"I'm all right, Charlie. It's Rose."

Joe Bettison's disappearance remained a mystery. He had certainly taken his eighteenpenny ordinary at the One Bull and there were several people who, relying upon what they usually saw rather than upon what they had seen on one special day, were prepared to swear that they had seen him in the cattle market late in the afternoon. Mrs. Bettison, who had long had reason to suspect him of infidelity, was sure that he had run off with some other woman, but that suspicion she kept to herself, laying a few false clues so that, if he repented and came back, there would be no scandal. He could very well have gone to Norwich, where some important cattle sales were about to take place. He'd left his horse and gig at the One Bull because somebody had offered him a lift. Such a pretence could not be kept up for long, and those who knew the family well said that poor old Joe had simply found his wife and her tongue too much to bear.

Mrs. Bettison did not grieve. Joe had taken nothing with him; she had land and money and a son of thirteen.

The person most worried about the missing man was George Gilderson, who had never actually faced up to what could be done with a corpse weighing fifteen stone. He had felt nothing save a sense of achievement as he bundled the body into a sack and dragged it away: now the thought of touching it filled him with repugnance and seemed to paralyse his thinking. If he could get it out of the house and on to the cart, he could hide it in the woods along Forest Way, or drive down to the river below Bosworth. But he doubted his ability to lift it, and the possibility of his getting it out of the house undetected, even in the dead of night, seemed remote. The foot of the stairway he must use was in the lobby between the kitchen and the private rooms—within a few feet of Charlie's bedroom.

Over and over in the sleepless night he visualised himself

overcoming his physical aversion, calling up hidden reserves of strength, and then meeting Charlie in that little lobby.

Yet he knew from experience how much stench the body of a rat, dead under a floorboard, could cause. Until it was found and removed, or corruption was complete, a room could be uninhabitable. And the spell of hot weather continued.

The floorboards of the bedrooms in this wing were exceptionally stout. He had proof of that in the fact that, though the thatch was rotten and the upper rooms very damp, there had never been a leak in the ground-floor rooms. The locked room had a window. If that were open, would the odour of the putrefaction dissipate? Be lost in the smell of stables and pigstye? And if the window, why not a section of the roof? He could only try.

"Charlie, that . . . that accident proved to me what a rotten state that roof is in. I'd better get back to work right away."

"I'd sooner you didn't, Dad. I don't reckon it's safe for you to go crawling about on. Do you realise that, if your ladder had been a foot further that way," he jerked his thumb, "you'd have gone down with that beam and broken your neck?"

"That I didn't shows how well I know that roof, and how careful I am."

"All right then, but be extra careful. We don't want another accident." Typical of Charlie, so easily argued down. Typical, too, that the boy had not yet realised what the one accident had done for him. He'd been upset. Seemed genuinely grieved. It wasn't that he was insincere; he was just easily swayed. The suddenness of Rose's death and the manner of it had made him forget a lot of things and remember others. That Rose Webber had been very pretty; that he'd loved her enough to marry her in face of the old man's objection; that the One Bull had been a disappointment to her, and so had the baby, and so had he.

George Gilderson, like most of the males of the family, had spent some time at the grammar school; he was therefore fairly familiar with his Bible, and though for much of his adult life he had had little time for reading, he occasionally read a chapter or two—the Old Testament mainly, the most stirring stories being there. Now a sentence recurred to him, "Where the carcass is, there will the vultures be gathered." Something like that. In England there were no vultures—or was it eagles?— but there were carrion crows, and cats, and horrible blue-bottle flies.

Before opening the window of the locked room to its fullest extent and removing some thatch, so that the sack—easier to think of it so—lay exposed to the sun and the air, George tacked muslin over both apertures. He used the curtains from this and the other disused rooms. In the exceptional heat and drought of that summer, Joe Bettison quietly mummified, and only stank in the old man's dreams.

The dreams were horrible, the more so because they always began happily and always involved people of whom George Gilderson had been fond: his parents, a sister who died at thirteen, one of the masters at school. Most often of all, his dear Susie. Occasionally he was with Charlie, too, but always Charlie as a little boy. Something pleasant and exciting was always just about to happen, a present to be unwrapped, some special treat in the way of food about to come to table, a new plant to be shown in the garden. All homely, undramatic things. Then, just as the crucial moment arrived, he—and apparently he only—would catch a whiff of the odour of corruption; he, and he only, knew what the parcel, the dish, the next step in the garden would reveal. He'd scream, with the soundless voice of dreams, "Don't look! Don't open the parcel! Don't raise the dish cover!" Then he would wake, streaming with sweat and with the stench still in his nostrils. It took a little time to fade, but once it had gone, it was gone. But the dreams came often enough to keep him perpetually aware of the body in the room just along the passage. And he knew that one day he must do something about it.

The very least he could do was to remove anything that might identify the corpse: the watch, the chain with its dangling ornaments. Joe Bettison would certainly have owned that symbol of prosperity. Had he worn a ring on any finger? Would the drying-out process, which alone could account for the absence of smell, have changed his face out of recognition? Must he then mutilate it?

The evil-scented dreams, the pre-occupation by day, affected his appearance. He'd always been thin; he now grew emaciated, and people who had considered him a wonderful man for his age, and very spry except when suffering from lumbago, now remarked that the years were catching up on old George. And what a pity that he should begin to decline just when his home life had taken a turn for the better! Charlie was all set to marry Emily after a decent interval, and she came from a very respectable, though poor, family.

The autumn came with its winds and its rains. Now he really must thatch in the last section of roof. And one day soon he must really do something about what lay below it.

He saw now that he'd been a fool. On that summer market-day afternoon, he should have confided in Charlie. Between them they could easily have disposed of the body, and Charlie wouldn't have felt all that hurt—or at least not for long. Maybe he wouldn't even have been much surprised—he must have known Rose for what she was.

Now and again, especially when he woke from one of those dreams, he considered making a clean breast of it to Charlie. But that seemed a shame, just when the boy was regaining some happiness and liveliness of spirit. Not an apt moment to go dragging up old unhappy things. He'd been a fool, and a fool must pay for his folly. Anyway, the nights were longer in winter. Fewer people about. Put off the dread task until after Christmas, when Charlie and Emily would be married and there'd be less risk of Charlie coming out and meeting him at the foot of the stairs, in that little lobby.

There was now a young charity girl to take care of poor Timothy. Only twelve and none too bright, but teachable. They played together rather like a couple of puppies. And Emily, also very teachable, was learning to cook. Already she was acquiring—or rather always had had, and now brought it to the surface—the gentle dignity so neccesary in a decent inn-keeper's wife.

All would have been well but for the constant nag-nag, not of conscience—never for one moment had he felt a qualm of guilt—but of responsibility. The facing of something which could not be endlessly deferred and must one day be faced.

Because . . . suppose I died . . .

He'd always thought, and once, in a burst of irritability, said to Charlie that the horse liniment didn't cure lumbago, it simply gave the sufferer something else to think about. And when the spring came—spring, and still nothing done about that sack—George Gilderson had something else to think about. A very well-dressed, slightly self-important man alighted from the coach, bespoke the best room in the New Wing, ate a good meal cooked almost entirely by Emily, and then said that he would like to speak to the landlord.

"Perhaps you'd better go, Charlie. It's most likely something to do with licensing or new taxes. Maybe I'm too old to be bothered."

"You own the place, Dad. You *are* the landlord."

That was where Charlie differed from so many sons only too anxious to take over, all too ready to push an old father aside. But at the same time Charlie said, kind and considerate as ever, "If it's a lot of facts and figures, just call me and I'll come."

George listened, and then made a blunder. And as soon as he'd made it he saw where he'd gone wrong. He should have said, tactfully, discreetly, "This is something that I and my son must talk over." But he didn't do that. He shouted, after an hour's quiet talk and reasoned argument, "Charlie, come here." And when Charlie came, thrust upon him in a few words the gist of an hour's talk.

"Look here, Charlie, this . . . gentleman is from London. He wants to buy this place and knock it down. Make a timber-yard or some such. I said, 'no.' Then it struck me, you should have some say. It'll be yours. You must say. But Charlie, we've been here since before Adam. Good times and bad, wars and revolutions and plagues. Always a Gilderson at the One Bull."

He sounded hysterical. At the back of his mind the gentleman from London made an observation—in extreme old age men often became like women, and women like men. With relief he turned to Charlie, so much younger, more likely to listen to reason. "Good morning, Mr. Gilderson. I have been trying to explain to your father, but of course, he has a sentimental attachment—quite understandable. The facts are these. The company in which I am interested has purchased some standing timber along Forest Way and in certain other places within easy reach of Mallow. What we need now is a large space, as central as possible, for a timber-yard. Few such sites are available, and my company is prepared to be generous. Perhaps you and I might have a talk." He hoped the old man would go away. But George stayed. He'd said that Charlie must say. But he knew Charlie's propensity for being talked round.

Charlie, however, stayed staunch, "It'd be a waste of time. My father has already given you his answer."

"Hastily. Without due thought. Surely it merits a moment's

consideration. I have no wish to be offensive, but it is evident that trade is not very brisk at the moment."

"We just about pay our way," Charlie said agreeably. "But, as Dad says, we've weathered bad times before. Something always turns up. And will again." He spoke with the confidence of a happy man, and the stranger looked at him sharply.

"One hopes so. What are you expecting?"

"Oh, nothing definite. Better times in general. Maybe a different arrangement concerning the coaches. Anyway, we don't want to sell."

"You have not even heard what my company would be prepared to offer."

"And don't want to, thanks all the same. It's always been in the family, and I hope to live to see my son take over."

As he said the last words he looked at his father with an expression which George rightly interpreted as being apologetic. Of course, poor Charlie! Thinking of that ugly, near-idiot child! For it was April now; the new happy marriage almost four months old and no sign yet!

They left the stranger pondering the failure of his mission and the exact wording of his report.

"You did well, Charlie. Very firm!"

"I had reason, Dad. I'd have told you before if I'd had a minute, but Emily only told me this morning. She's going to have a baby."

George Gilderson, hitherto the strong man in the family, was obliged to blink and swallow and blow his nose in order to forestall the onset of a bout of unmanly, senile tears. And as soon as he had mastered his emotions and congratulated Charlie and said, "We must take good care of Emily," back came the thought of the locked room and the sack. This good news justified, more than justified, the action he had taken. But there was one thing more to do.

Joe Bettison's putrefying carcass had not polluted the air, but it was a centre of evil, a reminder of what he wanted to forget, especially in the light of this happy news.

He'd move it tonight.

Everything played into his hands.

"Friday's a quiet evening, Dad," Charlie said. "You could manage if Emily and I went along to Hornden, couldn't you? She'd like her mother to know."

George could only hope that dismay didn't show on his face.

"You'll be taking the pony-cart?"

"Not if it stays fine. Emily felt like a walk. And we can cut through the woods."

"Take something with you, Charlie. A bottle, a ham . . . It's something to celebrate, after all." And though the Gildersons were poor by some standards—even by some bygone Gilderson standards—they were rich compared with Emily's family, and an inn, whether doing well or badly, must always have supplies in hand.

Friday was a quiet evening. No resident guest and only two drinkers in the tap-room, both self-employed men as able to buy a pint on Friday as on Saturday. The ordinary wage-earner was paid on Saturday and was prepared, poor fellow, to make a night out of it over a twopenny pint of small beer.

George served the two, and then said, "My son and his wife are gone to Hornden and I—I have something to do. But help yourselves. Leave the money on the bar, or settle next week."

Tottering off to bed, poor old man, they thought.

He went out and harnessed the fat pony to the old rickety cart, and brought it down to the door of the lobby. Even now, with everything made so easy—he was even appreciative of the fact that he could do this distasteful job in the lingering April twilight and not in the dead darkness of night—he allowed himself the indulgence of a little brandy, diluted with water. Amongst the myriad traditions, fact or myth, handed down from Gilderson father to son, was the belief that spirits, brandy, whisky, gin or rum, should not be swallowed raw.

He did not carry the key of the locked room about with him, nor did he keep it in his own room. His distaste for the whole thing, akin to his refusal to touch that banister rail, had led him to deposit that key on the out-jutting jamb of the door to which it belonged. He had, now and then, after one of his dreams, used it and opened the door just a crack, enough to reassure himself that the stench existed only in his dreams.

Now he took down the key, opened the door wide, and stepped in, carrying another, rather bigger sack. There'd be blood on the other in the short time that it had taken to drag it from one room to another, and in the long months of his procrastination heaven alone knew what might have happened. But he was justified, more than justified in what he had done.

Charlie happy; a proper child on its way. So face it! Do what must be done!

Nothing.

A completely empty room with dusty floorboards and bare walls.

But how? But when? But who?

A rational man, born into what was known as the Age of Reason, George Gilderson stood there, stunned, amazed, and reaching what seemed the only possible explanation. He was getting old and muddle-minded, had worried himself into a state where he'd locked more than one room, and had now opened the wrong door. Unlikely, but *just* possible, and a hope not to be discarded until he'd gone all along the passage. No other door was locked; all the rooms except his own were more or less empty, and none of them contained what he was looking for.

It could only have been Charlie.

And that meant that Charlie knew everything. Knew that his wife had been a whore and that his father was a murderer.

Somehow it didn't fit. He'd always understood Charlie, seen through him as though he were a pane of glass. Charlie wavered, listened, agreed, changed his mind. You couldn't call him deceitful or cunning; nothing like that; just a bit weak and over-anxious to be agreeable. So was Charlie capable of doing what had obviously been done and giving no sign?

If so... God Almighty! What about that timber-yard? If Charlie were capable... Even that little bit of sentiment about Rose, which George had thought *he* understood! A man so secretive, so *false*, could very well have seemed to stand firm in his father's presence, and all the time be planning...

Unaware that he was speaking aloud with no listener but himself, George said, "I must have this out with Charlie!"

They came in, eyes aglow with happiness, cheeks pink from brisk walking in the fresh night air. George thought: Surprise the best weapon. Charlie asked the expected question.

"What's the pony-cart doing out there at this time of night?"

Keeping his stare fixed on his son's face, and speaking with deliberation, George said, "There was something I wanted to move off the top floor: but I couldn't find it."

Nobody who knew could look so guileless, so entirely lacking in interest. Charlie's face did not change colour; his eyes did not flicker. He said in his easy comfortable way, accepting an old man's little lapse of memory, "Don't worry, Dad. You'll remember where you put it, tomorrow." The best actor in the world could not have given such a performance.

Emily said, in much her usual voice, but with just a little edge of warning in it saying under the ordinary words, the ordinary tone, "Be careful! Don't fail now!" "Oh, that sackful of old rubbish? I moved it, Dad. Don't you remember? We had that great bonfire of the rotten thatch and wood with the worm in it. It seemed to me a good time to get rid of—rubbish."

An *excellent* time; for that had been no ordinary bonfire. Oak, however worm-ridden, was a slow-burning wood, and rotten thatch, dry on the surface but in its lower layers damp from the rains of past years, had flared, smouldered, flared again, and again smouldered through three days and two nights. And people all around in this congested part of the town, people with little backyards or little gardens, had come trotting along saying, "Mr. Gilderson, I see you have a bonfire going. Would you mind if I put this on it?"

Charlie said, "Well, I'll put poor old Tubby back into his stable. Good night, Dad."

Left alone, George and his daughter-in-law—and God forgive him, though he had accepted her gladly, at the back of his mind there had always been a slight reservation—looked at each other in silence until Emily said, "I hope you sleep well."

"I shall," he said, and knew that he would. For with no word spoken, just eye communicating with eye, responsibility and authority had been transferred.

16 Vikky and Alan

1897

"MIND YOU, SIR, IT'S EIGHT, NINE YEARS AGO. AND A LOT can happen in nine years," the younger of the two men in the first-class carriage said as the train rattled over the points and began to slow down for the stop at Mallow station. "I may have sent you on a wild-goose chase."

"No matter. My time is my own, and I was bound to break my journey somewhere. As well Mallow as Triver or Thetford. I am indebted to you for a most entertaining conversation."

"And I to you. Seldom has that tedious journey from Colchester passed so quickly. And here we are!"

The train grated to a standstill and like a runner, the course completed but the breathing heavy, emitted a great burst of steam. A porter snatched open the door and said, "Carry your bag, sir?" Two bags, identical in shape, but not of the same quality. That belonging to the younger man, who must, inevitably, one day be Sir Francis Colman, but who needed, in order to inherit enough to support the rank, to ingratiate himself with his crusty old uncle—his bag was of pigskin, its fastenings solid brass. His fellow-traveller's was a carpet bag, a much inferior article.

The porter wished that everybody travelled with carpet bags. Twopence was twopence, and pigskin weighed more. Young Mr. Colman could have afforded to be lordly with sixpence, but he compromised with threepence as he stepped into the waiting carriage. A true chip off the old block. It was the owner of the carpet bag who produced sixpence and asked to be directed to the One Bull.

"It's a fair step, sir. But there is a conveyance." It stood waiting in the station yard. A small omnibus, capable of carrying eight passengers and their luggage. It was painted dark green, and on each side and on each of the two doors which opened at the back it proclaimed its identity—a white bull, head lowered to charge. There were three other passengers, one with a good deal of luggage. "All aboard, then," the driver cried cheerfully and slammed the doors. He then climbed into the driver's seat, called equally cheerfully to the horse, and they set off along Station Road, which had lost its earlier name of Forest Way together with every sign of its former rural character.

It was curious, Alan Merton reflected, how closely all railway stations and all Station Roads resembled each other. Always the coal-yard, the timber-yard, the livery stable, the cheap eating-house, the bed-and-breakfast establishments, the rows of narrow-faced terrace houses built for workers on the railway. Better than the average workmen's dwellings, but depressing in their uniformity and in their greyness. A faint film of grey lay over everything, even the flowers in the little front gardens.

He knew them all so well, for until lately he had been a commercial traveller. He had never been in East Anglia. The Midlands was his territory, and his wife came from Dover and liked to spend holidays there. She always claimed that a breath of your native air was a great restorative, and poor dear, she'd always been in great need of restoratives. In the end, even Dover had failed her and she'd died there, two years ago. They'd had no children.

Left alone, with only himself to support, he'd lived rather more comfortably; no house to maintain, no doctor's bills to pay. And then, just four months ago, he'd come into money; not a vast sum, a thousand pounds. His employer, the publisher, Frederick Hayes of St. Paul's Churchyard, had in his will remembered everybody, down to the old woman who cleaned the floors and flapped a duster so that the dust-motes could rise from one surface and settle on another.

Alan knew what a man of sense would do with such a legacy. Invest it. A safe five percent—a pound a week, bar two, for as long as he lived. Keep on with his job, which was in itself not distasteful to him; eat and live a little better, avoiding the cheapest places; let the money accumulate so that his retirement would bring no hardship. But that was not his way. He was by nature a drifter, a romantic, caught up in the economic net and forced since he was sixteen to work for a wage; something in him had always struggled to be free, to have leisure to stand and stare; to travel for pleasure, not for business; to indulge his taste for things of the past.

He'd been doing all this in a quiet way for the past four months and was now bound on a sentimental journey. He came of a Norfolk family and had actually been born in Burnham Thorpe—Nelson's own village. He'd left it too young to have any memories of it, but his mother talked of Norfolk a great deal, always nostalgically, mentioning particularly the quality of the light.

It was now August; presently he would make plans for the autumn; get himself to Italy, Crete, Rhodes—perhaps even to Jerusalem. As he had said to his fellow-traveller, his time was his own—for a year; two? After that? Well, he'd see. Back to the treadmill, unless . . . unless the impossible dream came true. The thing he had never mentioned to anybody, dared hardly face himself, for nobody knew better than a publisher's representative that there were too many books in the world.

The One Bull's bus turned to the left, crossed a bridge, and was in a different world. The amiable young man with whom he had shared a carriage had said that Mallow was fossilised, and so, to the unsympathetic eye, it might seem. The road widening into a space, neither oblong nor oval, was surrounded by buildings, all different, all bravely defying the prevalent craze for uniformity. There were some, Alan noted with a kind of pleasure, built before James I issued his decree against building upper floors jutting out beyond the lower. A fire risk in a narrow street, but acceptable here. Jumbled roofs of various heights and sizes, and beyond them, to the left, some towering grey ruins. All that remained of an abbey, famous in its day but now forgotten. Even Alan Merton, who knew a little about many things, had never heard of St. Cerdic.

The omnibus turned again, sharp left, and the horse knew exactly what to do. Go through the archway, over which the sign, rather unusual—not a painted board but a silhouette— hung motionless in the still afternoon light. No touch on the reins, no word was needed to bring the vehicle, which the horse pulled every day, level with the door, out of which lithe boys ran, strong and willing, ready to carry baggage, show travellers to their rooms, bring up copper cans of hot water, so that the stains of travel might be washed away, and inquiries about afternoon tea might be made. It could be served in your room, in the Garden Room or, on this fine afternoon, in the garden itself.

All the boys wore a kind of uniform, abbreviated jackets and tight trousers of green cloth, and each on his breast wore the same badge as did the omnibus.

Since coming into money, Alan had avoided the cheap accommodation of his working days, but had also shunned expensive places. When young Mr. Colman had casually mentioned the One Bull in Mallow, he had not dwelt upon its amenities as a hotel, merely mentioned its immense age and some wall-paintings which, in his opinion, were as good as those in Pompeii and other places which he had seen on his Grand Tour. It was that which had decided Alan to break his journey.

The green boy said, as an afterthought, "And dinner is served, sir, any time after seven o'clock." Knowing it to be foolish, Alan immediately thought of the deficiencies of his wardrobe. He had just the one suit that he was wearing, a greenish flecked tweed knickerbocker suit, eminently suitable for wear in rural Norfolk, quite unsuitable for dining in so sophisticated a place as the One Bull was proving itself to be. (He had even seen in the corridor a door marked W.C.) It was somewhat ironic to think that had he, during his working life, inadvertently strayed into such a hostelry, he would have looked less out of place after dusk, for representatives of certain firms— anything to do with books or clothing—were expected to dress with the utmost formality. Men travelling in other commodities were allowed more latitude. The tweed suit was the only new clothing that Alan had bought for himself since he received his legacy, and he liked it—it was a symbol of freedom.

Now he said to himself: Come, come! What does it matter? In any case, in a place this size there will certainly be somewhere to get a bite if the dining-room is barred to you because you are improperly dressed. Next month, God help you, you'll be forty. Don't be such a ninny!

The One Bull probably seemed larger than it was because, like many old places, it had been added to and altered: a few steps here, going up; a few there, going down; passages made by taking a bit off a room; rooms contrived by the incorporation of a landing. A jig-saw puzzle of a building, but all old, except for the obviously recent contrivances.

The young man in the train had said, "Talk to the landlady.

She's a bit of a martinet, I believe, but very knowledgeable. She's made quite a hobby of it. Quite fascinating."

He had also said that a lot could happen in nine years. A lot had.

Alan was well accustomed to making a tactful approach. Booksellers were odd fish; some were almost recluses, emerging from some dim, dusty lair, blinking, saying trade was bad. Mr. Mudie with his circulating library, and then Mr. Smith with his bookstalls on all the bigger stations had cut away the very roots of the ordinary bookseller's trade. Then there were men of the other kind, younger, tougher, more modern, more adjustable. Alan knew several, prepared to sell books as a sideline. The combination of tea-shop and bookshop was not unusual; bookshop and chinashop, bookshop and a little printing-works. And Alan knew—it was in Birmingham—a very enterprising young man who was, very successfully, combining a bookshop with his original tobacconist's business, and planning something else: a minor challenge to the great circulating libraries—a twopenny library. No subscription, just twopence down and the book was yours for a week.

All customers were to be greatly cherished, properly approached. So now, not exactly seeking custom, but anxious to make contact with the martinet who was knowledgeable, Alan, having found his way at last into the Garden Room and drunk his tea, said to the green boy who had served him, "Will you take this to Mrs. Gilderson, with my compliments, and say that I should greatly appreciate five minutes' conversation with her."

He had taken his tea in the Garden Room because the garden itself was full of ladies, gay as butterflies, sitting in little cane chairs and shaded from the sun by huge sunshades fixed into the centre of the small, green-painted tables. They were chattering and laughing like parrots.

Presently one rose and came towards him, the card which he had given the green boy delicately held between the thumb and first finger of her left hand.

"Mr. Merton?" she said. "How do you do? I am Mrs. Gilderson."

She was very pretty and very young. Her dress was of silk, the colour old rose—he knew, because he had been a travelling man, and, whereas he carried samples of books, he associated with men carrying samples of other kinds. Old rose was pink.

Mrs. Gilderson wore on her head a hat not unlike a pancake made of flattened roses of the same pink. A bit of a martinet. Knowledgeable. And the history of the old inn her hobby. Impossible!

He said, "I . . . I am interested in old things. And . . . well, somebody told me that the One Bull had a long and interesting history."

She looked at him with an expression as pretty and blank as a doll's.

"So I am given to understand. But I'm practically a stranger here myself." A little, tittering laugh. "Mr. Gilderson and I were only married last year. But," she added hastily, having already learned that unless a guest set out deliberately to be disagreeable one must try to please, "I am not responsible for the renovations. Mr. Gilderson had the place thoroughly overhauled as soon as . . . I mean when his mother passed away." Alan thought: how true to type! In her euphemistic little world, places were not altered, they were renovated, and people didn't die, they passed away.

The french window between the Garden Room and the garden stood open; a female voice, cutting through the chatter, called, "Sophie!"

Giving an excellent imitation of a woman wanted in several directions, but remaining calm and sweet-tempered, Mrs. Gilderson said, "Coming, dear. Well, Mr. . . . ." she glanced at the card again, an almost imperceptible pause, "Merton; if there is nothing else . . . This is my busy afternoon. I hope you will enjoy your stay with us." She was at the french window, duty done, when a thought struck her, and she half turned. "If I can get hold of Vikky—she is my stepdaughter. She shares your interest in old things. But she is very shy. Not easy to talk to, but very clever." She gave him her pretty, doll-like smile and went out to join the largest group of women in the garden.

Alan occupied the interval between tea and dinner by walking around the ruins of the abbey. Except for the great gateway, which a plaque informed him had been destroyed by the townsfolk in 1321 and rebuilt in 1328, there was nothing very spectacular remaining. Inside the grounds, backed by the grey wall and fronted by a handsome garden, were the Assembly Rooms, and to the south of them another stretch of wall had been incorporated into some near dwelling-houses. The sight of relatively modern windows and doors set into mediaeval apertures did not offend Alan's sense of fitness. He liked old things, but without pedantry.

An air of positive peace, not the mere absence of noise, brooded over the place, enhanced rather than destroyed by the voices of children playing on the rough grass near the river, and by the occasional bark of a dog. Alan sat on a stump of ruin and smoked a cigarette. Then, as it was still early for dinner, he turned, when he emerged into the street, away from the One Bull, crossed the mouth of Station Road and then the bridge over the river. He observed with pleasure that slightly upstream of the bridge which carried the road were the fairly well-preserved remains of a three-arched, very ancient stone bridge. He walked on and came to an inn called the King's Head. A pleasant, early-eighteenth-century building, but with a run-down look about it; dirty windows, flaking paint, a yard both untidy and deserted. In directing him to the One Bull, Mr. Colman had assured him of comfort, even if the main interest proved to be a wild-goose chase. And it was odd to think that so little as four months ago, when he was on the road, as the term was, he would not have aspired to a lodging even in such a place as this rather sleazy looking hostelry. He'd have been in Station Road, in a bed-and-breakfast place, thankful if it were merely clean. Publishers' representatives were notoriously badly paid, and publishers were always pleading poverty. A man could make more by selling bicycles or agricultural implements. He'd always known that, but he'd always liked books and liked dealing with people who liked them. Even the most go-ahead young men, propping up an ailing trade by subsidiary activities, were essentially book-lovers. With them he felt at home.

He turned back and re-entered the One Bull, bearing in mind that he must not allow himself to drift into the habit of living in luxury. A thousand pounds would not last forever; the holiday which a thousand pounds could buy would come to an end. Then he'd be back on the road again. Unless . . . He was so accustomed to shying away from that thought that he now did it automatically.

East Anglia was recognised as being one of the coldest areas in England. Even Alan's mother, that homesick Norfolk woman, had admitted that the east wind could be bitter and that it blew for at least two hundred days a year, but she had also said that the wind accounted for the exceptionally clear quality of the light and the hardiness of the people, and when there came a sunny day, without wind, then it could be like heaven.

This was such a day. But the dining-room at the One Bull had been planned not for those few days, but for the majority of days. It was all red. The walls were papered in crimson in the new paper called "flock," which looked like cloth. The floor was covered with Turkey carpet, mainly red; the windows had crimson-velvet curtains and all the lamp-shades were red, too. On a winter's day it would have given an illusion of cosiness. And Alan remembered, not inconsequently, a fellow-traveller who sold cloth and was disposed to chat about flannel. There was white flannel and red, and poor stupid women actually believed that the red had the virtue of warmth denied to the white. Weight for weight, the man had said, they were identical.

On this warm evening, in a room where red of various shades predominated, Alan understood. Despite the open windows, the room was stifling.

But the food was excellent. No brown windsor soup!

It was a joke. Doubtless at some time, long ago, before the late and much lamented Prince Albert had effected economies in the royal households, thus making himself very unpopular, a chef at Windsor had produced a tasty, game-flavoured, brown-coloured soup. Hotels and boarding-houses throughout the length and breadth of England had taken it up: brown windsor soup, thick, dark and completely tasteless. Once one of Alan's fellow-diners had said, "It's made of the paste they use to stick posters on hoardings, and coloured with hat dye." In another place, but over the same dish, another man had said, "Imperious Caesar, dead and turned to clay, might stop a hole to keep the wind away—suitably diluted, of course!"

None of that here. A crystal-clear liquid, magically combining the essence of beef with the flavour of onion and celery. After that, a fillet of sole with a piquant sauce; then a choice of roast saddle of mutton or chicken. Fresh fruit salad or sherry trifle; a variety of cheeses. Easy to see why this dining-room was crowded!

Near the service-door was a largish table occupied by Mrs. Gilderson, four women very much like her, and a man of about fifty. Plainly the landlord, and absolutely cut out for the job. Some people, on entering, greeted him. Two or three times during the meal he stood up and threw a benevolent yet critical gaze over the assembly. It said quite plainly, "Everybody happy? If not, why not?" Once he went through the service-door and was absent for about ten minutes. When he came back he must have said something amusing, for his wife and the other ladies laughed. He was a man well over average height, not fat but with just the hint of a paunch. What hair he still had was brightly silver and there was about him, quite indefinable, but unmistakable, the smack of the sea. Towards the end of the meal he stood up again and began to move about the room. At some tables just an inquiry: "Everything to your liking?" "Suffolk is certainly putting on its best face for you." "Very glad to see you again." He tended to linger longer at tables where a solitary diner sat. Very tactful; affable; yet . . . yet, not false exactly. Insincere? Patronising?

Basically, Alan Merton was a shy man, not quite in the ordinary sense of the word; if he'd ever had a tendency to hesitate in his speech or blush or fall over his own feet, he'd outgrown it long ago. And he'd grown a professional carapace; he could tackle a new, potential customer as well as the next man, and better than most. But on the whole he avoided, rather than sought, contact with people. It was Mr. Colman who had started the conversation in the train. Inspired by that, he had come to the One Bull and asked for a word with Mrs. Gilderson—who had turned out to be the wrong one. And he had probably made a false assumption. The Mrs. Gilderson who was a martinet and knowledgeable about the past had probably been this landlord's first wife. Mr. Colman had spoken of her as old, but he had also said that his one visit to the inn was eight or nine years ago, and then he must have been very young indeed, so young that anybody over thirty would seem old to him.

Anyway, Alan felt, for no explicable reason, that he did not particularly want to talk to Mr. Gilderson, but just as he was in the act of rising, a girl confronted him and said, "Mr. Merton? I'm Vikky Gilderson. My father seems to think that I should talk to you."

Her manner was abrupt to the point of being unfriendly, but before he could get to his feet and greet her properly, pull back the unoccupied chair and ask her to sit down, she'd done it herself. Seated, she called over her shoulder to one of the waitresses, dressed as parlourmaids, black and white, with streamers, "Mary, bring back the cheese, please. I'm famished.

I'd like coffee, too. And possibly Mr. Merton could drink another cup."

One of the new breed of woman, Alan thought with dismay. She even wore what was to them—and he'd met a few—practically a uniform: a close-necked blouse with no frills or furbelows, and a dark, narrow skirt. She had a great deal of bright yellow, absolutely golden hair, rather untidily bundled up, and her eyes were gooseberry green—no, that was unkind—emerald. And she was young; her eyelids and her lips had that moist look which, he had noticed, gave even ugly girls a brief beauty. Not that she was ugly; far from it. She'd have been beautiful had not her face already taken on an expression of discontent, a droop and a scowl which might have been, in a weaker face, rather pitiable. Allied to that high-bridged nose and square jaw, it was formidable.

"Sophie"—and his keen ear, tuned to nuances, informed him that the girl would more readily have said: My stepmother—"says that you are interested in old things."

"That is true. On the train I got into conversation with a young man who told me that this hotel was very old and had some quite unique wall-paintings."

"Did have."

"You mean . . . ?"

"Look around you," she said. Expanses of crimson paper, broken here and there by copies of well-known pictures and wall-mirrors in ornate frames.

"This was the room?"

"Yes. Tell me, is your interest in any way professional? I mean are you an architect or an archaeologist, or planning to write a book?"

"Oh, no. Nothing like that. I'm just . . . interested."

"Good! I couldn't talk to anybody very knowledgeable without betraying my ignorance. And there are such enormous gaps. You see, the only person I knew who cared about such things was my grandmother—and she died when I was twelve." She threw a look of distaste around the handsome, crowded room. "She, of course, would never have allowed this to happen to the Oak Room."

"That was its original name?"

"One of them, I should say. Actually the oak came from the abbey. The paintings were far older. Definitely Roman."

"So I was told. What a pity."

"Yes." She was silent, staring at him with a curious intentness. He thought: She is anything but shy; that was an euphemism for abruptness and—yes, sullenness.

"Look here, if you really are interested, I have pictures and a few other odds and ends. But they are in the only place I can call my own. Which happens to be my bedroom. If you would feel compromised..."

"Good Heavens! Of course not."

"Come on, then."

She led the way upstairs, along a passage, down a few steps, up another staircase, the standard of comfort declining as they climbed. Carpet gave way to floorcloth; red-shaded gas jets to bare, flaring ones, wallpaper to whitewash. Six steps, set at a sharp angle, ended in a tiny landing and a door. As she opened it, she said, "Please wait here a minute. I'll make a light."

He heard the scrape of a match; two gas jets popped, glass clinked on glass.

"Now," she said. "Come in and look to your right."

There, on the whitewashed wall, were the pictures he had broken his journey to see. Three scenes painted in glowing colours, the figures stylised, yet lifelike: a feast; a triumphal crowning with laurel; a sacrificial procession centring about a white bull with flowers on its horns and around its neck. Beautiful!

He had never seen Pompeii, but he had peddled, with some success, illustrated books on it and similar subjects. And because he had only seen pictures scaled down to page size it did not strike him that these pictures were small, less than life-size. And indeed everything here was in such exquisite proportion and portrayed with such meticulous detail that the whole display seemed rather more than life-size.

When he'd got his breath back he said, "How did you manage...?"

"Oh, I cheated a little. You see, Papa was in such a hurry. I had only just time to find a photographer. I made some hasty notes about colours and scribbled a few sketches. And of course there had been damage. What I call the Feast and the Laurel were tolerably well preserved. The Sacrifice, less fortunate. Probably *that* owes something to my imagination. And, of course, all the time I was obliged to persuade Papa that it would be quicker and cheaper to use the battens, have canvas stretched over them and the canvas papered, rather than uprooting the battens and having the paper slapped on the walls. Papa had waited so long, poor man. My grandmother was so opposed to any change . . . Odd, I'm the granddaughter of the one, the daughter of the other, and I see both points of view. I always do. And it makes life extremely *difficult*. Have you ever found it so? Oh, do forgive me. I am being inhospitable. Please sit down. That chair is more comfortable than it looks. And may I offer you something to drink? I disturbed you at your coffee with which brandy goes well. Allow me to make good." She moved over to an article of furniture which Alan recognised— again from pictures—as a Tudor court cupboard, the direct descendant of an earlier piece of furniture known as a livery table. An arrangement of shelves; a cupboard, once all open; then the lower shelves enclosed by doors, the two upper ones ornamented with carved pillars.

And while she was busy there he looked about the room: a converted attic, with a dormer window. It was starkly neat but at the same time very comfortable. A very old, very faded but still silken and beautiful rug covered most of the floor, and the bed, a narrow low divan, with a green serge cover, pushed close to the wall, with several cushions, was the only indication that this was a sleeping—as well as a living-room. There was a massive but narrow table placed under the window, and opposite to it a very up-to-date piece of furniture indeed; a glass-fronted china cabinet. It held, not the usual "best" tea-set, but upon its top shelf a statuette of the Virgin Mary with a small white dove at her feet and, lying flat on the lower shelves, some books and some papers in folders. Flanking this piece of modernity was an ancient prie-dieu.

"I salvaged everything I could lay hands on," Vikky said. "There seems to have been a hoarder in every other generation of Gildersons. I'm the present one. It was a grief to me not to use the huge family four-poster. It couldn't be got up those last crooked stairs. The prie-dieu and the statue I found in the lumber-room. I don't know to whom they belonged, but I imagine to someone who lived before the Reformation, or during Mary's time perhaps . . . And then, with all the no-popery nonsense, such things had to be hidden away. That I can never know." She sounded regretful. "Now the dove—it's really a scent-bottle—I know a great deal about. It belonged to a Marguerite Gilderson who lived in the early seventeenth century. She kept a journal—and very sad reading it makes." She checked herself abruptly and said, "I talk too much on these rare occasions when I find a sympathetic listener. Retaliate, Mr. Merton. Tell me something of yourself and *your* family."

"Nothing of much interest to tell. Unless you consider it worthy of mention that I was born in Burnham Thorpe."

"Nelson's village."

"Yes. My mother's family farmed there. My father was a tailor—quite prosperous, I believe, until cheap ready-made clothes came on to the market. Then he thought he'd do better in London, and so he did for a time. Well enough to keep me at school until I was almost sixteen; never well enough to take a holiday and go back to Norfolk, which my mother always longed for. In fact, he died young, almost certainly from overwork. And I got a job. I'd always liked books, so I went into a publisher's office, in a very humble capacity and—how can I put it?—*crept* my way up and became what is called a representative—a commercial traveller." His voice changed. "My mother died before I attained this elevated position. I married . . ." He would not say that he had drifted into marriage. Amy had been the kindly, capable woman who had looked after his mother during her last illness and then somehow stayed on, being kindly and capable, providing meals at odd hours, mending and laundering his linen, starching the collars and cuffs of his regulation shirts, sponging and pressing his formal clothes.

For her, at least, he had been able to do more than he had for his mother—repeated visits to Dover where Amy could show off. Amy and her family thought that she had done well for herself, and who was he to contradict? Her life had been short but, he comforted himself, as happy as he could make it. And any port, like Dover, was open to diseases which better sanitation had practically eradicated from England. Cholera had struck Amy down on one of those happy holidays.

"I married," he said. "My wife died seven years ago. In April of this year I received a legacy—enough to enable me to live as I please for a bit. What a very dull recital!"

"But for what—oh dear, romance is not quite the word—what interest I can squeeze out of this place, mine would sound even more prosaic. Though I certainly was born in what *sounds* a romantic place—Mauritius. Why do you look like that?"

"I wasn't aware of looking in any particular way. Just an

idle thought. Probably mistaken, but I thought your father had the look of a sea-faring man."

"You're very observant! Yes. He had his own ship. Family feuds are so boring, aren't they, and we seem to have had more than most. Very seldom have father and son, or mother and son, seen eye to eye. Papa went stamping off to sea, saying he'd come back when his mamma sent for him. But she accepted me and brought me up, shaped me, I suppose one might say. Finally she did send for him and he came home, thinking to get his own way, but he had to wait. I think myself that that is one reason why the changes he has made are so sweeping . . . Still, it is old things that interest you; not today's gossip."

She got up and went to the cabinet, opened its doors, lifted, with reverent fingers a small black-bound book. "Marguerite Gilderson's journal," she said. "Well written in both senses of the word. Oh, and this is interesting, at least to me. The records of the Florentine Club. It may seem to you difficult to believe, but that very red, sedate dining-room once housed a kind of Hell-Fire Club . . . Margaret, not to be confused with Marguerite, Gilderson, seems only to have kept accounts, but she never married, and left everything to a distant relative who married a woman called Isabel. Possibly inspired by this little black book, she also kept what she called a day book. And my grandmother—her name was Emily—kept some kind of record, too. I think she did not learn to write until she was married, and what she wrote hints at some mystery. Ferret as I may, I cannot explain it."

The door opened; a female voice said, "Oh, I'm sorry, miss. Can I just turn down your bed?"

The intruder not only turned down the covers and took two of the cushions out of their green serge covers, but also opened one of the cupboard doors, revealing a washstand, basin and ewer, a looking-glass fixed to the wall above it, a shelf bearing toilet articles. Finding all in order, she said, "Good night, miss. Good night, sir."

Vikky said, "Spy!" just as the door closed. All the animation had drained out of her face and the sullenness was very marked. "If you'd care to look at these," she took up the small black book and a larger one with a mottled cover, and handed them to him. "Next thing we know, Papa will be here, a cutlass between his teeth! I'd better go and play whist." She whirled away so quickly that, without breaking into a run, he could not keep up with her. He took two wrong turnings before reaching his own room.

It was still early, but he had something to read—and a good deal to think about. Adept at making himself as comfortable as possible in unpromising surroundings, he now prepared to be very comfortable indeed, donning his shabby dressing-gown and scuffed slippers, edging the well-padded, velvet-covered chair to a better position under the rose-shaded gas light. And why not a drink? There was a white china knob below a little white china label which said: Service. One of the green boys appeared, slightly breathless, and Alan said, "I'd like a brandy and soda. No hurry. Take your time." He meant it kindly, but the boy took it as sarcasm.

"I'm sorry, sir. Bit of a rush tonight. Old Grammar School Boys' Reunion in the Conference Room." He dashed away, and Alan began to read the journal of Marguerite Gilderson, which began with an undated entry. "Oh, I am so happy here at Highgate. And to think that I dreaded it! Yesterday Mrs. Houghton said it would be a good idea if we all kept journals. She said it would be good practice." Pages of similar girlish effusions. A concert, an outing; many mentions of Mrs. Houghton; somebody called Lucinda. His mind now oriented to Mallow and the One Bull, he read as he had read so much in his time, since a publisher's representative was supposed to have sampled all the wares he offered. Often enough he had been obliged to flip through three books on the train journey between London and Birmingham. So he was getting on, had reached the point where this long-dead woman had drawn a thick black line, when a tap, with something imperious about it sounded on the door, which then opened before he had time to say, "Come in."

It was Mr. Gilderson himself, his air of dignity and command in no way diminished by the fact that he carried a small lacquered tray and the drink Alan had requested. Taking immediate control of the situation he said, "Mr. Merton? Good evening. I brought your drink myself because I have an apology to make."

"Oh?" What Alan had long ago recognised as his own weak streak came uppermost. He was seated, the big man was standing; he was wearing a robe and slippers which had long since seen their best days; and he was slightly in the wrong. It was, now he came to think of it, indiscreet to say the least to go into a very young woman's bedroom and stay there for an hour.

"Yes. I don't know how long you intended to stay in Mallow, but I'm afraid the receptionist did not warn you—as she should have done—that this room was available only for tonight. We are fully booked for tomorrow."

Cutlass between teeth indeed. Stand by to repel boarders! But it was beautifully done. The surface affability was still there, alongside the cool assessing blue stare that belied it.

"That will not inconvenience me in the slightest," Alan said. "I had no real intention of staying in Mallow at all. A chance conversation in the train prompted a desire to see the One Bull, surely one of the oldest inns, if not *the* oldest, in England."

He was conscious of the black book in his hand, the one with the mottled cover on the table beside him. Mr. Gilderson must recognise them.

"It is old," Mr. Gilderson said with the air of one conceding a point. "But that is an aspect I have tried to change—with, I think, moderate success. For one person whom a musty atmosphere attracts, there are a hundred who appreciate comfort, modern conveniences—and good service."

"All in abundance here, if I may say so. I happen to enjoy both aspects; sitting in this very comfortable chair, with a good light and reading these, which Miss Gilderson so very kindly lent me." God! I sound ingratiating. Why?

"Ah, yes. So I see." The affable mask changed to something else, less pleasant but more real. "My daughter is another who likes to have things both ways. To live in the past while enjoying the amenities of the present. It is an attitude which leads, all too easily, to misunderstanding. I trust that you, Mr. Merton, are man-of-the-world enough not to misconstrue her invitation to her bedroom."

"I most certainly did not. She had a few things to show me and they happened to be in her room. So I went."

"I quite understand."

He did; he felt better now that he had seen the man whom Sophie had described as "young." He should by now be accustomed to Sophie's habit of relating youth to a good head of hair! This was no young man; no likely seducer. Fusty, musty, poor, scholarly, probably genuinely interested in a load of old rubbish, probably didn't even notice that it was Vikky's bedroom. Towards Alan, Ted Gilderson relented.

"If you wish to prolong your stay, there is a rival establishment, the King's Head, just along the road. If you mention my name to the owner, he will do his best for you, I am sure. And the hotel omnibus would deliver your bag for you."

Had Alan not already seen the King's Head, he could have told that the word "rival" was used mockingly, and that its best would be very inferior to One Bull standards.

"Very kind of you, I'm sure," he said. "My plans are uncertain."

Towards his daughter Ted Gilderson did not relent. It was time she learned some sense. Bringing her home as a baby and leaving her with his mother had seemed the wisest, the only thing, to do, but it meant that she'd been spoiled, allowed to run wild, and had imbibed all her grandmother's foibles and fancies, without a grain of her shrewdness. He had that to remember, and also his own hot-blooded youth. About Vikky's mother he preferred not to think, unless obliged to, as at this moment . . . Marie-Louise, unbelievably beautiful, with the French blood of which she was so proud and the strain of another breed, not to be mentioned. He'd been crazy about her; crazy enough to marry her, crazy enough to overlook one infidelity, two, three . . . And divorce out of the question with about fifteen female relatives—all fanatical Catholics—ready to swear on the cross that Marie-Louise had never gone outside the wide-verandahed, pink-painted house alone, no, not even to church, unchaperoned.

He could still hear, even above the roar of voices at the Grammar School Reunion which he was about to rejoin, the shrill female voices accusing *him* of being the deserter, the unfaithful husband. They said, and truly, that many ships' captains took their wives with them. But to put Marie-Louise aboard a ship with a crew of women-hungry men would be like throwing a naked flame into a hold packed with raw cotton. The cunning bitch had always declared her willingness, her eagerness, to share his life. And when, at last, his hardy old mother had written, not very humbly, to say that if he wanted to inherit the One Bull as a going concern he'd better come home, as it was getting beyond her, Marie-Louise had declared her willingness to come to England, bad as the climate was said to be. But not without her mother, at least two aunts, a few cousins and poor Uncle Joseph. Had they not always lived together? Were they not a family? How could he be so very

unkind as to suggest...Colour was an unpredictable thing;
even Marie-Louise was several shades darker than when he
married her. Poor Uncle Joseph was quite black.

Fortunately the family was willing to be bought off; fortunately he had the means with which to do the buying off.
He'd made a profit out of most of his voyages, and he sold his
ship well. Then he came home to find that the One Bull was
doing well in its sluggish, old-fashioned way. Nothing like the
roaring success it was now, of course. Still, he'd laid all his
plans during the eleven months of life which remained to his
mother, and immediately she was dead he went into action.
He now had, instead of an out-of-date inn, a tip-top modern
hotel, the best in Suffolk.

No son yet. But his second marriage was still young.

Alan was still reading when the note was slipped under his
door. It was brief. "Take the books to the little church across
the yard. If I can get away, I'll be there at ten. Don't wait.
Leave them on the back pew. V.G."

Self-mockery said wryly: A clandestine meeting! At *your*
age! Yet he did not feel his age when he asked for a piece of
paper and made the books into an anonymous parcel, nor when
he asked, slightly ostentatiously, that his bag should be taken
to the station and lodged in the left-luggage department. The
way in which Miss Gilderson had spat out the word "Spy!"
last night, and her father's subsequent behaviour, so amply
justifying the word, warned him to be careful, and when he
left the One Bull he turned right and walked as far as the great
gate of the abbey before turning, crossing the road, and going
back. It was all made easier by the fact that it was market day
in Mallow, with stalls already erected, or being erected, all
around the perimeter of the irregular market-place. The phrase,
"across the yard," had slightly misled him. St. Cerdic's church
was adjacent to the One Bull's yard, but separated from it by
a wall, and having its own entry, an archway alongside the one
with the inn sign, and then a walled walk turning at a right-
angle and leading to a small graveyard and a very small, very
old church. The clock in the tower of the newer church struck
ten as Alan pushed open the creaking door. But Miss Gilderson
was already there, and busy. Two tall jars of what were known
as madonna lilies, white, golden-centred and heavily scented,

stood on the altar, and she was arranging a small, low bowl, almost a trough, of flowers on the sill of the only window.

She whisked round and said, "Hullo. So you managed it. So did I, this being St. Lawrence's day, which Mr. Holloway, being a stickler, likes to observe. Papa, with good reason, hates anything that smacks of papism, but he likes to keep in with everybody. And arranging a few flowers is a permissible occupation." She turned back to the flowers and tweaked the single rose in the collection into a more prominent position. "When it is my turn to do the flowers, I try to match the remaining glass," she said, "but real rose colour is difficult in August. Well, did you have what they call a nice read?"

"I did indeed. I read till midnight. I'd hazard a guess that two more contrasting stories centred about the same subject were never written. And what mysteries! Why did Marguerite marry that pot-boy? And how could he change his very nature almost overnight?"

'Oh, I think I understood that. It would probably take a female eye . . . I think that wool-shearer called Captain and she had a love affair and she did not want an illegitimate baby. So she grabbed the first available man."

"That did occur to me, but in fact—she became much more scrupulous about dates as she went on—she had her first child a full two years later. I mean after what she refers to as a revelation like St. Paul's on the road to Damascus."

"You really did read it thoroughly."

"But of course."

"I entirely agree that she loved that man. And had what is called a false alarm, perhaps a miscarriage. What matters is that she had put herself into Jimmy's power, and he knew it. Quite fatal! But understandable. Now the other, Emily, my grandmother. What on earth did she do that was so secret that she wrote, years later, that it made her sick to remember it and avoid what she refers to as 'that room'? I can't think it was any lapse from virtue. She wasn't that kind of woman at all."

"People change very much as they age. You lived with her, Miss Gilderson. Did you ever notice her aversion to any particular room?"

"Never. But of course I knew nothing of it until I read her diary—after her death. There are vague, very vague stories about a haunted room, but I suppose every inn has those, invented if not real. Personally, I always suspect it is what is now the Garden Room. No real reason, except that once I was there and had a feeling of—of not being alone. Oh, and when Papa started his sweeping alterations I did hear one of the very old chambermaids say, 'And a good thing, too. Nobody need go alone into a *tea*-room after dark.' If my grandmother had still been alive then, I could have asked her about *that*. But, of course, Papa couldn't make the changes until she was dead...Oh, I entirely forgot. Papa! Did he say anything to *you* about coming to my room? I see he did. Was it *awful*?"

"Just banishment to the King's Head. Rather like being sent to Siberia. But with a mitigation. If I mentioned his name the rival hostelry would do its best for me."

She laughed, not very wholeheartedly. *"Folie de grandeur!* But they undoubtedly would. Whenever the One Bull is packed out, Papa sends people along there. And to think that, for years and years, the King's Head on one side and the Green Man on the other took all the trade and reduced the One Bull to almost nothing but a beer-house. I'd rejoice, I'd gladly applaud Papa's triumph... were I not tied to his chariot wheel."

"In what way?"

"One of those execrable promises that people on their death-beds sometimes exact. I was twelve; she was dying. I loved her. She'd been everything to me. Oh, let's not be maudlin! I just promised to stay, to look after the One Bull, get along with Papa as well as possible, regard myself as a...as a kind of trustee. And, you see, she did trust me absolutely. She'd left me enough in her will to make me independent for life. When Papa's more than usually intolerable I sometimes think...But it's no good. I'm like a gypsy's horse, turned out into a wide common, but hobbled." Her voice, her whole manner changed. "I simply cannot imagine why I am boring you with all this. It's just that, what with one thing and another, I have nobody to talk to. And I meant to show you so many interesting things. All those accounts, and some letters. And Thomas Gilderson's pictures."

"Where does Thomas fit in?"

"I'm not absolutely sure. He was never the owner. And he only dated two pictures, both 1750. All his pictures—he was very versatile—are in the Conference Room."

She wore—and it was her sole ornament—a gold chain supporting a watch, tucked into her belt. She pulled it out and said, "Heavens! I must go. For conduct unbecoming last evening I'm confined to barracks today. Are you going to sample the King's Head?"

"No. I can get a train to Lynn at half-past eleven."

"Oh." Her face resumed the expression which he called sullen. "I was only about to suggest that you could just look in at the Conference Room. I admire the pictures very much, but I'm no judge. Good-bye, then." She held out a firm narrow hand. "Give me two minutes to get clear." She tucked the wrapped books under her arm, picked up the basket which had held the flowers and the watering-can, and went briskly away.

Left alone in the cool, lily-scented church, he experienced two contrasting feelings: a kind of regret and a kind of relief. He'd failed her in some inexplicable way. He'd escaped any involvement. Relief gained the upper hand. He told himself that he'd broken his journey in order to see some ancient wall-paintings, not to get involved with a somewhat peculiar family.

He stood waiting for rather more than the two minutes she had requested, staring about the little church now, and finding it unrewarding. He liked an old church to show some evidence of antiquity—a crusader's tomb, a three-tiered pulpit, memorial plaques on walls. Nothing of that kind here. Just the remains of some old glass in the window and the sheer timelessness of the building itself.

"I try to match the remaining glass," Vikky Gilderson had said. She'd done it well, too; the pale yellow of the honeysuckle, the cornflower blue, the leaves of copper-beech, the one rose. An artist in the family. Marguerite Gilderson, in her grave for two hundred years, lettering signs . . . He had a feeling unknown to him hitherto. Almost a pang of remorse. Dutiful son, dutiful husband, dutiful employee, remorse had never touched him. He'd been—no other word for it—complacent. A nasty word for a nasty characteristic. That inner self-satisfaction, that secret pride; that making duty a virtue; thinking: I kept my mother in such comfort as I could afford; I gave Amy her holidays; I served old Hayes well.

But he realised, in a stunning flash, that to nobody had he given anything of himself. His time, his money, his consideration, his labour, but no more. Always Alan Merton had stood aside, a tight little self-enclosed nugget of Alan Merton watching another Alan Merton perform, and applauding the performance. And he'd done it again this morning, letting that poor girl down. She'd appealed for something and he'd backed away, talking about catching a train.

He stood there, mentally stripped naked and not liking what he saw any more than he would have liked an exposure of physical nakedness. And Alan Merton said to Alan Merton: This is simply absurd! Pull yourself together; there's something about this place . . . Get out!

He was doing it; he was getting out. He was actually at the door when a noise, a slight noise in fact but, in the stillness, loud, made him turn.

It was only one of the lilies, too hastily arranged, tipping over. He thought: The very least I can do, and walked towards it, standing, as he plunged the green stem into the vase, on one of those disappointingly unmarked slabs of stone which made this small church so disappointing to those who took history seriously. Constant trampling had worn away even the faint, shallow mark of the cross for which a monk, suddenly granted that boon to the old—close sight, so that you could read, or carve, practically with your nose—had made a little hollow, exactly fitting the silver cross which Cerdic had worn on the day of his martyrdom.

The lily back in place, Alan went out, and turning away from the One Bull, mingled with the market-day crowd.

Mallow was plainly a growing town; around the old Market Square and in two other shopping-streets the buildings were old, though some had been re-fronted. The shops themselves seemed busy and prosperous. Outside this central core there were streets of new houses, and more building going on. All houses designed for solid middle-class people. At the northern edge of the town was a huddle of slum dwellings, not tenements, just little low houses, and not all of them ill-kept. Beyond them a pub called the Green Man with the noisy crowded cattle-market behind it.

No bookshop.

He took his lunch in a pretty little restaurant which served teas and light luncheons. There again, trade seemed good, every table occupied, mostly by women, not quite so gaily or fashionably dressed as those in the Garden Room and the garden at the One Bull yesterday afternoon, but all exuding an air of affluence.

Paying, as he had been told to do, at the desk, he said to

the woman—obviously the proprietress, "Excuse me. I'm new to this town. Can you direct me to a bookshop?"

"I can't, because there isn't one. There's a stall at the station. If you call shilling shockers books. I don't." She released some of her disapproval by jabbing the slip upon which the waitress had scribbled evidence of his debt—a shilling— with rather unnecessary force, onto the spike which was in fact her cash register. He stood aside while she dealt with two more, but more gently. Representatives were well accustomed to giving way to customers. Then he said, "Books aside, madam, writing-paper, pens, ink, sealing-wax. Where could I obtain such things?"

"At Mr. Bridger's. Just along there. His is a general shop."

He was no believer in miracles, but once or twice in his life he had learned that, if you were looking out for something sharply enough, you found it. And now, with one Alan Merton cautious and indecisive, the other alert to explore possibilities, chance played a hand. In the one small area of Mallow which he had not explored there was a shop to let.

Small, very old; obviously a part of Mr. Bridger's extremely general shop.

"I'm having to pull in my horns," Mr. Bridger said. "That bit my father used, and I used till lately, simply for *cheese*. All laid out on this counter here, and a knife, and a box of biscuits. People'd come in, taste what they fancied and then give an order. People you could trust. But no longer! Troubled times, sir. People nowadays would come in, sample every cheese, eat half a tin of biscuits and be off. I realised I was giving free lunches. I still sell cheese, but in the main shop where I can keep an eye. And what, may I ask, if you hired this end bit, would you be selling?"

"Books."

"So that wouldn't interfere with me. Except notebooks, account-books . . . If you mean just reading-books, all right. Say thirty pounds a year, paid quarterly in advance."

Almost directly, but not quite—rather diagonally—across the Market Square, twelve men were enjoying a special lunch in the Conference Room. Thomas Gilderson had been very versatile, and had tried his hand at portraits as well as landscapes and pictures of flowers; he'd even attempted a self-portrait. Several unmistakable Gilderson faces looked down upon the

mixed company—one architect, one surveyor, two representatives of the Mid-Anglia Railway, a lawyer, the head of a
building-firm, and six gentlemen with money to invest. Few
of them would ever have met the other socially, but this was
a business luncheon and exactly right for a hot midsummer
day: lobster salad, roast duckling, gooseberry fool. And by
their choice of drinks ye shall know them! The builder chose
stout.

Mr. Gilderson looked in, affability disguising his faint sense
of patronage. He was not accustomed to hiring the Conference
Room to so small a company or to a body unidentified.

"I hope," he said,"that you have found everything to your
satisfaction, gentlemen."

Yes, they said; splendid, they said. And he did not—how
could he?—recognise them as his executioners. The men who
were going to finance and build the Station Hotel.

17 Gilda and Charles

1939

SIX PEOPLE WERE GATHERED AROUND THE MASSIVE FOUR-
poster bed, waiting for Vikky Merton to die. They all knew
that the watching was futile; they would all rather have been
elsewhere; they all felt an obscure guilt about their lack of
emotion. The truth was that Vikky—or Gran, as they most
often called her—had been a thoroughly unlovable character.
Also in the last six months she had suffered so much that of
her death it could be truly said that it was a happy release.

Two of the watchers were middle-aged and, though they
used the word "Gran," were actually the dying woman's children, Charles and Gilda. There'd been another son, Gilderson
Merton, but he'd died in the mass slaughter of the Somme.
He'd been just over eighteen, tall, golden-haired and hand-

some, a happy warrior in the old tradition, a soldier poet. His best published poem, *Mallow Remembered in Mud*, was included in all the war-poem anthologies and was regarded as important, bridging as it did the gap between the whole-hearted enthusiasm of poets like Rupert Brooke and the disillusionment of Owen and Sassoon.

Of Gilderson, her first-born, Vikky had been more tolerant, more almost affectionate than to the others, though she could speak sharply even to him at times. Charles had always been regarded, and inclined to regard himself, as a bad second best, and, save for her usefulness, Gilda had never counted at all.

The four young watchers were Charles's son, Edman, and his daughter Janet, now aged eighteen and sixteen, and Gilda's son, Gil—named for his dead uncle—and her daughter, Anthea. They were nineteen and eighteen. They had been brought up together, though outsiders distinguished between them, Edman and Janet being known as the Inn Children, Gil and Anthea as the Shop Children. All of them showed some sign of their Gilderson breed, but it was remarkable that Charles, who had married a pretty woman, should have produced two rather plain children, while Gilda, who had married a plain man, had a handsome son and a very pretty daughter. The four were bound by their family blood, by their shared childhood memories, and by the solidarity of a group suffering a common affliction—in their case, Gran. In all possible practical ways Vikky had been a most excellent grandmother, but her nature was sour and she had a tongue like a wasp's sting. Its sharpness had reached a point where it was unsafe to say such a simple thing as, "Isn't this a lovely day?"

"Yes. For those who can get out and enjoy it," she would retort, implying that it was your fault that such enjoyment was denied her.

As they sat or, rather, uneasily perched about the room, their thoughts and their memories differed.

Charles remembered how Vikky had snapped at him, "You are the spitting image of your father!" Which meant a failure. Three much-travelled but never published manuscripts, still gathering dust in a bottom drawer, testified to Alan Merton's failure, as did the bookshop which had never paid its way.

Vikky had shored the failing enterprise up, introducing novelties, leather goods, pottery, cheap jewellery. It was now known as the Gift Shop, rather than the Bookshop. Not, however named, a thriving place. Nor, when Vikky's father died—his second marriage childless—and Vikky inherited the One Bull, could that have been regarded as prosperous. The brand-new, right-on-the-spot Station Hotel had creamed off the best of the trade. But Vikky had been indomitable. She once said, scornful and angry, "I've worn a track across the market-place with my feet."

Gilda, at an early age, had been put in charge of the shop, and Vikky had presently scolded her about her marriage and presently about her pregnancies. And once, when Gil and Anthea were of an age to enjoy an outing, and there was a cheap excursion to London, Gilda had suggested closing the shop for one day. She had said, incautiously, "I want my children to remember a few happy days with me." Vikky said, "That may sound very well, but if I had taken that attitude where should we all have been? On poor relief! I may not have given you trips to London to gloat over: I *have* kept food in your mouths."

That was undeniable. They'd always been well fed and well clothed.

And surely nobody, having faced up to and fought a hard and disappointing life, had ever been so indomitable about illness and death. Two savage operations. Of the first she had said, "Oh, anything to be rid of this pain. It distracts my mind." Of the second she had said, "I suspect you are making a guinea-pig of me. But I have no choice. I still have a lot to do."

Even after that second, unavailing operation, she had not given in or accepted her fate. The pain she still suffered was from the scars where they'd hacked her. "At sixty one cannot expect to heal easily," she said. She said, "I should have done better to stick to aspirin!" And she said—actually to Doctor Holloway, "Next time I feel indisposed, I shall send for the vet."

And despite all the palliative doses and, later, the injections, she remained alert, in lucid intervals, to outside affairs, anything to do with the shop or with the One Bull, and with the gathering threat of war. She did not actually believe that war would come. She credited Hitler, whom she rather admired, with better sense. She said, "Look what he's done for Germany. He'd do the same for Poland if we'd just leave him alone. Last time it was Belgium—and I lost my son. I can't be the only person who remembers."

And even if war should come, she had thought to herself,

all those for whom she felt responsible would be safe enough. Charles was almost forty and had served at the very end of the last war, being wounded in the hand; who'd want him? Or Gilda, soon to be thirty-nine and fully occupied with the shop and helping at the One Bull. Gil would be safe if he chose to be, for he owned about thirty acres of land, inherited from his father. Gil could abandon his academic career and turn farmer— a reserved occupation. (But of course, Vikky admitted to herself, in her own mind, with Gil one never quite knew; he had never been easily or entirely dominated.) As for Edman, well, he was so completely short-sighted as to be almost blind without his glasses. And who had discovered that, when he was almost six? Not his father or his silly mother or any of his schoolteachers! No, his perpetually angry grandmother, who asked three times in half an hour what was the time, snapped, "Boy, are you dead stupid or blind? Look at the clock!" Edman said meekly, "I'm not blind, Gran, but I can't see far-away things." "Then you need glasses. I'll see about it tomorrow."

As for the girls—well, towards the end of the other war, some girls had volunteered for service; they had not been conscripted. Anthea, who was clever, would go, as arranged, to Homerton College in Cambridge, and Janet, who was practical and already a good cook, would stay at home and make herself useful.

These had been amongst Vikky's last conscious thoughts, her last arrangements for the family whom she had always regarded as her personal property. Now, at last stunned by morphia, to which she was so painfully resistant, she was dying, and the family waited.

Charles looked at the four young faces and thought: If the balloon does go up tomorrow, they'll see enough of death, poor things! He made an effort, and broke through the kind of hypnosis that had fallen upon them all, through the silence broken only by the ticking clock—and surely never had time moved so slowly—and the harsh, irregular breathing. He said, in a low voice, "There's no need for you all to wait. This may take hours."

Gilda, who was feeling the strain, said, "There is no need to whisper, Charlie."

"There is, Mum. They say the sense of hearing is the last to go." Anthea spoke in the dreamy, almost self-communicating way which Gran had derided as an affectation, but she stood up, glad to be dismissed.

Gil rose, too, and said, "It's time I locked up the shop." And Edman, with a matching phrase for once, said, "I expect Tom could do with a hand in the bar." Janet said nothing, but she stood up, too, and for a moment they looked at the bed, feeling no grief, and angry with themselves.

At the door Edman turned and asked softly, "How about a drink, Dad?" That might seem callous, too, but Edman knew that his father could find comfort in a good stiff whisky. Gran would watch, grudging and suspicious, and once she had said, "I wonder what would have happened to you all if *I*'d taken to the bottle!" That was Gran's way, making the most innocent pleasure seem to be a sin, and never, never failing to remind them what they owed.

"Yes, I would, son. A double."

"And you, Aunt Gilda? The usual?" Gilda drank gin-and-lime, holding that the lime had a neutralising effect on the alcohol, and once at a party—across at the shop, of course, a party celebrating one of Gil's many scholarships—Gilda had drunk six gin-and-limes and remained cold sober.

Gilda nodded and gave Edman the beginning of a grateful smile, then, remembering, smoothed it away. "That would be kind, Eddie."

The young, as they were called, went down the oldest staircase: shallow steps, all sloping but still sound. They huddled together rather, seeking comfort in their shared youth, their shared consciousness that they were being callous, their shared, adolescent ability to leave behind, to discard the old and look for the new. In the little lobby at the foot of the stairs, Gil said, "I must just lock up," and Janet said, "Don't be long. I'll rustle up something to eat." Edman said, "I'll see to the drinks," but once in the bar he knew that he did not want to go upstairs again until it was all over. He'd pour two double doubles and let Tom carry them up.

Tom was a relic of the old, glorious days. He'd once worn a green uniform with a white bull emblem on his chest. He'd been thirteen and Miss Vikky had been seventeen and he had adored her; still did in a way, though her tongue had been as abrasive towards staff as to family. He'd grown a bit deaf at a relatively early age, and Mrs. Merton had had him fitted with the latest of hearing aids, one he could switch on and off.

Often, when she began to scold, he'd switch off. But he had
learned to lip-read, and knew that she often called him a deaf
idiot and asked God to give her patience. But often it seemed
to him that he was the one person who understood or dared to
pity her. He knew what had gone wrong and embittered her
life. She'd married the wrong man. She'd have done better
with a more go-ahead fellow, somebody with something about
him. As it was, she'd married a virtual stranger who'd put his
money and her money into—of all silly things—a bookshop.
Then she'd inherited another ailing thing, this pub. And she'd
lost her eldest son in the war. Enough to make any woman
bitter. That and all the other troubles . . .

Tom handed in the drinks diffidently, and then looked pity-
ingly at the bed, and thought of funerals and the words about
man born of woman having but a short stay, coming up like a
flower and being cut down. Miss Vikky to Tom had once
seemed like a flower. And now the sad, the really shocking
thing was that, although he understood and pitied her, the
thought, "She is four years older," would intrude, giving him
another four years to go.

Gilda took her drink and went to the window. From it the
shop was visible with its elegant bow front. There she had been
born and in it she had spent much of her life, with little more
authority than a hireling would have had. Vikky, however
overworked, after the inn became hers, could always find time
to run across and make some criticism; the wrong book was
too prominent, the well-reviewed one tucked away. "And don't
tell me you have no time for reading. You've always got some
trashy magazine on the go." Gilda liked magazines which gave
knitting-patterns, sewing-hints and cookery recipes.

Now she watched as Gil approached the shop, studied the
window for a second, then went inside. In many ways he closely
resembled that other Gil, her brother whom she had adored.
And if war came tomorrow, and this Gil were killed, Gilda
wondered whether she could bear it as bravely as Gran had
done.

The thought might have softened her heart toward her mother,
but it did not; she'd suffered too much, too long. In the time
it took Gil to switch on the window light, lock the shop and
come loping back to the inn, Gilda had time to review her life,
more particularly her marriage.

She married to get away from her mother and to escape the

implication that she was unattractive. "If you can't be deco-
rative, be useful." Things like that. Ralph Bettison, the only
young man who had ever paid her any attention, was the youngest son of the Grindle Bettisons—the other branch was known
as the Curlew Bettisons. Gilda had imagined herself leaving
the shop, moving out to the Grindle, and employing all her
practical skills in being a good farmer's wife. And a mother;
she wanted children.

But old Mr. Bettison had no intention of losing his authority
by handing over to Ralph; as a wedding present he gave Ralph
thirty acres of the worst Grindle land, and it was understood
that Ralph would continue to spend most of his time working
on the main farm. Old Mrs. Bettison had no intention of having
Gilda live at the Grindle, though the house was big enough for
three families. And Vikky had no intention of letting the young
couple become independent. Making a sacrifice, she said, she
would give notice to the family who had been occupying the
rooms above the shop, and the young people could make their
home there. Rent-free in return for Gilda's work in the shop
and help at busy times in the inn. On a good horse, Ralph
could make the journey in half an hour, and she would stable
his horse free of charge, if he would help occasionally with
the heaving and hauling, things, which poor Charles, with half
a hand, could not manage. "I do not think highly of your choice,
my dear, but we must all pull together and make the best of a
bad job." Why bad? Gilda wondered, but did not dare to ask.
Ralph was far from being a typical Bettison; he was sensitive
and kind and, within his limited means, generous. But he never
spent a shilling on Gilda or on the improvement of their living-
quarters, but somehow Mother found out and had some acid
comment to make. "I thought farming was supposed to be in
the doldrums. How nice to think that some people have money
to fling around."

One idea which Gilda put forward tentatively when the shop
was going through a bad spell—that Ralph should devote his
small-holding entirely to market gardening and use the shop as
an outlet, Vikky had instantly repudiated. "How could you
possibly compete with the market-stalls in price? And a green-
grocer's shop needs a back entrance."

Over and over again, every attempt to attain independence
had been quelled. Now Mother was dying and Gilda was alive.
And if only, if only war could be averted . . .

"I don't know about you, Charlie, but I can't stand much more of this."

"You've done most of the nursing," Charles said in his kind understanding way. So she had, with the help of various nurses, one of whom was in the next room, beginning to pack, certain that her services would not be needed on this Saturday night. "It can't be long now . . ."

Janet said, "Just in time, Gil. And I remembered that you liked your eggs turned over."

"Bless you, darling," Gil said, and then remembered that he had promised Gran not to encourage Janet's infatuation for him.

"All girls go through a silly stage, and falling in love with cousins is quite a normal procedure. But believe me, I know. Janet looks very solid and stolid; actually she is extremely neurotic. You're not in love with her, are you?"

"Good God, no. Nothing further from my mind. What on earth gave you that idea?"

Gil was the only one of the grandchildren who would have dared ask such a challenging question. But then, unlike the others, he had had, since his father's death, a small but regular income from his thirty acres.

"The Mallinsons' dance," Vikky said. "I looked in, you may remember. You danced with Janet far too often—and with your cheek against her hair."

"Force of habit," Gil said flippantly. "No, I felt sorry for her, actually. She seemed rather out of it. And young as she is, she is a bit tall for most chaps." Not to mention hot-handed and heavy-footed, and so unsure of herself that she kept saying, "Sorry, my fault," all the time.

"An imaginary love affair, doomed to frustration, is not calculated to induce confidence or social grace, Gil."

"No. I see that. I promise you I'll discourage her, if you'll promise me something in return."

"And what is that?"

"Not to keep thumping home to Janet that she is not Helen of Troy."

"I have done no such thing. I admit I did suggest a different hair-style and I *paid* for her to go to Suzette's. Even you must admit that it was an improvement. Also, when she suffered from acne, I gave her a bottle of Skinclear. *You may remember, it worked for you.*"

Typical Gran! Cutting him down to size, reminding him that, not so long since, he'd been a spotty adolescent.

Gil remembered how once Gran had said, after some dispute with authority, "I have never yet lost a verbal battle. When I do, you may notify the undertaker."

Now here he was, breaking his word and calling Janet darling again, and the way her too-angular and yet too-heavy face brightened showed that Gran had been right, damn her! Well, where did a wise man hide a leaf? In a forest.

"Eddie darling! Lager! Just what was called for. Anthea, my sweet, wake up and take interest in what may well be the last meal we take together for some time."

Setting the glasses down, Edman said, "They'd had the news on in the bar. Nothing so far."

"And nothing from upstairs," Anthea said in her soft, self-communicating, seductive voice. "You know, I've often wondered what made her so disagreeable."

"Born with a chip on both shoulders, and never met anybody with guts enough to knock them off," Eddie said.

"Tom thinks otherwise. Once, some time ago, when she'd practically reduced him to tears, I happened to be there, and he said, quote, she was the nicest sweetest young woman, till marriage ruined her, unquote."

"That is sheer rot. Anthea, if you aren't going to clear up your plate like a good little girl, give it to me. We can't afford waste in this house!" From habit he imitated his grandmother's voice, realised what he was doing and looked horrified. "I can remember our grandfather. He died when I was five. He was a dear old boy. Wouldn't hurt a fly. He taught me to play draughts."

"That was where he made his mistake." Eddie's glasses glinted. "Maybe she'd have done better with a nasty old boy who'd have told her to shut up or . . . Oh, well, let's abandon this unprofitable subject and think of the future. Personally, I don't think they'll pull back *now*."

It occurred to them all that the future would now be their own, the decisions theirs to make. Neither Gilda nor Charles would interfere or rant and rave and denounce and browbeat. The prospect was slightly dizzying.

"I shall head straight for London and Steed-Kemp," Gil

said. "He knows all the ropes. We trained together and have certificates to prove our air-worthiness."

Eddie, without knowing it, pushed at his glasses, brooded a moment on the unfairness of things, and then said with wry good humour, "I suppose that even in these enlightened days they have a Pay Corps. Nice safe cushy job."

"Splendid idea," Gil said. "Try to get with my lot. Then you can fiddle the books and give Air Vice-Marshal Bettison a few extra noughts." He did not intend to sound patronising. But he did.

"Don't be so modest," Anthea said. "Air Marshal, surely."

"The difficult takes little longer. Just give me time."

Janet, having provided the food, consumed her share in silence. It tasted of nothing. She'd known all along that Gil would be one of the first, but, Oh God! Please God, let him be safe.

Upstairs in the shadowy bedroom, the stentorian breathing stopped, and then, as Charles and Gilda looked at each other and at the bed, out of the deeper shadow there Vikky said, "Help me up!" The doctor and the nurse had said very positively that she would not regain consciousness.

They went, one to each side of the bed, and raised her gently. Ignoring Gilda as usual and addressing Charles, Vikky said, "You'll find everything in order. Let the shop go. It was a mistake. From the first. Only the One Bull matters. You understand?"

"I shall regard it as a sacred trust, Mother." He was far the more emotional of the two. Near tears in fact.

"How very beautiful!" She seemed to be looking at some flowers on the far side of the room.

"The roses, Mother?"

"No. Everything . . ." Then she sagged between their hands and they laid her down. Charles put his hands to his face and began to sob, the harsh, reluctant sobs of a grown man.

Gilda went and put her arms round him. She said, with a kind of rough tenderness, "There, there, poor old boy. Don't take it too hard. Think . . . She'll never have to bear another injection."

"I know. But . . ."

"I know what you want, what we both want. Just a minute."

She went briskly to the communicating door and said, "Sister Salter. My mother is dead. Would you be good enough to find my son and tell him. He knows what to do." She came back and took her brother by the arm.

"You need a drink and something to eat. So do I. We'll go across."

In the comfortable living-room half of the kitchen behind the shop, Gilda poured drinks, gave Charlie his whisky and, carrying her own gin-and-lime in one hand, opened out the gate-leg table, set two places, went into the purely kitchen area, which was partly screened off, and within minutes came back with two plates of ham, some potato salad, some butter and a crusty loaf.

"I don't think I feel like eating, Gilda."

"Don't be so silly! Sentiment is all very well, but what have we lost? An incubus!"

"Gilda!"

"Well, isn't it true? Oh, don't tell me that she was a good mother."

"She provided for us all."

"Any slave-driver could claim that merit. Can you remember one single occasion when she said a truly kind or comforting word, to you or me, or the children? You can't, can you? Do you know, I well remember being asked to tea with a girl named Connie Vincent. And Mrs. Vincent said, 'Connie dear, pass Gilda's cup.' I found the idea that a mother should use an endearment to a daughter quite staggering. I never forgot it. And don't ignore the fact that she did as much to wreck your marriage as anything else. As for mine, she killed Ralph as surely as though she had shot him."

"Killed? Honey, I think that last drink . . . You can't mean . . ."

"I do. Ralph and I didn't go about hand in hand, but we . . . liked each other, and got along all right. And he wasn't as strong as he looked, and he was overworked. And it was a nasty journey, straight into the teeth of wind, even when he gave up the horse and bought the motor-bike. So that winter he had flu, and Old Doctor Holloway said he should stay in bed for twenty-four hours after his temperature was normal, and then be careful. So what did she do? She came along with something, calves'-foot jelly or custard, and she said how well he looked. She didn't actually say he was malingering, but as good as. She asked what would have happened to us all if she had gone to bed every time she had a cold . . . So Ralph got up. I did my best to stop him, but who ever listened to anybody when *she* was around? Ralph went to work in that bitter weather, and developed pneumonia . . . and died."

"I knew nothing of this."

Gilda's mouth twisted.

"If I remember rightly, you were having some slight trouble of your own just then."

"Yes," he said slowly. "Mother and Joyce never hit it off."

"Simply because Joyce had a little money of her own, so that she couldn't be bossed about."

"There was that, of course. And I admit that Mother interfered about the children—but often to their advantage. For instance, Eddie's eyes."

Gilda refused to be moved from her recriminatory mood.

"Frankly, I often wondered how Joyce stuck it as long as she did. She was lively and popular. And Mother saw to it that you never had time to take her out. The outcome was inevitable. And perhaps not unintentional."

Charles looked back upon the years of his troubled marriage, of the final ultimatum. Joyce wanted him to cut loose, use her money, and set up on their own. If not . . . And if Gilda's husband had lived a little longer, so that Mother was not left with no man to fall back upon, who knows?

He said, still amiably yet with a certain inner force, "That's all over and done with, Gilda. What we must be very careful of is not to become like her."

"You couldn't, my dear. I think I could. But I'll watch it." She switched on the wireless and no sound came. "Damn and blast. I asked Anthea especially to get a new battery. She is so care . . . Sorry dear, I mean absent-minded. How Mother ever imagined that she would make a teacher I never could understand."

It had been Vikky's choice for a granddaughter, clever enough to pass examinations, and although teachers were poorly paid, Anthea, once qualified, could find a job in Mallow and live at home very cheaply.

She had settled Edman's future in a similar arbitrary and sensible fashion. He was almost as clever as Gil, and had ended his schooldays in a blaze of glory: full marks in maths and physics. He, too, could have gone to Cambridge. But Vikky decided otherwise. Edman would go to Walker-Armstrong's and study accountancy and, when he qualified, set up on his own—probably using the shop as office—and he could help in the inn at odd times and also take charge of his grandmother's tax returns.

Vikky had organised everything—even her own burial-place. That had been one of her major victories over all vested authority.

St. Cerdic's little churchyard had been officially closed some years before First Lieutenant—acting Captain—Gilderson Merton died in the blood and mud which he had so vividly described in his poem. He was one of those, and sixteen thousand dead in one day took some imagining, who had been decently buried. But it did not suit his mother that he should lie in a numbered grave in a faraway place with a foreign name, when there was a Gilderson tomb in Mallow. Not strictly a family tomb, since it held only one member of the family, Isabel, beloved wife of Adam. Other Gildersons, including Adam himself, lay under less pretentious headstones. So, under that fine table-topped, rail-enclosed memorial there must be room, and Vikky intended to have Gilderson buried there.

There was opposition and there was support. The vicar of the day was opposed. "It may create a precedent, Mrs. Merton. I am not contesting your legal right, but to allow another interment on the grounds that there is room for another—er— funeral ceremony, could easily lead to similar claims."

"What others do, Mr. Dowse, is no concern of mine. I know what I want, and I intend to have it."

He tried another argument. "Mrs. Merton, your son, in his poem, his justifiably acclaimed poem, made special mention of his devotion to his men, and theirs to him. He died, leading them into battle. Do you not think it right and proper that he should lie with them, awaiting the great and glorious Day of Resurrection?"

"When I wish to hear a sermon, I shall attend church. It is quite useless to argue with me. I know that after Crécy, after Agincourt, men were brought back and buried with their own. Have we so far retrogressed as to make such a simple matter so difficult?"

When she had won, she found, as all victors do, allies in plenty. People who remembered that Gilderson had been awarded, posthumously, the D.S.O. and was entitled to a military funeral. Vikky wanted none of that nonsense. Gil was back where he belonged, and Isabel's grave was deep enough for three. She had made it plain to everybody that, when she died, she would be buried there.

"And surely," Charles said on the Sunday morning when the portentous words, the declaration of war against Germany, had been spoken, "you could wait until after the funeral. It is only three days."

Gil said, "Hitler can do a lot in three days, Uncle Charles. I'm catching the three o'clock."

"I'll be with you as far as Cambridge," Edman said. "I have to see a man about a job, not a dog." He thought of the man, Professor Coverdale, who a year ago had expressed an interest in such a bright boy.

And Charles thought about his links with the local territorials; he'd never really belonged, merely helped, instructed a few eager young men in gunnery, as far as he could from his out-dated experience. But he'd always felt that, when the next war came, it would be a push-button war, and a man with only one thumb could be very useful, given a chance.

"I'll drive you to the station," Charles said. "And then, Gilda, if you think you could manage, just with the girls, I'll go along and have a word with Colonel Thickthorn."

"We can manage," Gilda said, deliberately keeping the defiant element out of her voice. She would not, she simply would not, would *not* try to govern, to be another Gran.

Gilda, Anthea and Janet went into the inn which lay in its usual Sunday-afternoon quietude which, on this particular Sunday, after the bustle of the station, seemed an almost uncanny quietude. And sad.

One palliative for sadness was to get busy, and bracing herself, trying not to think of Gil, gone away for a time, if not for ever, Gilda said, "Come along, my dears, we have a lot to do. It'll probably be a busy evening. It's been a disrupted day for everybody and there'll be a demand for snacks."

It was always Janet who was helpful and handy, Anthea who dodged, but today it was different. Anthea positively whisked about, loading the dish-washer—one of Vikky's last innovations—and then turning her attention to the making of snacks, while Janet stood about as though in a dream. Gilda, less clear-sighted than her mother, had never seen anything special between her son and her niece, and imagined that the poor child was thinking, perhaps in equal terms and certainly understandably, about her father and brother.

"Janet, honey, you must not take this too hard. I don't imagine that Eddie's mothy old professor or Colonel Thickthorn can act as recruiting-sergeants! And Gil always said that if this war came it would be different." She wished she could believe that herself; that it would be a war of machines, tanks and aeroplanes, not the broken bodies of men. "How about making us a cup of tea?"

"Of course, Aunt Gilda." Janet made the tea, poured herself a cup, drank half of it and then vanished.

St. Cerdic's was cool even on this warm afternoon, deadly quiet and sweetly scented, for Mr. Dowse's successor was very high church indeed. He'd been an army chaplain in India, and knew, was convinced, that the more religion divested itself of ritual and mystery, the less effective it was. So, in this tiny church with its indisputably long history, he had made no effort to take religion down to the people by way of clubs, social gatherings and such. He had gone as far as he could in the other direction, and oddly, he had attracted the young, Janet Gilderson among them. He had also introduced incense, which now scented the church as the rather poor, early September flowers could not do.

Janet was going through a recognised phase, the adolescent turning away from the material world which had proved unsatisfactory, a searching for something beyond . . .

She'd often prayed: Oh God, let Gil come home for part of this holiday. Oh God, let Gil dance with me, just once. (That prayer, at least, had been abundantly answered. But after that delirious evening he seemed to have cooled off.) Anyway, those were trivial, selfish prayers. Now she knelt and asked God with all her heart to spare Gil. Spare him, even if not to me. Even if for one of those jolly girls he's met at Cambridge or at Steed-Kemp's. Oh God, omnipotent and all-merciful, keep Gil safe; and please, please, show me what to do.

And that prayer was answered, too; when she rose from her knees she knew exactly what to do. And how to go about it.

In the One Bull the telephone rang, and Gilda, more edgy than she realised, snatched it up and heard Eddie's voice. "Aunt Gilda? I wonder if you could send me a few things." The line crackled and his voice faded and then revived. "Birmingham," he said. "Yes, I said Birmingham. I'll read you the address." It was a perfectly ordinary address and she scribbled it down and asked him what exactly he wanted sent on there. Then she ventured to ask, "What is all this about, Eddie? Why Birmingham? And what are you doing there?"

"I'm not there yet. I'm on my way. And the whole thing is rather hush-hush. But I must have some clothes."

"Is it war-work, Eddie?" More than any other member of the family, his Aunt Gilda had sensed Eddie's smouldering discontent, and knew that only Gran's forceful personality had kept him at Walker-Armstrong's. Now the suburban-sounding address in Birmingham, the demand for civilian clothes, and the hint of secrecy inspired her curiosity.

The telephone gave a hoarse cackle and went dead.

"Eddie seems to have found himself some sort of occupation—in Birmingham," Gilda said. "He wants his clothes sent on."

Ordinarily it was a job which could have been entrusted to Janet—after all she was his sister—but Janet seemed to have vanished. Anthea said, "I'll see to it, first thing in the morning." Actually volunteering, and looking cheerful about it. In fact, this news of Eddie's going was exactly the cue Anthea needed.

She had never wanted to become a teacher, but the idea of being up at Cambridge with Gil had been attractive. She would get introductions to any number of young men and perhaps to some not so young, fourth-year students about to take up professional careers, and ripe for marriage. Anthea wanted a lot of fun, a lot of boy-friends, and then marriage. Away from this dreary pub, out of Gran's orbit.

Now the young men would be elsewhere. They'd be here. There were aerodromes at Triver and at Daneley, and others further inland.

Gran had been unscrupulous in her demands upon Anthea's free labour; the shop phone would ring, and Gran wanted help with this or that, all dull tasks like checking laundry lists. Anthea was never allowed in the bar or the dining-room. "Run along now, back to this so-important homework!"

Anthea waited about five minutes and then said, "Mum, I've been thinking. With Eddie gone, you're going to be very short-handed. Janet isn't allowed in the bar, even as a customer. Don't you think I should defer college and help out here?"

"My dear"—Gilda was free with endearments—"I simply couldn't dream of interfering with your education. We can manage, somehow. I shall give up the shop. That was Gran's wish."

To hell with Gran's wish! Homerton and school-teaching had been her idea! But Anthea said smoothly, "I'm pretty positive that, in the changed circumstances, Gran would have wished me to help out, *here*."

"I must think about that. Perhaps talk it over with your uncle." Gilda had always felt affection and sympathy for her brother, but seldom placed much value on his opinion, for there had been only one arbiter here, and now, with that arbiter gone, Gilda felt rather rudderless and would have been prepared to be guided by Charles, two years her senior and, after all, a man.

However, Charles, when he did return, rather later than expected, well after opening-time, was too much concerned with his own affairs to take Anthea's problems very seriously. Colonel Thickthorn had been most positive, most assuring. "My dear Gilderson, within a week, they'll be digging out Chelsea pensioners! Fellows like you and me, who have fired a shot in anger, are worth our weight in gold. A crisis like this sorts the men from the boys, doesn't it?"

Charlie's main concern that Sunday evening was his uniform, so gladly discarded just on twenty years earlier. Had it been preserved, and if so, would it fit him? If it did, it would—curious tribute—be due to his mother, who had held, amongst other biased but unsubstantiated opinions, that overweight, even the ordinary, comfortable, middle-aged spread, was proof of gluttony and sloth.

Thus preoccupied, given news of Eddie and told of Anthea's suggestion, Charles said, "I must say it sounds a good idea. I know I seem to have deserted. I know what I said to Mother . . . but that was before war was declared. Now I can only hope, Gilda, that with the girls—and Tom, of course—you can carry on."

Pushed back onto her own resources of energy and fortitude, Gilda could only say, "I'll do my best, Charlie. And I must say that Anthea has been most helpful today."

The value of Anthea took a sharp jump upwards on the Monday morning when Charles opened the till in the bar and was confronted by a folded paper, and recognised his daughter's handwriting, formalised as it was.

"Dear Dad—I've taken three pounds. I'm going to London to enlist, if I can, in the WAAF. I'm under age, but I'm big, and if they demand a birth certificate, I shall lie like the devil. And please, please, don't try to claw me back. It wouldn't work. I'll write when I can."

So, left with Anthea and Tom, Gilda prepared for war.

18 Jill and Steve

1975

ONE LAST DRAWER TO EMPTY. NEARBY STOOD A LARGE PAPER sack destined for the bonfire. Why not turn the drawer's contents into it, keeping your head averted? Keepsakes! Hurt lay in that drawer. That was why she was leaving it till last. Why invite painful memories? Why hoard? And now why select? There'd be no room for sentimental things where she was going.

Yet, somehow, to deal so summarily with things so long cherished seemed disrespectful. And cowardly. And in her quiet, self-effacing way, Gilda Bettison had always faced whatever was demanded of her. She opened the drawer with a firm hand.

Letters. A few beginning, "Dear Sis." They were from her brother Gil, killed in 1916. A few beginning, "Dear Mum." Letters from her son, another Gil, shot down in the Battle of Britain. "Dear Aunt Gilda": several of those. Eddie had been a very conscientious correspondent, and because he could never mention what exactly he was doing, he'd tried to make up by descriptions of Birmingham, and later of America.

Beneath the letters was a jumble. Gil's first baby shoe, still recognisably blue: Anthea's white. Somebody's first glove, small as a cat's paw. Two or three dance programmes with tiny pencils attached. Why had she kept them? She had not greatly enjoyed the few dances she had attended, and the man she married had never been to a dance in his life.

A scatter of photographs. She drew in her breath sharply. It would be impossible to consign them to the flames herself. Maybe Eddie... Then she heard him on the stairs. He lumbered; there was no other word for it. The truth was that he drank rather too much, but apart from a gentle, half-teasing hint, she had never said anything to him about it. As perhaps she should have done.

He came in, his florid face aglow. He always looked good-natured: now he looked jubilant.

"Did you hear the phone? Gilda, they've given in! Two hundred and fifty thousand pounds. A quarter of a million! Think of it. We're rich!"

"Well, dear, I thought they would. What choice did they have, with you sitting here like something off Easter Island?"

"That's true. Still, there were moments when I thought I'd opened my mouth too wide, but I sweated it out and I won."

"I'm very glad for your sake, Eddie. It was what you wanted."

"And now I want to talk to you, seriously." His gaze took in the preparations for departure: one suitcase packed and closed, another yawning, half filled. "You must give up this idea about going to Abbey House. I intend to buy the old Bumpstead place out at Layham. I'll have central heating, double-glazing, the lot. We're going to live in comfort."

"My dear, I'm not going to the Abbey House in search of *comfort*. I'm quite comfortable here. But I am seventy-four. I haven't pulled my weight about here for weeks now. I may soon need a bit of waiting on."

"And we'd all do it. Gladly."

"I know. But that is exactly what I don't want. It wouldn't be fair. Jill and Steve have their own lives to live. At Abbey House, looking after the decrepit is a job which they have chosen to do and for which they are paid."

Eddie had always worn glasses, very thick, and since the mysterious accident in America, soon after the war's end, they'd been tinted a pale beige. Now, behind them, his rather beautiful, myopic eyes narrowed, and he said, "Look, has this decision of yours anything to do with my decision to sell this place?"

"What on earth put that idea into your head?"

"Well, the two did coincide, didn't they?"

Curious, Gilda thought. Everybody had always underrated Eddie. Her own son, Gil, had always outshone him and, although in some quarters his ability had clearly been recognised, the subject was something that even now could not be talked about. But he was clever and shrewd.

"It was just that when you began to bargain with these supermarket people, I realised that one move was as much as I could face. And as Abbey House had a vacancy pending . . ."

"It wasn't anything to do with the thought that you'd be stuck away in the country? I mean . . . I shall be a free man: no more opening and closing hours. I'll buy a Jag, I think, and I'd chauffeur you about whenever, wherever you wanted."

"I know you would, dear. But . . ." To divert him, she asked, "Have you told Steve and Jill?"

"Yes. To be honest, I don't think they were much interested. Steve said the Bumpstead place was still on his books and down a thousand since last week. Then he went off to change. And Jill said, good for me and the nosh would be ready in half an hour. Which is now. What have you got there? Photographs? Let's take them down and show the young what we were like in our prime, eh? And think over what I've been saying, Gilda."

In *our* prime! It was one of Eddie's endearing traits to pretend that he and she were contemporaries. Until lately it had not seemed too much a pretence, for she had kept her hair and her figure; he had grown baldish and paunchy. But lately she'd aged suddenly, and now Eddie took the photographs in one hand and extended the other to help her up. Anything she had ever done, from being kind to a little boy who was bullied by his grandmother, offering a temporary refuge across at the shop, to keeping the One Bull on its legs through so many vicissitudes, was for Gilda, repaid in that gesture, and in what Eddie had said. Gilda knew of more than one case where a change of residence had been used as an excuse to oust some elderly relative.

"D'you think I'm too old to take up riding?" Eddie asked.

"Of course not. Maybe you're a bit heavy. It's the beer."

"I can change my poison now. In fact, we'll have champagne tonight."

They went down the one remaining staircase, the oldest, the one with shallow treads, all sloping. Once, counting the twisted stairs to the attic, the inn had boasted four flights.

Formica had allowed kitchens to become beautiful. The table at which Jill was about to dish up was covered with a pattern of red roses scattered on white; every working surface had been similarly treated. The casserole was pretty, too. The plates were old, dating back to the time when the One Bull could order its own ware, green with a white bull in a medallion.

"Hullo, darling," Gilda's granddaughter said. "And now where is Uncle Eddie off to?"

"He said something about champagne." A curious look crossed Jill's face, but all she said was, "They say it goes with everything. This is just hot-pot, tarted up."

"It smells delicious."

"I'll give Steve a shout. He had a sandwich lunch." She opened the door to the bar and said, inelegantly, "Steve! Grub up!"

Talk about dominant strains! Steve had been born in Indiana, of an American mother, but he so closely resembled Gilda's brother and son that sometimes the sight of him gave her a little pang.

"Did you have a good day, Steve?"

"Wonderful! A thousand pounds for a grandfather clock. And a hundred pounds each for some dining-chairs literally held together with string. Sad, though." He often said that, when he was called upon to sell up an old family home. Yet, curiously, he had made no protest when his father began to negotiate the sale of what must surely be one of the oldest buildings—what remained of it—and the oldest family businesses in England.

Eddie came out of the store-room, which was always called the cellar, bearing the symbolic bottle. At the One Bull there was not much call for champagne in the ordinary way. Sometimes somebody who had been lucky at Newmarket, and even more rarely people with long memories, still thinking of the Red Room at the One Bull as the height of splendour, would hire it for a party. So the inn kept a small stock. And champagne was unreliable; it could go off. Eddie was pleased by the pop and the foaming.

When it was poured—into ordinary tumblers—some word seemed to be called for and Gilda raised her glass and said, "Congratulations again, Eddie. Many happy days!"

"And to all of us," Eddie said. "I must admit I've had jittery moments—especially after that smoothie said something about an alternative site."

"Sheer bluff," Steve said. "I told you so at the time. There isn't a comparable site within two miles. And apart from being a bit far out, it'd involve agricultural land. And the planners are getting a bit cautious about that."

Gilda had brought to a fine art the pretence of eating heartily while surreptitiously slipping food to Jill's dachshund, Rudy. He was not supposed to beg at the table, and never did, but he knew where to station himself and how to take an offering quite noiselessly.

"Have you told everybody, Uncle Eddie?" Jill asked.

"Not yet. For one thing I didn't know, for certain, myself until about an hour ago. And—I know this sounds daft, but, well, a lot of fellows look on this as a home from home: they'd be upset. And some would be envious. Perfectly natural. What I thought I'd do was wait till I had the cheque—and they can't back out now, they've *signed*—and then gather all the old faithfuls and have a bit of a party in the Red Room; say what must be said and close down."

Gilda thought: This was my mother's legacy to us! A too-great fear of disapproval, practically a neurosis.

There was little further conversation. Eddie made two attempts to re-open the subject nearest his heart at the moment, but they fell rather flat, and when he had finished his hot-pot, which was in reality a superb goulash, he refused strawberries and cream, and rose to go back to the bar. He said good-humouredly, "No thanks, honey. I've recently had a reminder to watch my weight." He had put the photographs on the dresser, and he now picked them up and dropped them on the table.

"These may amuse you. No prize for identifying me. I'm the one with the specs."

"Poor old Dad," Steve said. "If that thing skips a generation and I have a short-sighted child, I'll have it fitted with contact lenses from the word go."

Jill said, "Oh, photographs! How interesting. Come to think of it, we're not much of a family for photographs, are we?"

"I never cared for them standing about," Gilda said. "Either you look at them and remember things best forgotten, or you look at them without really seeing, which seems worse."

"Would you sooner not look at these?" Steve asked.

"Oh, no. I was speaking generally. Now this..."

It had come uppermost. It would! The last picture taken of them as a family. Charles, Gil, Eddie, Anthea, Janet and herself. "Taken on the day war was declared," she said. "Somebody had a box Brownie. Small pictures, but very clear."

"My mother was exceptionally pretty," Jill said. Steve thought he detected a certain wistfulness in her voice, and, at the risk of offending Gilda, whose daughter the pretty girl had been, said, "It was a type. Fluffy blonde."

Unoffended, Gilda said, "Anthea's hair was naturally curly, and curly hair was then *de rigueur*. Look at me! Permanent waving was torture in those days, but we unlucky ones, with straight hair, had to endure it. Your mother had beautiful eyes, too. You have them, my dear."

Steve said, "There you are, Jill. And once, when I said you had nice eyes, you asked what I wanted to borrow."

"I was speaking from experience. A soft word and a hard touch!"

Time was not a constant thing. While the young people made that exchange, Gilda lived through what had happened to her beautiful daughter.

"Mum, I'm sorry, sorry, sorry. I've tried *everything*, but I'm pregnant."

"How long?"

"I think three months."

"Can the man not marry you?"

"He's dead."

Gilda had not been blind. "Is there any other man who could be regarded as responsible?"

"Two. One is dead. The other is married and I wouldn't want . . ."

"Of course not. We must manage."

Managing, Anthea went for a week-end in London and came back flaunting a mock sapphire ring. Gilda had decided that the mythical man whom other men envied, must be a naval officer; that would explain his non-appearance in Mallow and a hasty marriage in Plymouth. It was natural enough for a girl with a husband at sea to remain with her mother. And people had more to do, just then, than to count the gestation months on their fingers. In fact, the only thing that worried Gilda was Anthea's mention of having tried everything.

Exactly what? Well, drinking almost a bottle of gin in one

go; taking a fierce purgative; jumping downstairs; lifting heavy things. Nothing else? Well, yes, the married lover had provided some pills. They hadn't worked. But Gilda dreaded what effect they could have had. In her quiet, almost passive way, Gilda decided that a child, hideously malformed, should not live. Which meant that she and Anthea must be alone at the time of birth.

It was not such an extraordinary decision. She had borne two children herself, easily, conscious all the time. But to make certain, she'd bought a book on midwifery and studied it diligently. And all the time, taking the exactly opposite course from what she knew her own mother would have done, she spoke no denunciatory, scathing word. When Anthea went into labour, Gilda put notices on all the doors: SORRY. NO BEER. TRY TOMORROW.

The baby was born, complete and perfect. Infanticide was not required, but soon a doctor was, for the afterbirth did not come away and Anthea was hemorrhaging badly.

The only doctor functioning in Mallow at the time was a locum who, some years earlier, had just escaped disqualification for drunkenness by retiring early. He was never completely sober, and, mounting the sloping stairs, felt rather more drunk than usual, but once in the room he was prompt and sensible. "Force of gravity while we wait," he said and lifted the foot of the bed, "push that chair under here," he said. "Chuck out the pillows. Where's your phone?"

While he was demanding impossible things of the overstrained hospital service, the change of position resulted in Anthea's return to clear consciousness.

"Mum!"

"I'm here, darling. It's all over. Everything is all right."

"Boy or girl?"

"A lovely little girl."

"Then I want her named for you. You've been so good . . . About everything."

The ambulance was at least an hour too late.

Gilda registered the child herself and made sure of a produceable birth certificate: Father—John Scott, naval officer.

Two Gildas in a house could be confusion, so Gill became Jill. And within a year of the war's end, Eddie came home with Steve. Eddie had been "lent" to America, and in a small Midwestern town, chosen for its security, had, being English and engaged on some secret job, attained glamour enough to attract the daughter of a wealthy congressman. Naturally Eddie had described her as the sweetest, loveliest girl in the world, and the child, when it came, as the loveliest baby; he thought the family name, Stevenson, upon which his wife insisted, a bit of a mouthful when allied to Gilderson, but it shortened easily. Eddie had seemed happy and settled until the mysterious explosion took place. Then the break-through, hoped for in Indiana, was made in California and the dearest, sweetest girl in the world showed her bitchy face. She didn't want Steve, a child by one marriage was a handicap in the search for another. Eddie, hurt but resilient, had come home and recovered. Charles, his father, a prisoner of war since the fall of Singapore, was already home, still emaciated after months of feeding up, melancholic by day and given to terrible nightmares at night. Eddie had slipped into place, and Charles, his sacred charge handed over, had died peacefully.

Jill said, "And that must be Aunt Janet." Dangerous ground, for Janet was never mentioned by Gilda and rarely by Uncle Eddie, who would occasionally say, "Poor Janet could cook, too," or make some glancing reference to his sister, always in practical terms.

"Yes, that is Janet." Gilda's voice took a hard edge. Most unusual.

"What happened to her?"

"She joined the WAAF." Suddenly it was like a boil bursting. "She had a schoolgirl crush on Gil and I think she imagined being on the same station. They never were. She was posted to Amesbury, he to Biggin Hill. They never even had a leave together."

The two young, but only comparatively young, people (both around thirty but looking far younger, as many Gildersons did) were astonished at the spite in the voice of the old woman who was grandmother to one, great-aunt to the other. Always so kind, sweetly-spoken and, if anything, over-lavish with endearments.

So what had Janet done?

"When Gil was killed," Gilda, his mother, said, "Janet had a nervous breakdown. Naturally, as soon as I knew, I offered to have her here and look after her. But she chose, or *they* chose, to send her to a kind of convent near Brighton. She eventually became a nun and wrote a letter asking that we should regard her as dead to the world. It was for her to decide, but I still think that I was dealt with unfairly. It was *grossly* unfair!"

And this was Gilda, so mildly spoken, so kind, so reluctant to sit in judgement.

"Gil owned some few acres of land," Gilda said. "They were let, but the tenant went off to the war and I took over."

She thought of those harsh times, harsher than any her mother had known. Up early in winter, in the dark; drive out to the holding with a guggling swill-tub for pigs, dry scraps for fowls. If you received a meal ration, however meagre, then your pig and your fowls and your eggs must go into the common pool. She'd cheated, because the boys from Triver and Daneley had so enjoyed a meal of proper bacon, new-laid eggs. They were all boys like Gil, their time limited, and she had pampered them shamelessly, while warning them never to boast that you could always get egg and bacon at the One Bull.

Old people tended to repeat themselves; it was a thing to be wary of.

"Stop me if I have told you about the pig I stole from myself." Neither Jill nor Steve would have stopped her for anything in the world. Lately she'd been so quiet, so withdrawn, and now these photographs, which could have caused sadness, seemed instead to have evoked animation.

"I did draw rations for some pigs, but I took some swill every day, and I felt I was entitled to one. Tom, an old barman I had at the time, said he could kill it. My dears, it screamed so terribly! I was at the far end of the holding, digging potatoes, but I could hear only too well. Then we had to get it home, in a sack in the boot of the car, feeling like criminals. As to the smoking and curing, that was comic. We found an old smoke-house amongst the outbuildings and Tom said only the smoke from oak would do, so he took down shed doors, and sawed up some old stools. It was a great success. We never did it again, though, because of the squealing. I made an . . . arrangement with a butcher. All highly illegal, of course! And I was punished. The moment Janet was twenty-one, nineteen forty-four that was, her convent sold the place for some grossly inflated sum and without giving me the slightest consideration. I left some vegetables still in the ground."

She was ashamed that a sense of grievance should still be so lively and went through several pictures rather hurriedly:

Janet in uniform; Gil in flying kit; Gil at the wheel of a car; Anthea in various guises, usually with a man, never the same one twice. Then Steve said, "Gosh! I had no idea it was so huge!"

It was a photograph, taken from an angle, of the One Bull, taken either before the war or during the early days of it.

"It was an absolute warren, and mainly disused. Grand for hide-and-seek. We called that the New Wing and this the Old, but even the new was old. Of course, the part where we are now is the oldest of all. The core, so to speak."

"Incredible," Steve said, studying the photograph with a professional eye; he was a house-agent as well as an auctioneer.

"Both bombings were freaks," Gilda said. "The first was aimed at the station, or being jettisoned. There was a great stretch of abbey wall about six feet thick, and a bit of a tower to the south of the New Wing, just room enough between for people on foot or a barrel on a barrow. The bomb blew the wall and the tower up and they came down on us, at least on the New Wing. It went down like a pack of cards. Anthea and I and Tom were in the store-room, I suppose because we always thought of it as the cellar. And it was curious. There was a noise like the end of the world, and then rumblings as other pieces fell, but not a bottle in the store shifted an inch. The fire-bomb was even more freakish. It fell on St. Cerdic's. It was a blustery night and bits of burning debris blew about, hop-scotching as it were, from a shed to a stable to another shed and so to the house. We stand a bit high here, and there were other fires; water-pressure was dangerously low, but they were able to use the well in the forecourt." She had remembered and suggested it. One of her tiny victories in a lifetime of what, looking back upon it now, seemed to consist mainly of failures. She said, almost petulantly, "And if you wonder why no re-building was done, I can tell you. There was insurance, of course, and war damage, both derisory in the face of rising prices. And the One Bull was never *mine*. It belonged to Charles, and there were years when I didn't know whether he was alive or not. When he did get home he was too ill, too broken to care about building or expansion. And Eddie has been content to jog along."

"Maybe just as well," Jill said. "So much less work for the bulldozer."

Suddenly Gilda felt tired; she had talked too much, remembered too much. She shuffled the photographs together. "Look at them at your leisure," she said. "I don't want them any more. I'll go and tidy my room; it's like a pigstye."

Steve said, "I'm coming up. I want my jacket."

In the little lobby at the foot of the sloping stairs he said, "Ladies first," and from the kitchen Jill called, "I'll say good night when I bring your nightcap."

Steve was coming upstairs behind her in case she should stumble and fall; Jill would bring Ovaltine; Eddie had offered her a home. She thought: I may not, by Mother's standards, have done much with my life, but I've kept a happy family together and they are fond of me . . . Then she thought: How smug!

19 St. Cerdic and the One Bull

STEVE CAME DOWN, WEARING HIS JACKET, AND WENT STRAIGHT into the bar, returning with a trayful of glasses, all foam-streaked. Not for the One Bull the furtive little rinsing behind the bar in a bucket of dirty water with a cigarette-end afloat. Vikky had been dead for thirty-six years, but she had left her stamp.

The glasses, with the supper dishes, made a full load, and Steve switched on the dish-washer.

"I'm going out," he said. "There's something I want to look at. Care to come? It's only just across the yard."

"It'd give Rudy a bit of much-needed exercise," Jill said. Nobody would have guessed that, had Steve invited her to walk with him across hell's red-hot pavement, she'd have gone without a second thought.

In one way Gilda had shown foresight. In place of the huddle of buildings which had once surrounded the yard, there was now a line of twelve garages, eight let as lock-ups, four for the use of guests at the One Bull. Steve's battered but still roadworthy old car stood out in the open. It was a family joke that, if he put it under cover, somebody would arrive and need the garage.

The twelve garages did not stretch quite the whole width of the yard; between the end of one and a bit of rough masonry that hardly qualified for the name ruin, there was room to pass, and, having passed, one was in a jungle. Everything that flourished in neglected places flourished here: nettles and dandelions; docks and herb robert; self-sown saplings of oak, horse-chestnut, blackberry brambles, mountain ash, acacia and laburnum, wild rose and honeysuckle.

"Steve, what are you looking for, *here*?"

"Some sort of boundary line. It's never been established, you see. The pub has passed down, inherited, never sold; so what lawyers call a search has never been made. But I've looked up an old map or two, and I'm reasonably certain that Gilda didn't build the garages on the far end of our lot. I think that, before the bombing, our yard was bigger and St. Cerdic's correspondingly smaller."

"And you think Eddie might get an extra thousand or two?"

"It is possible. If we could establish a boundary. Some sort of fence, or wall."

"In this wilderness?"

From her window, Gilda watched them go, the two motherless children whom she had mothered and whom she loved. She was certain that they were in love with each other without knowing it. The brother-and-sister relationship obscured all else. But here they were, nearing thirty and neither settled. Steve had had innumerable affairs which had come to nothing. Jill had had two, seemingly serious, and one prestigious. For three months she had worn a grand ring, signifying her engagement to young Walker-Taylor, the heir to the accountancy kingdom in which she was a mere employee. That engagement had been ended; Jill had said vaguely that it didn't work.

Watching them disappear around the end of the garage block, Gilda wondered whether the coming upset would jerk them into some kind of self-knowledge. They were both extremely clever and should have gone to college, but both had elected to stay in Mallow, to stick to the One Bull. Maybe, being jerked out of it, out of the old way of life, the sheer continuity—nothing changes here and nothing ever will—might make them see sense. She could only hope so.

Steve said, "I didn't realise it would be so rough. I'll go first. I should have brought a stick." Jill followed, and the dog brought up the rear. It was not at all his idea of a walk. He didn't care for exercise at all, and, if he must walk, let it be pavement or the more frequented part of the abbey gardens.

Jill said, "A thought occurs. St. Cerdic's graveyard was closed, way back. A hundred years or more. Remember Gilda's story about our great-grandmother? That means it was full; so the graves would mark the boundary."

"Clever girl," Steve said, and trampled nettles.

"And I once read something about nettles," she said. "They favour, though perhaps not exclusively, domestic sites. Old middens and such."

"There must have been a plenitude of middens, then."

The scent of the trampled stuff, mingled with that of honeysuckle and briar rose, and the quietude made this seem like the depths of the country instead of the heart of a town grown big enough to interest a supermarket.

Raising her voice, words being so useful in combating sentiment, Jill said, "I have often wondered if Eddie quite realises how much he'll miss the bar."

"He'll find another and take up a firm stance on the customers' side of it." Coming from Steven, usually so mild in judgement—except when he lost his temper and did extraordinary things, like quarrelling with the senior partner of the firm where he was working, and setting up on his own, literally on a shoestring, but very successfully—that was a harsh remark.

Presently he half stumbled, recovered his balance, and said, "Yes, a headstone, half sunk." He turned and looked back, made a sound of satisfaction. "A good sixty yards. How wide, remains to be discovered."

Jill thought of the dead, many of them her own ancestors, and gave a little shiver.

"You're cold. Here, take this." He shrugged off his jacket and put it around her shoulders.

It smelt of him. Under the superficial odours of tobacco and sheep and old furniture, the distinct personal smell, of which perhaps only lovers and enemies were aware.

"Look," he said, "that bit of wall was obviously the limit on that side. You go and sit down; you look tired. I'll just pace this out."

She was glad to sit down. Lately all her days had been hectic: office, home, office, home, shopping, cooking. And sometimes she had wondered whether, if this deal went through, she wouldn't do better to live on her own, in a small flat, close to the office. Gilda, to whom she owed a great obligation, would be safe in Abbey House, and two men, one rich and not decrepit, one young and very attractive, would have no difficulty in finding a housekeeper.

Bleak, she thought, and, inside the warm coat, shivered again.

Steve came striding back and sat down.

"I make it forty, well demarked. This is going to cost them! And, better still, hold them up."

"Steve, does it matter all that much? Just a bit more money."

"It isn't that, Jill. It's Gilda. If I can possibly contrive it, she's going to die in her own bed."

"Die? You can't mean..."

"Look! Think back. She began to fail when Eddie started these negotiations. She didn't say anything, but she began to pine in advance, so to speak."

"It may be coincidence, Steve. She is seventy-four, and she hasn't had the easiest of lives. I actually thought she was looking forward to Abbey House. She always speaks of it very highly."

"Isn't that suspicious? She's so reticent about her feelings as a rule."

It was typical of Steve to be so observant about the non-obvious things, whereas she, always in a rush, had concentrated upon cooking Gilda's favourite dishes and supplying things like Ovaltine. Even now she was practical.

"Assuming that you gain a month's delay, it may not be enough. Or do you know something that I don't? *Is* she desperately ill?"

"I'm afraid so, honey. I happened to see—oh, why be so cagey?—I deliberately looked at her last prescription. It isn't something prescribed for toothache."

"I see." Jill's eyes, cool and greenish, filled with tears. She blinked and swallowed. "I suppose we all come to it."

"Not necessarily in exile," Steve said, thinking it wise to ignore this slight show of emotion. "And if a month or six weeks is not enough—well, I have another card up my sleeve. It's one I don't wish to use, though. Let's have a cigarette."

Gilda refreshed her make-up, the out-dated rouge rather high on the hollowing cheeks, powder a shade too light, lipstick slightly too vivid. Then she went down and into the bar, where she was greeted with some warmth. It was ten days since she had felt well enough to face it; more than a month since she had been really useful.

Once more the One Bull's clientele had changed, and most of the men in the bar were elderly, men who liked a local within strolling distance. Both the King's Head and the Green Man were noisy and full of youngsters who liked noise.

Those who thought she looked pretty ghastly hastened to say that she was looking very well. Eddie gave her a smile and hastened, forestalling all offers, to pour her usual drink, a double gin-and-lime. Her coming into the bar, the way she instantly slid into the trivial, rather boring, talk encouraged him to believe that she had taken notice of their pre-supper conversation. Maybe, after all, she had been regretting her decision about Abbey House and had been feeling depressed.

He reflected that, with a quarter of a million pounds, he'd be able to buy her all the attention she'd ever need. And then suddenly, in the midst of commiserating with old Major Ferrand whose retriever had had to be put down, Eddie's mind jumped aside, and he looked about and saw what he was about to exchange for mere money. The bar, cosy in winter, cool in summer, was a centre of good fellowship. Nothing remarkable was ever said there; nothing dramatic ever happened; men came for a drink, for a bit of a chat, to gratify a need to belong. He belonged here, too, and he had a nasty feeling that he'd never belong anywhere else quite so completely.

The poor old Bull had welcomed him back when the outer world had rejected him, when his always poor sight had been damaged by the explosion, and his work made obsolete by the break-through in California. And now, goddamn it, when fate had relented a little, he couldn't help feeling sentimental about it. "You need a good whisky, Major," he said to the man who

had lost the best dog in the world, and he poured two, hoping
that Gilda was not watching.

She was not. She was gathering herself together for the
effort of mounting the stairs. She said, "Good night, everybody." They all said, "Good night," and "Nice to see you
again," and "See you tomorrow." Eddie said, "I'll look in later
on."

She managed the stairs, went through all the almost me-
chanical preparations for bed, even winding her bedside clock.
She had no need to do something so glaringly obvious as taking
an overdose of the good pain-killers. Poor Charles, who had
survived where many younger and more able-bodied men had
died, had suffered terrible insomnia. Doctors, understanding
why, had been generous with the barbiturates favoured in the
fifties. And Gilda, always bearing in mind her mother's end,
had saved some in a bottle that had once contained indigestion
tablets. In twenty years they might have lost their efficacy; that
she must risk. She arranged herself in her usual posture, book
propped on one corner, so that it could be read by somebody
lying down. The print blurred almost immediately and she had,
not a sinking, but a floating, sensation. Over the hills and far
away. But I never saw a hill in my life. Steve and Jill . . . fond
of me . . . perhaps they'll turn . . . Here I go . . .

"Let's have a cigarette," Steve said, and perched himself beside
Jill on the bit of ruined wall. His cigarettes and lighter were
in the right-hand pocket of his jacket, which she wore slung
over her shoulders, the pocket farthest from him; so he reached
a long arm behind and around her.

When the roof rafter and the varnished pews of St. Cerdic's
burned, the heat had been sufficient to crack some of the pav-
ing-stones, and into a crack above the saint's unmarked and
forgotten tomb, a laburnum seed had rooted and grown and
proliferated. One of its offspring grew over the bit of ruined
wall on which Jill and Steve were sitting. Perhaps because its
seeds were poisonous and poison was connected with witches,
various superstitions had attached themselves to the laburnum.
The most common was that it was unlucky to uproot a sapling
unless you were giving it to a home where it would be cherished.

Neither Jill nor Steve bothered about such myths. Nor did
they know—and knowing would not have attached much im-

portance to the fact—that St. Cerdic's miracles, some of which were recorded, were psychological rather than physical. All they knew, in the stunned way that made accident victims such unsatisfactory witnesses, was that it happened, the thing they'd both wanted for so long. Steve's arm curved and tightened; Jill gave herself into its embrace. Their faces came together, their mouths met. Kissed and murmured inanities.

"Steve, I can't help it. I love you absolutely."

"I've loved you ever since I knew the meaning of the word."

"I thought I was to dwindle of unrequited love. You were always so damned brotherly."

"I thought I was doomed to marry Dorothy Hutton. You were always so damned sisterly. And I know I like all the wrong books, the wrong music. And there was that toffee-nosed young Walker-Armstrong. God! The time we've wasted."

They made up for a little of the wasted time while the sun went down, melting into rose and molten gold, crimson, dove-grey.

Rudy had stopped at the first gravestone. He belonged to Jill and she belonged to him, but there were places, two within the inn, some in the abbey gardens, where a dog should not set a paw. This was another such place, and, after waiting, he let loose the bark which convinced the uninitiated that the One Bull was patrolled by a mastiff.

"He's right," Jill said. "We must go. But now, darling, tell me just one thing. If you hold up the sale and Gilda lives on, what is the card you don't want to play?"

Steve looked towards the ornate table-tomb, just visible amongst the undergrowth.

"Our redoubtable great-grandmother made a peculiar will. You'd think she was disposing of a great estate, not a mere pub. Charles was to have it, and after him his heirs, but it was not to be sold without the consent of the next heir, providing he or she had reached the age of discretion."

"Giving you the power of veto."

"Which I don't want to exercise. I don't want to upset Eddie. Hence, the delaying tactic."

Jill considered for a moment. "Umm, I see. What a nice, tactful fellow you are! Personally I doubt if he would be upset. He enjoyed the struggle, but I think he'll regret it as soon as he's signed his name."

"On the other hand, we must admit that the place doesn't pay. I don't see much future for it."

"It would have, if I had my way. I mean if it were mine."

"Assume that it is—or will be."

"I'd make a restaurant of it. Very good food at reasonable prices. The Red Room would be ideal—without that tatty old wallpaper, of course."

"And who'd cook?"

"I should, of course. A nice change from dealing with other people's tax problems. And think what a kick Eddie would get out of saying he'd refused a quarter of a million! Not a bad advertisement, either."

Walking close together, his arm still around her shoulders, hers around his waist, they emerged into the inn yard. From this angle, what remained of the building looked very much the same, and *was* much the same, as it had been when somebody all those ages ago had said, "Deserted," and Paulus had pushed forward to see for himself. But tonight it did not look deserted. The bar window glowed and a light over the entry lit the yard, and upstairs Gilda's curtained window was faintly shining.

"We must tell her first," Steve said.

A little wind had sprung up and the inn sign creaked on its hinges. It made a lonely desolate sound as a rule, and everybody said somebody should get to work with the oil-can. Tonight, however, the creaking did not sound sad or plaintive, just blatantly triumphant.

About the Author

Bestselling author Nora Lofts lives in Bury St. Edmunds, Suffolk, an ancient city much like her fictional Mallow. She is married, has a son and grandchildren, and spends most of her time at the typewriter.